GILE

Za

faber and faber

First published in 2002
by Faber and Faber Limited
3 Queen Square London WC1N 3AU
This open market edition first published in 2003

Typeset by Faber and Faber Ltd
Printed in England by Bookmarque Ltd, Croydon

A CIP record for this book
is available from the British Library

ISBN 0–571–21420–7

2 4 6 8 10 9 7 5 3 1

Giles Foden, who grew up in Africa, was for three years an assistant editor of the *Times Literary Supplement* and then joined the staff of the *Guardian*. Foden won the 1998 Whitbread First Novel Award for *The Last King of Scotland* which was followed by *Ladysmith* in 1999; two novels which, according to Alan Massie, 'establish him as the most original and interesting novelist of his generation'.

Further praise for *Zanzibar*:

'Foden pulls off a difficult feat – he adds something fresh to the most reported news events of the last half century.'
Harry Mount, *The Spectator*

'An unusual and refreshing novel; it is willing to engage with important political issues, and does so without oversimplifying them.' William Skidelsky, *Times Literary Supplement*

'His sense of place is unerring, his details exact, felicitous, often rising to the luminosity of poetry – whether he is writing of coral reefs, or clove farms, or the markets of Zanzibar and Pemba. There is no trace of colonial, condescending or Orientalist attitudes in his writing.' Neel Mukherjee, *The Times*

'A rewarding intelligent novel that displays his now characteristic blend of experience, imagination and intimate research.'
Henry Hitchings, *Financial Times*

'He is a master of ambiguity where it is welcome, and discomfort where it is not. Above all, he knows how to use individual lives to dramatise and explain external events that impact on us all.'
Anthony Holden, *Observer*

'[His] fiction is so convincing that it is hard not to feel that you are reading the "real" inside story. In his hands, terrorists are no longer caricatures of fundamentalist evil, but men whose actions seem understandable, who exist in three dimensions.'
Edward Marriot, *Evening Standard*

by the same author

THE LAST KING OF SCOTLAND
LADYSMITH

For Tilly

Author's Note

This novel was, largely, written before the attacks on America of September 11, 2001. On that day, the Southern District Court of New York had not yet concluded its consideration of the events of 1998 upon which the story is based.

A small portion of this material appeared in *Arena* magazine in 1999. Another piece of work in progress was included in *The Weekenders* anthology (Random House, 2001).

. . . nor could his eye not ken
Th' empire of *Negus* to his utmost port
Ercoco and the less Maritine kings
Mombaza, and *Quiloa,* and *Melind,*
And *Sofala* thought *Ophir* . . .

JOHN MILTON, *Paradise Lost* (1667)

PART ONE

As the light broke, she stretched her hungry limbs after the night, entreating it for a mate. What the fugitive dark provided was a monstrous tree. It embraced mother earth in its branches, making her writhe in joy and pain. They struggled for mastery. After a vast lapse of time, it seemed the tree had won. When the goddess was released, however, it was the tree that gave birth. Green shoots issued from its gnarly roots. Birds squeezed out through cracks in its trunk and flew away. Animals, too, it spawned. The first of these – and the most esteemed by man and woman when they themselves emerged – was the turtle.

Some students of the Swahili creation myth say that all this happened on the island of Zanzibar. On the eastern seaboard of Africa, it is a place known for the tranquillity of its harbours, the sweetness of its fruit, and the scent of its spices. Other scholars, especially those from the neighbouring island of Pemba, maintain it was there, in fact, that the Tree of Life pushed down its roots and gave birth to the great turtles of the Indian Ocean.

The turtles are so rare today that many believe they are ghosts. But the ghosts of Zanzibar and Pemba live not in thalassia, or any other pavilion of the ocean. They live in the fragrant orchards of clove and ylang-ylang that cover the islands like a shroud. It is through these that nightly predations are said to be made by the *papabawa*, the islands' legendary pale-skinned vampire.

People say the *papabawa* is just a race memory of the slave trade. No one who has actually seen one of the great turtles, in any case, would call it a ghost. Khaled al-Khidr saw one on February 15, that year's Night of Power, when the Koran descended in its entirety into the soul of the Prophet. They should have been observing that holiest of occasions, not lying about on the beach.

It was 1996 – the year of his twenty-first birthday. There was a full moon, the time when the turtle laid her eggs, and he was with his friends Ali and Juba. They were camping out on an islet a few miles off the main island, a place his father patrolled from time to time on behalf of its new owner.

They were dozing on the beach in front of a bonfire. All members of a soccer team back on Pemba, they had spent the afternoon on the sand – practising penalties, shooting the ball between two fronds of leaf that made for a goal, or just kicking it around between the three of them. Now it was dark and they were tired. Normally they listened to music at night on these trips, but the batteries on Khaled's radio had run out.

The moon was shining brightly, its grey light mixing with the yellow of the fire. Khaled had just drunk a can of coke. Ali was chewing gum. Juba had been smoking – a fat roll of leaf that kept going out in the wind. He had been seized by a fit of coughing, and Khaled thought it was him again, but it wasn't. It was a deeper, stranger sound. There was another noise too, like digging.

They exchanged glances in the firelight, then jumped to their feet and ran in the direction of the sound. A strong wind was whipping the palm trees, but it was easy to tell where the noise was coming from – even for Juba, who was still deep in the thrall of *dagga*, as marijuana is known in Swahili.

The turtle was enormous, easily seven feet long. The dome of her shell rose at least four feet high. She was digging a hole. The repetitive, wheezy cough came with the effort of it, accompanying each thump of her back flippers as they sprayed out sand behind her. Her front flippers were pushed out like levers, to give her purchase; the whole manoeuvre was perfectly achieved.

4

They watched in awe, their figures casting shadows on the moonlit beach.

Once the hole had been dug, she started making another noise, more high-pitched, a sighing. With the culmination of each sigh, a glistening white egg dropped in the hole. Almost an hour passed, during which more than a hundred appeared, each about the size of a golf ball. Khaled lost count, gazing at every one as it fell.

When the hole was full, the turtle moved forwards a little and began shovelling sand back over the eggs, untroubled by the watching young men. Her glaucous eyes seemed to look straight through them, unseeing. Khaled saw oblivion there, a supreme indifference to everything except that universal law which bids all living things to eat and be eaten in their turn.

After the eggs were covered, they thought it was finished. But then the oddest thing of all happened. The turtle began executing a circle above the nest, pushing herself with each flipper in turn. Around she went, three times. When she finally shuffled away from the nesting ground, the sand was almost completely level. It would be hard for a predator to tell – at least by sight – where she had laid her treasure.

Under that bright full moon, with the sound of rustling palm trees and the rolling breakers all around, the three watched as the turtle progressed, heaving, down the beach. She paused for a moment in the surf and disappeared.

It was the following morning that Khaled al-Khidr, returning home, found his mother and father lying side by side on the floor of their living room. They looked as if they had been placed there deliberately, both of their arms extended above their heads. Across the throat of each was an abrupt, reversing stroke, like a Z on its side.

He tried to scream, but no sound issued. Gasping in anguish, feeling as if the earth itself were shaking, he reached out a hand

5

to steady himself, gripping the back of a chair. He forced himself to breathe, to look, to approach. The edges of each slash were encrusted with dried blood, as were his parents' shoulders. There were rubbery clots of it covering the mat upon which they lay.

For a few, shocked seconds, staring at the clots, he swayed. His mind wanted to shriek out again, but his voice once more disobeyed, offering only a horrified murmuring that, mounting upwards in the suffocating air, filling his throat and nostrils, choked his being with a sound of new-hatched evil. Unable to bear it, he fell, his legs buckling beneath him.

Queller's clock radio exploded into song. The time was 7 a.m., but he'd been awake already for half an hour. The numbers were pulsing, lime-green LED, and the speaker was belting out a jingle based on the letters WMVY. The date was April 1, 1997. The place was what he called his 'log cabin'. In truth it was far more luxurious, a pleasant wooden home on the island of Aquinnah, in Martha's Vineyard, off Cape Cod.

He reached over, sipped some water, swallowed it, then took a big swig. He swilled the water round in his mouth, then let it drop back into the glass. Why was it that however hard he scoured his teeth before going to bed, he woke up feeling as if two hundred elephants, six hundred camels and at least a thousand mules had camped in his mouth while he slept?

He lay back down, head thumping, knowing too well the reason: Scotch, the enemy he'd put in his mouth each night since she'd died, hoping it would be a friend. Glass after glass, night after night . . . he was bored by his own addiction now, but it continued to keep him in its grasp.

April 1, well . . . Lucy always used to play a trick on him. He lay staring at the ceiling, happy at the memory, sad at the loss. As he lay there, fixating on the curious duality that is death in life, the newscaster ran down the headlines. Queller wondered if they'd slip in a bogus story. Sometimes they did that.

Fools' day – he would know this – was named when the Muslims of Granada were tricked into leaving the besieged city. The forces of Spain's King Ferdinand promised them safe passage if they disarmed, then massacred them on the quayside.

Men and women, adults and children, some forty thousand, were all put to the sword. The Spaniards made no distinctions in the application of their cruelty.

In many ways, he thought, the Muslim armies of that time showed greater clemency than the Christian ones, even sparing vegetation. The Koran said: *When you fight the battles of the Lord, destroy no palm trees, nor burn any fields of grain. Cut down no fruit trees.*

April 1, 1492, was the date of the massacre – the same year Columbus sailed for America. It certainly made one think twice about practical jokes. Queller shut his ears to the voice of the WMVY newscaster. After over half a millennium what happened in Granada was hardly acknowledged as a fact, never mind an outrage. How rarely, he thought, justice overtook the crimes it was supposed to pursue, as it strolled down history's corridors. It was no wonder that many Islamic nations felt they had been violated by the West, no wonder that a strong madness tugged at the carefully woven threads of diplomacy. The US had broken nearly every treaty it had ever made with Arab countries.

The radio noise was persistent. As he lay, still staring at the ceiling, he learned that the Senate was going to ratify the chemical weapons convention, and that an Arkansas judge had thrown out a sexual harassment case against the President. Currently on a trip to Africa, Clinton had celebrated by playing a tribal drum and telling reporters that he was looking forward to going home and 'continuing the very ambitious agenda we've got there'.

Despairing, Queller rolled over on his stump, flailing at the radio's square white box with his remaining arm. He thought he'd hit the button, but the damn thing persevered. 'In other news this week, the President issued a memorandum prohibiting the use of federal funds for human cloning. He urged leaders of the scientific and medical community to adopt a voluntary moratorium on the subject.'

8

'But can we trust our leaders?' demanded a Catholic activist in the discussion afterwards. No, Queller growled, lifting thick, old man's fingers to hit the button again and switch it off successfully. Especially not that leader. He'd heard an account of another presidential liaison, involving an intern, that journalists were only just beginning to sniff round. His source was a secret service friend whose responsibilities included protection of the Oval Office.

Queller shook his grey head, trying to rid himself of the lurid image which his friend had described. He pondered the last time when he himself had had sexual relations with a woman. His wife. But lovemaking, like much happiness, occupies an elusive place in the structure of memory. Sometimes he could hardly summon her back. Lucy's face and body, the way she moved and spoke, drifted out of focus.

When it dissolved, that mental phantom, the pain was one of physical separation, like the reed cut from the reed bed in Rumi's poem. What came instead, sharply defined, was a sharded remembrance of another affliction, some fragment of what felt like a previous life, even though it had happened only eight years ago.

He did not need to look at the stump. The mere breath of memory stirred old fear in his veins. The bullet had taken off his elbow joint, leaving the forearm attached by very little. He'd been knocked down, body and blood tumbling together. He remembered stones, not much earth.

How was it, then, for Queller? After the fall, after the red spray? He'd taken one look – askance, through the distance of shock – and come to his senses. Attention was vital. He gripped the flesh above the wound, anxious to stop the flow. The pain – remembered now, across time, across borders – hit him. He uttered a series of sharp cries.

He laughed. Mr Sam, as he was known then (though he had many names), just laughed, getting back into his four-by-four.

Others followed suit, the remainder climbing onto the running-boards, guns at the ready. They moved off up the rocky track. Most were *wahhabi*, Arab fighters. Some were local mujahidin. The Arabs wore black turbans, the Afghans caps of rough brown wool.

Queller was left clutching his arm. The four Green Berets sat on the ground around him, as they had been ordered. It was all just a moment, but it broke down endlessly: him applying pressure to the bleeding, the soldiers in a circle, their guns piled in the middle, their frightened faces . . .

Green Berets don't always wear green berets. It's a fact. His companions were hooded, faces striped with camouflage cream: mottled blues and greys. There is a way to apply it, rubbing scree and boulders into a face until you achieve the same effect as the 'disruptive pattern material' of your mountain uniform.

Waves of agony throbbed through him, his companions' variegated faces flashing before his eyes. Above them, the sun was rising. A hot bar of iron, dragged up from behind snowy peaks, it might as well have been a cauterising tool applied to his wound. Pain is a vector, all the world and time collapsing to a bunch of nerves. He groaned and whimpered.

To stop these noises, he bit on his collar. It tasted of salt. Beside him, the lieutenant was cursing. None of them, not Queller, not the four soldiers, dared move until the convoy of mujahidin, numbering about fifty, had vanished into the mountain. There was too much risk the Arabs would kill them all. The cold seeping up through their haunches as they sat on the ground, the Americans watched the convoy move up a gulch in the morning sun.

Once it was safely out of sight, the lieutenant called in a chopper on his radio. They had to move to somewhere the Chinook could land. A dressing was unwrapped and wound round Queller's elbow. Another, tightly knotted at his bicep, served as a tourniquet. Two of the men made a bosun's chair to carry him to the rendezvous, a meadow further down. There was scree, and they stumbled on the way. Queller screamed as the rocks raked his bloody elbow. Then he passed out.

He awoke in Islamabad hospital some four hours later. There was some hope of saving the arm. They gave him six pints of blood immediately, a major from US Army Liaison Islamabad ordering whichever of his men had the same blood group to donate. Over the next two days, septicaemia developed. The stench became revolting, Queller delirious and amputation essential.

The arm was removed at the point where the bullet had shattered the bone, leaving some eight to nine inches of the humerus. It was anything but a neat job, with incisions constantly having to be made to release infection. Queller was unconscious for a few days, before waking up one morning to see a vivid circle being painted on the stump with iodine. The Pakistani surgeon explained that this marked the place where a cut was to be made. The hidden infection, the rot in the bone, he said, was called the *sequestrum*; and the holes it came up through, they were *cloaca*.

Staring, slack-mouthed, at the ceiling – more or less as he was now – Queller thought about those words a lot during the next few days. He also wondered why Mr Sam had not killed him outright. Did he want him to suffer? Or was it, he speculated as he lay in the sweat-soaked sheets, that Mr Sam acknowledged a debt to him? After all, he was Queller's creation, to some extent.

Queller turned over. The clock radio continued to blink its monstrous numbers at him, each one seeming to curdle before his eyes as it turned into the next. He sat up on the edge of the bed and looked at the rough-cut pine boards of the walls, whose tongue-and-groove he had fixed himself. How many nights had passed since he had built this place? How many nights had passed since that brief, beautiful hiatus between his retirement and her death? Before he had stopped work he had been at war with . . . *enemies of the State*. How ridiculous, how illusory that sounded now.

11

A small bird, possibly a lark, was singing in the locust tree outside the cabin. It seemed to be there almost every morning, and he should by now have determined its species. He looked through the window into the branches, where greenish-white flowers were starting to bud, but he couldn't see the bird. He loved these trees, which in the fall produced brown, twisted pods containing seeds and a sweet pulp. In what was something of a crux in both the Bible and the history of vegetarianism, it was said to be this pulp, not insects, that John the Baptist had eaten with wild honey in the wilderness. It was nutritious stuff, by all accounts. The squirrels and quail and white-tailed deer that roamed the island went crazy for it.

He stared through the pane. Beyond the tree was a small lawn that inclined, with a shallow curve, into a classic Aquinnah heathland. The word was an Indian one meaning 'beautiful colours by the sea'. It was certainly a glorious blue day. And in a short while he'd walk down to the beach, and do his exercises on the red sand. But it wasn't guaranteed that good would come of them, not any more. There was a time when he could rely on them making him happy.

His toes fidgeted with the pile of the rug. When would he be free of this feeling of being at war with himself? With the past that had made him – with certain actions, secretly done in the name of duty, about which he now had doubts?

The bird outside piped up again.

He was in conflict on several fronts, also carrying a powerful consciousness of neglect, which he connected to his wife's illness. He felt she might not have got cancer if he'd been at home more. It was, he knew, nonsense in medical terms. But he felt it all the same, and the feeling fed a deeper sense of insecurity about whether he had ever done any good in the world.

Survivor's guilt, the agency shrink had said. It wasn't as simple as that. For some time, Queller had felt he was on a penitential journey. He looked at his stump. The scar tissue was like a map.

3

1998. One year on, and another glorious blue day is born on the day of fools. It was, considering the state of Florida, the kind of day when the sky might be glad to see itself anew on the sea beach – in the silvery surface of the water, in mother-of-pearl, in gum foil even.

Nick Karolides didn't see any of this. He was in the kitchen, making his breakfast, pouring milk into a bowl of Cheerios. Pouring from the carton as he stood, bare feet on the floor tiles . . . A tall, dark-haired young man in boxer shorts, he was fit and well-proportioned; but not handsome, not exactly. The milk made a thin white snake into the bowl.

He sat down and ate them slowly, those 'one and only Cheerios', listening to the radio and reading the cereal box as he chewed: 'Cheerios has been an important part of all our lives for nearly 60 years. It's your kids' energy fuel, one of baby's first finger foods, and the perfect wholesome goodness for the whole family.'

An only child, even now he found this insistence on the triumphant healthy family, which he saw a lot in advertisements, kind of alienating. It wasn't that he'd had an unhappy childhood – the contrary in fact, at least until his father's death – but the way these ads made him feel he was lacking somehow. As if all those smiling faces on the packet or TV screen were America's normality and his family something else.

In his case, the whole thing was compounded by Sarasota's Greek community being relatively insular and he himself something of a loner. People always thought if you were a member of an ethnic community like that, it was close-knit. That was true up to a point, but he hadn't kept in contact with many of his childhood friends. Quite a few had drifted away and not even kept in touch with their own relations.

The radio announcer was prattling on about the Lewinsky thing. Again. He turned it off, a trace of anger on his brow. All that stuff depressed him. A lot depressed him. The one and only Cheerios depressed him. Familiar items in the kitchen – things he had seen since childhood, such as his mother's chrome juicer or, mainly and massively, the slightly curved door of the refrigerator – they depressed him, too. These days the letter magnets spelled 'Fiery Furnace', or 'It Is Written.' Or something else along those lines.

After finishing up his breakfast, he went back to his room, his long, toned limbs – he swam every day – moving with an easy grace that belied his spiky mood. He changed for work, putting on what Absal called his uniform: black jeans, elastic-sided boots, white T-shirt, black leather jacket. She said it was how the gangsters dressed back home.

As his head came through the neck of the T-shirt, he caught a sound that had become familiar in the household since his father's death. It was a muttering that rose in pitch once in a while, then fell again. He grimaced, raising his eyes to heaven. In the corridor, the muttering grew louder. He put his head round the door of her room. Inside, flickering under the light of a row of electric candles, he could see her back.

Blonde – rare for a Greek – and with a well-kept figure, still a source of pride for her, in spite of a temperament much altered since widowhood, she rocked to and fro as she mumbled. In front of her, above the row of candles and a heap of religious paraphernalia, was a large picture of Christ on the cross, surrounded by a ring of fire. Flashed across one corner were letters licked with flame: 'Holy Spirit Fire Church.'

He heard her intone: 'The day is thine, the night is thine, thou has prepared the light and the sun.'

Next to his mother, as she prayed – if it truly was praying: a suggestion that was offensive to some residual religious feeling in him – a cigarette burned in a green ashtray.

Nick watched the rocking figure for a few seconds, then – breaking into the Greek that remained the language of emotion in his rended family – whispered goodbye and shut the door behind him. He passed a cardboard box crammed with more religious items, mostly icons. Some, he knew, were quite valuable, but she had just chucked them in there. There was even an ancient wooden pyx, the small box in which the priest carries Holy Communion to the sick in their homes. He frowned, not so much at the way in which his mother had discarded these accoutrements of the old religion, as at the contents of the next box in the corridor. It was filled with materials for making artificial flowers, a hobby that had once made her happy.

Outside, he wheeled his motorbike from the garage, put on his helmet and sped away. He drove fast to clear his mind, weaving in and out of the traffic. A garbage truck was belching clouds of black fumes; he pulled down his visor. Swooping past a bright red hatchback, he saw the driver check her hair in the rear-view mirror. Next, the driver of an executive sedan was thumping the steering wheel in frustration at having to slacken his course for the pungent dumpster truck.

He made his way out of the suburbs. Past small-town lots and shops. Posters on steel shutters. Commercial signs – Belaion Bakery – and civic blunders: a bed of wilting flowers, laid out in curious knots. Once part of the mayor's regeneration programme, it was now a dumping ground for syringes.

Mr Belaion, a Libyan, had a daughter Nick went out with for a year. She was wild. Wearing a baker's white coat in the day, she wore ripped jeans and braided her hair with beads when they went out at night. Smelling of bread, she kneaded him like dough. She left him for a Cuban in the end, saying she would have married him, if only he'd let her inside his head. He knew it was a cliché of male puzzlement, but it was still strange how women put such a premium on opening up like that. Surely, he thought, the stronger bond would be the one without words. Having a person say 'I love you' over and over again, even in Arabic, made you question whether it was true.

Torrance Dry Cleaners. He was in the fire church: Mr Torrance who came with evangelical papers to the house, chewing odorous gum. Nick's mother would put the papers in envelopes for mailing to Africa, where – in common with other apocalyptic sects – the fire church was expanding in a big way. One day, Mr Torrance will go evangelise in Africa, his mother said.

He took a short cut near the railroad, and came down a ramp by the coal depot. Passing an Army surplus store and a joke shop, finally he hit the freeway, rejoining the line of commuters. He despised these people in their cars, already angry about something before they had even got to work. But he knew that also applied to him. He had that much self-knowledge, Nick Karolides.

A guy in a red convertible cut him up. He accelerated, followed, and – glancing back – passed the convertible at speed. On a bike the helmet can be expressive. Particular angles. Articulations of the neck. These can be used as insults. For an emotionally stunted person, for a fortified person, for a person who doesn't want to engage with the world directly, wearing a helmet can be liberating.

All this had to change. He knew that, too. Dino had said this. What he was doing now, it wasn't living, it was resisting. Not against the enemies of times long ago – like the men who forced his father to leave his homeland – but against a creeping enclosure, an oppression that shut down freedom in your head just as effectively. What made it all the worse was that people *wanted* it. They *desired* it. Given the appearance of choice, and a dependable stream of stimulating experiences, they were willing to be manipulated like a child's toy.

He twisted his hand on the throttle, powering up to overtake a Fedex van. A toy with movable limbs. Action Man. Barbie and Ken. My little fucking pony. Or some electronic gizmo: Tamagotchi, as promoted on Fox Kids. Fox Kids. That just about sums it up.

Nick Karolides very much wanted to isolate himself from all this. Perhaps it was a desire to affirm his Greekness – to forge a connection with that fallen land of lost gods and godlike men which his father left behind. Or maybe it was just a kind of condescension towards ordinary folk, some sense he'd been otherwise chosen. But he had too much self-doubt for that . . .

No, it could be, rather, that he simply felt there had to be more to life than a shimmering hurry of days, which sometimes he could hardly persuade himself had any reality at all. The whole thing sometimes seemed to him like a kind of fairground machine, operated from behind by pulleys and ropes. It was a suspicion that applied as much to his inward as to his outward experiences. Now and then he thought he presented a false self to the world, then found himself shocked to have been one of the observers who had taken it as real.

The truth was, Nick wasn't a man to analyse such things in depth. He was a marine biologist. He just knew he wanted out. He would be thirty-one next year. His hopes and anticipations were not unusual; they mainly involved escape. From, for instance, the smell of exhaust fumes seeping in through his visor.

Or – look! – these signs on the edge of the freeway, raised on poles and platforms so you couldn't miss them. Especially prominent that morning were a host of ones with an apocalyptic theme. They all had the familiar fiery writing of his mother's poster: *Then the fire of the Lord fell, and consumed the burnt sacrifice, and the wood, and the stones, and the dust, and licked up the water that was in the trench.*

He was weaving in and out with more abandon now. The signs were pissing him off. He could do himself an injury. He could do others an injury – like this guy in the Fedex van, who'd caught up and just given him the bird. *Then he shall say also unto them on the left hand, depart from me, ye cursed, into everlasting fire, prepared for the devil and his angels.*

And so on, all the way down to hell. Finally, when it seemed the freeway might run out of poles on which to speak the name of the Lord, by which time the text was written in Nick's speeding body as a burning fire shut up in his bones and he was so angered by the posters he felt he couldn't stay on his bike a moment longer, the pay-off came, the chosen ones' come-on-inside: *Holy Spirit Fire Church – join before the day comes . . . call toll-free F-I-E-R-Y.*

The next intersection brought, at last, another sign, its picture of snook and starfish and shells overlaid with the words: *Welcome to the Florida Institute of Marine Sciences, a partner in the National Estuary Program. Sarasota Bay: Reclaiming Paradise.*

He turned in and parked the bike near the entrance, setting it up on its stand and locking his helmet in the pillion box. As he walked across the quadrangle it struck him how much he had grown to resent this place, how quickly its mission had lost all its meaning for him. There was a pool with dolphins, and a little aquarium where skates and sharks skimmed the glass. He liked the skates, he hated the sharks. It wasn't a place that people visited. There were other places for that. This was a place for tests.

Someone called his name. It was Absal at reception, springing up from her revolving chair. He waved, and moved on, before she could engage him in conversation. Sometimes he enjoyed doing this kind of thing, giving people the slip, refusing to be anchored. It was probably a bad characteristic, one that didn't let much warmth into his life, but it was also protective. If you made yourself like an island, you couldn't be hurt.

It was true he hadn't a girlfriend right now and he'd thought about Absal. She was good-looking, but she wasn't his type. Absal was from Tajikistan and had a beautiful accent, but she wore too much make-up.

Woe unto those that striveth with their Maker!

It was that stuff again, getting inside his head. Those placards his ma had up around the house, the phrases she whispered while watching TV. *Let the potsherd strive with the potsherds of the earth. Shall the clay say to him that fashioneth it, what makest thou? Or thy work, he hath no hands? Look unto me . . .*

Christ. He went in, pulled on his lab coat, and spent the morning analysing samples of seawater from Sarasota Bay. It was part of a sewage control initiative. Septic systems played a significant role in nitrogen loading in the bay. More shit from the City of Sarasota meant more nitrogen in the ocean. More nitrogen meant increased levels of phytoplankton and epiphytic algae. More phytoplankton and algae meant more shading for seagrass blades. More shading for seagrass blades meant lower oxygen levels. And that, that left fish and other creatures gasping.

There were other problems. Stormwater run-off full of pollutants. Grow-fast from lawn care. Fertiliser from agriculture. Heavy metals in the creeks and bayous. But trying to stop or reverse all this, though a noble cause, didn't make him happy. During his training, he hadn't expected to end up here. He'd wanted to be out on the ocean. He'd wanted to be free.

At 1 o'clock he got back on his motorbike, picked up a pastrami, Emmental and mustard sandwich from the deli, and drove over to Dino's. This was the usual pattern for his lunch hour. Dino had been a Navy Seal with Nick's father, whose own father the Colonels' men had shot down in the street – which was why Georgiou Karolides had left. Dino had come with him. Before that, again with Nick's father, Dino had been in the Greek merchant service, shipping out of Piraeus.

Dino's Dive Shop. The owner, a wiry sixty-year-old with bushy eyebrows, was fiddling with a regulator when Nick came in. Head bent over the counter, under a fantastic array of masks, flippers and spear-guns, he just nodded, and carried on working. Nick munched on his sandwich.

'How is your mother, anyway?' Dino said, eventually.

'You mean Florida's premier religious maniac?' He pulled a face.

'She wasn't always like that, you know. Your ma was a very beautiful woman in her day. We all wanted her – us Greeks, I mean. Then I introduced her to your father . . .'

They both fell silent.

It was the day after his twenty-first birthday. A Sunday. Dino turned up at the door, grim-faced. He and Nick's father had been diving. The shark had come out of nowhere, taken off his father's arm. Still alive when Dino pulled him to the shore, he died on the way to the hospital.

'I've been thinking about what you were saying the other day,' continued Dino. 'About wanting to go. It is time you got out of this place. You're wasting your life. Dipping around in other people's shit!'

Nick laughed, but he knew the old guy was racked with guilt about his father's death. He didn't blame him for what had happened. It was a source of sorrow for them both. Dino was like an uncle now, which was why he gave these lectures.

The eyes beneath Dino's bushy brows were on him. They were surprisingly hard for a man with such a quiet voice. They seemed to know exactly what he was thinking: *you are holding yourself back.*

Or so Nick thought. His mind, too, had its cargo of guilt. Why was it his father, the hero, who'd been taken, not him – the failure, the stay-at-home?

'Fact is, I've something I wanted to show you.'

Dino came round the counter and approached a rack of sub-aqua and other marine-related journals. Picking out *Ocean* magazine, he flicked through the pages till he found what he was looking for, then handed it to Nick.

'I've marked it for you.'

In the middle of the page a recruitment advertisement had been ringed twice with a red felt-tip pen:

Ranger required for Zanzibar Reef Protection Scheme. USAID-funded project seeks trained marine conservator to take charge of coral and species-protected area management on islands in the Zanzibar archipelago. Apply soonest ZRPS, USAID, PO Box 331, NW Washington DC 20019

4

He sat on deck, on his bag, smoking and looking through the white rails at the ocean. The sun was fierce, and all around him were faces. People crossing his line of sight. Mouths talking a language he couldn't understand. Swahili. *Sawahil*. Arabic for littoral folk, for islanders and coastlanders, people of the sea. He had read a little about it.

The books didn't help him, though – he could have read every book on the subject and it wouldn't have helped him – when out of fellow feeling he tried to strike up a conversation with one of his neighbours, a big lady, wearing a turban of brightly patterned cloth. She responded to the unintelligible stream of white man's talk with a look of frank, self-assured incomprehension and not a little affront.

And then she uttered what he heard as: '*Papabawa! P-P-Papabawa!*' – which he supposed to be a greeting.

He put a hand to his lips. A small patch of skin had come away, pulled by the filter. He had left the cigarette there to block out the smell of the diesel from the engines.

Tired of watching the sea through a forest of legs, he decided he ought to stand up. A slight wave of nausea passed through him as he did so. He leaned back against a throbbing bulkhead and looked up at the sky. The fumes were making him feel woozy. His mind felt as if it were floating off on the ocean breeze with the gulls, into some illusory world. He went over to the rail and, leaning over, let the cigarette drop from his fingers into the water.

The *Smooth Hound* gave a little jump. Operated by an Australian company (what were *they* doing here?), the hydrofoil belied its name. It was a far from comfortable ride, and he was beginning to wish he had taken another flight from Dar-es-Salaam. The port there had been hellish, and the *Smooth Hound* was not much better. Rather than gliding, the craft did something more like chew its way across the water.

One passenger near him, an old African with a white eyepatch, was chewing for real. Every now and then he spat a long, red thread onto the deck. This manoeuvre, which left a pattern of scarlet arabesques on the fibreglass, made Nick feel sicker than ever. Why couldn't he spit over the side like everyone else? His nausea was intensified when the man cheerily offered him some of whatever it was he was chewing. Nick felt dizzy. Gestured-offering-by-man-with-patch was how his floating brain registered it. Some kind of nut. Wrapped up in a parcel of bright green leaves.

Nick smiled politely and, shaking his head, looked out over the waves, affecting an exaggerated search for sight of land.

'Top banana,' said the man with the eyepatch after a while, as if aggrieved.

Then he grinned, creasing the flesh near his covered eye. The patch was attached with strips of dirty tape.

'I learn speech from British Army.'

Nick stared at him.

'Fought with *wazungu*,' the man added proudly. He gave a brisk salute. 'Kill Hitler. Kill Mussolini. You are from London?'

'The US.'

The man grinned again, showing his red teeth.

'USA – top banana!'

Raising his eyebrows, Nick lit another cigarette.

He would smoke two more before Stone Town, the capital of Zanzibar, came into view. Cranes, minarets. He scanned the quays as they docked. The usual drama of arrival. Harbour people. Harbour equipment. The emptying and filling of vessels. Dhows, modern cargo ships. Longshoremen were working with lifting gear, extracting brightly coloured metal boxes out of the container ships and wooden crates from the dhows. Port officials spoke into walkie-talkies as distinguished Arab merchants, in long white gowns and Muslim skullcaps, waited patiently for their goods.

All this made it a wonderful place to someone like Nick, someone with the sea in his veins. But it was a wonderful place that was also fetid and slightly threatening. The older buildings, constructed out of massive coral blocks, once glittering and white, no doubt, were now almost as grey as the new concrete ones. As he disembarked, he was approached by several young men offering to carry his bag, one grabbing hold of the handle and tugging hard. He pulled it back sharply.

Sweating, he found himself being funnelled into a series of narrow offices amid a jostling crowd of other passengers. There were more hustlers here, leaning on door jambs or squatting on the floor of the customs hall. He was annoyed to have to fill out an immigration card and have his passport stamped for a second time. The official, a man with a deep, tubercular cough, looked more like a bar-keep than an immigration officer. The reason for the double stamp was, Nick gathered, something to do with Zanzibar's precarious federal status – a separate country, but in uneasy union with mainland Tanzania. He also had to show a yellow-fever inoculation certificate. Then there was some problem with his visa. The man in the booth at first said he could not enter. This turned out to be a ploy to earn a $20 bribe, which Nick duly paid, too tired to argue the point.

He finally emerged into the wider throng of the Stone Town dock area. Dino's tales of his merchant-seaman days came back to him. Piraeus, Port Said, old Marseilles . . . He could see those ancient wooden sailboats, the dhows, riding at their moorings in the slight swell. Fishermen were bringing in a catch, tipping silver fry from their nets into plastic boxes. Others were heading and tailing bigger fish, barracuda maybe, with machetes.

Elsewhere, a tall man, stripped to the waist, was gripping an octopus by a tentacle and whacking it against a rock.

Nick walked a little way along the breakwater, humping his green canvas bag, looking for some sense of where the town proper began. There was a boy tugging a donkey. He still felt disoriented as his eye followed the tight cord between the boy's black fist and the donkey's pink, flaring nostrils.

A clattering noise. Startled, he looked over his shoulder. A crane loading up a cargo ship had dropped a pallet of hessian bags. Some split, releasing a sudden strong smell into the air.

Cloves. The spice lay strewn about on the stone. He went over and picked some up. Little black tacks in his hand. He stared at the splintered pallet. He turned and the boy pulling the donkey crossed his field of vision again. From side to side, the cord in between, the boy and the donkey: it was like a tug of war.

The docks fed into the town through a network of winding alleys. Many of the shops seemed to sell only firewood and raisins. He passed a mosque, letting his eyes travel up the abstract patterns of its stone pillars. He had a headache. He would, he determined, get something to eat and drink before trying to find this guy. Chikambwa. A marine policeman, the Zanzibar government contact for his project. The USAID man in Dar-es-Salaam had given him the name, then warned him, off the record, that he shouldn't expect much help. 'You'll be pretty much left to your own devices . . .'

Extensive as his USAID briefings had been, he already felt unprepared. The organisation's mission statement – furthering America's foreign policy interests in expanding democracy and free markets while improving the lives of citizens of the developing world – was hardly going to be of help on a day-to-day basis. Nor were his fellow officers on the ground in East Africa. The chain of command went to Michael Nagle in Dar, then someone in Nairobi, then the Africa office in Washington. Nagle was an

agricultural economist with little sense of what marine conserva-
tion might be about.

Avoiding young African men buzzing by on old-fashioned
Italian scooters, he wandered through the narrow streets (one
even called 'Narrow Street') until he came to a crumbling hotel.
Its façade included a balustraded veranda overlooking the
esplanade. He climbed the steps and settled himself in a wicker
chair. From behind a carved wooden door of great antiquity, a
waiter appeared and took his order of shrimp and salad. The
waiter was very gaunt, and as soon as he'd gone Nick experienced a twinge of anxiety about eating raw food in such a place.

Waiting for his meal, Nick noticed a faded poster on the wall.
It declared that the building 'formerly housed part of the sultan's
harem', beneath a black-and-white photograph of a woman's
face, half-covered by a diaphanous veil. The exposed half
seemed, at first, to express corrupt and exotic sensuality – a sly
invitation to dangerous adventure. Under the heavy, kohl-ed
eyelids, however, was a glimpse of fierce intelligence quite out of
keeping with the impression of decadence the photographer had
clearly hoped to achieve.

Nick was still gazing at the photograph when his food arrived.
He set to – only to be disturbed a few minutes later by something
brushing against his leg. A glaring gang of cats had surrounded
him on the veranda. Smaller and mangier than ones back home,
they had sharp pointed ears and extravagant marmalade mark-
ings. They seemed wild, ancient, mystically Egyptian, and their
amber eyes looked at him, or more properly at his plate of
shrimp, with sphinx-like fascination. Picking a shrimp from his
plate, he tossed it into the road and watched as they chased after
it, fighting amongst themselves, cuffing and hissing.

Paying the bill, he asked the waiter where he might find the
offices of the Zanzibar Ministry of the Marine Environment. The
man looked back at him blankly.

'I have to find an Inspector Chikambwa.'

The waiter's thin face lit up. 'Oh, you mean Bwana Ernest. That is far. That is Ng'ambo.'

'What's that mean?'

The waiter looked very grave, as if the translation were a difficult one. 'It means – the other side.'

Nick paused.

'Ng'ambo is the other side of Creek Road,' the waiter explained.

That part of town, as he learned during a confused and sweltering search, was also called Michenzani. It was a poor area, shockingly poor, overrun with ragged children scrabbling round in the dust in front of old stone houses. In the centre of Michenzani, he rounded another derelict corner and encountered – against expectation – a thicket of modern tower blocks. They were dilapidated and discoloured, but they were at least a century newer than the houses. He approached one of these more recent ruins and peered in at the lower levels. The inhabitants seemed to be camping rather than living there. The glass was missing in the windows, and he could see right in to where they were cooking food in tin pots over open fires. Looking up, he saw smoke rising from the top of the block. Holes must have been made in the roofs of each successive level to let it pass through. He felt faintly disheartened. Somehow he hadn't expected to see this kind of poverty here, the kind of African poverty which he associated with Ethiopia and all those other places.

'So, you are the new American?'

Chikambwa's heels were on the desk when Nick entered the office. From the very start, he conceived a dislike of this sullen man in his charcoal-grey policeman's shirt and steel-rimmed spectacles.

'That's right. Nick Karolides.'

'Passport!'

The policeman examined it sternly.

'*Karro-lides*?' he said, as if practising the name, and then handed it back. 'They told me you were coming.'

There was an awkward silence. Nick became conscious of the breeze from the ceiling fan, stirring the hair on the nape of his neck.

'Well, I suppose I ought to explain your duties – although I should add that your predecessor overreached his role. Frankly, I'm not surprised he came to a bad end.'

'You mean the accident?'

In his interview, the USAID people had told Nick that the man he was replacing, George Darvil, had died in a boating accident.

Chikambwa looked at him.

'That is what they told you?'

'Why? Did something else happen?'

'We are not sure. His boat was found with holes.'

'They just said he drowned.'

'It is not important.'

'It is for me! What happened to him?'

Chikambwa gave him a hard stare. 'As I said, we are not sure. The reason may be that he did not do as he was told. He cut the nets of poachers.'

'And they killed him?'

'Who knows? What is clear is that it is vital for you foreign workers to remember that you are our guests. We are a socialist revolutionary republic. You are here, Karro-lides, by our invitation. You are *not* here to tell us what to do.'

'OK,' said Nick, still thinking about Darvil. Had they lied to him at USAID, to not discourage him from taking the post?

'So now I will show you.'

Chikambwa stood up and went to a noticeboard, on which was pinned a coloured map of Zanzibar.

'This area is called Nungwi.'

He fanned his hand across the northern part of the map.

'Here is your responsibility – from the point of Ras Nungwi down to Macpherson Cove.'

'What about those?' asked Nick, pointing to a speckle of small islands a few kilometres off the coast.

Chikambwa ignored him. 'The important reefs are here. You will patrol them, looking out for poachers, pollution and for rare species . . . I have a list.'

He went to a drawer and took out a laminated plastic sheet showing pictures of fish and other marine organisms, together with their English, Latin and Swahili names. It looked like a page from a child's textbook.

'Use the Swahili where possible. It is our national language. The fishermen will not understand you if you use fish names they do not know.' He paused. 'It is in this department that your predecessor may have gone wrong. To cut nets unilaterally is forbidden. You must only cut nets and traps with specific permission from me.'

The Inspector smiled, his teeth gleaming. 'Personally.'

'So . . .' said Nick, after a moment's silence. 'Where do I live?'

'A room has been reserved for you at the Macpherson Ruins Hotel.'

'That doesn't sound very promising,' Nick replied, not sure himself if he was being serious or making a joke.

'It is a good place. You are lucky to be able to live there. You should be grateful to your government. An African, Karro-lides, could not afford to live there.'

Nick nodded, his expression appropriately contrite.

'You will find the manager, Mr da Souza, a very helpful person. A Goan. There is a boat there, too, of which you will have the use. Although you will have to send dockets to the USAID office in Dar-es-Salaam for fuel, I am afraid. Do not come to me for fuel.

'I suggest you find a boy from one of the fishing villages to

29

help you with the boat. There are very many narrow channels on the coast which are difficult to navigate.'

'What about paying him?'

'The boy? That you will have to meet from your own salary.'

'And how do I get up to this . . . Macpherson?'

'Dala-dala. It is what we call taxi-minibus. You can fetch one on the street.'

'Right. Thanks. I guess I'll be seeing you.'

Nick shook the official's hand and turned for the door.

'Wait. One thing,' Chikambwa said.

'Yes?'

'You might see a man, Leggatt. European. He is a clove farmer who also does yacht charters and game fishing. Additionally he meddles in the marine affairs of our country. He is a nuisance. Keep away from him.'

'Right . . . OK.'

Perplexed and a little suspicious, Nick made his way outside into the heat.

It was twenty minutes before he could find a dala-dala heading to Macpherson Cove. He cheered up during the journey. The further north he progressed, the more beautiful the landscape became. Now there *were* palm trees and spice farms and monkeys and all those other elements – pieces of the jigsaw of every dreamer's golden land – that he had been eagerly expecting, that the name 'Zanzibar' had summoned in his head before he came. Even so, he also saw, from the cracked window of the motorised dustbox that was the dala-dala, things he hadn't been expecting – like a man riding a bicycle, with an enormous pelagic fish, perhaps a tuna, tied to the back. His heart soared, and his eyes grew dazed from squinting into the radiant light.

The dala-dala turned off the main road onto a sandy track. Here the leaves of the palm trees grew larger and, as if the sky were opening its robes to the sea breeze, the light changed perceptibly. He could tell he was by the ocean now. The wheels of the dála-dala jived in the sand, and then a sign flashed up. Macpherson Ruins Hotel. The remains of an ancient building stood in gardens nearby. It was more as if the garden was *in* the ruin. Lianas twisted about in the roof tiles. Big red blooms burst out between the masonry, covering the blocks and slabs with a network of shadows.

It was, in spite of the breeze, piercingly hot. Nick paid the driver and carried his bag down a sandy path to some newer buildings. These were simple constructions except for their roofs, which were tall, sweeping cones of straw thatch. He could feel the heat through the soles of his trainers. He entered one of the straw-hatted buildings, under a teak lintel into which the word 'RECEPTION' had been carved out.

Inside, it was cool and very dark. Relief from the sun was a gift given bodily – the skin round his eyes relaxed, his scalp and hair altered minutely as, like some finely calibrated scientific instrument, they took account of the change in atmosphere. There was no one behind the desk, and nothing on it save a leather-bound ledger and a battered bell, the kind you press to ring. So this was it then, this would be home for a year. He thought of his mother, of Dino at the dive shop, his work at the lab . . . the life he'd left behind. Then, with some panache, he pinged the old brass bell.

For a few moments there was silence. Then a voice came through the gloom.

'Guest!'

'Guest!'

He heard a door open. The hiss of a match. A small, elegant figure appeared, glowing in an off-white suit.

'That's right,' said Nick rather smartly. 'I *am* a guest.'

'Oh no, sir,' the match-lit figure replied. 'You misunderstand me. I was simply happy to have a guest. Bookings very down. I knew it was you. Chikambwa from the marine . . . he telephoned me.'

31

'So you are Mr da Souza? Aren't there any lights here?'

'Your first question, sir: yes, I am da Souza.'

He reached out and touched Nick's sleeve by way of introduction.

'To your second question, I am afraid I must offer a negative reply. No generator, sir, being fixed tomorrow.'

'You do have a room?'

'Yes, of course. A room. *The* room.'

Nick wondered if the manager was mocking him, imitating his previous tone.

'Please – come this way. Let me take your bag.'

'No, it's OK.'

The strange little man led him through a warren of corridors, each as shadowy as the reception, then out into a garden. Nick blinked in the sunlight. Enclosed by trees – mangoes, jacaranda, frangipanis – it was a kind of courtyard. Bordered by flowerbeds, paths of crushed pink coral radiated from a central gazebo. Each path led to a chalet beyond the trees. It was to one of these that Nick was led. As they walked, he saw that da Souza was, quite apart from being very short, extraordinarily beautiful. He had a smooth, mahogany-brown face; his tiny ears were set flush against his skull; his eyelashes were rather feminine; and his neatly parted black hair looked as if it had been oiled as well as combed.

He led Nick across the courtyard and up a flight of creaky wooden steps to one of the chalets. Da Souza walked, Nick noticed, like a dancer.

'This is the room,' said the manager, taking a key from his pocket and opening one of the doors.

Following him inside, Nick dumped his bag on the floor. Again, it was dark. But there was enough light filtering in through the open door and the inadequate curtains – big French windows behind them – for him to see that the room was neat and decent. The bed had its sheet crisply turned down and a couple of blankets folded at the foot. There was a table with an old-fashioned wooden chair pushed underneath it and, on the surface, leaning against the wall, a few marine biology textbooks and a novel called *The End of Eternity*.

'The room of the gentleman before,' explained da Souza, seeing him look at the books. 'The gentleman from United States like you, sir.'

'Those are his?' asked Nick. 'So, what happened to him exactly? I've been hearing conflicting stories.'

The manager appeared to ignore him. 'There are some clothes in the closet. I did not know what to do with them.'

'The USAID guy – what happened?' repeated Nick.

Da Souza went over to the window and drew the curtains. Through the glass came the intense glare of the beach and, beyond it, the green of the sea, calm and glittering except for a ruff of surf far out, folding voluptuously into its own foam.

'He drowned, sir.'

'I know that. But what were the circumstances?'

Da Souza had his back to him, his white suit framed by the seascape.

'It has been said he was chasing poachers, sir. But nobody knows for certain. His boat was stove in. Some say there was a storm and his boat hit rocks. It was seen, eventually, half full of water.' He hesitated. 'Mr Darvil's body – was on the reef.'

Da Souza turned and walked forward, taking Nick's hand like a child.

'Oh sir, it was very sad. You must take care in your employment. You will find the boat on the beach outside. The blue painted one. It needs to be fixed.'

He paused, then added brightly, 'Mr Leggatt, he towed it in. He has a clove farm at Mtoni.'

'Chikambwa mentioned him,' said Nick, disengaging himself politely.

He was still wondering why USAID hadn't gone into more detail about George Darvil. Maybe they, too, had never known the full story.

'Well, I suppose I should get settled in.' He pointed at a squat brown box in the wall. 'That an air conditioner?'

Da Souza smiled. 'Yes, sir, but it will work only when generator is running. Is best if you just open the window. Natural air conditioning.'

'Yeah, well. I always thought those things poisoned you anyway.'

The dapper little manager had crouched down; he was trying to open the French windows. One of the bolts was stuck. As he fiddled with it, he gave a little curse in a language Nick didn't understand. Chikambwa had said da Souza was Goan. What did they speak in Goa?

'Don't worry,' said Nick, crossing the room to look, over the creamy fabric of da Souza's shoulder. 'I've got a knife in my bag. I'll open them later.'

In fact, he did so as soon as da Souza had left him, quickly bundling snorkel, fins and swimming trunks out of his bag, onto the bed, delving for his Rapala clasp-knife. Opening it with his thumbnail, he knelt down and lifted the bolt with the back of the blade. Then, with a push, and some small resistance, the windows were wide open.

It was an exciting moment, those glass doors springing free; it seemed to clear his mind. He could smell the sea so strongly now. That, and the sight of it – the hypnotic return of waves of unnameable shades of blue, some craft, an outrigger maybe, traversing the distance – were at once humbling and intoxicating.

Changing quickly and grabbing his snorkelling gear, he stepped out onto the veranda. Now he could see it all. Either side of the veranda's flaking paintwork, the beach gave out – an expansive whiteness. It had a deceptive, almost liquid appearance in the heat, as if it were melting, constantly spreading on either side. Pulled up above the waterline, which was marked with straggles of black seaweed, were several Zanzibari fishing boats of the type he had glimpsed further out. He was right. They did have outriggers and, sticking out from their prows, paraffin lanterns for night fishing. There was another boat, too, on the ribbed sand, a blue one with a gash in its side . . . that must be Darvil's, he thought. Nick had a sudden vision of him – all sodden skin and glittering eyes, rising from the torn hull of the boat.

Dismissing the image, he looked out to sea again. Luminous, extending to a distant horizon of flat cloud, it gave an impression of incredible power. It was sound that did this – not the sound of the nearby waves, lightly throwing themselves forward and withdrawing on the shore, but the constant noise of the surf where, half a mile out, rollers crashed against the reef. The surf-line was like another bank of cloud, he reflected, his gaze following it under the horizon. Only this white wasn't flat; it was alive, moving – continuously, like a loop of film endlessly replaying itself.

With mask and snorkel pushed up over his forehead, fins and towel under his arm, Nick stepped out from under the veranda's straw roof, down some warped wooden steps, and onto the sand. It was as soft as talc, running hotly over the bridge of each foot as he walked.

Reaching the sea, he tossed the towel onto a twisted piece of driftwood and – with his fins under his arm – walked directly into the water. It covered his body, the waves so gentle that they hardly moved him as, sitting in the shallows, he put on the fins. He pulled down the mask and dived.

Sea light. Sea life, too, but not much of it. He looked from side to side through the oval of the mask. The first thing he saw was a starfish, clinging to a rock. They never failed to make him think of someone's hand, fingers outstretched. Then: nothing, just the

white bed of sand, dotted with more rocks. He swam on a little –
to where, edging down, the sea floor began to shelve. He felt
ghostly, knowing again that pull of the waves in his blood – an
immemorial, homeland sense that went beyond words, beyond
explanation.

The splash of a cormorant shook him from his reverie. He
watched its brown shadow trigger through the water. A flash of
silver signified the fish that was taken, the fish that he hadn't
even noticed; all this he realised later, once the bird had gone. At
least it meant there were fish about; he had been getting vaguely
anxious. He had seen more in Sarasota Bay.

Then, as if some whimsical deity of the deep had decided to
salve his anxiety, he spotted something intriguing. Below him on
the seabed were two glassy green lumps: as if somebody had
taken a couple of spoonfuls of jello and, very carefully, half covered them with sand. Taking a breath through the snorkel he
swam down, enjoying the familiar pressure in his head. He was
about half way to the lumps when the sand abruptly levered up
beneath him – lifted up flat before dispersing in a fizzing cloud.
Out of the turbulence – slowly appearing, then sliding away at
some speed – came a black rubbery triangle. Two metres across,
it tapered to a long, thin tail.

Exhilarated, Nick watched the ray scoot across the sand, tail
dragging behind it like an old-fashioned radio aerial. He powered himself forward in pursuit, kicking on until he was out of
breath and had to come to the surface, blowing water out of his
snorkel with an aggressive burst. He turned over and let the sun
play on his stomach for a while, then spun round once more, to
face the reef.

It took him about a quarter of an hour to reach it. Every
minute, as he approached the line of battered coral, was like a
revelation. As the skeleton of the main reef came closer, fish of
every description began to weave around him. Some were

breathtakingly beautiful, with names that told their story – butterfly fish, parrot fish, angel fish. Others were unlovely, but no less fascinating; and, once again, deserving of their names: groupers, puffer fish, goatfish, grunts . . .

At the reef itself, a school of blue-lined yellow snappers enveloped him, some hundred strong. The way they brushed him tenderly with their fins was almost like a greeting. He dived down to inspect the reef more closely, and the blue-yellow cloud billowed around him. There were different species amidst the coral. Many, such as the surgeon fish, with its sharp beak and beady eye, simply ignored him and kept on grazing. Others, like the nervous trigger fish, fled immediately on his approach. He swam along the vertical coral wall, glad that he had come without the full scuba gear. There was something liberating about doing this with light snorkelling tackle.

He felt blessed. It wasn't just the fish. The reef itself was no less absorbing. It had the massive, accumulated energy of a great building. Like something in Rome or London. Maybe it was the way a reef built up, trapping sunlight over hundreds of years to produce calcium carbonate, a cathedral of light. Even the dead parts of the wall were alive in their way, offering a surface on which algae could breed and, correspondingly, fish could feed.

The skeleton itself was fantastically complex: staghorn, plate, table, brain. Every type of coral he knew was here. Distinct yet conjoined, mainly white but streaked with the remnants of plant pigments, it really was like an edifice, the battlements of some elaborate castle out of a legend of doubtful authenticity – supreme production of a colossal empire, itself on the verge of a continuing, accelerating fall. But it was always changing its appearance: no comparison would hold. He floated along the side, holding his breath till, lungs bursting, he kicked his way to the surface.

He cleared his snorkel and swam on a little, enjoying the sun on his back. Then, taking in a giant breath, he dived again.

Round him now in shafts of sunlight were species of living soft corals, transparent, or the faintest pink and lilac. He watched where the polyps reached out to collect plankton, flailing like a blind person or a baby in its cot. Only they weren't blind. They *knew*. And the sponges knew, and the anemones, and the sea squirts. Everything was part of the system, and the system itself gave a kind of sentience, a sense of what they were about, to each of its constituent parts.

He floated up, letting the current carry him over the reef. And then, suddenly, it was blown away, the little fantasy world he had been building for himself. Here the reef had been destroyed. Here the wall was gone, missing for a good hundred metres. Broken pieces of coral were scattered on the ocean floor. There were no fish at all now. Nothing. The light had changed, too, become the fearful grey of a sea in mourning for itself.

Dismayed, he tried to imagine how it had happened: how the fishermen had come out one morning and, lighting the fuses in their waterproof casements, dropped the sticks over the side. How they had hurriedly rowed their boats to a safe distance to watch the water erupt in a foamy mushroom. Afterwards, the harvest: spreading their nets on the astounded surface and waiting for the dead fish to rise in their thousands. It made him feel sick, and he swam back to shore in a temper, kicking the water with his fins as if the ocean were to blame for its own destruction.

Da Souza was waiting for him on the beach with a tray of tea. 'Hello, sir!'

He pointed down at the lump of driftwood where Nick had left his towel. 'I saw your belongings . . . I trust you had a pleasant swim?'

Nick pushed the mask up off his face. 'Well, I did have. Until I saw what those shitheads have done with their dynamite. How long has that been going on?'

The Goan appeared shocked by his language. 'It has been happening for several years now, sir. When the fish are short.'

'The fish will be very short indeed if they carry on. Once the reef is gone, they won't come back.'

He picked up the towel, which was warm from the sun, and started to dry himself. 'Why doesn't Chikambwa put a stop to it?'

'He is very busy man, sir. And these fishermen, you know, they are poor and hungry.'

Then, to mollify him: 'Have some tea, sir.'

They stood in silence for a while, Asian and American, watching the surf line in the distance. As they looked, a wooden yacht, painted yellow, came into view from behind the green promontory that marked the edge of the cove.

'It is Mr Leggatt,' da Souza said, pointing with a white-sleeved arm.

'Chikambwa warned me off him,' Nick said in reply, watching the boat begin to cross the bay. He turned to da Souza. 'Any idea why?'

Looking embarrassed, the manager shook his head. 'I don't know these things.'

That night, Nick watched the news on CNN in the Macpherson's TV lounge. The top story, delivered with some drama, concerned independent counsel Kenneth Starr's extension of his investigation into President Clinton's alleged perversion of justice. The President was denying that he had had an affair with Monica Lewinsky. Nick listened for a while, then turned it off and went to bed, feeling despondent. Not about the state of the Presidency, which to his mind was far less important, but about the coral.

He saw the yellow yacht again the following morning, after inspecting the damaged USAID boat. The hull was badly stoved in, and there was no motor – but da Souza said he would lend him the hotel's spare outboard. It was, the manager said, in perfect working order except for a broken starting cord. He saw the yellow yacht once more later that day, returning, and twice the following day, too. He realised it was a pattern. Every day the yacht passed at the same times – on its outward journey and its return – and from the same direction: an east–west bearing.

This continued over the next fortnight. As he gathered his resources and laid out his quadrants at low water for what he had determined would be his first project – a survey of mollusc life on the intertidal flats – the yellow yacht, passing to and fro, became a regular fixture of his days.

Nick used his binoculars to try to get its name, but it was too far out. He could just make out the letters C-H-U-R-C-H, and see the pipe-smoking helmsman leaning over the wheel, scanning the horizon.

He was intrigued. 'I mean, where does that Leggatt guy go?' he asked da Souza, one night over dinner.

The Goan shook his head. 'I don't know. He just travels.'

'Eastwards every morning – what lies east of here?'

Again, as if the distances were too far, or the question involved too great a mental effort, Mr da Souza shook his elegant head.

5

It was almost dusk. A pink light covered the mountain called, in Pashtun, the Eagle's Nest. Soon, like lamps in a cave, stars would hang above its snow-capped peak. Soon darkness would settle everything. For now, however, the prospect was majestic, enlightening: the kind of view that seemed to forbid disillusionment. It was no wonder that earlier conquerors had given Afghanistan names such as 'the roof of the world' or 'the heart of Asia'.

In truth, these fierce mountains resisted their human names. Or so it appeared, against his holier nature, to the young man lying on his belly among them. Take oil through my sides, they seemed to say to him, call – if you like – these patterns in my rocks, the ninety-nine names of Allah. Bring me your dynasties, bring me your petty plans. Bring me your hydroelectric schemes. Bring me your fabulous conspiracies. I will outlast them all.

This is what, impiously, the mountains said to the young man lying on his belly, some twenty others by his side. They might also have said that Khaled al-Khidr didn't have much of a belly these days. Months of intensive training had seen to that.

It was three and a half years since his parents' death. The scene remained engraved on his mind, as if the killer's keen blade had touched there also. He had spent many months struggling to find out what had happened, or make the police find it out. But they weren't interested, characterising it as a robbery, even though nothing was taken. They would do nothing without a bribe. Most were more interested in illegal selling of turtleshell and other products than in investigating crimes.

He had to sell his father's boats to survive. Despair gnawing away at him, he sought refuge in fornication and drinking, spending his bloody inheritance, hoping to forget. Once its brief pleasure ceased, every lapse screamed the dread memory in his ears like a monkey – telling, one by one, how each of his deeds of shame brought dishonour on the memory of his mother and father. He suffered agonies of remorse, knowing he should instead be revenging them, and then comforted himself with more shameful acts, piling up a weight of guilt.

Then he came, Zayn – tendering support, a chance to repent, to arrive again at Allah. That was in the January of the following year. Khaled had known Zayn previously as an associate of his father. Zayn was the man who'd asked his father to be caretaker of the little island, having bought it off him, in a manner of speaking. He was also someone who arrived, from time to time, to give *zakat*, Muslim alms, to the village.

Zayn told Khaled that his father had for many years been working for a Muslim jihadi organisation, as what was known as a sleeper. That the organisation's purpose was to free the sacred places of Islam from the influence of the American *kufr*. That his father was a hero whom US agents had come and killed because of his work. It was now, Zayn said, time for him to join the jihad like his father before him.

It was an easy decision, a relief to have someone to hate. His life had been spiralling downwards. Islam could, he was persuaded, provide an explanation for the tragedy that had befallen him. Zayn told him there was no major sin once you have opened the door of acceptance and Allah's grace confronts you.

After leaving the island, following Zayn's instructions, he embarked on a year's religious education in Sudan. He worked on one of the Sheikh's farms outside Khartoum, driving a tractor in the mornings and taking instruction in the Koran in the afternoons. He'd enjoyed both types of work. The sound of the bright green maize cobs tumbling into the bin of the cutter behind him, the sound of his fingers as they leafed the pages of the Book . . . these things came back to him often.

So did other sounds, but not with pleasure: the din of faithful people being attacked by the military machines of the *kufr*. Helicopters and missiles, machine guns and rocket-propelled grenades . . . Every night, video tapes of Muslims being maimed and killed by infidel forces – by Americans in Iraq, by Russians in Chechnya, by Serbs in Bosnia – were shown to all the trainees.

Now he lay at the firing range, with a clattering in his ears and his comrades by his side. He was used to it, having been six months in Afghanistan, although he still wished they provided earmuffs. The Pashtuns who fed the belts were half deaf from having performed this service for wave upon wave of the fighters who came through the camp. It gave Khaled pleasure to see the fresh jihadis arrive at the headquarters; he felt benevolent towards them, but enjoyed accommodating himself to their inferior state.

They would, he knew, have two months of tough physical training – push-ups, sit-ups, running and crawling – before they were allowed to make their *bayat*, their oath of allegiance to al-Qaida, as he had recently done. He had memorised the words: 'I give my oath with Allah that I am ready to be a martyr in order to attain the high goals of jihad and to strive with all my heart to the last drop of my blood, and with a pure mind and a sweet patience endure every kind of difficulty. And if I should be there, in the gardens of delight, I shall not die, but wear the belt of eternal life, eating the choicest fruit at the wedding feast, together with my companions.'

Afterwards his mentor told him, privately, that he had been chosen a long time ago, as a superior figure to those who'd trained with him, and that soon his talents would be called upon in a special way. Zayn added that Khaled must nonetheless remember that knowing when to conceal superiority is a further proof of it; he wasn't to tell anyone else about his special status at the camp.

The headquarters used to be in Peshawar, in Pakistan. In those days al-Qaida was something like a charitable foundation, providing funds and facilities for volunteers on their way to Afghanistan to do battle with the Soviets. The Emir had run a number of safe houses and hostels in the city, offering accommodation for fighters from abroad, together with health care for refugees from the war. The CIA had helped him in that time, Khaled had heard, before the Russians left in '89.

Now they were the enemy, and the camp was in Afghanistan itself. Khaled raised his eyes to find the sight at the end of the barrel. Before the rock face opposite him was a line of targets. They weren't Americans, these black-lined sketches of charging soldiers, but he, like all the trainees, was encouraged to believe they were. Once, a magazine picture of the queen of the *kufr*, Madeleine Albright, was pinned up for them to shoot at. The previous night, they had been shown videotape from a news programme called *60 Minutes*, in which the Secretary of State said she thought sanctions against Iraq were worth the price of the half million children they had killed.

Zayn blew his whistle loudly. Khaled and the others pulled their triggers. The valley erupted with bursts of automatic gunfire. Splinters of rock flew up ahead as the bullets passed through the images and hit boulders on the mountain beyond. The young man squinted to see how he had done. It was a good set of rounds: one line across the chest, another raked across the lower abdomen. These were killing shots. Zayn Mujuj would be satisfied.

Khaled waited – lying on the ground, rifle in hand – as the leader of their cell, walking behind them with binoculars, checked their shots. Although he often found Zayn frightening – with his shaven dark head and heavy shoulders, and those intense, coal-black eyes – to Khaled this brooding figure was all

44

the same a kind of surrogate father. For it was Zayn Mujuj who had cared for him, bringing him off Pemba, Zanzibar's second island, and giving him a new life.

His benefactor made an approving noise behind him.

'This is sufficient,' he said, tapping the youngest member of his cadre on the ankle with his foot.

Khaled rose and Zayn, clutching him to his huge chest, kissed him on both cheeks, laughing.

'More than sufficient! Soon, my little greenfinch, you will be as good a marksman as I.'

Then the cell leader spoke more loudly, so all the fighters could hear.

'Return now. Make your ablutions and your prayers. Tonight the Sheikh will see us.'

The Sheikh. The Prince. The Emir. The Director. Khaled had not seen him. He had another name, but it was rarely spoken.

The man in question was sitting in his tent in conference with one of his closest advisers, who was also his personal cameraman. Leaning on the wall next to him was the 7.62-millimetre-calibre Kalashnikov that rarely left his side. It was well worn, with little dents and abrasions on its laminated wooden stock. It might be thought something of a trophy, gained as it was during the course of a three-day assault on a Russian position.

The adviser was known as Ahmed the German simply to distinguish him from other Ahmeds in the organisation. His true nationality was Jordanian and he had picked up the nickname because he had spent time studying in Germany. He was slightly fairer than most Arabic people – a hint of blue in his eyes, a touch of blond in his hair. He was more or less the only person in the camp who wore Western dress as a matter of course – including a trademark baseball cap with the words 'SPORT TEAM OSNABRÜCK' across it. He was permitted this indulgence because he frequently travelled in Europe and America on al-Qaida business, and because he was one of the Sheikh's favourites.

Ahmed knew the leader of al-Qaida well enough to speak to him in familiar terms. 'You are looking a bit weary, Sheikh. Your face has more lines in it.'

The face to which he was referring was long and thin. Its most striking feature was a pair of sharply arched eyebrows, which curved a good way down the side. The Sheikh's lips were rather full, and he had a straggly, longish black beard with a fork of grey directly under the chin. Otherwise, it would be noted that his eyes were light brown – with a range of expression that included a distant stare, burning anger and a certain dreaminess of aspect. It was true, too, that the Sheikh smiled a good deal.

He was smiling now, as he spoke to his colleague in Arabic. 'It is the burden of the work. And what the work might provoke. We do not yet know what the consequences of our action will be. Only Allah has foreknowledge. But I predict that when this thing is done, the Americans will put a price on my head, offering millions for my capture. Or they will send people or missiles here to kill me. Whatever is the case, I will accept my fate, relying on Allah.'

'*Inshallah*, you will be safe. But you must not tire yourself.'

The Sheikh laughed. 'Your concern is touching.'

The cameraman shook his head doggedly. 'We need you. All of us need you. You are the only one whom all respect. You are our cornerstone.'

The Sheikh lifted a hand to Ahmed's cheek. On one of his fingers he wore a gold ring with a large ruby set in the centre.

'I am just the instrument of Allah, as this is my own hand. No more. This work we are doing will not stop if I am gone.'

The Sheikh let his hand fall. 'Now, you are ready for the surveillance? I am also relying on you to marshal the activities of the forward teams, and extract them without notice. This is a crucial factor.'

'I will leave after the instruction,' Ahmed said. 'Nairobi first, then Dar-es-Salaam. I will have the tapes sent here by courier, using one of our own people.'

The Sheikh fixed his eyes upon him. 'I have decided to fast until you reach the continent of Africa. Let me know when you do.'

Ahmed nodded slowly, looking back at his master. 'It is good. Now, we must prepare. They will be coming for instruction soon. First I will fetch the others and we will pray.'

'Prayer is Allah's due.'

'It does belong to him and him only.'

With that, Ahmed salaamed and left the tent. The Sheikh walked over to the place where he made his ablutions, lifting up a canvas flap to reveal a china bowl on a wooden stand, half full of water. There was also a small square hand mirror, set in a plastic frame. With long, thin fingers, he picked it up and gazed into the glass, examining his own reflection, in the surround of soft pink plastic.

'And so it begins,' he said to himself.

But even as the words passed his lips, they were swallowed by the prayer call, echoing through the camp.

Allaaaahu akbar allaaaahu akbar!

The Sheikh made a mental note to have someone fix the Tannoy more securely to its wooden post.

* * *

With his lecture notes resting on his lap, Queller sat in a rented Lexus. He was in the car park at the Bureau of Diplomatic Security headquarters, Washington. On the seat beside him was a volume of Persian poetry and a bottle of mineral water. Only he wasn't studying his notes, or even thinking of opening the plastic top of the bottle, or the book at a page of Hafiz or Attar. He was watching girls.

Two, playing tennis on a court adjoining the car park. They were pretty evenly matched. Pretty, too. Although it was not given to him to know it, they had played together nearly every morning of the year-long DS training course.

As the blonde called out 'Forty–love,' the other – a darker, more intense, luxuriant type whom Queller liked better – picked up the ball where it had run to the edge of the fence. She turned and approached the baseline. She looked good as, holding out her racquet arm, she tossed the ball up freely. She brought the racquet back over her shoulder. Queller gazed in frank admiration as the girl's white sports smock, already sleeveless, tightened with the motion.

Man, she looked good. Oval green eyes. Rich dark-brown hair, a pale, clear complexion. She reminded him of his wife. Strong, but easy on her feet at the same time. Beautiful, but not in the way magazines or Hollywood conceived it: something more particular to do with the curve of the cheek, the shape of mouth (a pomegranate, opening) and a curl of hair at the nape of the neck. Just a minute, and he was back in a world of hope. A refuge where she existed still, before the terror had crept – like a long, slow serpent – over the horizon.

He spun silently in his memories, feeling worn down, craving the taste of times gone by, wishing his body could have hers beside it once more. And be itself again, not denounced, over every inch of skin, by its own history. Queller was sixty next year and he thought a lot about decay. Time was getting to him: his hair was oyster-grey, his skin chalky, there were deep lines cut in his face and heavy swags of flesh under his eyes. Yet all people noticed was that one particular VDM. A Visual Distinguishing Mark, as the intelligence dossier would put it. Something missing. Today, however, he was wearing the artificial. He hated it, but he had a reason. He had a show to put on.

The serve was an ace. It whipped right past the receiver and hit the fence with a rattle. Queller clapped softly, flesh against plastic, and watched the two young women walk towards the bench and pick up their kitbags.

He heard their voices through the open window.

'Probably our last game, Miranda,' said the blonde, as they passed along the edge of the court.

'Unless we both get posted here,' replied Queller's favourite, wiping her face with a towel.

The movement stung his memory, and for a few brief seconds she lived again: *Lucy*.

And then his wife's ghost and her companion passed out of earshot. Once more the darkness came into his head like a stain. With a last farewell that scarcely reached his ears, she died a second death, falling back again into that same place from which she had come.

* * *

They marched along the spine of the ridge. The rifles – sights folded flush against the barrel – were heavy across their shoulders. At the head of the column was Zayn's forbidding broad beam. At the back were the three Pashtun bearers with the bandoliers. Their loads were less heavy now that several hundred bright copper cartridge cases had, once again, been spilled in the mountains of Central Asia. Between Zayn and the bearers came the cadre. It included Khaled with his curly hair and young, Arab–African face, and Yousef, the pale Syrian with the awkward body and pencil moustache – silent Yousef who had been with the Sheikh's organisation for years and was an expert bombmaker.

Khaled shivered as he walked. Through ragged, scarlet clouds, the sun was beginning to set. It was growing cold. Above the flanks of the valley, covered now with an angry red light, stood the Eagle's Nest and the other peaks of the area. Below him he saw a bleak compound of grey, industrial-style concrete huts surrounded by wire fences and topped with razor coils. It looked like a prison – but for the past year it had been his home.

It was not a very comfortable place, but it was clean and they were well fed, receiving a ration of potatoes, onions, rice and tea every day.

Beyond the fence, on the slope of one of the treeless hills that are a feature of this region of Afghanistan, were the ruins of a mud-hut village and a cluster of green tents. Next to the tents stood an anti-aircraft battery. Two long barrels, gleaming in the dying sun, emerged from the sandbagged dais. This was the Taliban encampment, here to watch the al-Qaida men as protectors but also, Khaled sometimes felt, as guards.

He found them strange, these silent men with their dark beards and wool caps. He could not understand them, and not just because they spoke Pashtun; he could not understand their fierceness, their inflexibility, their intensity. They shared these qualities with Zayn, but there was something else about these fellows. Some of the older ones hunched in blankets over the bonfires had, he knew, been mujahidin, Afghan freedom fighters. They would remember the days when the Russians came in helicopter gunships and hunted them like dogs. But most were in their early twenties, as young as Khaled himself. He wondered what drove them. They had no scar of experience to remind them, to drive them on always in the service of Allah and hatred of a great enemy.

Whereas he – an alien here under these slate-grey skies – he had that. Written in blood on his memory, never to be forgiven. It had nurtured him during the arduous months of his training. All the while – as he fought with knife, or ran with pack, or squeezed the trigger of an automatic weapon – it was the image of his dead parents, lying on the floor of their house on Pemba, throats cut in a zigzag shape, that had given him strength.

Allahu akbar allaaahu akbar . . .

Hearing the prayer call from the camp, the column hurried its step.

The tennis players passed into a kind of tabernacle: the asphalt frontage of the Bureau of Diplomatic Security. The Bureau – DS as it was known – was charged with the protection of US personnel overseas. Its primary function being to provide a safe environment for the conduct of foreign affairs, it also had a role in protecting the Secretary of State, the staff of foreign embassies, and visiting foreign dignitaries. It was, in fact, these subsidiary aspects of DS work that the young women were discussing.

'Some *do* stay, you know, to work in the department and look after the foreign missions. Though I wouldn't want it myself. I couldn't see the point of going through all that training just to stick in Washington.'

'I wouldn't mind. I could still see Frank . . . Well, guess we better find out where they sent us.'

'Shower first?'

They looked at each other, shook their heads in unison, and ran helter-skelter in their tennis kit to the noticeboard in the corridor of the central building.

The blonde girl traced her finger down the list of names. Graham, Kirsteen.

'Hell, I am sticking here after all. Well, I guess that means another year of Frank. What about you?'

Her companion read it out.

'Powers, Miranda. American embassy, Dar-es-Salaam, Tanzania. Executive Assistant (Logistical and Security) . . .'

'Wow,' said Kirsteen. 'That's Africa! How do you feel?'

She looked at her friend.

Miranda pursed her lips. 'Kind of funny. You know, all the time we were doing this stuff, the weapons training, personnel review, construction security, the whole thing . . . all the time I knew I would end up going somewhere out of the way. Like, I knew it wasn't going to be London or Paris.'

Kirsteen pulled a face. 'The shops won't be so good. Talking of which, I guess we better go get ready. Who are the speakers?'

'One's Jack Queller – used to be the top Arabist under Reagan.'

'The one-armed bandit?'

Miranda nodded, feeling a bit aggrieved that her friend already had this piece of information. 'They say he's a kind of genius. A bit weird. Apparently he meditates every day.'

'What about the others?'

'Don't know. Someone from the FBI, I think. We'll find out at the door. Better get going.'

The two young women emerged from the central complex and headed for their room. Half an hour later, freshly showered and soberly dressed, the roommates were back again, lining up with the other graduates of the DS training scheme outside the lecture theatre.

Miranda felt excited. It was the last stage in the long journey of her training. With this over, she would be able to take possession of that coveted boon, a job in State. She hoped desperately that it wouldn't be one of those experiences of which the anticipation proved more special and satisfying than the actuality. Her father, although generally an optimistic person, used to say all of life was like that: that only in heaven would we get everything we had been anticipating – and more besides, to be sure.

But then, he was a devout Catholic and she suspected this had been drummed into him by a priest. She heard him saying the word 'anticipating' again in her head as she and Kirsteen approached the door of the theatre. There was a printed sheet pinned up on the wall-board outside, detailing the imminent proceedings.

* * *

Khaled and the others assembled for prayers. The Sheikh's construction workers had built a mosque at the camp. The small garrison of Taliban soldiers joined them. As for the Sheikh himself, he prayed alone in his tent.

Khaled knelt on the mat, trying to find some still point in the clamour: the clamour of his mind – any woven material like this still disturbed him – and that of his co-worshippers. The Talibs were very noisy when they prayed. Weeping and wailing, they rocked to and fro with such fervour they sometimes knocked into him. He suspected it was vanity that made them so ostentatious in their worship, rather than true righteousness. For did not the Prophet specifically enjoin us to recite the Koran slowly, so that our merely human ears might hear Allah speak to us with true profundity? And did he not say also that our Lord's impression upon us was deepest in the silent hours of the night, when his words came to us with genuine eloquence?

But everywhere was the sound of battle. Zayn said politics and fighting happened because of the power of the *kufr* and the weakness of Muslim leaders. Like the rest of them, he saw America as the Satan of the age, but for him it was specific – the matter of Palestine and its freedom, and US support for Israel. Yousef had told him Zayn's parents had been killed by the Israelis. So they shared something there, as the Americans and the Jews were one and the same. It was what the Sheikh said in his messages; it was what bound al-Qaida together; it all came down to history.

He could see Zayn now in front of him – could see the stubbly hair on the back of that huge head; it bristled most where his neck bulged over his collar. Sometimes he found it hard to love his saviour. But most of the time Zayn was warm and endearing, looking after him like a favourite son, always making sure he had the best food and equipment.

They'd had many happy days together in Sudan – every

Friday visiting the camel market in Omdurman to see the desert tribesmen bargaining, or going to Al Haj Yousif to join the large crowd of spectators for Nubian wrestling. On the way back, they would buy sweet pastries in the souk and stand eating them with sticky fingers, watching the snake charmers coax their swaying animals out of wicker baskets.

Zayn explained many things to him, putting straight what seemed tangled in his head. Once, near the Mogran, the confluence of the Blue and White Niles where it was possible to see a defining line between the two pieces of water, Zayn had put his arm over his shoulder – they were standing on the White Nile Bridge – and told him that his life should be like that now: once you committed yourself to God, your life would never flow in the same direction again.

He said nothing must get in the way of that, especially not women or wealth. 'You remember what the Koran tells us – how Sheba visiting Solomon saw a shiny surface which she thought was water and bared her legs to swim. And then he told her it was only a reflection in glass and she was covered in shame. Well, that is how you must see the world from now, my little greenfinch: just glass, a reflection . . . That is what it means to surrender yourself to Allah.'

It was comforting to have a nickname. Arabs always made jokes about his surname meaning 'the green one', because he shared it with a legendary figure who came out of the spirit world to help Moses and other holy men. Some people said 'Salaam aleikum' to an empty room when they entered it, because al-Khidr lived in the void and had to be greeted. So most of the jokes were about Khaled being not there, or being an empty person. No one had ever called him a greenfinch before.

* * *

Guest Speakers:

Altenburg, Morton, Director of Operations (Justice/Counter-Terrorism), Federal Bureau of Investigation, Chairman (Interagency) Counter-Terrorism Group, National Security Council

Kirby, Tom, General, Joint Staff, Department of Defense (Special Operations and Low-Intensity Conflict)

Queller, Jack, Consultant, Middle Eastern Issues (State/Counter-Terrorism), formerly Chairman (Interagency) Counter-Terrorism Group, National Security Council and CIA Senior Ranker

The trainees took to their seats – the moulded red plastic chairs that had been unstacked beforehand and would be restacked at the end. In front of them, raised on a platform and spread with green baize, was a longish table, behind which were the three speakers. One, Queller it must be, sat at a slight angle to the table – on the edge of which, as if laid down like a challenge, rested the flesh-coloured, polyurethane hand of a prosthetic arm.

The course convenor, David Cronin, introduced them.

'I'm very pleased to welcome here, on the eve of your graduation from DS training, three senior experts. They will, I hope, give you a snapshot of the multi-dimensional terrorist threat affecting US diplomatic interests. First to speak will be Mort Altenburg, the FBI's chief adviser in this field. I don't think I'm telling tales out of school when I say he's seen by some as the main contender to be the next deputy director.'

At this Altenburg, a tall, bespectacled forty-year-old wearing a pale blue suit, gave a wry smile and shook his head in a show of self-deprecation.

Cronin continued. 'Mr Altenburg will be speaking about intelligence and threat analysis. We are also joined by General Tom Kirby from the Department of Defense. General Kirby has directed a number of counter-terrorism operations around the world – but I can't tell you too much about these as they're all classified.'

People laughed, looking at the soldier.

'General Kirby will speak on the military aspects of diplomatic security.'

Miranda frowned as she considered Kirby. The buzz cut, the hard eyes, the neat lines of the uniform. It was abundantly clear what kind of man he was. Her father, whose word had been like holy writ to her, had told her he always distrusted men who cut their hair too short. She knew it was silly – it would count against half the US Army for starters – but it was hard to forget.

'Finally I would like to introduce Jack Queller, late of the CIA and the National Security Council's Counter-Terrorism Group, of which he was Chairman – an interagency role which Mr Altenburg now holds. Having recently taken early retirement, Mr Queller has seen service with a number of agencies and now holds a prime consultancy role in the State Department. He is still rated as the country's premier expert on Arab affairs, and it is on this subject that he will talk.'

Her gaze settled on Queller. Grey-haired and modest, he looked more like an academic than an intelligence operative. Only a craggy face, and the arm – its unnatural contours clearly visible beneath his jacket – marked him out as unusual.

Or so she thought at first. On closer inspection, there was something unnerving about Queller. She believed herself quite a shrewd person, but the elements of his physiognomy, especially his soft eyes – ashen, like his hair – were quite hard to read. It was, all at once, the face of a man of blood and the face of a man of mercy.

'First though, Mort Altenburg . . .'

The FBI man stood up to applause – a sound of frightened pigeons – and began to speak. 'It is a commonplace to say, with the end of the Cold War and the fall of the Berlin Wall almost a decade ago . . .'

Miranda was certain she saw Queller give a thin smile. She looked back at the speaker. Altenburg was clearly far less interesting, just another Washington blue-suit guy. But the eager will to power, the commanding sweep his eyes made of the room before he spoke, those chimed – uncomfortably – with something in her. So, she had plans, she wanted to fulfil her father's expectations: that didn't mean she had to be pressed out by the Washington cookie-cutter. Hadn't he always said there was no virtue in sameness – that you always should walk up a different side of the street to everyone else?

She felt as if Altenburg was talking down to them. 'We all know that a nuclear conflict is less likely these days, and that our country faces other dangers – smaller ones, but no less dangerous for all that. From Damascus and Tripoli to Tehran and Baghdad, transnational groups such as the Abu Nidal organisation can find willing sponsors and supplies of arms. As the Gulf War, Somalia and Bosnia showed, there are also still governments – well, really we ought to call them dictators and warlords – out there willing to challenge the civilised nation states.'

Again Miranda saw Queller's face change, his expression more disdainful this time. He wasn't as dispassionate as she'd thought.

'General Kirby will talk more about taking the battle to these people, as we did with Qaddafi in Libya and Saddam in Iraq. My role here is to alert you, as those who will be taking charge of security in our embassies worldwide, to the threats you might face. People call it international terrorism, but we're chiefly talking about violent Islamic militancy. This is very different from nationalist separatist terrorism, such as the IRA and PLO. Or from the Marxist–Leninist people . . . Red Army Faction,

Baader–Meinhof, Shining Path. You've heard all the names. What I'm talking about elevates a spiritual rather than political program to the position of paramount importance. It's a pretty twisted spirituality, I grant you, and one that hopes to crush the West and certain Middle Eastern allies, but that is how they see it. How we see it doesn't matter, not to them. These guys are not killing for a Western audience. They are killing in the name of Allah. Allah will know what they have done. Because of this, so their warped thinking goes, they'll go to paradise if they sacrifice themselves in his cause.'

Altenburg looked over the faces in the room.

'Crazy stuff, isn't it?'

He paused, and then took up his thread again.

'And it's coming, this life-and-death struggle. Believe me when I tell you there's a evil wind blowing through the East. People snigger at the idea of a Holy War, the so-called jihad. But you shouldn't underestimate that threat. The bombing of the World Trade Center in 1993 was, I'm afraid to say, only the beginning. Last year there were over a thousand threats or incidents from Islamic groups against American interests. We're expecting many more. It's just parched grass out there, waiting for the spark, the man from the mountain or the desert about whom those flames will gather . . .'

Miranda shifted in her seat. She had heard much of this before. It was the kind of stuff they had been fed all year by Cronin. If this was one of America's leading experts on terrorism, then God help America. She felt sure, if there were so many threats, that a more sophisticated exposition was needed. Another thing her father always used to say was when it looks too simple, that probably means there's something more complicated under the surface. Altenburg must have known that the situation was complex; it was almost as if there was an element of deliberate parody in the way he spoke and presented his material.

'God is one; God is eternal. He has given birth to no one, and no one gave birth to Him. No one is equal to Him . . .

'He is the Lord of the east and the west, and there is no God but Him . . .

'He created human beings, and gave them language. The sun and the moon follow the course He has ordained. The herbs and the trees bow down in adoration.'

Khaled began to sway with gentle movements, chanting the verses quietly as he did so.

'He raised up the sky, and set all things in balance. He commanded you not to upset that balance, but to respect it. He laid out the earth for all creatures; and He planted upon it trees that bear blossom and fruit, husks that carry grain, and herbs that emit fragrance. Which of the Lord's blessings would you deny? He created human beings from dry clay, as a potter creates pots; and He created spirits from the flames of fire. Which of the Lord's blessings would you deny?'

Khaled emerged from the mosque with an easy spirit. It was all true, what the Book said. No one could doubt it. Unbelievers too would see that one day. There was no need to crack their heads against rocks. Was not the beauty of the Book a testament to its truth? Surely this was a sign for thoughtful people. He knew that many in the West misrepresented the Book out of fear and ignorance, unable to perceive even dimly the mysteries to which it was a righteous guide.

Sometimes, when he felt as calm as an inland sea, as now, as sweet as clarified butter, as now, he doubted al-Qaida and its work. There were other parts of the Koran. Such as that which commands the righteous to shun all those who divide religion into sects. Or that which outlaws intrigue as the work of Satan, who uses it to upset the faithful. The Prophet forbids us to plot in secret, the young man from Africa would say to himself. What we are doing, rather than making us the heirs of paradise, may indeed prevent us from entering it, vast as the sky and earth and watered by running streams as it is.

And then he would remember his parents – exactly as he had found them, with the zigzag slash across their throats, and their heads thrown back on the mat. And confronted by those horrible memories, his mind would clear and become strong again, filled with a hard-edged certainty.

Yet though he felt he knew his destiny now, somewhere deep inside, doubt still fluttered, summoning ensnaring sounds and figures from the mist of memory. Things half blanked out, a residue of fear, an unaccountable oppression. Earlier visits by Zayn, when he was much younger. The passing of money. Conversations in Arabic on the telephone, some angry.

Most disturbing of all was how agitated his father had been in the months leading up to his death. Once during that time, Khaled remembered, he had mentioned the future, in respect of them acquiring another fishing boat. His father had looked him in the eye and said: 'I have nothing but terror about the future.'

* * *

'Myself, I favour going in. Dealing with these people. Clamping down on illegal activities, restricting travel, disrupting training, breaking up support cells . . . bringing suspects to justice whatever the cost. We have to clip their wings; or, better still, wring their necks. I'm talking metaphorically here but – this is the real thing.'

He faltered slightly, before adopting a sterner, more admonitory tone.

'You realise the danger we face. Of course you do. It's our job, it's our duty.'

General Kirby was proving, to Miranda's ears, to be no more enlightening than Altenburg, saving the entertainment afforded by gung-ho soldier-speak.

'I don't make policy on what actions we take or don't take. That's for politicians. What I'm concerned for you folks to learn is that you must consider the embassies of the United States as de facto military establishments. Positions that have to be defended. Car bombs, mortars, Molotov cocktails, anti-tank rockets, surface-to-air missiles, close-order assassinations with handguns, rifles and grenades. That is the scope of the threat we are facing. That's why, as you know, at every US diplomatic institution you'll find a gunnery sergeant and his MSG, his detachment of Marines. The MSG, the Marine Security Guard, stands at the heart of the defence of our embassies.'

He paused to take a sip of water.

'But you can't leave everything to the MSG. It's down to you to be vigilant. Follow procedures. Never allow uncleared walk-ins. Take note of threat letters, anonymous phone calls, attempts at surveillance. Use the Tempest protection facility on your computers. Encrypt your messages. Shred your classified material. Initiate, every day, alarm-and-react drills. Make sure your X-ray units, your VCR control, and your radios are all in good order. Screen *everyone*. Because terrorists, enemies of the state, do not necessarily look like murderers. They mask themselves, pass as ordinary. That regular guy, in line for his visa . . .'

* * *

With prayers over, it was time to make their audience with the Sheikh. The three of them – Khaled, Zayn and Yousef – filed into his tent. It was large and had several sections divided by hanging flaps. Inside one, where the audience was to take place, lamps had been hung and carpets laid out, together with embroidered cushions and round trays carrying small metal goblets of sweet

61

black tea. Several of the Sheikh's senior lieutenants were already assembled, sitting cross-legged on the carpets or lying stretched out on the cushions. They included Ayman al-Zawahiri, the former paediatrician, leader of Egyptian Jihad; Muhammad Atef, al-Qaida's military commander; and Ahmed the German, al-Qaida's cameraman. Zayn was almost as high in the Sheikh's affections as Ahmed: he was at the core of al-Qaida's second echelon, followed by Yousef, the bombmaker who even now sat at Khaled's side.

After making their salaams, all waited in silence for their leader to emerge from his sleeping place, his inner sanctum. Khaled sipped his tea nervously. For a long time they had trained for some kind of mission. Soon they would find out what it was, albeit only in the vaguest terms. Security must be kept tight. Then would come the special training, related to their particular task, which Zayn had warned him could take another two months.

Khaled fiddled with the edge of the carpet, feeling the weave between finger and thumb. He saw Zayn turn his big head, look down, frown. Not sure if he was the reason for the frown, he stilled his fidgeting hand all the same.

Finally, a tent flap moved and a tall, slender figure emerged from the shadows. Well over six feet, he carried a cane and wore a spotless white *shalwar kameez*: the same long cotton shirt and roomy trousers favoured by many of the Talibs. Watching the great man enter, Khaled wondered whether the cane confirmed rumours of illness. It seemed to him the Sheikh looked in very good health. Bright eyes burned in a long, olive-coloured face. A dark, softly curling beard flowed over his neck and chest. There was, however, Khaled noticed, a fork of grey in it. On the Sheikh's head was a neatly wrapped black turban. On his feet, as if to say that this heir of paradise was indeed a humble man, were a pair of green plastic flip-flops.

The tent was silent as he moved across it, the lanterns making his shadow loom large against the canvas. The Sheikh sat on a small stool at the back of the tent. In spite of his height and his long thin limbs, he looked diminutive and surprisingly insignificant, sitting with his cane between his knees and one foot crossed over the other. But there was an unmistakable strength behind the modesty. The same was true of the Sheikh's voice, which, when it came, drew authority from its quietness. He began with an invocation.

* * *

'God bless America!'

The General sat down to perfunctory applause, and Queller approached the microphone. There was a pause, some amplified fumbling . . . Cronin adjusting the height. Miranda thought the final speaker looked tired and unwell. He had quite a large frame, but his shoulders had begun to round, and he stooped a little. There were deep lines in his face, as if every service he had done the state were written there. But his soft, pearl-grey eyes were pages from another kind of book, and when he spoke, he spoke softly, too.

'If there is to be a blaze in the East – and, speaking for myself, I hope that there will not be one – we had better put our hand in the fire while the coals are still smouldering.'

* * *

'Praise belong to Allah, the Lord of all Being, the All-merciful, the All-compassionate, the Master of the Day of Doom. Thee only we serve; to Thee alone we pray for succour. Guide us in the straight path, the path of those whom Thou hast blessed, not of those against whom Thou art wrathful, nor of those who are astray . . .'

A murmur of assent rippled through the company, and then the Sheikh took up his theme.

'My brothers, wherever your homeland, wherever you come from in the community of the Muslim world, I welcome you. Especially I wish to welcome Zayn and Yousef, they of brave and honourable service over many years, and their new recruit, Khaled al-Khidr. He is from Zanzibar, gentlemen, and is an essential element in a venture that will make us famous throughout the umma, bringing glory on our cause and all the doings of the faithful.'

Zayn clapped Khaled on the shoulder. There was a burst of applause, and the young Zanzibari hung his head with embarrassment.

The Sheikh smiled broadly. 'How good it is to see faithful people gathered. It reminds me of the old times, when Russians came on Muslim soil. I did not know then that it was just the beginning of a long campaign against the *kufr* of many nations. I only intended to expel the Soviet Union. But as it is revealed: antecedent intentions cannot pierce the walls of predestined decrees.'

He held up a copy of the Koran. 'Because nothing happens in the world or in your souls that is not written in the Book.'

Khaled fell into some confusion then. He had only been to a basic religious school in Stone Town, but he had studied more deeply in Sudan. He knew that the unpierceable walls were not in the Koran itself, but in a collection of mystical aphorisms. They were not God's will made manifest, as was the Book, they were simply sayings intended to arouse holy feelings in disciples. Yet it was not for him to question the interpretations of someone like the Sheikh. He was not a mullah.

* * *

Miranda saw Altenburg exchange looks with General Kirby. About their eyes, there was certainly nothing soft.

'What I mean to say is that we need to understand people,' said Queller. 'Sure, you have to accept that Foreign Service entails risks.

You have no choice there. But perhaps the worst risk of all is to misunderstand those, fellow human beings all, to whom your mission is directed. Embassies used to be called that: missions. Personally, I think it is a shame the habit has fallen away. Mr Altenburg is correct to warn you of the dangers of Islamic fundamentalism. But remember too that Islam is a broad church, though that's hardly the right way of putting it. Only a tiny proportion of the many billions who follow the Koran are fundamentalists. An even smaller proportion are likely to commit acts of terrorism. Bear in mind that a fundamentalist is not, per se, a terrorist; there may, moreover, be elements of fundamentalism one might admire. Purity of thought, single-mindedness, the patriarchal rigour of Islam – in which not to fear the Great Father, the Protector, the Bestower, is to be like a reed blowing in the wind – these things are alluring to the same degree that they are dangerous.'

* * *

'To counter these atheist Russians, the Saudis chose me as their representative in this part of the world. I settled in Pakistan first, in the border region. There I received volunteers who came from the Kingdom and from all over the Arab and Muslim countries. I set up my first camp where these volunteers were trained by Pakistani and American officers . . . You must understand that we were being cunning in dealing with Americans in this way, for while they thought they were using us to attack communism, we were using them to get arms. To prepare our strength . . .'

He smiled, looking directly at Khaled. 'It may seem strange now, to our younger members, that Americans came here to Afghanistan in person, their top men. They tried to make us part of their plots. To worship their idols and take up their evil ways. But we were smarter than them. We sent them away, with something to remember. And what we will do now, their nation will never forget. And other nations: all those who bow to America do not bow to our excellent Master, the Bringer Forward. Even now He is determining their fate, yes, from London to Moscow to the cities of Australia, he is preparing to sift them as wheat.'

* * *

Miranda sat up. This was more like it. This guy wasn't a fantasist or a hawk or a bigot. Queller had a brain.

'If the main threat to world peace is to emerge out of Islam, at least let's understand it. It is because it is misunderstood that Islam as a whole is feared, that it is perceived as extreme in its totality. That's way off target.

'Of course, there is genuine extremism. But that is what it is, an aberration. There are many different streams in a faith, even a monotheistic one. Different cultures, different practices . . .

'You might have heard some pretty horrible things about Islamic countries. But – don't we need to look at ourselves before we are too hasty to condemn? So, in one or two places, they cut off the hands of criminals . . .'

At this moment he lifted up his artificial arm, pulling the jacket so it slipped down, revealing the joint where the hand clipped onto the arm. A muted gasp was heard in the audience.

'Sorry,' he said, with a grin. 'Just wanted to get your attention. Yeah, they cut off hands and heads, but Uncle Sam puts criminals on death row and gives them lethal injections. Which would you prefer? My point is that if you view the Arab world as a stereotype, you'll never glimpse the sense of social justice and compassion that is also part of Islam.

'Now, saying that, there is a threat. It's a worldwide network known, in Arabic, as al-Qaida. That translates as the Base, or the Foundation. The Base – it refers not to the moral virtue of that network, though it well could, but to the organisation of an individual called Osama bin Laden. This is a man who has sworn to undermine American security worldwide.'

'So,' said the Sheikh. 'That is how it was. The weapons were supplied by the Americans and transported to the mujahidin by the Pakistanis. Some of these weapons we use even today.'

He pulled an automatic pistol from under his *kameez* and held it flat on his hands in front of the gathering, like an offering.

'Or we took them from the Russians. The money for our struggle came from both the CIA and the Saudis, and from my own reserves and those of other Muslims. The Soviets were the enemy then. But as I was telling you, my brothers, I soon discovered that to promote Allah it was not enough to fight communism alone. We had to fight Americans also. They wanted to take control here as they had in Saudi, Jordan and many places elsewhere. Helped by hypocrite rulers in those countries, they wanted us to take up their godless ways, their Cadillacs and McDonald's, their Las Vegas and their drugs and their pornographic films.

'Soon after we had chased away the last Russian from Afghanistan, the CIA sent their man here again from Peshawar with soldiers. He wanted to bribe the Taliban to fall in love with American companies. He wanted me to talk to them, to let them pass oil through the country in a pipeline. He was arrogant. He had to be shown that Muslim people will no longer be moved around by Americans like pieces on a chessboard.

'Later, in 1990, I returned to Saudi Arabia and gave my all in charity work for veterans of the Soviet fight. All that time I was discovering further how the American cancer had worked its way deep into the heart of the Kingdom. When Iraq invaded Kuwait the following year, I went to King Fahd myself and said, let the fighters of Afghanistan come and defend Saudi Arabia. But to my horror he opened the doors to American forces and their soldiers came. Half a million infidels sullying the land of the Ka'ba with the heels of their *kufr* boots. And some of them remain there still. It is a grave disgrace, directly disobeying the will of the Prophet.'

* * *

'He exerts control over his followers by misinterpreting portions of the Koran to justify violent actions . . . The perfect copy of that document, as dictated by Allah to Muhammad, is said to be kept in paradise. Well, bin Laden talks as if he has seen it himself. In plain view. Do you see?'

He took a sip of water. 'This assumption, this aping of infallibility is the key to him personally, and the reason for his success – he acts, in a profoundly symbolic and foundational way, as if he were the Prophet himself. It is deeply heretical, but it works. He is quite capable of persuading his followers to engage in suicide bombs. So Tom and Mort . . .'

Miranda was sure Queller had used their first names on purpose, as if he were saying 'Tom and Jerry'. Altenburg looked furious.

'– are right. *Be* vigilant. But do so from a position of strength. From a position of knowledge. Don't position Islam as negation. Be reflexive, provisional. Undo your own expectations. Get comfortable with the principle of contingency. If you pick up some item of intelligence, don't think because it is *this* type of intelligence, it carries *this* implication. With the information in hand, drawing out your scenarios, you have to be like a potter making a vessel whose shape he doesn't yet know.'

Once Queller's talk was over, there was enthusiastic applause. Having fulfilled the last requirement of their course, most of the trainees started filing out of the room. The keen ones buttonholed the speakers and started asking them questions.

Miranda picked Queller, phrasing an enquiry in her mind as she made her way swiftly towards him.

'Hi,' he said, smiling as she approached.

'Miranda Powers.' She reached for his hand, then realised it was the false one.

'Don't worry,' he said. 'Happens all the time.'

'I was just wondering,' she asked, nervously, 'if you could explain to me why, if bin Laden is really such a threat, we don't just send in a team, like General Kirby was saying.'

Queller sucked his teeth. 'It's tricky. Look at what happened in Iran when Carter sent people in to get the hostages. Look at Mogadishu. These things can go badly wrong. Besides, if you are talking assassination, there's a moral issue. The CIA has an ordinance about that now. Congress got wise, laid it down after attempts on Castro. I don't know what the answer is. The old "just war" line doesn't quite hold with terrorists under foreign sovereignty. Not that that's exactly what I'd call it, not in places like Afghanistan or Somalia. In any case, the problem is worldwide. London, Cape Town, Malaysia . . . this kind of terrorism's transnational, fluid. Its structure is the whole globe.'

* * *

'Now the Americans, who had so recently been seeking my assistance, were determined to hinder my holy work. They sent people to kill me in Sudan. When that failed they put pressure on the government there to eject me from the country. So in 1996 I returned here to Afghanistan with some of my children and many loyal followers, many of whom are with us here tonight.'

Several of the lieutenants, Khaled noticed, nodded self-importantly at this remark.

'The leaders of other holy organisations, like the good doctor here, they joined me. And we made our plans.'

Khaled looked at Dr Zawahiri, the Egyptian who had become al-Qaida's chief strategist. He was a plump, toad-like man whose face registered no expression as he was mentioned.

The Sheikh smiled. 'It was in August of that year that we first declared jihad, knowing the walls of oppression and humiliation could not be demolished except in a rain of bullets.'

He paused expectantly. A shout duly went up round the tent. Fists and fingers were raised.

'Jihad! Allah be praised!'

Then all was silent again, except for the hissing of the lamps. They waited for the Sheikh to continue.

'We had come here to Khost by that time. We were ready. We issued a manifesto that all Muslims should confront, fight and kill all American and British installations. Our object being to free every place in the Muslim world that suffers foreign oppression. By which I mean Iraq, by which I mean Bosnia, by which I mean Chechnya, by which I mean, most importantly of all, the Holy Places of Saudi Arabia. Which brings me to the forthcoming operations . . .'

Khaled listened intently as the Emir outlined the tasks for which Zayn and Yousef and himself, and the other team, had been selected.

* * *

'Where's your first post?'

'Tanzania,' Miranda said, feeling pleased she'd managed to successfully isolate him from the other students.

'You'll have fun out there,' said Queller. 'Head across the water to Zanzibar if you can. Beautiful place – I spent some of my childhood there. My father was US consul in Stone Town, the capital, after the war.'

'What was it like?' She asked the question with what might be thought an excess of urgency, which she immediately regretted, fearing that he might think her pushy.

'I was about seven when we first went. There for six years. I just have this image in my head of sea and sand. And, strangely enough, bullfights.'

70

'Bullfights? In Zanzibar?'

'I guess it must have been a Portuguese thing. They ruled the place once. We went to one. They don't kill them there though.'

'I guess that's something.'

'Anyway. I envy you having the chance to go. That place had a big effect on me. Hell, I even named my cabin after it. I've got this place on Cape Cod, you see. An island . . . that was the connection.'

'You've got your own island?'

Queller laughed. 'Not at all. Aquinnah, it's in the bottom corner of Martha's Vineyard, I've just got a little patch. Since, ah, this . . .'

With a twitch of his shoulders he crooked the prosthetic arm. She supposed there must have been straps around his back.

'. . . and my retirement, I find I'm happier there than in the city.'

They began walking towards the entrance, where Kirsteen was waiting. Miranda saw she had begun talking to Altenburg.

Queller followed her glance. 'You enjoy the lectures?'

'Yes. Of course.'

'You didn't think they were a bit *Sesame Street*?'

Miranda laughed and gave him a shy look. 'You did seem to have some interpretive disagreements.'

'I knew Altenburg when he was an intern. He's done amazingly well, hasn't he?'

She didn't know how to reply. 'Amazingly well' was exactly how she wanted to do in her life – to be one of those people who leaped off their little parcel of earth to touch the highest peaks.

'For one so young I mean,' Queller continued. 'Perhaps I should have been more of an empire builder. Got to the top of the tree. Is that what you want?'

She laughed uneasily, shocked at how instantly he'd seen through her. 'I guess. I haven't got it quite mapped out yet. But – yes. I'm not, like, ruthless though.'

'You don't need to be. You just need to be fluid. Hang on to the right coat-tails at the right time.'

She wasn't sure if this was a dig at Altenburg or a veiled invitation. There was another silence. Could Queller be the kind of mentor she'd been looking for since her father died? This was not something Miranda consciously wondered. Its apprehension happened at a very deep level – two notions coming together like loose matter floating in the brain, a meeting on one of those perpetual deviations of the mind of which the consciousness is hardly aware.

'Where you from anyway?' Queller said.

'Massachusetts too, as a matter of fact. Boston.'

'Really? You should come over if you ever get down my way. I'll give you my card.'

He dug in a pocket.

'And keep up the tennis.'

She blushed. 'You saw us!'

'Waiting in the car park.'

He handed her the card.

'And that's where I'll head back now, if you don't mind. I feel like a senior citizen round these guys. Good luck.'

'Thanks. Bye.'

She watched him walk towards Kirsteen and the two other men. He nodded politely at both but didn't stop to talk.

* * *

'Queller hates me,' Altenburg told General Kirby in the car park. 'He thinks I've risen too far too fast.'

'You're a talented guy. There must be more to it than that. Where are you?'

Altenburg pointed across the deserted tennis court to one of the ranks of parked cars. Nearer to his vehicle than Kirby's, they gravitated towards it.

'There is more. I'm on a committee that wound up an operation he was still running in retirement.'

They walked alongside the edge of the tennis court in the direction of Altenburg's Chrysler. All the while the General was trying to get his driver's attention, some twenty cars down.

'In retirement? How'd he get the funding for that?'

'Oil companies.'

'But there must've been some State connection.'

'Of course. The usual kind of thing. Back channels, old accounts. He's well connected, Jack. Been around a long time. And was good in his day, too.'

'I always heard of him as a bit of a maverick. His talk was a bit idealistic I thought. What was the op?'

The General made a five-minutes sign at his driver. The car was a black Lincoln. The driver was in uniform. He touched his cap in response. He knew better than to drive over.

'It concerns that bin Laden he was holding up as a figurehead of world terror, which is something of an exaggeration in my view. His plan was to get someone into bin Laden's organisation and have them kill him.'

'Where did the oil come in?'

'Some sort of contra-deal. He would get them access to fields in southern Sudan if they put up the money to get bin Laden. That way it couldn't be traced back to the executive by Congress.'

The General, who had a ring on his finger, touched Altenburg's metallic blue hood.

'Sounds a great plan. What was the problem?'

'It was too messy. It went too far back. We'd already been burned by bin Laden once. Queller himself was the point of contact in the field with him during covert operations in Afghanistan. Once the war was over, bin Laden turned. I reckon he was using Queller the whole time – gaining knowledge, gaining expertise he would later use against us. He was just an engineer before, albeit a multimillionaire engineer.'

'So that's the deal, Queller chasing a lost asset?'

Altenburg shook his head. 'It's more personal than that. They had some kind of shoot-out on a mountain. That's how Queller lost the arm. Some Army guys gave him blood. Saved his life.'

'You know, that rings a bell. I remember hearing something about that.'

'Then his wife got cancer and that just about did for him. He's always been a bit strange. But now it's bin Laden till kingdom come. If he had his way, we'd put all our resources in that particular pot.'

'So you pulled the plug?'

Altenburg pressed his remote key. His car gave a little whoop and flashed its indicators.

'With some difficulty. He fought back. It went right to the NSC. He has powerful friends.'

'What swung it?'

Altenburg folded up his Brooks Brothers raincoat and put it in the back of his car.

'I told them he reads too much Arab poetry.'

6

About a month after he arrived in Zanzibar, Nick Karolides was sitting in a bar in Stone Town. He had just been into a chandler's and bought a new starting cord for da Souza's outboard. It had been more difficult to patch up the damaged USAID boat than he'd expected, and eventually he'd paid a boatman to come from the docks in Stone Town and do it – a highly pessimistic guy who seemed to doubt that the whole process of repair was possible at all.

The only subject on which the boatman expressed any enthusiasm was Allah: he *inshallah*-ed everything – the hammer, the spatula, the fibreglass, the blowtorch – as if all were entirely dependent on God for their material operation. When there was nothing left in the repair for him to *inshallah*, he even *inshallah*-ed Nick, saying that the boat would carry him safely now, but only if the Almighty wished it.

Nick lit a cigarette, watching the calm sea from an old wooden table by the window, as he waited for his lunch. A dhow was creaking by in the bay, moving drowsily through the haze of heat above the water. He could see his reflection in a cracked mirror on the wall. He quite liked the look of himself these days: his hair had grown lighter and his Florida tan had deepened under the African sun. With so much swimming the tone of his muscles, too, had improved. Strengthening and suppling, the sea had worked on his long limbs like a masseur.

He was getting into the swing of things at work. If truth be told, he was enjoying himself enormously. A chance discovery had soothed his dismay at the damage the dynamite had done to

75

the reef. Continuing his mollusc survey, he'd found, by chance, while digging, some turtle nests on the Macpherson beach. Several turtles, perhaps four or five, must have come ashore in the night and laid their eggs. At least that meant there were some still around, that they hadn't been hunted out of existence. Their shells were sold for ornaments – buttons, jewellery– and the eggs were a popular delicacy in Asia. The meat was either eaten by the hunters, or rendered to make oil, for which there was also a good market. It had an extremely high viscosity and was used for skin-softening cream and various industrial processes.

He signalled for another beer. Horrible as it was, the turtle trade somehow fitted into the experience of Zanzibar, along with its magnificent, glittering bays and sweeping lines of palm – all that fuel for wistful fancy which, for a century at least, had made the place attractive to romantic wanderers. There had to be a flip side, something dark and cruel beneath.

He was perfectly aware of how he himself fell prey to such dreams, but allowed it to continue all the same. Sometimes, he wondered if it was those stories his father used to read him as a child – simple tales, full of heroes to admire and devils to despise – combined with a tendency, which he could not escape, to want to escape, which had brought him here.

To a bar in Zanzibar! He sipped the new beer, and looked across the dazzling water, contemplating the idea of a new self – the old one shed, like the delicate, translucent snake skin found on the beach that very morning, near the turtle nests.

There were still some connections to the old world that Nick was happy to maintain. He had his laptop with him. Electricity and phone line permitting, he had been able to log on to a number of websites full of useful information about Zanzibar. One represented Stone Town's fabulous carved Arab doors in its iconography: you had to 'open' them to move from one part of the site to another. He had also looked at specialist turtle sites, particularly on leatherbacks, of which Zanzibar boasted one of the highest populations in the world – although if things went on the way they were, it wouldn't for much longer.

The green Florida turtle, which he knew more about, faced different threats. There the danger came not from hunters but from sewage and chemicals: lead and cadmium from vehicle emissions and the deterioration of brakes and tyres. The particles collected on sidewalks and ran into Sarasota Bay when it rained. It wasn't all bad news, though: one of the things that had lifted his spirits before he left was a report of an increase of sea-grass coverage in Longboat Pass. Oddly enough, this was caused by dredging, which had opened up new shoals. The new grass was of a different type because of this. Thalassia, turtle grass, was being replaced by Halodule and Ruppia, or shoal grass and widgeon grass.

He didn't see that there could be any supplementary benefit to Zanzibar's ecological problems, the dynamite fishing and the breaking of coral by the keels of boats. There was dredging here, too, though on nothing like the same scale as at home: what had happened to the Florida coastline was, to his mind, a form of terrorism. Something the turtles in particular suffered from was floating plastic bags, which they tried to eat and choked on, thinking they were jellyfish.

A lot of Florida turtles had tumours: nasty looking grey-white lumps, like two or three small, uneven apples, stuck to the side of the neck. These fibropapillomas, as they were called, often excited attention from fish, which tried to graze on them, mistaking them for coral. No one knew what caused the cancer but its incidence had a clear relation to levels of pollution.

It struck him that a comparative treatment of the dangers to turtles in the two places might make a useful topic for his next talk at Matembwe School, where he was fulfilling the educational outreach part of his job. He quite enjoyed the weekly sessions, and had already given talks on the shaping of shore lines through the ages, how the moon causes tides on the earth, and the secrets of the deeps of the sea. The friendliness of the children was heartening. There was something genial and life-affirming about their eagerness to learn.

Teaching also gave him something to do while waiting for his heavier diving equipment to arrive from the US, care of the embassy in Dar. He'd had long discussions with Dino about exactly what apparatus he should bring, at first thinking not too much. But the wise old Greek had persuaded him he was crazy not to have whatever he might need. They had come to an arrangement about the cost, one which involved the selling of his motorbike. Dino had kindly agreed to take care of the shipping. Nick missed the bike, though. He couldn't afford to buy one, still less a car, at Zanzibar prices.

Which reminded him. What he did need to buy, and could afford, was a twelve-volt car battery and an inverter, so that he could use his laptop when the power went out at the Macpherson.

His lunch arrived. Grilled snapper and coconut rice. He began to eat, glancing round the bar as he chewed on the succulent fish and sticky, perfumed grains. There were three African youths sprawled on the parapet looking out to sea, and a couple of whites inside. One of them was a chunky, pasty-faced man in a blue short-sleeved shirt and chinos. He was seated on a bar stool drinking a bottle of Bell lager. The other, smoking a pipe, was across the room, half hidden behind a copy of the airmail edition of the London *Times*.

Getting up to pay, Nick was greeted by the beer drinker.

'Hello. What brings you to the land of Zinj?'

The guy held out his hand and Nick shook it. His name, he said in a strong British accent, was Tim Catmull.

'Let me get you another,' he added, leaning on the bar with his elbows. 'Freeman, another beer for . . .?'

Raising a finger, Catmull turned his compact body to Nick.

'Nick. Nick Karolides.'

'Get Nick another Bell.'

He turned again, spinning on the stool so that he faced Nick.

'That a Greek name then?'

'That's right,' said Nick. 'But I'm American.'

'Young American . . .' crooned the Englishman in his strange voice.

Nick couldn't help grinning, more at the accent, which he couldn't place, than at the supposedly comic gambit.

'Catmull's not such a common name itself,' he countered, not wanting to be left on the touchline. 'Least, not in my country.'

'To be honest,' Catmull said, 'I hate it. But what can you do?'

He held up his hands in a gesture of helpless resignation that was, it seemed to Nick, only half genuine.

'So . . . what did you mean by – Zinj?' Nick asked, climbing on to one of the bar stools.

'It's what the Arabs called this place. That's how you get Zanzibar. Zinj is from zang, the Persian word for black, barr is the Arab for coast. Or – land.'

'Right . . .'

'So what dropped you on the island then?'

'I'm here on a reef protection scheme.'

'The USAID thing?'

'Yeah.' He took a swig from the bottle Catmull had bought him.

'Didn't something happen to the bloke before you?'

Nick nodded. 'Boating accident.'

He didn't elaborate. His predecessor's death still seemed something of a mystery, and he had tried to find out more about George Darvil. Short of confronting Chikambwa on the matter again, which he suspected wouldn't bring him much joy, there didn't seem much he could do. After a while, when he hadn't been able to discover anything more, he'd tried to put Darvil out of his mind. He felt that he had a special affinity with the sea, and nothing like that could ever happen to him. Yet sometimes, on sleepless nights, he would be haunted by a ghastly image of a drowned man. He saw it now, where he gripped the bottle: Darvil's hand reaching through weed-scum, its skin white as leprosy.

'What about you?' he asked.

Catmull gave a hollow laugh. 'Me? I'm an expert in – Sudden Death.'

'What?'

'It's a disease of cloves. I'm with DFID. British international development.'

'Produce a lot of cloves here, don't they?'

'It used to be about 90 per cent of the world supply. Once the slave trade stopped, the island got most of its wealth from them. But this fungus keeps cropping up, killing the trees. That's why I'm here.'

'How do you find it?'

Catmull inclined his cropped head. 'Tricky. After the revolution they nationalised nearly all the farms. They've let a few small blokes start up again . . . but mostly I have to deal with officials from the Clove Board. Lot of corruption. You run into that?'

Nick shook his head.

'Hey, you don't play football do you?'

Nick paused. 'Soccer? No . . . I'd give it a shot though.'

'Great. I'll sign you up. As a defender, mind, not a striker. We've got a little league going, see. Sponsored by the drop people.'

'The what people?'

'The *drop* people. The water company.'

'I haven't seen them.'

Catmull looked surprised. 'Zanzibar Drop. The mineral water. How long you been here? Hey, Freeman! Toss us a bottle of Drop, will you?'

The barman put down the glass he was cleaning and, leaning down into the refrigerator, took out a small bottle of mineral water. Glistening with icebox dew, under the lighting fixtures it looked – ever so briefly – like a prized, secret object: something of great presence.

'Get a move on, Freeman,' Catmull shouted down the bar. Nick winced. He disliked the sneer of cold command with which many expatriates treated the Zanzibaris.

The barman wiped off the condensation with a cloth and, placing the bottle on a battered silver tray, began to walk – very slowly – towards them.

'This is it.'

'Yes, bwana.'

'I'm talking to the other bwana . . . This is the water I referred to.'

Catmull handed Nick the bottle. There was a blue-tinted photograph of a soccer player on the label. *Zanzibar Drop. Cold and delicious!*

'That's George Weah,' said Catmull. 'Liberian. He's in the European leagues now. Big hero in Africa. It's a good sign. Times have changed. I think we're moving into a period when most of football's heroes will come from here.'

Catmull talked on, but Nick was easing into a nether world of his own. It was an old habit, to slip like this into a world peopled by another sort of hero, as in his father's stories: Hercules, Theseus, Jason . . . Or the defenders of the Achaean League – islanders and coastlanders of ancient Greece, those people of the sea who beached at Troy with Achilles and won the long siege. Then destroyed their own civilisation through accumulation of power.

'Another?'

Nick realised they had been sitting side by side in silence for a few seconds. 'I believe it's my round. What'll you have?'

'No, mate. Got to get off. Just thought I'd offer, seeing as you were looking so thoughtful.'

'Sure?' Nick asked, embarrassed.

Catmull shook his head. 'Can't. Off up north this afternoon. Got to see someone from the Board. But give us your number for the football.'

Nick took out a pen and wrote the number of the Macpherson Ruins on a beer mat.

'Cheers. I'll give you a ring.'

'Good luck with the sudden death,' Nick said, as Catmull slid off his bar stool. 'Say, you don't know a guy called Leggatt, do you? I think he's a clove farmer. Also a yachtsman. People keep mentioning his name.'

'Ralph Leggatt? That's him over there.' Catmull pointed at the man with the newspaper, then leaned over and whispered in Nick's ear. 'Watch out, though. He's a bit of a grouch in my experience – right. Must go.'

He fanned himself with the beermat. 'Bloody hell, it's hot. Hasn't rained all week.'

Having said goodbye to Catmull, Nick went over to the man behind the newspaper. The brown, liver-spotted hands lowered slightly as he approached. The face that appeared – sun-dried, scowling, furrowed – was draped with dirty blond hair of a length one wouldn't normally associate with someone of his age, which must have been mid-sixties.

'Mr Leggatt? My name's Nick Karolides. I'm the new guy on the USAID reef scheme. I keep seeing your boat go by the Macpherson and I thought –'

The newspaper folded. A pair of eyes – deeply recessed and as yellow as the hair above them – regarded him balefully. The man's skin was so darkly tanned it might have been dipped in tea.

'American?'

'That's right,' said Nick. 'USAID.'

'Useless-aid more like. I haven't a word to say to you, young man.'

'Why? What have I done?'

'What have you done? Nothing. Your predecessor, on the other hand, drove his boat into the reef.'

'I thought he was chasing poachers.'

'He was, and a damn silly idea that was, too. But it was he who smashed the reef – this time.'

Nick was taken aback. 'He's dead, for chrissake. Don't you think you're being a little harsh?'

Leggatt drained his beer. 'You lot, you greens, NGOs, development people . . . You always think you're so right. Up there on the moral high ground. You can't see what's in front of you.'

'He drowned trying to stop poachers. If that was misguided, fine. But there's no need to blacken his name.'

'Friend of yours was he?'

Nick stuttered. 'No, but . . .'

Leggatt stood up, folding his newspaper. 'You're right. He did drown. He fell out of the boat when it hit the reef. I pulled him out and he died in my arms. Coral had cracked his head open.'

He fixed Nick with his mustard-coloured eyes. 'Mind, it would have been a lot worse if the poachers had got him. They'd have cut him to pieces.'

With that, he turned on his heel and headed for the door.

'Wait,' said Nick, going after him and catching his sleeve. 'I didn't mean to . . .'

'Bugger off.'

Leggatt shook himself free and went outside. Nick followed a moment or so later but the Englishman had already disappeared in the maze of narrow streets.

* * *

The river was like silk. Some kid had a remote-control boat. Miranda Powers sat on the bank under a tree and watched it for a while. Her last day in America. She was glad to be leaving

Washington, but she wanted to fix the city in her head before she did, so she'd decided to take a long walk around it.

Kirsteen had gone over to see Frank. Miranda felt strange, not having any more coursework to do, and not having a boyfriend of her own. She was packed and ready to go. Without activity, without something to aim at, she felt compressed in her own narrow being. And it was that feeling which had brought her, first, to the Potomac.

After a while, tiring of the noise of the boy's buzzing boat, she stood up and made her way to the Museum of American History. She did not stop there long, as it was very busy, checking out only the toy hall, where there were some fun automata, and the music section, where there was a life-size replica of David Byrne in his white suit.

She walked north then, skirting the edge of Federal Triangle, past the Justice Department and the Old Post Office. Finding herself by the studio of Matthew Brady, the Civil War photographer, she went inside. It was a fascinating old building, cool and dark. She looked at Ulysses Grant and his staff; some destroyed gun carriages from the siege of Fort Fisher; some Union soldiers chowing down; Pinkerton of the Secret Service on horseback at Antietam.

Coming out of the Brady studio, she went back on herself, crossing Federal Triangle and entering the National Aquarium. There were seventy or so tanks, but only two caught her interest. One was a touch tank, where you could handle turtles and docile crabs; the other was the shark tank. She'd happened to come at feeding time, and it was thrilling to watch the sharks gape and swallow the bucketfuls of mackerel as the assistants tipped them in.

The sharks took the fish on the run in the round tank – just swallowed, then passed 360 degrees round the glass before returning for the next mouthful. There was an opportunity, included in the $2 fee, to see a continuously running film about marine life around the world, but she demurred at that and stepped outside into the daylight again.

At Metro Center she caught the orange line north-east, thinking she'd pick up some capsules from a health-food shop Kirsteen had recommended. Nutraceutica: an all-round wholefood vitamin and mineral supplement that wouldn't, she reckoned, be available in Africa. Just before the door closed, a derelict woman in a flapping black coat swept in off the platform and sat directly opposite her. She smelt of bonfires and urine and looked weirdly like Madeleine Albright.

The train had hardly got going before the woman began lifting her dirty sleeve, pointing at Miranda and crying out, 'She has a perfect complexion! She has a perfect complexion!' The other passengers looked away; the woman kept repeating the words, with varying intonations.

Miranda was relieved to reach her stop and leave the train. The health-food store was, however, in a rather grim and desolate area. She felt uncomfortable walking along there. People were just sitting out on stoops doing nothing. Weeds on the sidewalk, potholes in the road. She felt that she stood out very conspicuously.

The store was next to a dance studio. *African Heritage Dancers and Drummers*. On the other side was a gas station, and a row of garages with their dull steel shutters pulled down. Each shutter was covered in graffiti so knotted and overlaid it was impossible to tell where one design ended and the next began.

She went in and bought the supplements. Walking back to the metro, she became aware of a dark green Acura Legend driving past her slowly. Its windows were down and there were four youths in it. One of them, his eyes drug wild, called out, 'Hey babe, wanna new man?'

They pulled over a little way ahead of her. Realising she had to get out of there fast, she turned tail and ran back the way she had come. She stopped, breathless, outside a soup kitchen next to the New Bethel Baptist Church. There was a queue of vagrants there, waiting for meals, which were being doled out by a plump, smiling lady in an apron.

Miranda turned and looked behind her. There was no sign of the green car or the youths. Turning back, she saw that the foul-smelling woman from the train had suddenly appeared on the sidewalk next to her.

'All lost!' the derelict said abruptly, showing an ink-blue tongue and pointing at a sign on the church noticeboard. 'TO HIM THAT OVERCOMETH WILL I GIVE TO EAT OF THE TREE OF LIFE, WHICH IS IN THE MIDST OF THE PARADISE OF GOD.'

Thrusting her hands deep into the pockets of her greatcoat, she produced a little bottle containing brown liquid.

'It shall dissolve,' she said to Miranda, assuringly. 'This machinery's entirely new to you?'

Without waiting for an answer the madwoman said, 'Be not afeared,' and shook the bottle vigorously.

As quickly as she could, Miranda made her way back to the station. Everyone talked about how crazy and chaotic Africa was, what a region of sorrow and despair it was, but were these run-down parts of Washington really any much better? By the time she got back home, to be greeted by her suitcases sitting ready in the hall, she was quite ready to make the substitution. But that was tomorrow. Tonight Kirsteen and Frank, who were chamber-music fanatics, were taking her to listen to an outfit called the Washington Viols, and then out for a farewell meal.

* * *

The episode with Leggatt put Nick in an anxious frame of mind and, walking along the beach that evening, he made a discovery which stirred his anxiety still further. The turtle nests had been dug up and their eggs removed. He couldn't figure out how whoever had taken the eggs had been able to pinpoint the nests with such accuracy.

As the sun lowered in the sky, he sat down by one of the empty holes. He found himself trying to compute the human time in which the eggs had been removed – five minutes? ten? – against the vaster spans the species itself inhabited. They might have been coming for tens of thousands of years. Every July. Nesting season across the ages. Plying up the beach to lay just here, since the time of the dinosaurs even. The struggle for life most severe when faced by man, with his false conceptions of progress and civilisation . . . little wonder, from Longboat Pass to Macpherson Cove, that time was running out for the turtles.

After a while he stood up and followed the swerve of the shore. Some way on, there was an inlet where a stream came down, breaking the smoothness of the sand with rocks and mangroves. The tide was coming in, washing about in the knotted roots, sending sodden leaves and bits of rotten weed to and fro. He leant on one of the trunks and watched the pieces sway in the eddy. Black and green, grey and yellow, the feculent fragments moved across the surface. They struck him as counters in some imponderable game, chaos its only umpire, turbulence its only rule.

Feeling a pressure in his bladder, he pulled himself out of his shorts and pissed in the stream. His water merged with the other water, tinkling like a little bell. As he tucked himself back in, he happened to look up into the tree on which he had been leaning. To his horror, he saw a large number of bats hanging upside down on the branch directly above his head – twenty or thirty bundles of fur, leather and dried fruit gripping the bark with their claws. He backed away quickly, then stood and stared at the roosting place.

It was getting dark. The stars were rushing in. Night would be upon him any minute. He began walking briskly back to the hotel, musing as he did so on what it might be like to be a bat. To feel the air rushing by you as you flew through it. To have a head full of blood as you roosted.

Wondering if perhaps he was going a little crazy, he tramped across the beach. Far in the distance, he heard a prayer call from a mosque in Stone Town. It drifted eerily out over the sands like the thin, piping cry of a seabird. The sound irresistibly led his mind up to the greater mind of God – away from the brute mechanism and clutter of the material world. He was sure the creator of the world in which we lived and moved could never abandon it; or look on his creatures, in the long run, with anything but concern. Evil had to be partial, Nick was convinced, a way of securing some greater good. Some regularity had to exist, a pattern of direction, even if one could not see it.

Darkness closed in with every stride, all the same. He started tracing his own footprints – following, at a speedier pace, and in reverse, the solitary, slow steps of his earlier passage – till, just in time, he saw the friendly gleam of the Macpherson's thatched portals, heard the chug of the generator and, finally, the faint chatter of hotel guests at dinner.

Not feeling hungry, he walked across the courtyard to his room, which was more like a little chalet. Turning on the light, he saw a neoprene and rubber pile of scuba stuff on the floor and, directly in front of him on the wall, a calendar. *Disabled American Veterans 1998: America the Beautiful.* The photograph that month was of Washington's Lincoln Memorial and Reflecting Pool. Hanging nearby, on a string between two nails, were some sponges he'd brought up from the ocean floor.

On the desk, next to his laptop and a Walkman, was something else he'd swum up with: a large conch. Beside it lay a U2 cassette (*The Joshua Tree*) and two issues of *Kids Discover* magazine ('Weather' and 'United States History') which he'd had his mother send him and planned to take to the school.

Also on the desk was a plastic 'PLEASE DO NOT DISTURB' sign with a hole for the door handle, and a postcard from Dino showing the actress Drew Barrymore in an old-fashioned dress, with the words *Ever After* at the bottom. He picked up the postcard and stared at it. The movie was clearly some kind of costume drama. But all sense of the past was destroyed by the card's own laminated surface: so shiny and slick – the thought struck him – it might have been done with turtle oil.

7

Breakfasting on the veranda at the Macpherson the next day, Nick saw the familiar yacht pass by again. A crescent moon was still visible in the grey morning sky as the yellow craft made its way across the edge of the bay. Between moon and sun, he realised, he could get a pretty fair idea of the yacht's bearing. He pushed aside his plate of papaya and drank up his coffee. Then he went back to his room and took out a map and compass from his gear. He spread out the map on his bed. If the bearing was right, the yacht was heading here. Tiny letters marked the spot his finger had found on the map. *Lyly* – one of the small atolls that Chikambwa had told him wasn't worth bothering with.

Suddenly excited, grabbing his knife, the new starting cord he had bought the previous day, and a pair of binoculars, he rushed over to the boathouse. Pulling da Souza's outboard from the musty shed, he humped it down the beach to where, newly repaired, the USAID boat was sitting on the sun-baked sand. Attaching the motor to the stern, he dragged the dinghy further down the shore into the shallows.

He paused with his bare legs in the water and the boat knocking against his thighs. The tide was incoming, pulsing slowly, indolently. He looked back at the furrow the dinghy had made through the sand, his own splayed footprints either side of the trough.

Then he stepped in and, sitting on the cross-bench, began unwinding the new starting cord from its spool. The dinghy was rocking gently. He began rewinding the cord onto the dynamo of the outboard. He had only pulled it a couple of times when he heard a shout behind him.

'Sir! Sir!'

Nick looked up. It was the Goan, running down from the veranda. He was carrying something.

'What?'

'Sir, if you are taking the boat, you *must* have these.'

'What?'

Da Souza was carrying a tattered and dusty lifejacket and an old canvas bag, from which he produced what looked like an antique pistol.

'A gun?' said Nick, looking at the pistol. It hung on a belt stuffed with fat cardboard cartridges. He splashed back through the shallows, keeping hold of the lanyard.

'Flare, sir,' said da Souza, handing it over. 'If you use the hotel engine, I must insist you have this for safety. Insurance.'

Nick inspected the ancient firearm. 'Does it work? It looks like it came from the Second World War.'

'That is right, sir.' Da Souza smiled with gleaming teeth. 'Second World War it is. I found them in stores. And this too.'

Nick gave him a quizzical look and, returning the gun to its bag, took the life jacket. He returned to the dinghy.

'I'll be a couple of hours.'

'Be careful, sir. I do not want another death from this boat.'

The engine gave out a puff of blue smoke and then, as the cord snickered back into its housing, started up with a satisfying whump. Nick manoeuvred the small craft out into the bay, checked his bearing, and set off.

Enjoying the feeling of the cool air on his face, and the vibrations of the motor as they came up through his hand and arm, he watched the clouds drift across the horizon. In the wide, blue expanse, he couldn't see any sign of the yacht.

A flock of white birds passed, skimming low and calling out, then swiftly disappeared above the folding waves. He thought of the muezzin he'd heard the previous night. Its ancient sound had called the faithful to prayer for generations, promising them a life after this life. Which, if he understood it correctly, Muslims thought an illusion.

Half an hour went by before the island came into view: a green lump sitting on a line of exposed coral. Nick scanned it with his binoculars. The green, he knew, must be coral-rag forest. What surprised him was the tall white building rising from the middle. He hadn't expected a lighthouse.

As he got closer he spotted the yellow yacht, moored outside the reef. Within the curl of foam that marked the coral was a lagoon skirted by a small beach. As well as the lighthouse, there were a couple of other buildings on the island – one a dilapidated house, the other a small church. Then a line of trees behind. He looked again. The church had a little minaret. It wasn't a church. It was a mosque.

Thinking he had best approach quietly, he cut the engine and rowed round to the other side of the island – with some difficulty, since the oars were heavy and the tide more insistent now. Eventually, by chance rather than design, he managed to land the dinghy after passing through a rough gap between the coral.

As he pulled the boat up and looked for somewhere to secure it, he noticed a spike of metal sticking up out of the rock. It was some kind of cable. The metal was copper, Nick reckoned, although most of its colour had gone, disguised under verdigris and the jelly-like attachments of algae. Still, it would do as a mooring.

After tying up, he turned to face the rag forest, which arced round him like a curtain. There was no sign of cultivation, and no activity except for two big, orange coconut crabs, moving slowly across the sand like a pair of halting dancers towards a fringe of undergrowth.

He set off through the rag, a little uncertain which direction would take him to the place where the yacht was moored. Eventually, emerging from the green-clad walls, he saw –

crouched down in the sand not some sixty feet away from him – the figure of Ralph Leggatt.

Nick lifted his binoculars. Through the roundels he saw that Leggatt was digging up turtle eggs. He felt a tide of anger rise. So that was why the sour old man had been so antagonistic towards him. He watched the Englishman for a moment, unsure what to do. Just as he was about to go and confront him, he heard a sound across the water. He looked over.

It was a small dhow. Narrower than Leggatt's yacht, it had been able to come right into the lagoon. Two men and a boy jumped out and started swimming towards the shore. Nick swung the binoculars back round: Leggatt had seen them too. He was running away across the sand. The three figures reached the beach, splashing through the surf. Nick recognised the large, muscular man as the octopus whacker he'd seen on the quay when he first arrived. Now he was carrying a panga, a machete. But it was the other guy who caught Leggatt first, tackling him like a football player.

Transfixed, Nick watched the man lay into Leggatt. The big one joined in too, hitting Leggatt with the flat of the machete, while the boy began gathering up the turtle eggs which the Englishman had unearthed. Perhaps these were Chikambwa's men, marine wardens . . . but they were beating the hell out of the Englishman.

Nick was about to come forward and show himself when they stopped. One of the men shouted an instruction in Swahili to the boy, before dragging Leggatt to a palm tree. He began tying him to it with a length of coconut fibre.

They meant to leave him there, Nick could see. Now they were taking off their ragged shirts and placing the eggs inside.

The binoculars found Leggatt. There was blood running from the old man's mouth. Something was wrong. Wardens wouldn't do this. He let the binoculars fall in confusion, then took them up again.

Balancing their precious packages on their heads, the Africans were swimming back to their boat; the one with the machéte was holding it between his teeth. The boy was swimming in a different direction – towards Leggatt's boat.

As soon as they were a safe distance away, Nick ran over to Leggatt and undid his bonds.

'You!' cried the old man, falling forward.

'I would have come earlier, only . . .'

'It doesn't matter now. Quick, before they get my boat. Where's yours?'

'You're hurt!'

'I'm all right. Where's your boat?'

Nick gestured over his shoulder, and then the two of them were running, crashing through the undergrowth back to where Nick had moored. They hurled themselves in. At first the motor wouldn't start.

'Get out the way,' spat Leggatt from his broken mouth.

He reached over and fiddled with the filter on the outboard's fuel supply.

'Now try it.'

Nick pulled, and the motor coughed into life.

By the time they had rounded the island, the boy was already on Leggatt's yacht. He was up in the rigging, tearing at the sails with a knife.

'Little bastard!' cursed the Englishman. 'Can't this go any faster? If they haul the anchor she'll drift onto the coral.'

Two small rivers of blood ran down his chin.

'I'm trying as best I can,' said Nick, squeezing the throttle. In his head he was trying, too – trying to work out exactly who was the villain in all this.

The men on the dhow had seen them by now, and were wheeling round.

'Come on!' cried Leggatt. 'They'll get there before us!'

94

'She's at full throttle,' said Nick.

They were about two hundred metres from the dhow. With the wind behind it, it was clear that it would get to Leggatt's yacht before them, even though they were closing rapidly.

'We're not going to stop them,' said the Englishman grimly. 'Unless you happen to have a shotgun.'

Nick paused for a moment. 'Down there,' he said.

'This?' Leggatt picked up da Souza's canvas satchel. 'What's in it?'

'Flare,' said Nick.

'What? No one will get here in time to save the boat.'

'At them, I meant.'

'Ah,' Leggatt said, with a sudden grin. 'I see what you're up to.'

He introduced one of the cartridges into the breech of the flare gun, took aim at the dhow, and pulled the trigger. Nothing happened.

'Bloody hell!' said Leggatt. 'Give me your knife.'

Nick tossed it to him, and looked up at the dhow. They were close now. He could see the faces of the sailors. The bare-chested man with the panga was standing up on the deck.

Leggatt finished scratching the end of the cartridge with the serrated edge of Nick's fishing knife. Then he closed up the breech and took aim again. This time, a tongue of flame came out of the muzzle of the old gun – a tongue of flame and a phosphorescent projectile, not unlike a firework, but brighter. It whizzed across the water into the rigging of the dhow. Almost immediately, flames began to snatch at the ragged sails.

'Ha!' Leggatt shouted triumphantly as the strong wind fanned the flames. 'That'll give us a bit of breathing space.'

They drew away from the dhow. Its crew, fearing the loss of their ship, had dropped anchor and were trying to haul down the burning sails. Nick and Leggatt reached the yacht in the meantime, tying a line and boarding by means of the rope ladder that ran up the side.

As Nick climbed, he saw clearly, in front of his nose, the full name of the craft, which he had half glimpsed from the shore. Painted in blue on the yellow background were the words *Winston Churchill*, together with a little cartoon of a man with bullfrog eyes, smoking a cigar.

'Right,' said Leggatt, looking up at his tattered sails. 'I'll go and start the engine. She's not going to sail anywhere now. Get that monkey out of the rigging before he does any more damage.'

Nick looked up at the boy. He was too high to jump, but too frightened to come down either. A little dubiously, Nick began climbing. They chased around – Nick cursing, the boy yelping – as the diesel motor chugged into life and the yacht began to move. They had left the island and the dhow well behind, before Nick, reaching across the rigging, could lay hands on him.

'Please, bwana, please!' cried the young African. He was anything between seven and eleven, and kept shouting and struggling as he was brought down. 'Please . . .'

'I've a good mind to whip the living daylights out of him,' said Leggatt, once they joined him in the wheelhouse.

The boy clung to Nick's shirt.

'Let's just take him to the police. Chikambwa.'

He looked at Leggatt's bleeding face. 'You need a doctor anyhow.'

'I'll be all right.' The long-haired old man spat some blood out of the wheelhouse window.

'Anyway,' continued Nick, 'what was going on out there? What were you doing with those eggs? Why were you digging them up?'

Ignoring him, Leggatt took out his pipe with a liver-spotted hand, lit it and – between puffs of smoke – began to question the boy in brusque Swahili. Nick looked out of the back window of

96

the wheelhouse, where he could see his own little boat bobbing away on its line in the wake of the *Churchill*.

'As I thought,' Leggatt said to Nick after a while. 'Chikambwa it is.'

'So what do we do, take the boy to his office?'

The old man leant over from behind the wheel and spat more blood out of the window. Then he took a good suck on his pipe, as if hoping the smoke would staunch the bleeding. Finally he looked at Nick.

'You still don't understand, do you? These are Chikambwa's men. It's him that's taking the eggs and, worse still, the shells.'

'He's a poacher?'

'Yes, that's it. Gamekeeper turned poacher. Policeman turned thief. The usual thing. Except that he's still gamekeeper.'

'There must be other police we can go to.'

'My dear boy, this is Africa. They'll be on the take as well, like as not.'

'I don't think like that.'

'Think how you want, but take my advice. Keep your head down. Look to where you can make a difference. Zanzibar is in the process of being sold off. You ecologists are too late. Always too late. There'll be hotels everywhere soon. Costa del Africa. Glad I'm too old to see the worst of it.'

Nick was confused. 'So what were you doing with those eggs?'

'Oh, moving them. I take them off Zanzibar and rebury them. They have a much greater chance of survival. Or would have done if that lot hadn't rumbled me.'

He looked at the poachers' boy, who had curled up in a corner of the wheelhouse.

Nick followed his gaze. 'Do you think they'll be back?'

'Not for a while. But eventually, yes. Really it needs someone to guard the place. I've buried a lot more eggs on there. In fact, maybe that's what you should do.'

'What?'

'Concentrate your efforts there. It's a pristine coral-rag island. Do you know how rare that is? A perfect reef ecology. Some of the most spectacular coral gardens to be found anywhere in the world. That's something worth protecting. You see that buoy?'

Nick looked at the child on the floor.

'The plastic thing, the red thing.'

'Ah,' said Nick, looking where it was hung in a swirl of rope on the wall. 'We say *boo-ey*.'

Leggatt grunted. 'It takes twenty years for a colony of coral of even that size to grow. Twenty years!'

'I know that,' said Nick. 'I'm a marine biologist.'

The old man gave him a hard look. 'You people have a lot to learn. Scientists . . .'

There was silence in the cabin, except for the chugging of the engine.

Eventually Leggatt spoke up. 'I'm sorry. I'm not much cop at getting along with people. I owe you one. Where do you want me to take you?'

'Macpherson, please.'

'Right-ho . . .'

He changed course, then repeated his apology.

'Forget it,' said Nick. 'So, how come Lyly has survived?'

'It's pronounced Lala. Swahili for sleep. Corrupted into English when we were here. The good old days. There's a lullaby actually . . .' He began to sing softly. '*Lala, lala salama* . . . Salama is peace. It means, sleep peacefully. More or less. It survived because of the Cold War. The pursuit of error sometimes leads to good. Happens all the time.'

'I don't get you.'

'It was part of a military zone. When the East German navy was here in the seventies and eighties. The fishermen weren't allowed near the island.'

'What about that house?'

Leggatt turned the wheel with his brown hands. 'It was built for a British lighthouse-keeper . . . in the thirties.'

'And the mosque?'

'Much earlier. The Omanis ran Zanzibar for centuries. Before that Zanzibar, Kilwa, Mombasa, were all part of the Kingdom of Saba. What's now the Yemen. That lasted from, oh, about 1000 BC to AD 300 . . . There's lots of legends. Saba, so they say, was the kingdom that the Queen of Sheba came from to visit Solomon.'

'As in King Solomon's mines?'

'That's it. Anyway, even when we were officially in charge, when Britain took over from the sultan, it was still the Arabs' show really. They hoped to keep control after independence. Then the revolution happened and the Africans rose up, killing the Arabs on the beaches. It was pure slaughter.'

'So who does the island belong to now?'

'Lyly?'

'Yes.'

'A rich Arab. A Saudi, not an Omani though, which is unusual. He doesn't seem to bother with it. He bought it off the Africans, who took it over from the Omanis. The original Omani family fled to Muscat.'

'So not all the Arabs were killed?'

'They started coming back. They were needed for the economy. But there are rules about how long they can stay. Although, as a matter of fact, there was so much intermarriage over the years it's hard to say who's Arab, who's African . . .'

Leggatt cut the engine. 'Looks like we're here.'

They had, indeed, reached Macpherson Bay. It was two o'clock in the afternoon. The beach and hotel buildings were glaring in the sun. There was no one about. Da Souza would be having his siesta.

'Well . . .' said the Englishman. 'I ought to thank you.'

'It's OK. What about him?'

They looked at the boy, who was rubbing his eyes.

'I'll see if he has any parents. If not, I'll find him some jobs on my farm, try to work some sense into him.'

Leggatt restarted the engine as Nick climbed down into the dinghy.

'Tell you what,' shouted Leggatt, 'why don't you come round to my place on Sunday? Mtoni. Ask anyone, you'll find it. Ten o'clock. We'll have a wander round, then maybe I'll get you some lunch.'

'OK. Sure – see you there.'

Standing in the little boat, rocking from side to side and redistributing his weight accordingly, Nick watched the *Winston Churchill* move away. He could see Leggatt in the wheelhouse, one hand on the wheel as he turned the boat in the bay to face the open sea. There was a worrying amount of blood on the old man's shirt. He really ought to see a doctor.

As he sat down and put out the oars, Nick realised why he felt so concerned. He started to pull. There was something about Leggatt that reminded him of his father; or how his father might have been if he had survived. Still, the old guy seemed to be OK.

Nick rowed back to the hotel in a little ecstasy of athletic precision, trying to make all the energy go into the stroke – not into the splash, or the eddy, or the noise of the rowlocks. It wasn't just the stroke itself he enjoyed, it was the way everything connected: arm and ocean, wood and water, the tug the oars made in the muscles of the back – they all came together in a single action. Then, what was also pleasurable, came the putting up of oars, like a bird folding its wings. Followed by a smooth coasting into the beach, the glide of it so sweet, so carefully judged, that the keel touched the sand with barely a sound.

After pulling up the boat, he picked a mango from one of the trees in the hotel courtyard, and went to his room to eat it. The air conditioning, which gave off a faint smell of stagnant water, had broken down, but when he turned on the ceiling fan, it began to revolve, slowly at first, then gathering speed. He drew the curtains. Lying on the bed in the darkened room, he ate the mango as if it were stolen fruit and he the boy eternal. It tasted good. He sucked the fibres on the stone. Despite the fan, it was still, so still.

Once the stone was dry, he reached over, put it on the bedside table, and promptly fell asleep. There he remained, as the white horses of the sea rode so, and so, still so – until, lulled by the spell of their own resumption, they became the horses of the night.

8

Executive Assistant (Logistical and Security). It is not a glamorous position in the Foreign Service, and not a lucrative one either. Starting salaries range from $33,000 to $45,911, depending on qualifications and location of assignment. Miranda was right at the bottom of the scale.

The post in Tanzania entailed work as a security specialist in the areas of facility protection, investigation, information management, and retention and training of local staff. The core of the job was ensuring protection for embassy facilities and personnel from technical espionage, acts of terrorism and crime.

She hoped, before long, to move on to the DS training scheme for special agents, who pursued counter-intelligence, anti-terrorist and other investigations from US embassies worldwide. In the meantime, she spent much of her time checking electronic and electromagnetic security systems, filling in forms and a daily security register (called the day book), making sure the local staff were performing their functions – and, in the evenings, going to parties, of which there were many.

With her long dark hair and green eyes, Miranda attracted much male attention at the round of diplomatic functions which substituted for a social life in a posting like Dar. The African diplomats, many of whom preferred the direct approach ('Do you have a husband?' – 'Will you marry me?'), often just startled her. She found it troublesome coping with their physical frankness, but also faintly amusing. She felt a little guilty about this, but it couldn't be helped. It was just one of the many ways in which the colour bar continued to operate subliminally.

Nobly, she allowed herself to feel a slight thrill, not sexual exactly, but something approaching it, about Abdi, the tall Somali deputy ambassador, who followed her across the room at parties like a long brown greyhound.

'Never was anything better named,' Ray had remarked drily, on first observing this now familiar scene, 'than a cocktail party.'

At first she hadn't understood what he meant, then flushed with embarrassment when he'd explained.

'Cocks tailing tail. Not mine, I'm afraid. Larry Durrell.'

Miranda didn't know who Larry Durrell was, but she had got to know Ray Delahoya pretty well in those first few months of her posting. Big, plaid-shirted Ray was the embassy comms man, the communications specialist who maintained the forest of satellite dishes and other aerials that covered the roof of the building. He had a little moustache and was excitably inquisitive, with a habit of asking personal questions. Ray wasn't regarded as a team player by the more senior members of chancery. He encouraged her to take her training – especially the intelligence, 'tradecraft' side of it – with a pinch of salt.

'You don't want to get too overawed by the mystique of all that,' he said one morning, when they happened to arrive together at the embassy car park.

They were walking across the lawn in front of the chancery, along a path scattered with chipped bark. Either side, rows of oleander and agapanthus broadcast their blossom, vivid pinks and blues.

'If you do, you'll end up seeing things. Threats in every corner. Truth is, most of our job here is just routine management.'

The path was sodden with sprinkler water. In the flower beds, she noticed, translucent droplets beaded the spear-like leaves of the agapanthus. Holding their position, as if they might never fall, they fixed hypnotically on the eye, making one want to stand and stare.

'What do you mean?' she asked. Feeling light-headed, she chided herself for not having had enough for breakfast.

'We just have to keep the machine rolling. The great machine of state.'

She gathered herself, businesslike. 'But there are dangers, Ray. That's why I'm here, that's the point of my job. America has only five per cent of the world's population but is the subject of thirty-six per cent of terrorist attacks.'

Another bloom caught her eye. Red, long-stemmed and volu-minous, it was one of a distinct variety of hibiscus planted in the embassy gardens. Again her mind dissolved – into Gauguin, *South Pacific*, the love flower in the hair of Polynesian girls – such totemic maidens, determined by men for their pleasure, as she knew she never could be.

'Nifty numbers, baby. I don't know. Sometimes I think the administration *needs* to have enemies in order to function.'

They had reached the entrance to the chancery. Forgetting about the red spray as suddenly as it had gripped her, Miranda found herself bristling at his cynicism.

'We have to defend our way of life. That's nothing to be ashamed of.'

She paused at the electronic turnstile. Both searched for their pass cards.

'Really got to you in training, didn't they?' Ray chuckled, as they passed through.

They stopped on the other side. 'Listen,' he said. He pulled a handkerchief out of his pocket with a flourish and began clean-ing his spectacles. '. . . you'll be disappointed with a career in foreign service if you go about thinking you're a mixture of George Washington and Mata Hari.'

'I don't think like that! I just want to take my job seriously.'

'Hey, take it easy.' Ray replaced his spectacles. 'I didn't mean to upset you. Sorry – guess I'm just getting my own anxieties off my chest. You know, I've wanted to work in foreign service ever since I could tell time. Now I am, and it doesn't really live up to all I hoped. It doesn't help my being . . .'

He dried up.

Miranda smiled and patted him on the arm. 'Come on, let's get some coffee.'

They began climbing the stairs, past windows which, cut like tombstones in the concrete, cast long, thin slices of light on the opposite wall.

Delahoya was funny, and most of the time she liked being round him. She enjoyed the way Ray would suddenly surf off on the wave of his own conversation. Like a conjuring trick – some sleight of hand with a tin tray and handkerchiefs – it would whisk the two of them out of the pious diplomatic environment. There was nobody else at the embassy with whom she could conceivably find herself talking *Pocahontas* action-figure dolls, Starbucks or the Olsen twins.

She and Ray often went shopping together at the PX, as the embassy store was called: it was a military acronym for 'Post Exchange', generally a store on a military base, which the embassy counted as, because of the presence of the Marines.

Ray was promiscuous in his cultural references. She couldn't keep up. 'The dons live well in the kawledge,' he'd say, whenever their trolleys bumped in the aisles of the PX, between racks filled with everything from vacuum-packed steaks to track shoes and the latest CDs. It was a line of poetry, apparently, that he told her always came into his head when he saw all the products on the shelves.

If there was profusion inside the compound, the opposite was true outside. They were in one of the poorest countries in the world. She had seen the beggars on the streets: the aged ones a pile of rag and limb on the sidewalk, the children lifting filthy hand to filthy mouth as they ran beside her car. She had grown accustomed to carrying the thick wads of bills that signified gross inflation. She had seen (though never tasted) the bowls of white maize meal that was most people's daily diet. Only a few were fortunate enough to supplement it with bits of meat, goat mostly, a horrid brown stew stirred up over charcoal fires in a ragged oil tin.

Sure, there was industry here – local products such as soap, paint, cigarettes – but only a tiny percentage of the population could afford them. Most were peasant farmers, eking out a fragile existence on their *shambas*, as these little farms were called in Swahili. A bad harvest or a natural disaster – flood one year, drought the next – could mean the difference between life and death.

Yes, Miranda knew all about it. It was a vicious circle. The worse things got, the more the farmers abandoned the production of cash crops – the coffee and sisal and groundnuts which represented Tanzania's main chance to earn foreign exchange. The less foreign money there was, the slimmer the country's chance of climbing out of poverty. For that, no conjuring trick, no poetry, nothing but an entire overhaul in the system of things, would suffice.

In spite of the rural poverty surrounding it, the city was still a city, a busy port connecting the interior to the trade routes of the world – as it had done since the bad old days of the slave trade, in which it played a central role. Dar-es-Salaam had its dives and traffic, its banks and hustle. But in the main it was laid-back, easy-going. Miranda liked to go to the Salamander Café for English-style fish and chips, and to eat ice cream at a place called the Sno-Cream Parlour. She had also become a member of something called the Yacht Club, which had a superb little private beach near her embassy-supplied house in Oyster Bay.

The house itself, a bungalow, stood among some old coconut groves on the fringes of the northern suburbs. It gave her a great deal of pleasure, although in the first few weeks she was burgled so often – nothing major, just a few things here and there – that she had to employ a nightwatchman. He only carried a staff, and to begin with she doubted whether such a simple weapon would deter any thieves. But the pilfering stopped, so his presence clearly had some effect. He also opened and closed the gate for her car.

Miranda soon found the small, interconnected world of expat life rather lonely, and the constant have/have-not interactions with the poverty-stricken Tanzanians difficult to handle with dignity. At first she threw herself into making her house nice, which meant cleaning out the remnants of the previous occupant – the person she had replaced at the embassy: spilt popcorn at the back of one of the kitchen cupboards, a packet of out-of-date condoms under the bed. Jerry Mintz clearly hadn't been much of a cleaner, since many of the kitchen utensils were dusty and there was mildew in the bathroom. She took on a housegirl, Florence – who slapped round the teak floors in flip-flops, following her instructions to the letter, but very slowly – and began to make lists of things she needed: fabric for new curtains; sink and bath stoppers (none in the house whatsoever); bug spray; a high-powered flashlight for when there was a power outage. Another problem was the air conditioner, one of those old-fashioned, water-extraction types. She was sure it was bad for her health.

The air conditioner was replaced. Other things were purchased, installed, utilised. Nisha Ghai, an Asian lady who worked at the embassy, took her to a shop to buy a rug for the lounge parquet – showing her how, on the good ones, the design on the back was as complex as the design on the front. The shopkeeper, a wonderful old Parsee with a goatee beard, piled the carpets one upon the other, unrolling each with a showman-like flourish.

So a sort of life took shape. The months and days came and went, and she slipped easily into the routine of existence in what are called the tropics. Months and days, and hours and minutes and seconds. Slow, monsoon-country time, carrying her along in its stream like a leaf in a culvert.

She learned, quickly, that this time was measured not by clocks and calendars but by a change in the weather, by coursings of dry and damp air, by the endless renewals, the constant cycles of heat and fecundity that were governed by the coming and going of the rains. She'd caught the mid-March ones just after she arrived. The old hands at the embassy said they were coming but she had felt it in herself anyway, during those first, hot, dusty days – felt, as the plants seemed to in their trembling leaves and nodes, faint animations of the future, a feeling that some urgently needful release was on its way.

The first visible sign was the sky's upturned blue platter turning rusty brown, and the few white clouds upon it gradually changing colour like a gathering bruise: pink, yellow, black. Then the first raindrops fell: heavy single drops, lookouts for the massed battalions to come, dashing and pocking the ground like bullets. Finally the full armour of the sky was loosed, as the pregnant, discoloured clouds delivered their long-held burdens.

When the turbid water curtain came down, it was as if the land itself were breached. The dropping green surge swept all before it, sending rats and twigs scurrying into holes, men and women into houses. The massive panel of water would begin gnawing at the laterite roads, which the grader's tooth had so valiantly sharpened all through the dry season. Everywhere it fell it brought new life, but at the time it seemed like damage, this sopping of maize and cassava plantations, this felling of the very saplings last year's rains had nourished. At river banks, on mountain sides, whole chunks of earth fell away as if bitten by some giant beast, dispersing in the torrent or tumbling down the escarpment.

Nature tried to revenge itself on man, it seemed to her – the storms battering the tin roof of her bungalow and beating brisk tattoos on the embassy's satellite dishes – but inflicted the worst of its wild turmoil on itself. Yet it was afterwards, in the calm, that its true power was revealed, forcing green shoots and riotous blossoms upwards in a mass of vegetation – out of land that, just yesterday, had been scorched earth.

She loved to watch the charged, electric storms and listen to them drumming on the roof *rat-tat-tat* like that. But it was an uneasy wonder, one that gave her pause. To some, she knew, the spectacle was no spectacle, but something of great necessity. The coming of the rains was of far more importance to ordinary Tanzanians on their *shambas* than to Miranda or her colleagues. For them the rains were not just a show or a mere inconvenience. Many expatriates she'd met seemed, on the other hand, to regard the rains – the whole of Africa in fact – as a springboard for their own fantasies. Fantasies of fulfilment or annihilation, desire or death, each according to their particular suggestion.

Miranda prided herself on having resisted this decadent, illusory view of the continent. Work was the perfect remedy for that kind of thing. Application to the diurnal round, daily life and its chores. But her tasks at the embassy were not absorbing enough to support such an ethic. Lying on the beach at the Yacht Club in Oyster Bay, surrounded by aid workers and the diplomatic corps of various nations, she sometimes wondered if she were not letting her ambitions drain away. As the weeks passed, she no longer thought quite so much about building a grand, successful career, or even about finding a husband and raising a family. The twin poles of her hopes began to wilt slightly, like the candy bars she sometimes brought back from the PX for the kids who clamoured round her gates when she arrived home. She didn't feel unhappy exactly, just a bit aimless. There was something about living on the edge of a warm ocean like this that undermined her ambition. It wasn't surprising. Stretched out on the sand at the Yacht Club, looking out over the ocean at sunset, it took no effort to feel that you might, like the merchantmen of old, drift all the way to India.

Ray liked to play golf, and sometimes she accompanied him to another club, the Gymkhana, which had nine holes of 'black' greens – that is to say, oiled sand rather than grass at the holes, so they could be easily maintained during the dry season. The Gymkhana's name went back to the days when English colonials used to run horse-racing and dressage competitions, but that was all gone now, like most vestiges of the British Empire in Tanzania, which had not been as anglicised as she'd heard Kenya to be. It did have tennis courts, however, made of the same red clay as the murram roads. But after one frustrating encounter it became clear Ray was so far below her in ability that it wasn't worth them pursuing that sport together. Miranda missed Kirsteen. Not just for tennis; she needed a girlfriend to run her dreams by, or to let her down gently in the wake of disappointments.

As gently as she herself, at lunchtime that day, or any other, would step down to the refectory, her shadow interfering with the light of the tombstone windows as she took the concrete stairway down into the corridor . . . leading to her customary seat in full view of the gardens (oleander: beautiful, poisonous), where she'd eat rice salad (grains unburnished), fruit (a Zanzibar apple) and drink a polystyrene cup of cranberry juice (good for the urinary tract).

Always too, this lunchtime or any other, Miranda would push her dark hair behind her ear to stop it falling into her food, and she'd likely be wishing, as fork came to mouth, she could cope better with being alone. But being in a sunny place and near the ocean made one want to be with someone, just as much as it sapped one's will to work.

Ray – she reflected, this lunchtime, seeing him come in – he was happy in his own company. He made much use of the embassy library, which was well stocked with everything from Shakespeare to science fiction.

She watched him walk over now, tray piled high with burger and fries and a carton of milk. He sat down, winking at her.

'What –' he asked forcefully, as he opened the carton, 'are you doing tonight?' He began jigging around. 'Dancing? Glancing? Backing and advancing?'

'Ray . . . you'll spill it on me!' She shook her head. 'Not much.'

'There's a great-looking new Nintendo game in the PX. *Yoshi's Story*. The character's this friendly, lizard-like dinosaur who eats fruit. Bit like you.'

He eyed her apple core, and took a long draught of milk from the carton. 'If I get it, I *might* let you have a go.'

'Excuse me, just how old are you?' she said.

He smiled wolfishly, milk on his moustache. 'Look, it's either dino capers with Yoshi or rowing with Virginia Woolf for me tonight, and I know which I prefer.'

He paused, then frowned, shaking his head. 'Actually, I don't think I do.'

Nourished by junk food and low culture as he was, Ray favoured more highbrow stuff so far as his borrowings from the library went. It was not unusual to find him sitting on a bench in the courtyard deep in something difficult. He ordered other books via Amazon.com, and when the cardboard boxes arrived at his desk, he would whoop with delight.

'So whaddya say, my little fruit bat?'

9

'Barracuda!'

Leggatt pointed with his pipe. About fifty yards away from the boat, Nick saw a pair of powerful, gun-metal fish leap out of the water.

'Chasing sardines,' said the old man, putting the smoking pipe back in his mouth. 'See there?'

Nick looked more closely. The water, which had been clear and calm, was now boiling with small fish. He watched in silence as the surface became increasingly agitated by the panic-stricken shoal. Thousands strong and densely packed, it was ripping to and fro in an attempt to avoid the predators. As their relentless pursuers drove back underneath, the top layers of the sardine shoal began to leap out of the water, forced up by the seething mass below.

Hundreds upon hundreds of the little silver fish plumed up in a shining cascade. Again Nick saw the gleaming torpedo of one of the barracuda, this time taking an unfortunate sardine in its teeth in mid-air before splashing back down.

Just as suddenly as it had happened, the commotion was over.

'I think we'll have some of that,' said Leggatt, with a grin.

He cast out. Nick followed suit. They both waited for the three-ounce spinners with their wire traces – those powerful jaws would cut through any nylon line – to sink a little.

After a few moments, winding their reel handles, they began to retrieve.

'*Pole-pole*,' Leggatt said, in Swahili. Nick had learned the phrase already. Slowly, slowly.

He hadn't expected to come fishing, but when Leggatt had greeted him at the clove farm, and said they were going to have to catch their lunch, he'd readily assented. He hadn't been fishing since he'd arrived. It was something he had used to enjoy doing with Dino and – in the long-distant and sweetly remembered past – with his father. He had no problems with it as a conservationist, either, since it struck him as illogical to eat fish at a restaurant yet refuse on principle to go fishing. So long as you ate what you caught, that was his law.

It is written, he thought to himself, with a chuckle. Weren't things looking up?

In addition to a small beach, the clove farm had its own slipway, bigger than the one at the Macpherson. Rather than taking the *Winston Churchill*, which was too large for their purposes, they had pulled down a speedboat belonging to the old man. It was a fine piece of work, with brass and walnut fittings and a powerful motor. Leggatt said he had bought it off an Italian hotel owner who was retiring.

Now, as they stood winding back in, the sun gleamed on the brass and the varnished wood. Nick stared out in front of him. In an instant the sea seemed to have turned from clear to jade-green. It was also calm again, and he found it hard not to imagine the spectacle he had just witnessed as some kind of vision. Once more the ocean had simply folded its secrets back into itself. All he could hear was the faint lapping of water against the side, and the clicking of their geared reels.

Then Leggatt spoke up. 'They might not be in the mood to bite after such a feed. Cautious as a housewife sometimes. But they're greedy sods, too, and when you hook one you'll know about it.'

Nick's line was in. Streaming bright droplets back down into the water, it swung about wildly in front of them.

'Careful,' said Leggatt. 'You'll have me snagged.'

Reaching out, Nick grabbed the line a few feet above the

glistening lure, with its poor representation of an open-mouthed, wide-eyed, small-sized fish; then he brought the whole complex arrangement, swivel, barrel sinker, second swivel, finally the wire trace and artificial lure, over his shoulder. Steadying himself against the rocking of the boat, and turning slightly to one side, he cast out.

A fishing cast is a strange tract of time, and even the most proficient fisherman cannot be quite sure how it will turn out. So when Nick's spinner found the right spot, hitting the water almost exactly where the sardine shoal had been convulsing, he felt a sense of pride and accomplishment.

He was about to say something to Leggatt, but hadn't uttered a word before there was a drag on the line.

'Something there, I . . .' But the pull was gone. 'Thought I had one,' he explained with some embarrassment, beginning the retrieve again.

'Sometimes they just explore it,' said Leggatt, on the point of casting himself. 'Take it in their mouths and test it.'

Pausing on the reel, Nick watched the arc of Leggatt's cast. It was to the left of his and, landing with a faint splash, went a good deal further out. He imagined the bright-eyed lure, a mixture of chrome and moulded plastic, sinking below the surface, swaying a little in the current. A couple of curious seabirds flew over the place where the water had broken, drifting down on white motionless wings.

Suddenly Nick's own line thumped hard. He felt the impact of the take between his shoulder blades, as energy was transferred down the line. He gave out a little cry as, at a terrific rate, the line span off the reel.

'Don't strike!' said Leggatt, urgently from his side.

'Why not?' replied Nick, anxiously, watching the line unspool.

'He's rushing with it. Let him go awhile or you'll snap the line. Now . . . slowly, mind, take the strain.'

Nick did as he was told, lifting the rod gently so that the force was transferred to it gradually. The rod began to bend and for a few seconds the fish appeared to check. Then it was off, darting to left and right, covering a lot of water until checked again.

It was running at speed. Nick arched his back against the pull and put his foot against the gunwhale to stop himself going off balance. Reeling in his own line, Leggatt came and stood behind him, all the while murmuring softly, like a mother to an infant.

The fish battled ferociously for a good ten minutes, swimming strongly in every direction. Once, coming up near the surface, it seemed to shake its head like a dog, sending a different kind of vibration down the line. At another moment it appeared to have given up, and the line slackened. Nick gave the rod a brisk tug.

'Don't force it,' insisted Leggatt. 'Let it run about.'

But it was already off again. The line sang as Nick pumped and dragged. The strain was constant now. His wrists began to ache.

After ten to fifteen minutes had elapsed, the fish began to weaken. Nick was able to bring it closer to the boat. Leggatt stepped forward with the gaff in one hand and the landing net in the other.

'Careful now,' said the old man. 'Lines this close can snap like sewing thread. Leave the brake off just in case.'

He was right to warn Nick, because the barracuda – they could see it now, swirling angrily just beneath the surface – gave a final determined fight for freedom, switching left and right and even going under the boat before it was eventually subdued. Leggatt plunged the gaff into its neck and scooped it, still struggling, up inside the net.

'Must be twenty pound or so,' said the Englishman as he boated the fish. 'You ought to be proud of yourself.'

But Nick didn't feel proud, he felt exhausted. And, as his quarry lay gasping at his feet, slightly ashamed.

'Damn,' said Leggatt as he used a pair of rusty old pliers to extract the hook from the lower jaw. He had scraped his hand on the sharp teeth.

He sucked the wound hard as they rode back. 'I've seen blokes lose a finger from inflammation,' he explained, holding it out.

Nick looked at the red gash in the old man's puckered skin. It didn't look so bad.

Back at his farm, Leggatt made them gin and tonic as his cook prepared the fish. They talked in the cool of the living room. There was no glass in the windows, just lattice screens that filtered the light and allowed a pleasant breeze to pass through. The place was decorated with an array of fearsome tribal masks and spears and other artefacts, including a matching pair of sea chests inlaid with brass and ivory, and an old grandfather clock telling the wrong time.

'So, what are your plans?' asked the old man, who had changed into a white linen shirt.

'I thought', said Nick, 'that I might go and camp out on Lyly for a bit – if you don't mind, that is. Reckoned I'd fix up that house. Live there for a week or two. Get some real study done on the turtles.'

'I don't mind,' said Leggatt. 'It's not my place to mind – frankly I'd welcome a bit of a break from keeping an eye on them. Strictly speaking the house is owned by an Arab as I said, but he's never there. It's ages since I've seen anyone go there. There's some African family from the main island who visit from time to time. Saw them out there once. Father and son. But that was . . . goodness, it must be seven or eight years ago now. You could probably get away with it.'

He refreshed their drinks then, and began telling stories of fishing trips of the past.

'Before I came out here, we used to fish Mafia Island in the channel. You could get everything. Wahoo, black marlin, bluefin tunny . . . even sharks, white-tips. Sometimes the sharks would take the fish off the line and all you would get was the severed tunny head. But then the dynamite fishing started and you didn't see so much.'

Nick remembered the white expanse of smashed dead coral. In Florida, too, he had seen dead corals, damaged by the anchors and keels of tourist boats, or bleached from pollution. All that was just as bad over time, but the effect of the dynamite was far more dramatic.

'You'd think the authorities would do more about it,' he said, distractedly, suddenly thinking about home. Ma. He ought to write her soon.

'They used to,' said Leggatt, knocking out his pipe in a flurry of sparks. 'Here as well, before Chikambwa was in charge. They once machine-gunned the canoes of some dynamite fishers, which was perhaps a little *de trop*. But now it's open house. They're even mining coral for building materials.'

At that point the cook brought in the barracuda and they moved to a table behind a screen woven from coconut leaves. To Nick's surprise, the cook shook out the thick pink napkins and placed them on their laps personally before serving the fish. Cut into slices and grilled, accompanied by rice and salad, it looked delicious. Already planning his sojourn on Lyly, Nick followed Leggatt's suit in dabbing the rice with tabasco sauce, then picked up his knife and fork and, faltering only when one of the thin little bones caught in his teeth, set to consuming his late adversary. It tasted just as good as it looked.

Afterwards, Leggatt took him round the spice farm, which involved a bracing climb into the terraces behind the house. It was strange to see exotic spices like nutmeg and coriander and cumin, which one normally saw in packets, growing like that. There were also peanuts and sesame plants there. But mostly the plantations were cloves. The pungent scent of these wasn't so

noticeable outside, but when Leggatt took him down to the drying shed, it was overpowering, even at the doorway.

Nick took a deep breath and stepped inside. In the darkness,
he could just make out long mats with the cloves spread on them.
But the aroma, catching at his throat and making his eyes run,
soon forced him back outside.

'Too much for you, eh?' chuckled Leggatt. 'You should stay in
here awhile, it's good for the tubes.'

A young African, who must have been in the very depths of the
shed, emerged from the shadows after them. His eyes were red-
raw with clove vapour. Nick recognised him as the poacher's boy.

'I gave him a job,' explained Leggatt, gruffly. 'Didn't I,
Sayeed?'

'Yes, bwana,' said the boy, grinning broadly and wiping his
streaming nose on the back of his hand.

Nick nodded at him and then, leaning against the edge of the
shed, saw something that made his heart leap. It was an old
green motorbike.

'That bike –' he said, turning to Leggatt. 'I don't suppose you
want to sell it?'

Leggatt laughed, throwing back his yellow hair. 'That old
thing? I haven't used it in years. You're welcome to it if you can
get it going – though I doubt you'll find any parts, and it'll surely need some. It's a Norton.'

Nick, ever the optimist, tried to turn the throttle, but it hardly
moved.

'Best British bike ever made. Bought it off a fellow called Mike
Drayton in Malawi. Chancellor of Zomba University no less. I've a
helmet somewhere, too. You can have that as well, if I can find it.'

They dragged out the bike and, with much difficulty, pushed
it over to Leggatt's workshop.

'Do you think you'll ever go back?' Nick asked as he bent over
the old machine, trying to undo the fuel cap.

'To England you mean?'

'Yes. Don't you miss it?'

Leggatt gazed out to sea, as if looking for the answer. He shook his dirty locks.

'Not now. Wasn't there much, anyway, except when I was young. And last time I was back it seemed a pretty poorly place.'

'Have you got any oil? The cap's stuck.'

'Up there on the bench. That was the seventies.'

'That's nearly thirty years!'

'Yes. I suppose it is.'

The nozzle of the oil can was covered with dead flies. Nick brushed them off and began squirting oil on the fuel cap of the Norton. He smiled to himself as Leggatt continued speaking. The old guy, he was nice really. As fouled up as his oil can, but interesting, and funny. The way he talked – that English accent of his – it was entertaining to listen to, regardless of what he was saying.

Above him, Leggatt took a tobacco-stained handkerchief from his pocket and blew his nose.

'It'll ease if you let it sit a while. No, I'll stay put. I've got – what? – ten years at most to master my fate, before I go gaga. Then I might go home. In a zinc-lined coffin. My dreadful relatives can fight over my will like dogs over a bone.'

He gave a loud cackle. 'I've told them there'll be millions. Zambian silver! Malawi gold!'

'I thought that was a type of marijuana,' Nick said.

'You're looking at the man who gave it that name. Never got into smuggling *that* though, even if it is the best hemp known to man or beast. Did you know that chimpanzees eat it when they've got a wound?'

He sighed, and blew his nose again.

'No, not with President Banda about. He'd have strung us up. Knew someone who that happened to actually. No, I was just a private smoker. I liked to think of myself as a connoisseur. Gave it up a few years back. There was this particular devil kept following me around.'

'DEA?'

Leggatt looked down at him, puzzled, then burst out laughing. 'You mean the drugs squad? No: an *imaginary* devil. An hallucination. A shade. Dope!'

For a second, Nick thought he was addressing him, then realised Leggatt was explaining the genesis of his demon.

'He looked rather like my dear departed dad, as a matter of fact. Except he was black as your hat, and that would have been difficult considering that *his* father fought for the Afrikaners in the Boer War – traitor to dear old Albion, I'm afraid, poorly even then. And afterwards his son grew up more in love with apartheid than the Dutchmen were.'

Nick, lost again, glanced up at him quizzically. Leggatt winked, and patted his pockets for his tobacco pouch.

'My pop I mean. Am I rambling? I'm telling you it exactly as it happened. We've always been a bad lot, till I came along. Beat the hell out of me. I jumped ship from South Africa and from him when Vorster came in. Headed home, by which I mean England. Took a degree at the Canford School of Mines, worked in Cornwall till that went down the pan, then came back out here. Or hereabouts.'

'Tanzania you mean?'

Leggatt frowned, looking into his tobacco pouch.

'Well, first it was Zambia. Up at Ndola. Copper and silver. Then Malawi. Copper and gold. I was nearly twenty years there. That was where I got into the boats. On the lake. This place, and the *Winston*, they were my retirement present to myself. The farm is just a hobby really.'

He sighed again, looking rather sombre.

'This isn't coming,' said Nick, whose new acquisition continued to frustrate him. 'Hey, what if we use that blowtorch? You know . . . heat expands.'

Leggatt favoured him with a look that garnered the full remaining potency of English disdain.

'Brilliant idea.' He paused to light his pipe. 'If you want to blow us up. OK, I haven't used it for a decade, but there could still be remnants of fuel in the tank.'

Nick blushed. 'You're right. Dumb idea.'

He continued trying to twist off the fuel cap, using up a bit of rag to give him more purchase.

'You must have made quite a bit of money to buy this place and the yacht too.'

'Ah, yes. The fabulous riches, explanation of. Diamonds is the answer. I hit the jackpot in Sierra Leone in the early eighties. Myself and a chap called Bailey – well done that man!'

The fuel cap had finally given. As if it contained the mystery of all things, from the trees and flowers, to the stars and atoms, to the infinite duration of eternity itself, Nick peered into the ancient tank.

10

Incident report #1: Miranda Powers

The alternate security guard (Juma Bagaya) reported to me the following. At approx. 0234 hours on Monday morning 04/05/98, he noticed two youths in their late teens in the motor pool. One with a bomber jacket, the other with a kikoi tied round his waist. One of the youths was tampering with the driver-side window of an automobile.

Juma pressed the alarm to alert the Marine Security Guard and proceeded outside with his weapon, having first turned on the spotlights. But by this stage the youths had already run across the pool and he could not see on account of the lights reflecting off the vehicles.

By the time the marine (Corporal Rossetti) arrived from his post, the youths had climbed over the wall and were running up Laibon Road. Police were called and arrived within fifteen minutes of the phone call.

Corporal Rossetti checked camera B2, which was on rotate at the time, but the incident was not covered.

Action taken: I sent a memo to John Herlihy asking if the technical department could fit some kind of filtering device to the lights in the motor pool.

Incident report #2: Miranda Powers

Approx 1530 Wednesday 10/06/98 the rear guard (Innocent Phiri) reported a burning smell coming from the air-conditioning fans by the generator in the yard behind chancery. I phoned John Herlihy and informed him of the situation. He came down and the two of us proceeded to the yard. JH turned off one of the fans by the isolator switches, as this seemed to be the cause of the smell – the fan motor was overheating, John said.

We returned to our respective offices. After fifteen minutes a humidity alarm sounded in the south computer room due to the fact that the fan had been turned off. We went back down to the fans. John said the fan would have to be replaced, but that it was in fact best to turn it back on now since it would turn off automatically if it overheated dangerously.

Action taken: fan in question to be replaced, occasional checks to be made on temperature in south computer room.

Incident report #3: Miranda Powers

At approx 1032 Friday 07/07/98 the alternate security guard (Juma Bagaya) called me to say a man was video-taping the gate near his post. I went down myself at once, but the man had gone by the time I arrived.

Juma had approached the man, he said, and asked him what he was doing. The man had replied he was a tourist and shortly afterwards continued on his way down Laibon Road. Juma said the man was brown-skinned and about five foot six and dressed in slacks, a collared shirt and a baseball cap with the words 'SPORT TEAM OSNABRÜCK' on it. He was unable to give any exact racial description except to say the man was 'not African'.

For the record I note that Juma is honest and I believe his account. However, he does lack analytical acuity and I would not recommend him for promotion to senior alternate guard.

As it turned out, the man was partially captured on camera B2 during its rotate, but his face was obscured by his own camera and then a bus passed.

Action taken: none.

11

Zanzibar . . . The name itself, languid and conspiratorial, was a kind of illusion. It seemed to speak of the heart's desire, of that yearning for paradise which is itself a sign we are fallen – that we are in the dirty realm of history, of actuality, of fact. The state of disgrace is not one of which we like to be reminded. It was little wonder, then, that when Nick – later in his stay and brown as a nut – saw Clinton on the television again, he turned it off and headed back to his room.

Having let himself in, he fiddled with the array of switches till he had the two bedside lamps on and the centre one off. It brought in the mosquitoes: there were enough tears in the grille already without making it easier for them. The walls were decorated with a much larger number of yellow sponges now. The *America the Beautiful* calendar had turned on a page – colour-enhanced Tranquillity Base – and the place smelled like a locker room. It was more untidy, too, not least through the addition of some underwater breathing apparatus he'd rented from a man called Turtle Mo. He was still waiting for his own sub-aqua gear to arrive. Dino, whose Drew Barrymore postcard now sported three Olympian coffee rings, had sworn blind on the telephone that the gear had been sent. But Nick was beginning to wonder.

He sniffed. The place really did smell. He turned on the fan, which started with its usual eastern-mystic *om-mmm* routine, and then went over to the window to let in some fresh air. The culprit, what was making the room smell so badly, was his wetsuit. Arms stretched out as if crucified, it was hung on the wall, drying from that morning's expedition with Turtle Mo's tank.

He pulled off his T-shirt. It hadn't been much help, Mo's anti-quated machine, which was really just an old reserve one, hooked up to an emergency mouthpiece. The mixture was slightly off and the supply tube leaked badly. In the end he'd just had to dive down holding his breath, like the Greek sponge diver his great-grandfather had been, so his father said.

Nick wondered how much of great-grandfather Karolides's lung capacity had come down to him. He'd found it difficult to stay down for very long. He'd hoped to attach numbered identification tags to a pair of breeding lobsters in a cavity at the bottom of the reef, but would have to wait until his own apparatus arrived – by which time, he reflected, they would probably have moved on.

Or been caught and boiled. Going through into the bathroom and turning on the tap, he thought of Turtle Mo again, imagining his big brown hand reaching for a lobster claw – perhaps even the same one that had waved at him from the coral cavity that morning, as he'd hovered there with his bursting lungs and a handful of steel tags. As if to say: you're not putting one of those on *me*!

The lobsters' tendrils, coiled up and moving in the water, swaying in the eddies, had made the entrance to their little cave seem like a kind of radio antenna. That was what he remembered thinking at the time, but now they transmitted a different message to his mind. It came to him with a slight pang while he was brushing his teeth. The lobsters' home, with the two of them just sitting there, was such an appealing scene of domesticity that he suddenly felt a bit lonely. Maybe he should try to get himself a girlfriend? He twisted as he brushed, looking at his torso in the mirror and thinking it over. He spat pink into the sink. He did not like clove-flavoured toothpaste at all – the tube he'd brought having long since run out, he'd had to buy local.

He went back through to the bedroom and, taking off his shorts, lay down, thinking about the tank. The sign above Turtle Mo's shop had read 'M. Gandhi Trading Pty'. A famous East African trawler baron whose freezer depots were dotted right down the coast, he originally came from Durban. Mo claimed descent from the great Indian leader through a rogue line established by Gandhi during his South African days, before his time of greater celebrity in India.

Nick doubted whether it was true. Large and bearded, Mo certainly didn't *look* like Gandhi, not like he was in the film anyhow. Nor did his booming voice, heavy gold watch, and the half bottle of brandy and box of cigars that had been on his desk when Nick went to see him suggest that Mo had inherited any of his reputed ancestor's self-denial.

As well as trawlers and fish-freezing plants, Mo had interests in everything to do with the sea in Zanzibar, from the export of salt – which villagers brought to him from the pans in wonderful, asteroid-like lumps and he sent in hessian bags to Dar – to the import of marine engines, small ones for outboards and big ones for trawlers. Mo also had a few cargo ships of his own.

His eyes found the wall. An image. Neil and Buzz bouncing about. On Tranquillity Base. On the calendar. On the moon.

It was his earliest memory, his father holding him and pointing at the television, saying: 'Remember this . . . this is history being made.' He would only have been something like two years old at the time – too young to take in the significance of such an event, or even understand what his father was saying – so he reckoned this must have been related to him later. But he certainly remembered something.

Tranquillity Base. It sounded neat, he thought. So did Lyly. *Lala.* Meaning sleep. The island of sleep, to which he kept meaning to return. He had been delaying because he wanted to explore it with his own scuba equipment, rather than spoil the experience by using the shoddy stuff Turtle Mo had supplied. In some ways he didn't mind having to wait. The island had taken up a place of special importance in his mind – it was beginning to oust Zanzibar itself as the focus of his interest. Going there for a spell would, he told himself, be all the better for the anticipation. In his imagination, Lyly now sat alongside that volume of Greek myths and history, simplified for children, which his father used to read him. Lyly, or the idea of Lyly, put him in mind of some of the stories: Odysseus stranded on the island with Calypso; Aphrodite, the love goddess born of the foam of the sea; Delphi and its mysteries, the sacred groves where time appeared to stand still peacefully.

While the planned trip to Lyly and the tagging of the lobsters would have to wait till his gear came, he'd had some successes. Modest as it was, his survey of molluscs on the intertidal flats had been well received when he sent the results to Washington. He had also, at last, seen one of the elusive leatherbacks – almost bumped into it, in fact, during his evening swim. Huge, about six feet long and four feet wide, it had lifted its head out of the water, regarded him for a moment, then dived, paddling strongly with its broad front flippers and trailing out its back ones behind, using them to steer. It disappeared swiftly. He'd swum back to shore feeling sublimely happy, as if he'd fulfilled his aim in coming to Zanzibar; although he knew really to do that he would have to save one or two of the glorious animals.

He recorded the sighting in his notebook, an old green-leather accounts ledger he'd bought in a junk shop in Stone Town. It was mostly lists of fish species that he logged there – triangular box-fish, barred needlefish, starry dragonet – but other observations went in too. Different to the work he did on his computer, his real work of charts and graphs and reports to Washington, this was where he doodled great spirals of nothing in particular, listed fanciful objectives for his future life and career, and recorded his impressions of people he met.

It was in the ledger, too, that he wrote up a little private project he was doing on life and death among the sponges. Just a short distance out into the bay from the Macpherson was a whole field of these multicellular members of the sub-kingdom Parazoa, all waving eerily in the undersea currents. They lived their passive lives subject to ebb and flow, the water constantly filtering through them. Somehow they fascinated him, and he had even gone to the trouble of drawing, in pencil and not very well, the olynthus of a simple calcareous sponge with part of the wall cut away to expose the paragaster, the central cavity of the body. It was through here that water left the sponge, having entered via the pores and washed around, feeding it with oxygen and microscopic nutrients. Sponges were, he'd come to believe, among the strangest creatures in the ocean.

There were others. The most exciting thing he had done lately – an account of which had gone into both ledger and laptop – was to sew a twenty-centimetre transmitter into the belly of a shark. For this he'd had to catch it (which he'd got some Zanzibari fisherman to do), and turn it upside down. Then it stopped thrashing about and became manageable, going into a trance-like state known as tonic immobility. The transmitter sent signals to a satellite, which in turn bounced the shark's location back to Washington, enabling scientists to track its movements. The whole thing had been fascinating, but his satisfaction in doing it right was chilled by the memories the shark brought of his father, that dark page of earlier life that he tried to keep shut but which still, sometimes, brought secret tears.

He knew that activity was the cure, not standing around dreaming of some imaginary perfection in which he wasn't bereaved. And so, notwithstanding his new attachment to Lyly, he had given himself over to a full exploration of Zanzibar itself.

After much tinkering, he had managed to get Leggatt's bike working. The boy, Sayeed, had helped.

The repair of the Norton opened up the place to him. Every weekend he would take a long tour, up to Nungwi in the north or down to the stretch of road that ran between Pingwe and Makunduchi village on the far south-western tip, stopping on the way to look at the hulk of the East German warship that had been abandoned here at the end of the Cold War.

Sometimes he'd ride on the beach, wild and bare-headed. Then dismount to sit in solitude by the billows, listening under the deeper boom of that heavier water for how the sea-spray's mesh of falling droplets boiled and hissed on the Norton's engine.

The ritual ended with the obligatory sunset, and then there was the homecoming on winding tracks, the two brown lines and cockscomb of frazzled grass that led him all the way back here: to see the sign, *Macpherson Ruins Hotel*, through gritty eyes. To see also da Souza, fastidiously preparing a gin and tonic for him behind the teak-wood bar. Or the woman whose head-to-toe black chador, as she swept the courtyard or turned down the beds each evening, struck a blow for chambermaids everywhere with its resistance to the male eye. In spite of his fascination with this Darth Vader-like character, Nick took care not to stare at her. Yet he often wondered how it must feel to be separated from the reality of things like that by the net of the veil.

The hotel itself was more revealing, releasing its staggered secrets like the split vanilla pods he sometimes ran over on his bike. While the main building was modern – though in a tasteful way, unlike so many of the horrors that developers all over the island were cooking up – the ruins, which stood in majestic gardens, were full of history. He had learned from da Souza that during the nineteenth century the ruined buildings had been a missionary school run by Caroline Thackeray. The Goan said that this lady was the cousin of a famous novelist from England and that the purpose of the school was to educate orphaned girls. Macpherson himself had been the bishop under whose aegis the mission school fell.

It was only a few weeks later, after he had wandered around the gardens and the crumbling, creeper-covered buildings several times, that Nick discovered these orphaned girls had been freed from slave-dhows captured by British warships. Now, whenever he wound his way under the ancient palms or large old mango trees, he would imagine the spirits of these poor creatures learning to read and write, or how to sew or cook rice.

The gardens themselves had been neatly laid out, with labels giving the names of the plants. Sometimes the reason for the name was obvious: elephant ear, powder-puff tree, umbrella plant, African hat plant, Dutchman's pipe, woman's tongue. Others were more arbitrary. He could stand looking at these stranger flowers for ages, wondering about their stories: beefsteak begonia, St Anthony's rick rack, bullock's heart . . . There was one, which the label said was from Peru, which was just called 'four o'clock'.

Nick was now officially an 'expert'. Most African countries suffered from a surfeit of these, and mostly they were white. But Zanzibar had surprisingly few. Nick only knew two or three, including the British specialist in Sudden Death he'd met in the bar in Stone Town, and for whose team he now played soccer on Wednesday evenings. Not very well, but he was coming along under Catmull's tuition. Tim was also teaching him to play snooker at the Africa House hotel, a regular night-time gig, with beer, after the soccer. They planned a trip to Pemba, Zanzibar's second island, where Tim often took weekend breaks. There was a good marina there, he said.

Another member of the soccer team was Olivier Pastoureau, a melancholy Belgian land reclaimer who worked down at Makunduchi. He had the best boat on the island, a handsome white motor cruiser paid for by the European Development Fund, the agency running his project. He was understandably proud of it, in particular the electronic gadgetry, which included an echo sounder and side-scan sonar to map the shape of the seabed.

Olivier had shown him how they worked during one of the Sunday-lunch barbecues for which the foredeck of the *Cythère*, as she was called, was splendidly equipped, having a minibar and a small gas brazier. The echo sounder gave an aerial view of the seabed, looking straight down, while the side-scan gave a horizontal view. Lowered by cables off the edge of the boat, the side-scan looked like a kind of torpedo or cruise missile. Then they would go back in the cabin and see the patterns of the ocean floor transmitted to the screen, its undersea hills and declivities all mapped out in glowing purple patterns.

Olivier needed to know the shape of the seabed so that his dredgers avoided the reefs when they went in to get the sand on which the planned new port at Makunduchi would be built. This conservationist impulse, which made the whole thing fantastically expensive, as the dredgers had to range much further, was to Nick's mind misplaced. Dredging would stir up so much sediment that it would block out the light the coral needed to live. So it would die anyway, in time.

The whole project sounded crazy – building on *sand*? – but obviously it wasn't possible for him to get into that in a big way with Olivier. He'd offered to look at ways of limiting the sediment drift on the bigger reefs by taking account of seasonal currents, which the Belgian said he would put to his superiors back in Brussels.

'But then,' Olivier added with a shrug, 'the project will be delayed further because we have to wait for this current or that, like a bunch of . . . how do you say, *bonnes femmes*, waiting to do their washing.'

Even when he was sitting out in a sapphire sea, drinking bottles of beer and turning over swordfish steaks on the brazier, Olivier always, though with some self-deprecation, saw the glass of life as half empty. Tim said the Belgian was mad as a snake. This might have been jealousy. Olivier was very attractive and had a funny effect on women. His wife – his ex-wife – was very beautiful. According to Tim, he had found the decline in her sexual desire after marriage difficult to accept. Nick and Olivier never spoke of this matter. They spoke of science and politics and higher things, from the creation of plastic to the Gulf War – oil, in that case, being the link.

So they had talked, that particular day, and so it unspooled again in his head. The history of our century was, Nick recalled the Belgian saying solemnly, the disgrace of humanity. All that was good, he said, had become like a dream flickering in the mind of a sleeping person: the future held only catastrophe, the triumph of death and sin. When he asked Olivier what exactly he meant, the Belgian simply shook his head gloomily and said the world was a wrecked vessel.

The phrase came back to Nick again at breakfast as he contemplated his little orange canoe of papaya. Served every morning, it had ceased to be exotic. He had almost begun to miss his bowl of Cheerios. After all (he remembered the ad), 'There's a lot of goodness in those little Os.'

Da Souza sailed toward the table, all smiles and hair oil, bearing the coffee jug for a refill.

'And how are we today, sir?'

'The same.'

'You are unhappy, sir?'

'Just . . . papaya again.'

'You don't like?'

'Forget it. I only mention it to illustrate a point.'

'This came, sir.' The manager produced a letter from his jacket pocket.

The envelope had a State Department seal. And a Dar postmark.

'This has taken over a month!' cried Nick, looking at the stamp.

'I am sorry, sir, but –'

Nick raised his hand. 'I know, stop there. It's Zanzibar.'

He tore open the letter. Brief, formal, and to the point, it was from the US embassy in Dar-es-Salaam, notifying him of the arrival of his scuba equipment.

PART TWO

12

They travelled to Pakistan in a battered green minibus. The journey through Afghanistan had been mortally slow, since the road
from Kandahar to Kabul was full of potholes. There were also
many checkpoints, but Zayn had all the correct papers and pass-
words to satisfy the Talibs. Having skirted the capital itself and
crossed the Kabul river in the dark, they spent a night at Khost,
where the Sheikh had a complex of camps. It was there they were
shown Ahmed the German's videotape surveillance of the target.

The following day, after winding through fields of scree along
a narrow road packed with lorries belching black smoke and
piled high with produce, they crossed the border without incident. There was nothing in their baggage to arouse the suspicions of the Pakistani authorities. The ordnance for the task had
followed a different route: from Italy and the Czech Republic to
Oman, using the services of a Russian freight company called Air
Yazikov, with which al-Qaida had connections. Then across the
Gulf by boat down to the East African coast, trade routes that had
been used for centuries.

*Loads carried to far-off lands . . . Ships whose cargoes bring pleasure
to peoples* . . . The holy words jostled with the thoughts in
Khaled's head as he looked out of the window of the minibus at
the rocky hilltops of northern Pakistan. He told himself to be
strong. Was it not true that only God knows what lies before people? Human beings can only understand those parts of His truth
that He chooses them to understand.

In Peshawar, they booked into a hotel owned by the Sheikh. It
was known as the Bait al Ansar, the House of Support, and many

people from al-Qaida and other Islamic groups stayed there as they passed through, before and after operations. Zayn had told them to keep a low profile, but Khaled managed to slip out – after a breakfast of bitter coffee, dates and yogurt – to wander round the streets, which were thick with people and traffic and dirt.

The crumbling yellow walls of many of the buildings were covered with brightly coloured posters of Pakistani film stars. There was a large garrison of soldiers and, testament to what years of war can do to a region, a large army of limbless beggars. Those who had lost legs scooted about through the black clouds of exhaust fumes on low wooden boards fixed with wheels, pushing themselves along on fists wrapped in bundles of filthy cloth.

The bazaars were full of all manner of goods, including a fear-some array of weaponry. He saw one stall where grenades were piled up like pomegranates. Peshawar was said to be full of smugglers. He suspected that these people were mostly ordinary traders, but it was certainly true that besides the local Pashtuns, the streets were busy with men from all over Central Asia: Uzbeks with florid whiskers, Turcomans in black woollen hats that looked like wigs, Nuristanis with blond hair and pale blue eyes . . .

He bought a glass of black tea and sat watching the faces pass-ing by the tea-house window. The variety of countenances pleased him. For although there is no God but God Himself, are not the most glorious places under Allah's sky those that are like this? Places where it is not one thing or the other that counts, as the Talibs would have it, but the great thronging mixture itself. His homeland was like that. Zanzibar, Pemba, Lamu . . . The whole coastline, Kilwa, Mombasa and Malindi, all the way down to Sofala in Mozambique, the port which the old men said was once the gateway to a fabulously wealthy African kingdom, long before white men came.

Home. Soon he would be there. The plan was that they would fly to Dubai. There, in the transit lounge, they would switch passports covertly with al-Qaida members inbound to Pakistan. Some of the passports were false, some were real. There was a facility within al-Qaida, a man who forged the documents. From Dubai they would fly on to Muscat to catch the Gulf Air plane that flew directly between the Omani capital and Zanzibar. This flight served those Arab families that divided their time between the island and the desert – subject, as always since the Revolution, to the residence laws that prevented Arabs from living on Zanzibar for longer than one month in four.

This aspect had been one of Khaled's own contributions to the operation. He liked to put a braver gloss on it, but sometimes he suspected he had been brought on board simply because he had the correct passport and visa, and the local knowledge. His documents had all been copied by al-Qaida's forgers. Zayn, a Palestinian by birth, and Yousef the Syrian were now fellow Zanzibaris of Omani extraction. Together with Khaled they could pass through the minimal controls at Zanzibar's tiny airport without hindrance. No one ever checked properly, Khaled had explained. By taking the direct Gulf flight they avoided having to go through immigration on the Tanzanian mainland.

This was important. In keeping with the semi-fiction that Zanzibar was a separate state in federation with the mainland, the authorities on the island had their own immigration service. But it was underfunded. Most important of all, it had no computers. Paper records of exit and entry to the island were rarely made either. Effectively, the representatives of al-Qaida would be entering the country invisibly.

Zayn was angry when Khaled returned from his wander round Peshawar.

He shouted. 'You are a young fool! What if a Pakistani policeman had stopped and questioned you?'

Khaled simply bowed his head miserably and waited for the stinging blow which the flat of Zayn's hand delivered on such occasions. There had been many.

After lunch, Zayn sent him into town to buy more units for the satellite phone that they would use in the course of the operation. It struck Khaled as something of a contradiction: surely he was far more likely to be noticed at the satellite agency than sitting in the window of a tea-house?

Later in the afternoon, feeling wronged, he went up on to the flat roof of the hotel. As he walked out onto the squared concrete, he saw a small figure. It was a boy flying a kite – one of the hundreds of little paper triangles that fluttered above the city every afternoon. Most were made of green or red tissue. Some of them were covered in pictures, though these could hardly be seen from the ground. Khaled stood watching. Kite-flying was a craze in this part of the world. The boys glued ground glass to the strings of their kites and engaged in fights, sawing away at the string of the other.

He sat down on the low, rough-plastered parapet of the roof wall and continued watching, to the boy's great pride and pleasure. Along with satellite television, videos, football and chess, the Taliban had banned kite-flying over the border. Khaled could not begin to fathom the reason. Perhaps they thought kites were in some way idolatrous. But kite-flying seemed such a harmless pastime.

As he studied the boy skilfully swerving his craft through the air, deft movements of the hand producing corresponding swirls and flourishes in the sky, Khaled felt happy again. Breaking through the clouds above the hills round the city, sunlight was bathing the whole place, making the yellow-brick town reflect upwards with a golden glow, in the midst of which danced the red and green dabs of the kites. It gave – he had to confess his thoughts took this shape – what could only be described as the impression of a painting.

The feeling soon passed however. Later Khaled could again feel Zayn's hot eyes upon him when, as dusk fell, they inaugurated their evening prayers in the hotel room. Khaled knelt and lowered his head. A fan whirred above. He heard Yousef's whispering voice beside him, and joined in the recitation.

'Praise be to Allah, Lord of the two worlds . . .'

* * *

High above the three men, higher than the ceiling, higher than the flat roof and the forest of kites over Peshawar, higher and knowing and seeing – but not omniscient – spun the machinery of satellite reconnaissance of the United States government. A few days previously, before the battered green minibus had left the camp, a long-range camera had taken a digital photograph of the vehicle. It had just taken another picture of the vehicle, outside the hotel in Peshawar, and this had provoked a reaction.

Passing the information through various critical filters, the computer that controlled the camera determined whether it was worth forwarding to intelligence analysts. Since one of the filters tested the movement of vehicles, the program for forwarding began to run. An encrypted message flashed its way from a joint NSA/CIA data-collection facility to the desks of a number of US officials.

These included Jack Queller. As part of the consultancy package he had hammered out with the CIA when he retired, he had the full complement of communications equipment installed in his home office in the cabin on Aquinnah. For all that, he still communicated in more traditional ways as well. The island was in the south-west corner of the Vineyard, near enough to the Haven for him to pick up his mail every morning in his modest speedboat. There was rarely much – statements from his broker, occasional copies of the journals to which he subscribed. But he liked to make the trip, just to prevent himself from getting too solitary.

There were two fishermen he drank with, Lanford Bourne and

Todd Stubens, but otherwise he didn't mix. Especially not with all the people who were coming in from New York and building houses in the area. There had lately been some trouble between a real-estate developer and the local Native American lobby, which was Wampanoag and fairly militant.

Half Wampanoag himself, Todd had an old Navy lighter from which he ran lobster lines. Queller loved this boat and sometimes the two of them would go out together to check no one had been messing with the trap lines. Todd liked to do this in the early morning. Then, when the place was quiet, you got a real sense of what the Haven must have been like in the old days, when it was full of tall ships – whalers and slavers, traders from Europe and the East. Todd had given Queller an old harpoon point he had found in a cove. It took pride of place on the window sill in his lounge, next to a photograph of Lucy.

That was where he was now, surrounded by bookshelves and wearing only his boxer shorts. As the 'incoming message' tone sounded on his computer and the corresponding dialogue box appeared on the screen – 'You have new mail, open mail?' – he was lying on the sofa reading, as he did every morning, a verse from Omar or one of the other great Persian poets.

Putting down the book, Queller went over to the computer and affirmed the dialogue prompt. With his hand on the back of the swivel chair, he read the message, taking notice of the co-respondents. These changed according to the status and subject area of the message.

To: Jack Queller
cc: Mort Altenburg, Sylvia Chavez, Edwin Elliott
From: Data collection
Subject: al-Qaida activity
Message: View portal 99142/3/A and advise. Control decision: Altenburg.

Frowning when he saw the last part of the message, Queller spun the chair round and went through to the kitchen to fix himself some breakfast. It made him feel low to have to file his reports to a younger man. Altenburg had a mere fraction of his experience of terrorism and hostage-taking, yet supposed himself an expert. He put some bread in the toaster and turned on the kettle. Whatever was in the message, it could wait. He felt his stump twitch with pain, as if the glowing bars of the toaster had been pressed against it. The cut nerves hurt like this from time to time; the cause was partly physiological, partly psychosomatic – but the pain, that was always the same.

He had, he felt, good reason to be down on Altenburg. The FBI man had recently vetoed an operation he had half set up and wanted to run 'dark' through the Counter-Terrorism Group. He had persuaded the representatives of two oil companies (both former agency men, as so many in the oil business were) to put up $500,000 each for a speculative unofficial project. Queller would fix them up with 30,000 square kilometres of concessions through a contact of his in Sudan. He planned to use the money to set up an unofficial operation to kill Osama bin Laden. But – even though the money was sitting in an escrow account in London and things were ready to roll – Altenburg had blocked the plan. Furious, Queller was sorely tempted to run the operation privately. He was an adept of dark ops, however, and knew that they tended to go wrong without covert official backing. Only agencies had the resources, deniable and undeniable, to run such things in a proper fashion.

Queller had another reason to dislike Altenburg. He suspected him of scheming to terminate his consultancy contract. Officially, they both came under the aegis of the recently established Counter-Terrorism Group, whose inter-agency team of officers produced tactical intelligence with the aim of thwarting terrorist attacks. The CTG itself came under the direction of Secretary of

State Albright – with whom Queller was on familiar terms – but she couldn't be drawn into a dispute of this nature, a dispute that wasn't even supposed to exist. It was a fiction that State took the lead in the CTG anyway. There was the usual power vacuum of an inter-agency function, and this gave guys like Altenburg a chance to extend their influence.

Balancing a slice of toast with raspberry jam on top of his mug of coffee, Queller went back through to the office and sat down at his desk, rereading the message. He had thought, when he began the consultancy, of keeping up his apartment in Washington or the house outside Langley – but these days, with intelligence gathering and analysis totally coherent with the electronic revolution, it wasn't necessary. So he had let out the apartment and sold the house. The place was full of ghosts, anyway. He glanced over at the silver-framed photograph of Lucy – smiling outside the Institut du Monde Arabe in Paris, their final vacation together – and felt the familiar stab of grief.

Now he spent nearly all his time on Aquinnah. He left the Cape only to attend meetings in Washington and Langley, and to give lectures to students at the FBI's Quantico and the training centres of other government agencies – such as, lately, that of the Bureau of Diplomatic Security.

He thought about the bright young woman he had met there – the one with the deep green eyes to whom he'd denied any such operation as the one that had recently fallen through. The woman heading for Dar. What was her name?

He noticed a scribble on the notepad next to his computer. *Termite dust.* He would buy some next time he went into Vineyard Haven. A few days ago he had noticed that some of the wooden cladding on the old part of the cabin (he had built an extension) was bulging. He had reached up to touch it and the whole thing had fallen off, baring a long thin nest of insects. Hundreds of the little creatures had fallen onto his face and hair.

Queller sipped his coffee and read the glowing screen. He once tried to use his prosthesis to type, moving a single latex-covered finger by stimulating sensor pads in the socket which responded to the flexing of muscles in the stump – but it was laborious and painful.

So today the arm dangled from its straps over the back of one of the lounge chairs next door. The flesh-coloured hand, which could be removed, lay on the chair in front. He hated the prosthetic. However much the socket was repadded (and he saw a specialist every six months), it rubbed against the stump. He hardly wore it these days, except when he went up to Washington. He told himself he did this for the sake of appearances, but suspected it might be that he enjoyed the shocked expression on people's faces when, reaching to shake his hand, they realised it wasn't real. Like the young woman whose name he had forgotten. He called it the revenge of the unhanded.

Miranda Powers! The name came back, like a tiny charge going off in the brain.

Queller actually had quite a few hands, a whole drawer full of the damn things, all of various capabilities and textures. They had been given him by the hospital and he had put them in the drawer and left them there. The prosthetics did not feel part of him in any way, each one being a ready-to-hand – as he liked to think of it – reminder of absence. Not just of the physical existence of what had been taken from him, but of the actions he could no longer do, like tying shoelaces, for example – he had to wear slip-ons – or the many ways in which having two hands assisted one to express oneself.

He had also been given a couple of metal hooks, but he never wore them. There was too much of the cartoon about them.

As a matter of fact, everything seemed cartoon to him now, the whole gamut of life – comedy, tragedy and everything in between. It was the condition to which things tended these days:

colour without tone, a flattening of dimensions, the false dynamism of something that was actually fixed, storyboarded.

Bin Laden's adoption of a singular perspective, the stuff he had covered in the lecture, that was part of the same thing, the same caricature. And so, perhaps, were people like Altenburg and Kirby . . . There was no room for grain and texture in it all, not like the lichen on the boulders of Aquinnah. Yet somehow the cartoons touched on, were part of, the rawness of existence. That was the mystery: how the inauthentic clicked into the authentic as easily as the prongs on his various hooks and hands picked up the ratchet of the main limb.

Queller enjoyed musing on the material aspects of his afflic-tion, turning them ever to the abstract. It filled the absence for him: by treating his condition in this way, he reduced its power over him. This was something that only those who were 'dif-ferently abled', as the PC police insisted, could fully under-stand: a way of bending the otherwise abled world to one's own needs.

For all that, right then and there, naked except for his boxers, it was with his live hand that Queller pointed the cursor at the hypertext link in the middle of the email:

View portal *99142/3/A* and advise.

Meaning, what? The message, which had come over the CIA's secure, proprietary system rather than a commercial link, was instructing him to log on to Langley's direct feed and view the satellite images. It took a few seconds once he had clicked. Then the picture popped up. It showed a green minibus parked outside a building with a flat roof. On the bottom left of the screen, super-imposed on the image, text was flashing with hypnotic vigour:

New location, arrival 1730 hrs local time. Departed camp three days previously.

Queller sipped his coffee and looked at the green minibus for a while. Then he began typing, with one finger:

Advise field surveillance from Peshawar onwards. High threat priority. They are starting on a journey. Refer to my earlier report citing alleged threats from al-Qaida, Egyptian Islamic Jihad and other terrorist groups against US targets.

The email flashed up on Altenburg's screen in Washington almost immediately: the CIA net was much more efficient than its commercial counterparts. This also meant that the reply came back quickly, and it wasn't one calculated to make Queller happy:

No dice Jack. We have been through this. I don't really see that we can divert resources to this kind of surveillance at the present time.

Queller stood up. That ever-vigilant sentinel of stress, his stump, began to throb agonisingly again. He walked out of the room, leaving Altenburg's message on the screen. Passing through the lounge with its cane chairs and cushions, he stepped out onto the porch. He was still just wearing his boxer shorts, and even though it was summer there was a morning chill. But he didn't care. Who was there to see him? To see him walk down the steps and out into the clearing in the pine wood that surrounded his cabin – the cabin on which, when she was alive, as Lucy grilled trout inside, he had used a soldering iron to burn the word *Zanzibar* into a plank next to the door. Because? Because being by the sea reminded him of his childhood in East Africa. Albeit most of the time it was a hell of a lot colder here on the Cape.

As he walked, he was conscious of the breeze on his chest and the pine needles under the soles of his feet. He came to a fork in the declining path and made for the shore, his feet like little ploughs for pine needles now, pushing up a green river round his ankles. Once he was out of the pitch pines there was a pretty piece of upland where gorse and broom and juniper grew on the edge of some pasture. He could see the remains of some old stone walls marking a former division. He walked on, enjoying the springy turf and the calls of the greenfinches that nested in the juniper. Far away, on a hill on a spur of mainland, he could see an old church, a narrow road winding up to it. It was Catholic, Portuguese, an old mission station. No one went there to worship now. The only visitors were tourists who passed it on the way to some strange cliffs nearby, famous for the multicoloured striations in their clay.

A verse from the Koran, which he knew intimately, came into his head. *Do you not see that Allah sends down from the clouds water, then brings forth with it fruits of different kinds or colours? And in the mountains there are streaks, white and red, of different colours, and others intensely black. And of people and animals and cattle there are different colours likewise. Only those of His servants fear Allah who possess knowledge* . . . It was a plea for equality, except for the crucial distinction between believers and non-believers, and it was an unveiling. Colour was nothing but an illusion in man's mind, even the many shades of white suggested by the use of the plural form in the original.

He walked on. There was another little piece of wood – maples, more locust trees, a venerable oak. Then sudden sand and a widening: the amazing way the sky opened up. He was in the dunes now, which usually made him feel better, but the bad feelings were still there, his fist was still clenched. His only fist. On his other side, he felt a dull ache. The stump hurting . . . below, ghost limbs. All that was missing: the hand itself, the hand it would hold were it there. Lucy's.

Queller looked out over the rolling sea. The wind was heavier here, and there was spray. That was why the bad feelings would go at last, beaten out of his chest by that wind and that spray and by each incoming wave as, marvellous, they came to see him. Each seemed like proof, as it rolled in, that just because a man was lonely and one-armed, had grey hairs on his chest and was standing in his underwear on an ocean beach, it didn't mean he was past his prime.

He eased himself down, sitting cross-legged in the sand, and began his meditations.

13

Miranda Powers looked from her desk, down at the courtyard of chancery. The extreme heat of the day, now diminishing, had released aromatic oils from a lavender hedge below. It amazed her they could rise thirty or forty feet like that. But then, there was no breeze.

She delved for an elastic hairband in the clutter on her desk, ran her fingers through her hair then scooped it up into the band, which she twisted over three times. Her work was nearly over. The day book was done. Protocols had been observed. The garden was safe for tomorrow. There was the bench where Ray liked to read, there was the fountain's silvery plume. The sun casting shadows with the struts of the bench made a little prison-house on the concrete slabs. As she stared half asleep at the pattern of the bars, absorbing how they lay at harmonious angles to the ordered ranks of a nearby bougainvillea trellis, she saw a figure cross.

A tall young man with dark, curly hair and a tanned face, he had a swimmer's body. None of that was so extraordinary, except that he had a large double scuba tank strapped to his back. She watched in surprise as he checked himself through the marine post and headed on to Laibon Road.

It was, she conceded to herself as she glanced at the papers on her desk, just about the most interesting thing that had happened to her all day. Dar itself was pretty limiting, she'd found. To spice things up a bit, she and Ray had got into the habit of taking tours at the weekend. Already, they'd been on a camel safari in the Arusha National Park and watched cheetahs hunting. They'd also been for a picnic in a part of the Rift Valley, at a hardly pronounceable but nonetheless idyllic place called Mto Wa Mbu. It was on Lake Manyara and the words meant 'Mosquito Creek' – though the mosquitoes weren't so bad really. They had stayed at the Fig Lodge hotel and seen wildebeest and zebras and giraffe in the game reserve. A baboon had jumped up on the hood of the car.

More extensive trips had been planned to Zanzibar, the Serengeti and Mount Kilimanjaro, which was said to be a punishing but exhilarating climb. She liked travelling with Ray, he was fun. But often, on these journeys or at home in her little bungalow, she still experienced something like loneliness. She missed her father a great deal. At night, in the last moments before sleep, the image of his face would often flit before her eyes: a big, tough mug, full of beer and laughter lines, crowned with prematurely white hair. She kept two pictures with her always, one of him in uniform, holding his policeman's cap before his chest, another of him at home, bare-armed, aproned, cooking a barbecue. But the most powerful revenance of Joe Powers that came to her was the hoarse, deathbed voice that said, *Make something of yourself, Miranda, be strong . . .*

She was in constant email correspondence with Kirsteen back in Washington, and with other friends. But having no parents, no living family that she knew of apart from some cousins in Ireland, and, though she had had several boyfriends in the past, no 'great love', as Ray once put it – these things made her feel as if she lacked an anchor in her life.

Strangely, she saw the young man again a little later, on her way home, overtaking him in her car. The lights changed and, as he crossed the road, they exchanged glances. He looked so odd, there in the middle of the city with that scuba pack on his back. Her foot on the pedal, she thought momentarily about pulling over, offering him a lift – but the traffic had already whisked her along and the chance had passed.

The following day was a Saturday and as usual she drove to Kunduchi Beach. This was the main resort on the coast and she liked to come swimming up here. It was less of a 'scene' than the Yacht Club, and safer than Oyster Bay beach outside her house, where there had lately been some attacks and burglaries perpetrated on Western tourists. She didn't like to be constantly worrying about her towel and sunglasses being stolen while she was in the water. So she had got into the habit of going up to the Kunduchi Beach Hotel, which was secure and sea-facing and anonymous. For a small fee, the hotel allowed people to change in its swimming-pool cubicles, and to rent a locker in which they could store their belongings.

After a brisk swim she went for a walk along the beach. It was quite crowded, being the weekend. Locals and tourists were out in force, picnicking and lying in the sun. She passed a group of boys splashing about in the water and struck out for a quieter patch of sand. Bound for this, with her eye trained on a finger of rock, she hardly noticed the figure approaching her; they had almost passed each other when she looked across and realised it was the young man she had seen the previous day. He seemed to notice her at the same moment.

Miranda, turning and hardly sure of what she was saying or why, spoke first.

'Hey, didn't I see you at the embassy yesterday?'

The man, who was wearing a pair of white shorts, received this overture with a puzzled stare. He took his hands out of his pockets.

'Have we met?'

Now that they were facing each other Miranda was conscious of his height, his imposing tanned face and, mostly, the smooth skin on his chest.

'I passed you in my car a little time after,' she explained, hurriedly. 'You were wearing a scuba tank.'

She gave him a mischievous look, a nuanced movement of the head. 'Pretty alternative dress code.'

'You think so?' said the man, standing on his dignity. 'I figured it was the most sensible way to carry it. You are?'

'Miranda Powers. I work at the embassy.'

'Right,' said the tall brown man, nodding.

His wariness lessening, his face broke into a smile. He held out his hand in greeting.

'Nick Karolides. I'm USAID on Zanzibar.'

She shook his hand. 'I've been told it's lovely over there.'

He nodded again. 'Yeah, it's fine. I'm on a reef protection scheme. Hence the tanks. I'm here about them now, getting them filled at the hotel. It's cheaper than Zanz.'

'Zanz? Is that what you call it?'

'Er, I just made that up in fact,' he said, looking a little sheepish. 'Though I think it was called Zinj by the Arabs. Zinj el Barr. Coast of the black people. A guy told me . . . some such story.'

They had fallen into step side by side.

'The tanks will be a while. Where you headed? Catching some rays?'

'Guess. Over there, I thought.'

She pointed. She was acutely aware of the falling waves, of her bare feet in the sand, and the shouts of the children behind them.

After a few moments, he spoke again, vouchsafing something unexpected. 'I used to come to the beach and play like that as a kid.'

'Where did you grow up?'

'Florida. Born and bred. But my family's Greek. You?'

'New York. Irish.'

'Don't tell me, your dad's a cop.'

She laughed, then mimicked him, reproducing his tone. 'My pa's a cop, I'm telling you. Well, he was. Then he became a security guard when he retired.'

'Safer.'

Her face darkened as she shook her head. 'Uh-uh. The building he was guarding was a bank. He was shot in a robbery. In the chest.'

He stopped walking. 'Christ, I'm sorry. I was only kidding around.'

She smiled slightly at this display of concern. 'No problem. Why should you have known?'

He made a sucking noise with his teeth, and lifted one of his hands, as if unable to express himself properly.

'It's all right,' she repeated, thinking he was rather unusual.

'I lost my father too,' he blurted.

'Ah,' she said, understanding now. 'I'm sorry. Guess it's what we have to put up with – at a certain age I mean.'

He strode forward, kicking the sand with his feet. 'Guess so. It's a demographic, right?'

'Yeah, it's a demographic,' she said in agreement, although there was something a little challenging about the way he was speaking now.

'My dad died violently too. What's the demographic for a shark attack?'

'You mean he was killed by a shark?'

'That's right.'

Falling silent, she processed the information.

'I didn't mean anything by it,' she said, eventually.

He shrugged. 'Don't worry. Just bad luck, I guess. Same as you.'

She looked out to sea. 'Are there sharks here?'

'Here?' He gave a cruel laugh. 'Of course. There are sharks everywhere. But it's kind of rare to see one close to the coast. There's so much fishing, they learn to keep away.'

'Good,' she said, and gave him a smile.

They had reached a rock that jutted into the sea, then curved back on itself to form the shape of a question mark. As naturally as if they had known each other for years, they made themselves comfortable on its smooth warm flanks – Nick sitting in his shorts, feet dangling in the water, Miranda, her skin pale gold, stretched out like an odalisque on her side.

He circled his feet in the swell. He seemed quite distracted, she thought, gazing out to the horizon's blue shimmer. The intense, near-blinding appearance of infinity was broken only by a container ship crossing to Dar port.

'Kind of makes you think, doesn't it?' she said, following the direction of his gaze. 'Makes you feel small – as a human being I mean. I always think that.'

'Me too. And of all those stories about cities under the sea. The whole civilisation going under.'

'That's just legend, isn't it? The deluge.'

'It's a hell of a legend to just make up. The idea of it, all those millions drowning. Imagine if you were the only one to survive. Like Charlton Heston in *Planet of the Apes*. Walking along the beach under the Statue of Liberty. The last man.

'Or woman,' he added. 'Though I guess it wouldn't make much difference. Unless you were pregnant.'

There was a pause before he said, 'I mean, she.'

His clumsiness touched her. 'Do you usually get talking to a girl like this?' she asked, slyly. 'When you've only just met her?'

'You spoke to me first,' he said defensively.

There was another embarrassed pause. Miranda tried to read the thoughts behind his face. Closer, its imposing qualities seemed more plainly cut; not ugly exactly, but there was a drift that way, a tendency: wide mouth, broad forehead, a nose that was slightly flat. Still, she reflected, he had something.

The tension was broken by the descent of a swarm of large African sandflies, which bit like pincers. Nick and Miranda started slapping at their flesh as the insects gathered round hungrily. Then, without thinking, they both ran shrieking and laughing into the sea.

It was rougher than they might have expected. Miranda fell under a breaking wave, turning upside down and catching her shoulder on the rough sand. She thrashed her limbs, panicking and choking.

Suddenly there they were, strong arms scooping her up. He held her gently under the armpits as she coughed sea water. She steadied herself, planting her feet wide in the sand.

'I'm OK, I'm OK.'

He released her. 'Careful. Like this.' He balanced himself with his arms. 'There's strong currents in this ocean. You better get out.'

She shook her head, frowning. 'Thanks,' she said, 'but I want to swim.'

'In that case you better come further out. It's much safer away from where the current hits the beach.'

She was about to reply, but he was already swimming. She could see the white soles of his feet as they kicked up. She followed at a slower pace, breaststroke in the wake of his freestyle. She was conscious of the place where the sand had rubbed her shoulder – conscious of that, and of the memory of his hands, holding her, then letting her go.

Further out, they trod water, facing each other, droplets on their hair and faces. Here the sea was calmer. Around them the water shifted from side to side, reflecting the sunlight in iridiscent panels.

'What do you do at the embassy?'

'I'm Diplomatic Security,' she announced, somewhat formally.

'No shit? You're some kind of spook?'

'No! We're in charge of security procedures there, well, some of them. The Marines do the hard-nosed stuff. My job's mostly hiring and firing, and technical stuff. You know, making sure we have the right kind of walls and fences and alarms. And the right local employees. No one who's a threat.'

Nick laughed. 'Who's a threat to us these days? Not here, anyway. Well, I heard the Tanzanians were trained up to see us as the evil empire by Nyerere and his East German advisers, but I don't think they ever took that very seriously.'

'We have to do it by the book everywhere, you know.'

'Suppose so,' he replied. 'Hey, I better get moving. I've got to collect those tanks.'

They swam back together. She matched him stroke for stroke.

'Any chance you could give me a lift back to town?' he asked, as they waded out of the water. 'Save me getting a taxi.'

'Sure, where d'you want to go?'

'Well, I need to do some shopping. Food mainly . . . there's things I can't get on Zanzibar.'

'Why don't you come to the PX?' offered Miranda. 'The store at the embassy. I can get you in. You can get some good stuff there.'

'Great,' he said, smiling at her. 'You're certain it's no trouble?'

'No trouble at all. On Sundays it's self-service and you just put it on your chit card. You can give me the money.'

'I've only got shillings, not dollars.'

'Don't worry. I'll swap you. Unless you're planning on buying the whole shop.'

'Uh-uh. Just a little variety. I'm tired of fish and rice, rice and fish.'

'Good for you.'

'Sure, but what I *want* is chocolate, steak, ice cream.'

'We've got 'em all,' she said, in a crazy shopkeeper voice.

The sun dried them off as they continued down the beach, laughing and chatting. He went to collect his tanks from the dive facility. She retrieved her belongings from a wooden locker, the lock of which opened with the tired ease of overuse. Once she had towelled and dressed, she took a bit longer than normal doing her hair before coming out. Her eyes asked themselves questions in the mirror, and she wished she'd brought some make-up.

When she emerged, he was standing there with the twin cylinders beside him.

'Sorry I took so long . . .' The lie came so easy it shocked her. 'I couldn't get into my locker.'

'No problem. I only just got done myself.'

He wore a T-shirt with pictures of fishes on it, the same white shorts he had swum in, and a pair of black sandals that fastened at the ankle with velcro strips. She thought she liked the look of him as he waited there, but she wasn't sure. Not *sure* sure.

She opened up the trunk and he lifted the tanks inside. Then they drove back to Dar. A storm broke on the way, with attendant claps of thunder and flashes of lightning. Soon sheets of brown water were planing across the murram.

'This isn't monsoon time,' he said, as the car splashed through the puddles. 'Must be a freak.'

The rain brought a chill with it. She reached to turn off the air conditioning. Driving, she suddenly found herself amazed that her day had turned out like this. What would Ray say when she told him?

At the embassy, the marines let them in without Miranda having to wind down her window.

'They know the vehicle,' she explained. 'Though really they should come out and check no one else is in it.'

'Can't blame them in this weather,' he said, looking across at the camouflage outline of the Marine in his booth.

They ran across the sodden lawn as fast as they could, but were soaked all the same. As they went round the PX aisles, she was conscious of his gaze on her body through the wet cotton dress. She wasn't sure if she liked it, although there was a kind of enjoyment in catching him looking away guiltily. But she was tempted, then, to consign him to the general run of male attention. Nothing special.

When they came outside, the storm was over. The sun was shining strongly once more, although the air still smelt wet and vegetal. It was a smell of death and decay which, like the poisonous flowers she had seen at Mto Wa Mbu, was another aspect of rain in the tropics. After he'd packed his stuff, they stood under the open, dripping hatchback, writing down each other's telephone numbers and email addresses on bits of paper – under the watchful eye of one of the chancery security cameras, which had swivelled round to observe them.

The atmosphere had shifted subtly. After exchanging contacts, they parted with some formality. She dropped him off at his hotel, the Kilimanjaro in the centre of Dar. Through her rear mirror, she saw him standing in the exterior lobby with his tanks, as if waiting for her to wave. But she didn't, and by the time she got home, the whole episode seemed like a strange dream. She barely gave him a second thought for a couple of weeks, neglecting even to tell Ray what had happened. Which wasn't much, after all.

14

Nick thought a lot about Miranda Powers on his return to
Zanzibar. But he only had the vaguest intention to follow up their
meeting. He didn't know what he felt about her, exactly. She was
certainly very desirable and smart, and they seemed to bond a little
even in the short time they were together. But, well, he didn't know.
His positive feelings were clouded by that solitary, self-sufficient
tendency in him which refused claims on his affections. Yet she
had not made any such claims, and perhaps it was ridiculous for
him to assume she might do so. He wondered whether the truth
was that he quite liked leaving it up in the air, all in potential.

In any case, another kind of adventure was at hand. Now his
scuba tanks had arrived, he could go to Lyly. It was easy to clear
this with Nagel at the USAID office in Dar as legitimate work.
Having ascertained from Leggatt that there was fresh water on
the island, he was looking forward to spending a week, if not
longer, alone there.

He laid his plans carefully, drawing up lists of what he would
need. Leggatt helped with fishing equipment, lending him two
rods and an array of hooks, weights and lures. Then there was
food: he had all the stuff he'd bought in Dar, which included
chocolate and a variety of tinned soups. To this he added various
provisions acquired in Stone Town market, namely a small sack
of best basmati rice, a packet of macaroni, a box of biscuits, a
plastic bottle of Mazo oil, salt, pepper, curry powder and two
large boxes of matches.

Da Souza, who made it clear that he thought the enterprise
nothing short of lunacy, supplied him with a jar of instant coffee,

some tea bags, powdered milk and, since he was sceptical of the water supply, a crate of bottled water from the hotel bar. He also added some bottles of beer at Nick's request, although these, the Goan reminded him with some seriousness, would have to go on his monthly bill. As far as tools and other equipment went, he had only his fishing knife. So on his trip into town he also bought a pair of pliers, a machete, a small axe, a mess tin, a frying pan, a tin cup, knife, fork and spoon, and a boiling billy. For lighting, he thought candles and a storm lamp, together with a tin of paraffin oil, would probably suffice. For writing, he had his ledger and a few ballpoint pens.

He packed his sleeping bag and also another lighter one that he'd had run up out of cotton sheets by a Stone Town tailor. He added a roll of something he had always found useful on camping trips back home – black plastic garbage sacks. Before packing the roll, he tore off a couple of sacks and put a few items of clothing into them: jeans, a heavy sweater, two T-shirts, extra shorts, and a pair of heavy boots – his father's old Marine issue. Inside the boots, to stop them getting wet, he stowed the big essential: ten packets of cigarettes.

Nick said goodbye to da Souza and set off, full of excitement. He made the crossing quicker than before. He was following the same bearing he had taken off Leggatt's yacht, when the island of sleep was unknown to him, and Leggatt himself an enigma. This time he felt confident, secure, able to let the throttle out and bounce along the waves more rapidly than previously. On he went, under a canopy of sun-gilt cloud, until he saw the island appear in the distance above the prow of his boat, gathering in mass above the succession of waves. Coming closer, he saw the tip of the lighthouse poke out from the forest, then the outlines of the other buildings.

He turned off the engine and upended the outboard, allowing the dinghy to coast into the beach. Once it had nosed its way onto the sand, he jumped out and waded up. He stood for a moment on the shore, hands on hips, sniffing the air, taking it all in, then went back and pulled the dinghy up behind him. He tied it, very carefully, to a palm tree whose cluster of young green coconuts looked like a necklace on a slender young girl. Thinking again of Miranda – he was conscious he at least ought to have emailed her to say thanks for letting him shop at the PX – he began unloading his cardboard boxes of food and equipment onto the warm sand. As he did so, he realised he'd scratched his ankle on something – a sea urchin? – getting out of the boat. The saltwater made it sting painfully.

He carried the first of his boxes up the beach. Square and solid, built of coral block that gleamed in the sunlight, a white house faced him as he made his way up, with the box against his chest. At first the house looked splendid, there in the sun. But on closer inspection, it turned out to be rather forlorn and tumbledown.

He put down his box and went inside. The ceiling in the living room had caved in. There was plaster all over the floor, and a smell of damp from where rain had fallen. Small black spiders were running over the debris. He found a cabinet with a drawer full of old seashells, mainly trochus and conch. In the lower cupboard was an old-fashioned wind-up phonograph and two 78s, warped and covered in a thick layer of dust. Their labels were indecipherable.

He went back to collect the remainder of his boxes and other equipment before exploring the rest of the house. In the kitchen, which was a palace of dust, he discovered an ancient yellow refrigerator. Paraffin-driven, its door was open: he could see the clapped-out old burner and heat-exchange tubes underneath. There was also a table and three chairs, with tattered wicker seats.

He returned to the door and brought in his boxes one by one, piling them up by the table. Pieces of tarnished cutlery lay about on the floor, amid leaves and the husks of coconuts.

The house had two bedrooms. One was empty – except for a nesting bird, which fluttered round the room as he entered, then made its escape through the hatch-like window. There was no glass, and from the solid coral frame it looked as if there never had been. In the other bedroom, which was larger, the remains of a black-and-white striped mattress were decaying in a corner. There didn't appear to be any kind of bathroom.

He wondered when the place had last been inhabited. Perhaps not for thirty years. Later, he discovered signs of more recent occupancy: a rusty Coke can and some silver foil, maybe a chewing-gum wrapper. Other objects slowly revealed themselves as he went over the house again. A ragged mess that might once have been a blanket; a framed photograph, its glass all cracked, of the young British queen; a dented stove-kettle; a vase, surprisingly intact; the wooden frame of a hand-mirror . . . Eventually he abandoned his search, conscious that he ought to make arrangements for sleeping and eating before nightfall. He also wanted to find the spring that Leggatt had mentioned.

He set off into the deep thickets of the coral-rag forest, savouring the moist greenness that filled his nostrils. There were no paths to be seen, just the rag's curtain of close-knit leaf, punctuated every now and then by taller jack-fruits, banyans and frangipanis. Every way he chose seemed closed. He pressed on till mounting obstructions – fallen trees, binding branches of giant fern, large, slippery rocks covered in moss – and gathering darkness (it was later than he thought) forced him to turn back. There was no sign of any spring. He realised that a proper survey of the island would need time and planning. Tonight, he reasoned, he would drink bottled water.

He decided to sleep in the tiny little mosque adjoining the house. It was cleaner and less decrepit than the house, despite being much older. He wondered about making a fire and heating some proper food. But in the end he just ate some beans from a can, washed down with swigs of beer. He lit the hurricane lamp, using more matches than he would have liked. He laid out his sleeping bag on the stone floor of the narrow building, then spread his sheet sleeping bag on top of that and, after removing his T-shirt, climbed inside.

The hurricane lamp guttered beside him. For about half an hour, he just lay there on his side, looking at the lamp and listening to the waves, which were much louder than at the Macpherson. He seemed to see the pattern of the waves in the reflected flames of the lamp – shifting from side to side, impossible to fix as they engulfed the wick or crept up over the mantle. He closed his eyes and tried to think of Miranda, but all he could see (even behind his closed lids) were the sinister giggles of the flame.

In the morning, he woke with a start to a rustling sound. Through the arched doorway he saw, caught in a shaft of sunlight, a very large, pinkish-brown crab dragging a fragment of coconut shell across the clearing. He sat up and watched it for a while. Then, summoning resolve from drowsiness, he stood up and wandered outside. The crab, about the size and colour of a baseball glove, reacted with alarm to his presence and began to sidle away.

He couldn't decide what to do first. Go fishing – make sure he'd got some protein? Do the big tour? Dig a latrine? Clean up the house and move in properly? He decided to go for a swim and a wash while he thought about it. Then he realised that he had forgotten to bring any soap or shampoo, or even his toothbrush. He would have to swill out his mouth with saltwater instead. He walked down to the beach – into the surf, then, thinking something, retreated and took off his shorts, dropping them on the sand. Who was there to see him, after all? He dived in.

After swimming a while, he began to rub his naked body in the ocean: his face, under his arms, his butt, his genitals. Then he swam up and down some more, to wake himself up. He was conscious of a peculiar feeling, the drag of his dick in the water in the cold currents. Then he realised something else about his body. The ankle he had scratched on arrival was stinging again. On getting out, he knelt down on the beach, just above the surf-line, and inspected the cut. It was bright red and, he could see, in danger of becoming infected. He regretted that he had not packed any antiseptic cream in his supplies either.

He replaced his shorts and put on a T-shirt. The sun was already up. He pulled on some socks and his heavy boots, feeling how strange it was to do this in sunlight. Then he went into the forest again, this time carrying the hand-axe. He had been planning to cut some wood for a fire – but there was plenty simply to be gathered up. He picked some dry pieces. These – when he returned to the house some ten minutes later, having gathered some tinder grass and applied his cigarette lighter to the pile on the beach – kindled pretty easily. He boiled some water for coffee, wondering what to eat for his breakfast. Settling in the end for another cookie, he sat on a piece of driftwood dipping it into the lukewarm coffee. His food supplies were woefully inadequate, he was beginning to realise. Time to get fishing then. He looked at the sea and, unlacing his boots, considered the prospect. Using a spinner or lure, that would be easiest. That would save him having to dig for bait.

Fishing turned out to be far more difficult than he had imagined. He spent most of the morning sitting on a rock by the boat, without a single bite. Finally, after much changing of lures, he pulled out a small parrotfish. He wondered whether to eat it or to use it as a bait-fish, eventually deciding to cut off the head and use only that for bait. The rest he saved, wrapping it up in a palm frond and putting it in the shade to keep fresh. Returning to the beach, he took off the lure and tied on a big hook. At least he wouldn't have to keep recasting now.

The head of the parrotfish yielded startling results. In quick succession he pulled out two wahoo and a baby shark. He now had too much. *Too much wahoo,* he said to himself. But he was happy that he had proved it was possible, happy that he had proved he could be a survivor. He filleted one wahoo. *One wahoo is enough for you,* he sang, out loud this time, before frying it in cooking oil and pepper. Accompanied by boiled rice and a cup of black tea, it made a passable lunch.

He felt, however, that he shouldn't have boiled his bottled water for the rice. This little self-chastisement spurred him on to search for the spring. He donned jeans for the expedition and put his boots back on. Off he set, panga in hand, aping the intrepid explorer. There was something maze-like about the rag forest, and it was half an hour before he found the semblance of an old path. At the end was an algae-covered rock, with water running over it. Someone, long ago, had hacked out a space in the rock to enable a utensil to be placed underneath. It was then he realised that the intrepid explorer had brought no container. He retraced his steps to fetch the boiling billy and an empty plastic water bottle. The bottle would not fit in the space in the rock, and he spilt a little from the billy on the way back.

The sun was very hot now. He became aware of other omissions: he hadn't brought sunblock, or a hat. He really was very unprepared. Why did he think things would just pan out for him? All life's experience said otherwise.

His head aching, he went to the mosque for a sleep, feeling a bit foolish. It really was very hot. He could hear thumping, and could hardly tell if this was the noise of the water in coral caverns beneath the island or the blood in his head.

He slept for longer than he meant to. It was almost dusk when he woke. Lighting the storm lamp, he went into the house. The lamp made antler shapes on the rough plastered walls. He saw the horn of the phonograph, and decided he would try to get it working. He took the machine, which was surprisingly heavy, into the kitchen. Opening another bottle of beer, he sat there supping and fiddling. Eventually, somewhat to his surprise, he fixed the spring back into the winder. After wiping the dust off it with his shirt, he put on one of the 78s. What came out of the horn was tum-tum music, ukelele, and that made him happy. He drank more beer and lit a cigarette. Right now, he reflected, some marijuana would be nice too, what with the superb darkness outside and the noise of the breakers and the palm trees. He wondered if any grew wild on the island. He played the tum-tum again and then put on the other record. This time it was an Englishwoman's voice, high and reedy, and much scratchier than the ukelele. He couldn't make out all the words but the chorus was clear enough:

> This demon desert lover
> You don't want to discover
> Mustapha! The Moor!
> He does things you'll abhor.

At the end the accompaniment, which was piano and sax, suddenly stopped; the woman's voice, in a hoarse, over-dramatic whisper, reprised the chorus with a twist . . .

> This demon desert lover
> You keep him under cover
> Mustapha! The Moor!
> Take care you don't want more.

The song gave him the creeps. There was something disturbing about the Englishwoman's voice. He played the tum-tum a third time to get the other one out of his head before bunking down in the mosque.

The island was about two miles in diameter. It was dominated by the lighthouse. On the morning of the second day, he climbed to the top. The edifice was built from the same material as the house: crushed coral mixed with cement and painted white. The wooden door at the bottom was stuck. On getting inside, which took a hard shove, he found a dead fish eagle on the first step. It had obviously flown in and got trapped.

He counted as he climbed: thirty-three steps in all. In the room at the top, he was surprised to find the lamp and its reflectors unbroken. The instrument, he divined, was oil-powered. He wondered whether he could get it going with his paraffin.

He stayed up there for almost an hour, surveying the sea's terrifying immensity. Only the vague haze of Zanzibar proper rescued him from sensations of being utterly alone. Yet there was also something appealing in the spectacle. The idea that through hermit-like withdrawal suffering might be avoided attracted him so powerfully it was almost frightening.

But what had he suffered, after all, he reflected on making his way down the winding stairway. The loss of a father? That came to everyone in the end, as Miranda had said. It struck him it was something they had in common. She'd seemed a bit raw and vulnerable about it when they'd talked. In his case, the pain had lessened some lately, but his dad's death remained a kind of watershed, a moment when everything changed.

Later in the day, he walked out onto an amazing bar of sand that appeared as the tide receded. Cresting the reef and several miles in length, it seemed to reveal itself as he walked along, as if his footsteps made the water retreat. It fell away, waves in the ocean on the left of the reef, ripples in the lagoon on the right. With a certain narcissism, perceived and readily conceded, he introduced himself into two episodes of a Biblical nature, stories his mother's sect were apt to link: Moses's parting of the waters, Jesus's walking upon them. Except . . . except that winding his way back along that tremendous bar, the sand became really too hot to walk on at all. He was soon hopping, hopping, hopping: Nick the dervish, Nick the whirling sufi.

Elsewhere on the island, in the cool of early evening, he rediscovered the same nub of copper he'd moored his boat to during the business with Leggatt and the poachers. He remembered, again, something the old man had told him about the stump of metal: how it was part of the old telegraph system that connected the mainland to imperial Britain. Cape Town–Durban–Mombasa–Dar–Zanzibar–Aden–Cyprus . . . London. The old order, connected by thousands of miles of steel on the seabed, a wired world that existed long before fibre optics and the Internet.

Walking back to the house, he realised his ankle was throbbing. Crouching down again, but in the jungle path this time, he saw that it had become infected. He squeezed a little pus out of it. Delicately, using the edge of a leaf, he scraped it off before continuing on his journey.

That evening, opening his ledger, he made an account of the food that would have been available to the true castaway. He'd opened a coconut but the milk tasted gross, and the flesh no better. Neither were the young pawpaws edible, being still bitter and milky. He had considered trapping or spearing one of the big crabs. But it was easier to fish, now that he had the knack for it. And the way the crabs hung round rotting vegetation made him think they would probably taste rank. Eyes darting sideways as they hunkered over white shreds of coconut flesh, they looked like hoodlums at a street corner.

He read over his paltry list of produce. Relying on nature left much to be desired. Inadequate as they'd previously appeared, he was now very glad of his supplies. Of the lemons especially. He liked the way they stung his lips, which had become cracked from the sun. He thought of it as a punishment, that sting, but he didn't know what for. Before going to bed, he daubed some of the juice on his suppurating ankle. Maybe it could help that, too.

The third day. A day to dive, and this proved some experience. Leggatt was right. The Lyly reef was spectacular indeed: a mass of colours, richer than any coral he'd yet seen, and populated by a wide variety of sea life. In one place a moray eel, lunging from a hole, bared its fangs at him. Elsewhere he saw a labyrinth fish of the genus *Anabas*: the rare climbing fish that resembled a perch except that it could travel over land on its spiny gill covers and pectoral fins.

He didn't plan to stay down a long time; but it was very tempting. Luckily, the highlight of the dive was one that saved him using up his tank. Where the reef joined the base of the island, he noticed that the current sucked in and out in an unusual manner. He swam closer. On further investigation, he discovered an opening. It was just big enough for a man's body to fit through – a man's body without scuba tanks on his back. He hovered there for a few minutes, watching the water go in and out. The noise of his own breathing was loud in his skull. Then he thought he'd risk it.

Taking a deep gasp of the mixture, he reached and turned off his regulator. He shrugged off the tank harness and tied it to a spur of coral. He knew that what he was doing was dangerous. He just needed to keep calm, he thought. But already, during the time it had taken to remove the harness, he had begun to run out of air. He had done things the wrong way round. His head pounding, his chest feeling as if a heavy weight had been dropped on it, he held the mouthpiece to his lips and, turning on the supply again, took another burst. Bubbles flew up. Waste. But he hadn't time to think about that. Already he was insinuating himself into the hole, the fear he would run out of breath strong inside him.

Now he was inside, and there was a small space above him. Air! He dared not believe it . . . but it was too late, anyway. He was already taking in a big, joyous, double lungful. Humectant was the word for it, since it was stale, marine air he was sucking in so powerfully, air born of too long a contact with the green-dripping walls of the place. He swam forward a little in the slosh-ing water, till he came to a shelving bank of smooth, slippery rock. He had to take off his fins to stand. His toes sank into an oozing substance.

There was a dim light. He could see that the cave was about four metres wide and some twenty or thirty twisting metres in length. Perhaps it was longer, there may have been further cham-bers and corridors. It was hard to see. What he could see was about three to four metres high in some parts, less elsewhere. He shivered. The source of the light was deeper in the cave. He moved forward carefully, edging his toes through the ooze on the floor. Obscured by what seemed like vegetation, the light came from a circular space in the ceiling. He considered trying to climb up, but on touching the walls he found them to be covered with thick green slime.

As he removed his hand, he was shocked to see that there were chisel marks, some kind of writing there. He scraped away the mucus, dark green goo, flicking it from his palm. Yes. Curling Arabic script, etched into the rock. What did it say? He felt his lack of knowledge like a pressure on the temples – an almost painful sense of whole worlds and cultures that had been closed off to him.

The next morning, he discovered that all trace of infection had gone from his ankle wound. The lemon juice had done its work. Or maybe it was the ooze in the cave. He'd heard of stuff like that. Whatever was the case, there was no sign of suppuration any longer, just a thin red tick: a nice scab. He traced it, that night, with his finger, under the flickering storm lamp, under the roof of the crumbling house.

Something about the script, the writing on the wall, had made him move into the house, leaving the mosque to its ancient holiness. It didn't seem proper to doss down in a place where people had once prayed.

The cave gave him something on which to focus. He went down there again the following day, with his ledger and a ballpoint pen sealed in several garbage bags, thinking he might copy out some of the writing. But it was no good. The pages of the ledger immediately began to absorb moisture from the wet air, like a sponge. He put it back in the bags. He couldn't really make out the characters, anyway. They were too subtle and seemed to change in the sea-green light even as he looked at them.

It was just as difficult to work out where, on the surface, the opening that gave the scanty light would be. He tried to triangulate it, but as soon as he was back up top, the geometry seemed different.

He began to build a search for the opening into his day. It was exhausting and his hand began to blister from using the panga in the forest. He was out there for hours over the next few days, chopping and stomping about, sweating and wild-eyed. The trees let through far more sunlight than he imagined, dappling him with fierce rays. His hair became bleached, his skin papery, a template for the sun's experiments. Now he really wished he had brought some sun cream. He started to use the Mazo oil instead; except that he had knocked the bottle over while cutting one of his paths, and if he wasn't careful he would find himself short of it for cooking.

Soon, he started to feel guilty about cutting down so much of the undergrowth. He told himself he must slow down, then laughed at himself for thinking this. Executive desert-island stress. It's a cave, so what, no need to go nuts is there? Anyway, he had proper work to do.

He had, in fact, spotted some turtles, watched them laying eggs on the beach under a full moon. It was a glorious sight, a sight for the blessed, but all he could really think about was finding the opening to the cave. Other tasks, necessary ones like fishing, got done in double time. He was good at it now, pulling fat fish out of the water like rabbits from a magician's hat, disdainful of his own skill. The garbage clearing and house tidying he simply abandoned. Cooking was routine now too. Fire, fish, oil, pan. He would suck on a lemon afterwards and savour the way his lips stung.

He never found the opening. He gave up the search. On what, he decided, would be his last evening on Lyly, he climbed to the top of the lighthouse. Almost as an afterthought, he picked up the can of paraffin oil and a box of matches on the way. Having climbed the thirty-three steps and entered the lamp room, he doused the wick with paraffin, pouring in most of the can. In spite of the years that must have passed, it lit almost immediately. He pulled down the mantle and reflectors and was dazzled by the light that suddenly flared. He had to leave the room.

The blindness stuck. On the way down, he nearly tripped and fell on the steps. He caught a splinter in his hand from the rail and barked his shin on the stone.

Swearing, he made his way outside. Night had fallen. He may have had a lighthouse, but right now he needed a flashlight. He used his cigarette lighter to guide him, cursing again when the flame scorched his thumb. And the lighthouse beam – it didn't seem to be showing.

Back at the house he could see it, however. Something to do with angles. He lay down in the bedroom on his sleeping bag and sucked at the splinter in his thumb. Through a window frame, which also enclosed stars and a crescent moon, he watched the lighthouse cast its widening ray over the ocean till it faded and died. But he was dreaming by then, Nick Karolides, peaceful at last on the island of sleep.

Morning brought a pink, refulgent dawn, in the midst of which he walked round the island one last time, before seating himself by the stub of copper, which stuck out of the rock like the nib of a giant fountain pen. He must have stayed beside it for – what? Half an hour? An hour? Time was mysterious beside water, it seemed to him. It flowed in a different manner, taking on all the sea's varieties of blue. By the shore it was pale and limpid, lighter than turquoise; further out it grew dark, more solid and inky, becoming almost black near the horizon. Shade after shade ran upon the surface, perpetually varying hues altering the general pattern.

Everything, as he sat there by the cable-end, came to his eye with meticulous definition. A large white bird, like a gull but different, landing on a tree nearby, seemed to show the very grain of its beak to him – and, no less definite, the scales of the small, steely fish that struggled in those yellow tongs. The bird walked along the branch and bent over its spiky nest. High-pitched sounds announced fledglings in the nest, puckered and urgent.

Was he himself, he wondered, still quite so hungry for alternative experience? He looked up into the sky as if it might furnish some answer. The morning light was stranger than he had thought. The flesh-pink shade had gone. A blood-orange colour was in the clouds now. He wondered if it meant a storm was coming.

He stood up, using the cable-end to push himself, and sighed like an old man. He turned his hand as he walked. The nub of the cable had left a mark on his palm. Cape Town–Durban–Dar–Zanzibar . . . the other names he couldn't remember. His mind tried to plumb the network below, all those messages of the past. It struck him how, in history, so much was incalculable, so much was lost.

He went back to the cottage and began collecting up his stuff, feeling low. He was tired of being alone – not just here on Lyly, but generally. Walking down to the boat with his tanks strapped to his back, he thought about Miranda, teasing him for wearing them in Dar, and smiled at the memory. It was then he knew he would like to be around her some more.

15

– I thought that since your messages had got shorter and more infrequent you must be working hard. That I should leave you in peace. As for me, I've been considering my position here. Not sure if this job is right for my future happiness. Not challenging enough.

– I thought I had offended you and you were giving me the silent treatment!

– Not at all. By the way, that something you sent me underlined means it's a hypertext link? It didn't work.

– Works for me. What did you do?

– Just clicked it as normal.

– At the weekend I mean.

– Ate loads of spaghetti. I am now made of pasta.

– The Maid of Pasta. Bet you still look good.

– You wouldn't say that if you caught a glimpse of my legs. Ape-woman. Am off to get them done now at the Kili. Catch you later.

* * *

– Who've you got your legs done for? Sugar and lemon juice sounds nice on a pancake but less nice to have torn off you. Don't they have Imac? Is that what it's called? As for your future happiness, I refer you to Nietzsche: The secret for harvesting from your life the greatest fruitfulness and the greatest enjoyment is to live dangerously. Fire walk with me.

– ??????

* * *

– Have just been for drinks and cake at the Ocean Watch party in Stone Town. It is a reef protection charity. They had a cake in the shape of a fish. It wasn't a very nice cake: too much sugar, not enough flavor. My friends Olivier, who is belgian and depressed, and Tim Catmull, who is British and british, came too. Sorry. can't seem to be bothered to use the cap key. Will try harder. How are you Miranda? I feel sorry for you there in the middle of dusty Dar. Forgive me, I think I must be a little bit drunk. Not much news here. Would you like to come and visit me?

– I have a mouth ulcer. Ow ow ow. But if that doesn't put you off, in answer to your question: yes! I'd like to see Zanzibar.

– Try pawpaw for the ulcer. Pleased that you are coming.

– Will do (pawpaw). Can I add, though, that you shouldn't make anything of my visit?

– What you are talking about?

– Don't get any ideas about a holiday romance.

– I see. Well, at least you are brutally honest. Hadn't any, as a matter of fact.

* * *

– Nick?

– Sorry, been busy. Am not not writing to you.

– Do you still want me to come? Could do a long weekend.

16

With her hands around his hips, she felt odd sitting on the back of the motorbike. And none too safe, either, as they weaved through the narrow streets – her rucksack strapped crossways on the pillion, her hair streaming out behind. There was only one helmet, and it was too big for her when she tried it. In the end they both rode bare-headed; he tied the helmet to the pillion with little bungees.

She had thought a lot about seeing him again, conjuring the figure on the beach in her mind during their exchange of emails. Reality didn't disappoint, and her senses quickened when she saw him there waiting for her at the airport, smiling and bronzed, with the helmet under his arm. As they went out to his bike in the sunlit car park, all her smoky imaginings of what this moment would be like kindled into flame, springing spontaneously in the heart. Yet behind the glow of warm feelings, there was a warning voice telling her to be prudent, to keep her self-possession.

He took her for coffee at the Livingstonia Hotel. Two cannons at the entrance door. Very British. Very colonial. Inside was a weary snooker table and an age-dimmed indication in wood relief: ☞ The Ladies' Powder Room. Two things rescued this run-down and slightly sad establishment, where even the hunting trophies looked mournful, as if the animals had known they were going to be killed. The first was a wonderful balcony, opening out to the sea, high above the rusty, corrugated-iron roofs of the town. The second was an old library, full of red and brown hardback English books with titles like *Tales from the Mysterious East* and *Memoirs of the Boer War*.

'Ray would like it here,' she said, as they peered through the glass of the dusty cabinets. *The Effect of Tropical Light on the Skin of White Men. Fortune My Foe.*

'Who's Ray?'

'A guy at the embassy. He's kind of a bookworm.'

'Right,' said Nick, nodding.

She wondered if he suspected Ray was a rival for her attentions, which was crazy, considering, but then he wouldn't know. Yet the moment had already passed at which to put him at his ease . . . in any case, the insistence would have created too obvious an invitation.

She wasn't sure if she herself liked Stone Town. Its crumbling coral houses seemed slightly hostile. Especially the former residence of Tippu Tip. Nick said Tippu Tip was a famous slave trader who had helped Livingstone and Stanley make their explorations. Now a private house, it had a large carved front door, in front of which sat an old bearded man in turban and robes. On the steps beside him, a noisy crowd of children were playing with wooden models of aeroplanes and cars. They were imitating the sounds of the engines, careening the models through the air close to the old man's face. He remained unmoved.

They left the old man and snaked through the busy streets, under carved wooden balconies. Electricity cables were looped from house to house, and she worried they might hit one. From the doors of the Indian curio shops, some of which were studded with brass knobs or lines of cowrie shells, tourists emerged sporting old silver bracelets or cradling antique nautical instruments. She also saw basketfuls of crabs and shrimps, sitting in the open sunlight, their contents still twitching, and street vendors grilling chunks of squid or lobster on wooden skewers over charcoal fires. Everywhere was the smell of fish and spices and flowers. At one point the bike sped down a street whose surface was covered with hibiscus petals. Miranda guessed there must have been a wedding there, or some other kind of feast.

Further on, he stopped to show her some iron rings where slaves had been chained.

'Is this where they were sold?' she asked him, staring at the scarred old metal.

'Don't think so,' he said, putting out a foot to steady the bike. 'I heard a church was built on the site of the old market. I guess they just . . . kind of waited here.'

There was a pause during which she was conscious of his body in front of her, between her knees, and the hair on the nape of his neck. He kicked the pedal and restarted the engine.

The next place they visited was the Old Arab Fort, which a sign said had been built between 1698 and 1701. It was a large stone building with medieval-style battlements. It now contained a restaurant.

Over his shoulder, Nick said: 'And Leggatt – he's a British guy I met, maybe we'll go see him – told me the Arabs built *that* on the site of a Portuguese church, so I guess it's a case of what goes around comes around.'

They also visited an edifice called the House of Wonders. A large balustraded building with a clock tower and lots of tiers and fretwork, it had once been the Sultan's ceremonial palace.

'There's a story that the skull of a slave was buried under each of those columns,' he informed her, as they dismounted. 'It's going to be a museum, once the government finds the money to do it up.'

'Everything here seems to be in transit,' she observed, gazing at one of the columns.

'How do you mean?'

'On its way to becoming something else.'

He nodded thoughtfully. 'Yeah. I guess. Polymorphous. Going through different stages.'

As he spoke, she couldn't get the image of the suffering, despairing slaves out of her head. The columns, fluted and massive, were stone, not coral, and they must have had quartz or something in them since they glittered in a way she found malicious. Slavery seemed such a vast and forbidding area of human experience to consider that she was almost glad when an African businessman, wearing a suit and clutching a purple briefcase to his chest, rushed between her and the awful columns.

'They don't seem kind of, so *poor* here as on the mainland,' she said, watching the man dash away.

'Tourists,' said Nick. 'There's more money coming in here now than ever. It's the mainstay of the economy since the price of cloves went down.'

'Why did it drop?'

'I'm not sure. I'll have to ask Leggatt. He's a clove farmer. I think people used to smoke clove-flavoured cigarettes in the Far East and now they don't.'

They remounted. He took her down Creek Road, past lines of fishermen carrying nets on their backs, to a place that really was a museum. Its exhibits included snakes in jars, Dr Livingstone's medicine chest, and a skeleton said to be the bones of a dodo. They looked more like those of a large hound.

They spent some time looking at carved doors on a street of Arab houses. Larger, darker and more ornate than the ones on the Indian shops, which Miranda suspected must have been modern imitations, these doors were covered with black metal roundels and spikes. In between, curled lines of calligraphy were etched into the wood like some kind of code. The carving was very elaborate. It was hard to pull one's eyes away from it, and the doors seemed to speak not only of all the labour absorbed in their making, but also of all the hours others might have spent looking at them. The geometric motifs themselves, she realised at once, expressed the logic and order of the Islamic world view: it was as if the repeating patterns and endless divisions were trying to represent God's unchanging laws.

They got back on the bike and drove around a bit more. For all Nick's efforts, Miranda still wasn't that impressed by Stone Town. There was a sweltering, squalid quality to the place, and there were mosquitoes everywhere. The town didn't conform to how she had imagined Zanzibar, which was, well – long white beach, spread of palms at the water's edge, etc. Her mood wasn't improved by a waiter in the restaurant they went to for dinner sneezing as he brought their food, nor by Nick's awkward attempts to flatter her.

After eating, they went dancing at Spices Nite-Club. The live music – twangling, Afro-style guitars – cheered her up. As they whirled around together, the awkwardness lessened. She realised, as the music hummed about her ears, that she hadn't danced since coming to Africa. At one point, when the music was appropriate, he held her hips. It excited her, she wanted to feel his hard chest's weight on her – and it made her wonder, too, whether he just hoped for sex, or thought more of her.

They sat down and talked a little. In spite of the compliments, which kept coming, it was still quite hard to sense whether he was hopeful of anything serious developing. It was strange how men could be so closed off like that, voice and eyes ever alert to the betrayal of emotion. It was as if they were addicted to secrecy. Of course, women concealed their feelings too – it was a necessary part of life – but men seemed to do it as a matter of course, as if to open up at all made them entirely vulnerable.

By the time they arrived at the Macpherson – he'd booked a room for her there – the lights had gone out. They had to make their way to her chalet, guided only by Nick's cigarette lighter and the moon and stars coming down into the courtyard between the chalets, reflecting up off the pink coral gravel.

He sprung a tentative kiss on her cheek as they said goodnight on the step. Again, it was hard to read, in itself as much as in the semi-darkness. She could see his eyes well enough in the flame, and they were surely expectant.

Her wondering – that glorious uncertainty which affects all those whose hearts are stirring – took too long. His shoulder had already begun to turn as he made to go down the steps. She said goodnight a second time – he turned again, said goodnight once more himself – and then she went inside, shutting the door, perhaps a little slowly, perhaps a little slyly, behind her.

Moonlight, and a hushed sound of waves, filled the room. She went over to the French windows and stood for a moment, looking at the silvered sea: a mixture of pearl, soot and polished metal. The sky near the moon was illuminated by a skirt of clear, grey calmness; the rest was a deep, impenetrable black, utter but for the pinpoints of stars, which shone much more brightly than at home.

She thought of her father, her mind settling on the blue felt policeman's cap he kept as a memento after leaving the job and which she still had. She had put the cap into storage for safe keeping when she came to Africa. Its main feature was the badge: 'BOSTON POLICE', silver letters on a blue background. There was a tiny emblem of Paul Revere on his horse between the words, commemorating his ride to warn the revolutionaries that the British were coming. Beneath 'POLICE' was the civic crest, a depiction of the city skyline from the harbour with three boats. Under that were the words *Bostonia Condita* AD *1630*.

Her mother, who died when she was just three years old, might just as well have come from such a distant period of history. Everything about her was hazy. Whatever memory of a happy family Miranda retained came through her father. She remembered the smell of the cap and the cap remembered his smell: fried bacon, oil and exhaust, soap, tobacco, beer.

He was a good man. Apart from when he'd drunk too much, which was only very occasionally, he was sweet and kind, a slight frown sufficing for his anger. Recalling talking about him with Nick back on the beach in Dar, she wondered if that was what had drawn them together. He had, in a way, something similar.

She began to undress, feeling strange, divorced from herself, excited still but a little solemn also, happy, yet oddly forlorn. Nevertheless, it was nice to go to sleep with the noise of the ocean in her ears.

In the morning, she met da Souza at breakfast, after which Nick took her down to the beach, to show her his dinghy and a mangrove stream and some places where turtle eggs had been. After that she once again hitched up her skirt over the back of his motorbike.

They drove to somewhere called Jozani Forest, which was shadowy and slightly frightening. Monkeys rattled the trees; the blooms of the flowers, purple and deep blue, oozed with mysterious secretions. On one tree at the edge of the forest, four or five large birds, a little like peacocks, were perched side by side; their long, spangled tails gave the impression of a light curtain or veil where they hung down from the branch, with the sun shining through and indistinct green hills beyond.

For lunch they rode across to another little hotel on the west of the island, run by two gay Germans. It was a lovely place, at last delivering what she had hoped for. Something exalted happened to the acoustics on the beach, which ran at least ten miles either side of the hotel. The reef surf seemed to place its distant roar behind you as well as – out there, where you could see its proud-standing, always-moving line of white – in front.

'Surround sound,' said Nick, and suddenly she felt pleased that she was with him rather than with Ray.

She took off her sandals so that she could feel the sand between her toes and ran down to where an outrigger canoe was washing to and fro in the surf, tugging at its coconut-fibre mooring.

'I wouldn't want to go to sea in one of these,' she said, when Nick caught up with her.

'They're pretty stable actually. But don't worry, I'll take you out in my boat tomorrow. You can spend your last day on my island.'

'*Your* island?'

'Not really,' he laughed. 'Just somewhere I go to work. Well, to chill out really. It's called Lyly. Spelt L-Y, L-Y.'

'How far is it?'

'You worried?'

'It's not a very big boat.'

'We could go in the British guy's yacht, if he'd take us. You more comfortable with that idea?'

'A yacht? Sure.'

'We'll go and ask him tomorrow.'

They walked, mainly in silence, up the beach for a while – to where some women, squatting down, were harvesting seaweed into deep baskets. They watched for a while before turning round and heading back.

After eating lobster salad at the German place, they returned to the Macpherson, by which time it was almost evening. Kicking out the stand, Nick parked the motorbike under a tamarind. The sun was coming down through the big tree's branches, throwing leopard-skin shadows on the sand round the larger patch cast by the leaning motorbike.

Nick said, 'Do you want to go for a walk in the gardens? They've got all the species. The local plants, I mean.'

'OK,' she responded, evenly, and they walked over to the garden under the deep red sun.

Soon they were moving along the paths between the trees and shrubs and flowers. Between philippine violets and wild custard apples and, so the label said, though it was hard to read in the fading light, hop-headed barleria. She felt drowsy as she walked

186

beside him, which was probably, she reasoned idly, all the oxygen from riding on the back of the motorbike. But it could have been the smells of the plants which were making her feel so sleepy and warm – the tropical blue sage, or the cinnamon, or the star jasmine . . .

Or may it have been, as their hands brushed, that the air was simply thick with possibility, heavy with prepared likelihood that he would turn and, bolder now, kiss her beside the flower of love or the rub-rub berry?

But he didn't. He kissed her beside the false globe amaranth. All those other names that might have been germane – on the one side the hare's foot fern, the fire bush, the convolvulus, the purple grenadilla and the java plum; on the other, the flowering banana, the ashok mast tree, the snake plant and the silver quill – all those other names were beside the point. They'd lifted clear of earth, it seemed, for a brief passage were beyond the Macpherson gardens and the deep red sun suffusing them, beyond, even, their own mouths as they met.

This wasn't supposed to happen, she thought, as he kissed her. How on God's sweet earth, she sweated, had she let it? How had she been brought into the arms of a man she hardly knew, on an island on the edge of the world? She realised she could hear water in the glade someplace, the sound of a stream in an upland part of the garden, rolling down towards them over twisted roots. They kissed some more. The sun's rim dipped.

It was almost dark by the time – brows and armpits prickling in the intense heat, lips and earlobes full of bee-stung lovers' blood – they made their way back to the hotel building. She was rationalising now, thinking that it hadn't been so sudden since there'd been so much anticipation. The emails were just part of a deeper seam of inchoate, half-willed plans which had been laid down long before. It had begun weeks ago, at the embassy, the moment their eyes had met. Watching over them, back then, the security camera on the chancery wall could not have picked it up – but something had happened, a change had taken place, the needle had swung round in the compass of the heart.

17

They arrived at Leggatt's in a heavy storm. Once again, Miranda sat behind Nick on the motorbike. But this time it was unpleasant. Grit from the wet dirt road spattered her bare legs. Her clothes were soaked through. As they turned off the main road, the clove farm appeared before them, with its long barns and tin-roofed cottage. It was an eerie place in the bad weather. Once Nick switched off the engine, the sound of what, she was sure, was piano music came distinctly through the noise of the rain. The sky was almost black with cloud as they dismounted.

'Can you hear music?' she called, as they splashed towards a small porch housing a glass-paned front door.

'Strange, I never had him down as a piano player.'

Nick banged on the door. There was no reply. 'Probably can't hear us.'

'This is a bit spooky,' she said, smiling at him, tendrils of wet hair round her face.

He knocked again, then tried the handle. The door opened and they entered a hallway, droplets of water falling from them onto the wooden floor. The music was louder now, coming from behind the curtain of cowrie shells that separated the hall from the living room. They went through. The cowries made a ticking noise.

Leggatt sat with his back to them, hands fanning to and fro over the keys, nap of dirty blond hair framed by the black wood of the upright. The room, Miranda saw, was hung with rough-carved African masks and other strange items. In one corner, hanging from the ceiling like a gigantic mobile, was something made of twisted fibres and strung on a wooden frame. It was, she thought, a little like an old-fashioned box kite, but without any fabric. On the other side of the room stood a coconut-leaf screen, partially hiding the dining table.

'Do you think he can hear us?' she whispered.

'I certainly *can* hear you.'

The music stopped suddenly and the old man spun round on his revolving stool. He crossed the parquet floor. Miranda stared at the ancient, rheumy-eyed figure. He was wearing a fawn safari suit. Discoloured, wizened skin and white hairs showed through the opening of the shirt.

'Hello, Nick,' he said, smiling. 'Bach . . .' He admired Miranda. 'This is a nice surprise.'

'A friend of mine,' Nick explained. 'Miranda Powers.'

'Leggatt. Ralph,' the old man said, sternly. 'Raphael, strictly speaking.'

There was an interval of a few seconds during which no one spoke, the three of them standing in a circle as if waiting for something to happen.

Anxious to break the impasse, the reason for which was inexplicable, Miranda exclaimed, 'Wow, you've got some great stuff here!'

She pointed at the array of sticks and fibres hanging from the ceiling. 'What *is* that?'

'That, my dear,' said Leggatt proudly, 'is a soul trap.'

'You can catch fish? With that? Wouldn't they swim through the holes?'

Leggatt gave her a peculiar look, then chuckled. 'Oh no. The other kind of soul. I picked it up in the Congo. There's a tribe there, way out in the back country, which believes insects steal the souls of men. It's like this. A chap has done something bad, polluted himself in some way. He goes to consult the witch doctor, who hangs that thing in a tree and waits for hours, staring till he's boss-eyed, to see whether an insect flies through it. The idea is that this business will trap the soul as the insect flies through. I had myself

190

done. Then bought the contraption off the *féticheur* once he had given me a clean bill of spiritual health. So, there you have it . . . now what can an ageing gentleman like me do for you two?'

Nick smiled gauchely. He seemed, to Miranda, to be a little nervous of Leggatt. 'I was wondering . . . if there was any chance you might take us out in the *Winston*. I thought – I mean if you don't mind – we might go out to Lyly, maybe have a picnic? I want to teach Miranda how to dive.'

'In this weather? You must be joking.'

The old man walked back across the room and, sitting at the piano stool, began to play again. It was something in a very different style, almost vaudeville. Nick looked at Miranda and grinned. The two of them went over and stood behind him. The skin wrinkled over his knuckles as his fingers slid across the keys.

Nick raised his voice above the gliding music. 'I meant tomorrow.'

'Right-ho!' shouted the Englishman. 'Eleven.'

Understanding that they were dismissed, Nick and Miranda left the music-filled room, lifting aside the cowrie curtain. They stood in the hall, looking at the glass-paned door, the outside of which was running with water where the wind pounded rain into the porch. Through the storm-darkened air, they could make out the shape of the bike. On top of it all, overlaid on the streaming black light of the pane and the vague, slightly menacing shape of the Norton, they could see their own reflections too. They stood as if frozen, peering gloomily into the glass, anticipating a second soaking.

'I hope it isn't like this tomorrow.'

Miranda shook her head. 'It won't be. Rain before seven, fine before eleven.'

'That's seven in the morning,' Nick said, 'not seven in the evening.'

'Oh,' Miranda replied, feeling foolish, realising she'd misunderstood the proverb as long as she'd known it.

18

She sat in the gentle surf, pulling on a fin. In front of her lay the *Winston Churchill*, at anchor just off Lyly, beyond the reef. Nearer, half up on the beach, was the dinghy in which they had landed. It was surrounded by the lagoon's horseshoe beach, and was rocking slightly in a pool of blue-green water. The approach had looked like a kind of mirage – especially the white-tipped pinnacle of the lighthouse rising out of the dense green forest. She had almost finished a roll of camera film before setting foot on the island.

Nick had laid out the equipment on deck during the voyage: tank, regulator, fins, mask, something that looked like a life-vest. He had then explained the purpose of each individual item to her. Now was the moment to put the theory into practice. Above her, his thigh close to her face, he was fitting a snorkel to the side strap of her mask. Further away, she could see Leggatt sitting in a canvas chair on the deck of the *Churchill*. He was smoking his pipe and watching them. Behind him, as if standing to attention, was the young Zanzibari, Sayeed. He was rather shy and silent, but Miranda had drawn him out of himself on the way, answering his halting questions about America. And she had learned about his village, which was called Potoa.

'Up you get,' commanded Nick.

Like an explorer offering his domain, he cast a hand over the water, the surface of which was ruffling gently in the breeze. It looked idyllic, she thought, but also slightly sinister, as if some great beast were stirring beneath, waiting for its moment to rise.

She stood, unsteady in the surf, as he tightened the straps.

Having finished fitting the life-vest thing, which he called a buoyancy jacket and was like a kind of bladder, he began attaching the breathing apparatus.

'I feel like a turtle!' she exclaimed, as he lifted the heavy tank onto her back. 'Why do I need the snorkel if I've got this?'

She waved the air tube.

'Just safety really. Some people don't bother, and keep their regulator in their mouth right until they break the surface. But if you're in trouble, then the snorkel is near when you need it. OK, you ready?'

She nodded, and was about to say something when he handed her the regulator to place in her mouth. It was slightly too big, pressing against her teeth. She drew in a breath. The air tasted metallic. She felt a rising panic and fancied she could feel her heart beating faster. But there also came, in that moment, a sense of wonder as the air roared in her ears. They waded a little further out and she put her face below the surface.

Blinking behind the glass screen, her eyes adjusted to the underwater light. The sand was yellow-grey. Nick joined her in the water, which was pleasantly warm. They swam out a little, to where the ocean bed began to fall away. She was beginning to get out of her depth – felt herself rolling slightly in the current. He showed her how to release air from the convoluted hose of her buoyancy jacket, and suddenly she was sinking. The surface of the water closed over her head. It made her feel uneasy. Nick, as if perceiving this, reached out and took her hand. He motioned her to add more air to the jacket, until she achieved neutral buoyancy.

At first there wasn't much to see: just the shelving expanse of sand, dotted with black rocks. Still hand in hand, they finned out further at a steady pace, to where the reef began. The cylinder shifted a little on her back, and it was difficult to keep upright. Gradually, however, she began to enjoy it, though it was comforting to have Nick beside her.

Her eyes were now fully adjusted. Up ahead, she could see the crevices of the reef where brightly hued fish were darting in and out. Elsewhere there were clumps of kelp and other strangely fronded weeds. In one place, an area of clear sand, some twenty or thirty sponges were attached to the ocean floor, swaying slowly from side to side. More confident now, and enjoying the power her fins gave her, she kicked vigorously then felt a squeeze from Nick's hand. She couldn't tell if it was meant to be restraining or encouraging.

On one side the reef dropped sharply away into sheer blue water. Close up to the wall, which was full of natural archways, she was amazed to see how much life there could be in one place. It was as if the fish were swimming up to be counted. Nick told her the names later, pointing them out on his T-shirt: catfish, sunfish, clownfish, cuttlefish with their flat internal shells – as if they were riding their own surfboards. The most astonishing thing, endearingly small, was a sea horse. She stared at the living little curl: an evanescent 'S' drifting slowly through the water, a weirdly vertical shape in that predominantly horizontal world.

Further below, in miniature caves or crawling across the ocean floor, they found lobsters and crabs. Miranda could see that the crustaceans' cryptic tangle of antenna, tendril, and large limbs fascinated Nick. To her they spoke of millennia gone by, of the ancient secrets of living things. She hovered in the water, maintaining buoyancy with her breathing as Nick had shown her.

She didn't drift, didn't change position. But around her, the water changed. Suddenly she was in a swarm of krill, tiny and genital pink. And then they were gone, and she could see the reef again. The depth made the rubber flanges of her mask squeeze her temples.

She saw a shadow pass over the seabed and, turning on her side, looked up. It was the dinghy of the *Churchill*. Leggatt must have sent Sayeed to fetch it, to bring him to shore. Or maybe he was fishing. He'd said he was going to. Miranda, rocking in the amniotic sac of the ocean, started worrying about the hooks.

She realised that Nick was beckoning her. She swam on a little, catching up with him. Below her she could see a splendid kind of sea flower. An anemone or something . . . It was difficult to say what was vegetable and what was animal.

But not always: later in the dive Nick pointed out a pair of turtles swimming. It was one of the most wonderful sights she'd ever seen, even though they were only small green ones, not the leatherbacks he had mentioned. Their very ungainliness, the way they held their heads up like myopic old people, their crazy-paving shell, the odd movement of their flippers – these things were also the source of their grace. When they came to the surface, Nick told her even these small green turtles could live for up to 150 years.

They emerged from the water to find Leggatt, who had caught a wrasse while they were down below, spreading slices of bread with margarine from a tin of Stork. They sat with him in the shade of some palm trees eating fish-steak sandwiches cooked on an open fire, and drinking bottled beer. Stretched out in the sun, Miranda felt relaxed and happy: the embassy, with all its weight of mighty administrative power, felt an age away.

She heard Leggatt's low voice. 'Dolphin.'

Her eye followed his pointing finger. Nick, who had been stoking the fire with a piece of wood, looked up too. About twenty feet out could be seen a dorsal fin topping a thickset, grey-blue shape, part of which was visible in the clear water. It was about seven foot in length and moving through the water at speed.

'Lone male,' said Leggatt.

'Come on,' said Nick excitedly, and got to his feet.

The two of them rushed in like children, and started swimming out towards the leaping, diving shape. Miranda was expecting all the while that it would flee on the approach of

195

humans. It didn't. It came to greet them, swerving from side to side and then swimming under them. She reached out to touch it, imagining the feel of its skin on her fingertips – but then, with a flick of its tail, it was gone.

It returned minutes later, its snout breaking the surface just in front of her, emitting a crescendo of sharp clicks. She could see its rows of sharp teeth and the tip of a black tongue. Again she wanted to reach out, and again it vanished.

The dolphin stayed in the warm water near them for a good hour, circling or diving under the keel of the *Churchill* and then leaping wildly into the air – or retreating to fossick about at the edge of a reed bank nearer the shore.

'I think he's sulking,' said Miranda, when it disappeared among the reeds.

'Teasing you,' Nick said, swimming up close behind her.

They trod water side by side. The dolphin blew and dived. Seconds later they saw it leap, far out now.

'There he goes,' Nick said.

'I don't know whether I like it or the sea horse best,' she said, looking thoughtful.

'Did you know that the male sea horse puffs out its chest to attract a mate?' he enquired, assuming an air of innocence.

Miranda inclined her head, with its thick, dark hair, to one side, then pushed him playfully and began swimming to the shore as fast as she could. He followed a little later, cutting through the water in swift freestyle till he caught up with her.

They swam together round an outcrop of rock, till they came to a place out of view of Leggatt and Sayeed, who were still sitting by the fire.

Nick caught her heel as the beach shelved up, and the two of them began tumbling about in the shallows, wrestling and howling with laughter. She remembered the beach on the mainland, how he'd scooped her out of the rough water. She liked the memory, and she liked his touch now. Impulsively, she held his face and kissed him on the lips, then took his hand and dragged him out of the foam up on to the beach, where they lay down.

Later, they walked back round to the fire. Leggatt had boiled a kettle and was making tea.

'You missed the fish eagle,' he said, gruffly. 'Sayeed threw a bit of fish up and she swooped down for it. Lovely sight.'

After tea, Nick and Miranda walked round the island together. He showed her the ruined cottage, with its record player and photograph of the British queen.

'We could dance,' he said, picking up one of the 78s and waving it at her.

'You kidding?'

They came out and went over to the little mosque, which she said was neat. Then he led her up to the top of the lighthouse and explained how everything worked. Through its square, glassless window, they looked out over the island, to where the forest faltered down to a mess of rocks.

'See those?' said Nick, pointing to the rocks. 'Just about near there, a little way out, there's an underwater cave. I swam into it. You can breathe in there, and there's writing on the wall.'

They started climbing down the steps. 'What kind of writing?'

'I don't know. Arabic maybe. I must ask Leggatt.'

She liked being near him. It felt natural, strolling back along the beach, for him to hold her hand in his.

He pointed up ahead. 'There's a turtle nest over there somewhere. I saw the females lay their eggs when I was last here. In the moonlight.'

'I can't see anything.'

'You're not meant to.'

'What the hell –?'

He broke into a run. In front of her, where he had indicated, she caught sight of a winding green shape and froze. The snake was using its body to flick up sand. It was a very peculiar movement, a kind of drilling action, as if it were a corkscrew or mechanical worm. The sand came up in a wide, fine fan. Nick was approaching the place, but when he was about three foot away, he changed direction. He began jogging away to the right, towards a scrubby dune bank at the edge of the beach. The snake was still twisting in the sand. She saw Nick break a branch off a weatherbeaten bush that looked like a candelabrum.

Coming back down onto the beach, he returned to the nest, forked branch in hand. The snake was still twisting away. It seemed relentless. Then it suddenly stopped: the white domes of the eggs, four or five of them, were partially visible. The snake changed its position, curling round so that its head faced the eggs. Then it became aware of Nick, who was bearing down on it, holding out the branch. He seemed to stumble as he came down the bank. Miranda turned pale.

The hinged mouth was opening, ready to bite and squirt out venom. But already he was on it, pinning it down with the V of the broken branch before it could do anything, pressing the fork hard into the sand. She cried out again, but Nick, unfazed, was bending down. The snake's tail slapped against his calf. Then, watchful, he caught it tightly between finger and thumb and lifted it up. He held it away from him gingerly, at arm's length, its tail thrashing. She watched him begin walking back up towards the treeline, and she felt both impressed and angry at his foolhardiness.

Then she smelt pipe smoke, and heard a voice.

'I think he'll find that's a mamba.'

It was Leggatt.

'Not terribly good eating, I'm afraid,' he added, languidly. 'But very poisonous. Perhaps the most venomous on these islands.'

The two figures stood side by side in the open ground of the beach, Leggatt in a stained canvas jacket and a peaked sailor's cap of indeterminate authority, Miranda in trainers, shorts and a cotton blouse. Nick was up beyond them, on the crest of the dune. With the underarm action of a bowler, he tossed the writhing snake into the scrub.

'I rather wish he had despatched it more permanently,' observed Leggatt. 'Those things will hunt a man down. I'd be surprised if it doesn't make an attempt to follow him.'

He removed his pipe from his mouth and shouted up towards the dunes. 'Don't hang about, old boy!'

She lifted a hand to shield her brow. Nick was silhouetted against the skyline. He seemed to have heard Leggatt's warning, but didn't quicken his pace.

Leggatt walked over to the eggs and began scuffing sand back on top of them with his shoe.

'Anyway,' he said, 'it will only be back at nightfall to dig these up. We'll fight them on the beaches. Ha!'

Miranda was irritated by the old man's manner. Having felt it was stupid at the time, she now experienced a glow of admiration, pride even, at what Nick had done. All the same, when he joined them, she chided him.

'That was foolish. Mr Leggatt says they are very dangerous.'

'Not as dangerous to us as they are to turtles,' said Nick, grinning.

'I think that's the most wrong-headed thing I ever heard,' said Leggatt.

He tapped out his pipe on a rock, making a shower of angry red sparks.

'Anyway, what you did was pointless. I was just saying, to the young lady here, that that creature will be back during the night. Or one of its chums. You should have killed it.'

Nick looked dismayed. 'Is there nothing we can do?'

'Part of me feels one should just let nature take its course. But if you insist, we've got two choices. Either we move the eggs, which raises the question of where we put them, not to mention the likelihood of disturbing their hatch. Or we build a fence around them, which means we have to guess when they are going to hatch and come and dismantle it before they do.'

After some discussion, they settled on the fence option, and started gathering up driftwood. Once they had enough, they drew a circle round the nest, of about a metre in diameter, and began driving in the crooked stakes. Nick added some rocks, and in the end they made a pretty nice little palisade.

Or so Miranda thought in any case. Leggatt remained pessimistic about the chances of the baby turtles.

'I still don't think those little fellows are going to see the light of day,' he said, lugubriously.

He took off his cap and wiped the sweat from his forehead with the back of his wrist. 'It's hard enough for them anyway, with gulls and rats, and fish in the water . . . Well, I suppose we should be wending our way.'

'Before we do,' said Nick, as they walked back towards the fire, 'there's something I wanted to ask you.'

'Yes?'

'I found a cave.'

Leggatt gave him a penetrating look. 'So, you found, that did you?'

'I was diving round the edge of the island and went into it. There seemed to be an opening to the surface but I haven't been able to find it. There was writing inside, too. I think it might have been Arabic.'

'Thought it was my secret. Come on then, I suppose I can show you. We'll need a panga though.'

He went over to the dinghy and, after fetching the machete, began cutting a path through the deep bush. Nick and Miranda followed him, stepping over broken ferns and branches. After about ten minutes they came to an outcrop of rock.

'This is the opening,' said Leggatt. 'Well, one of them anyway. There's a couple of holes elsewhere that plunge straight down into the system, but this is the only one you can actually get through without breaking a leg. I don't think we should go in without proper lights.'

'The system?' queried Nick. 'You mean there's more than one cave?'

'Certainly. There's a whole network down there.'

He cleared away undergrowth to reveal the ragged entrance. 'Pretty nasty story actually. One of the sultans used to keep escaped slaves on this island. They threw them down the hole as a punishment if they tried to escape again.'

'But they couldn't have done the writing, surely?'

'I don't know. Maybe. Some of the slaves were pretty accomplished. Clerks and so on. They weren't all hewers of wood and drawers of water. I suppose it could have been a troublesome courtier who did it. Or it could be some kind of invocation. Anyway, we should be getting back.'

Returning to the beach in silence, they pulled the dinghy into the sea and got inside. Miranda felt subdued by the story of the caves. Still, it had been an exciting day. She watched Nick row, and wondered if she would miss him on her return to the mainland. She had to catch a flight very early in the morning if she was to get back to work on time.

Back on the yacht, Sayeed, who must have swum out, was scrubbing the deck. Miranda smiled at him brightly as she climbed up. But the whole idea of having an African servant made her feel uncomfortable.

Once the yacht got under way, she shared a bottle of beer with Nick at the front of the boat. Leggatt had taken up his position back in the wheelhouse. The sun was beginning to set. In the distance, some way to starboard but at an angle, they could just make out the white fuzz of another craft. It was moving swiftly.

'Probably customs,' said Nick.

'Hey,' he added, reaching into the pocket of his shorts. 'I picked up this for you on the dune.'

He handed her an object, about the size of a take-out coffee lid and almost as weightless. It was the empty shell of a baby turtle.

'A keepsake,' Nick said.

She held it up to the dying sun. It was exquisite, amber light gathering in the delicate, serrated layers.

'Do you think . . .?' She didn't need to tell him that she was thinking of the snake.

'Not necessarily. Birds take them too.'

She pulled a face. The thought of a bird's beak pecking the flesh of such a tiny creature was just as horrible to contemplate.

'It is a beauty, isn't it?' said Nick, a little too encouragingly. 'Keep it.'

She put the shell in her bag. His enthusiasm was slightly off-putting. But he was, she thought, looking kind of handsome in the evening sunlight, and she responded when he leaned over and kissed her.

At that moment, with a slight jolt, they suddenly changed direction. Miranda and Nick heard Leggatt swear. Looking up, they saw that the boat they had spotted earlier was coming towards them. Drilling powerfully through the water, it was a sleek white motor cruiser with a covered cabin.

They heard Leggatt again. 'What the hell are these buggers playing at?'

About twenty metres away from them, the cruiser suddenly veered sharply and cut its throttle. The wake rocked the *Winston Churchill*. Leggatt clattered out of the wheelhouse and started waving his arms about, cursing. There was no response from the cruiser, whose engine spluttered in the water. Through the glass of its cabin, Miranda could see three faces – all dark-skinned, but only one who could be said to be African – observing her in their turn. She picked up her camera and used the zoom to get a closer look. One of the men, she noticed, had a pencil moustache and a long thin face; another was much bigger and beefier than his companions; the third was the African one, who was also younger. Almost unconsciously, she put her finger on the shutter. Focusing on the man with the moustache, she was just about to take a picture when he pulled a curtain across the window of the cabin. Then, its engine gunning up loud and quick, the cruiser moved off again.

'What was all that about?' Nick asked Leggatt, who was watching the cruiser through binoculars.

'I haven't a clue, but I'm sure as dammit going to come out tomorrow and see what they're up to, since they seem to be heading for Lyly.'

The journey back, in a low swell, was otherwise uneventful. It was dark by the time they arrived at Leggatt's farm, and Miranda wondered how they would be able to dock. But even with no visible shore lights, the old man was able to steer them alongside the jetty. Sayeed jumped out with a flashlight. After mooring, he pulled down the rope ladder on the side of the yacht. Nick and Miranda climbed down carefully while the young Zanzibari played the beam over their feet. Then Leggatt lit a storm lamp and Sayeed began unloading the gear while Leggatt went into his house to start the generator.

Miranda and Nick stood on the jetty in the warm night air, which was filled with the smell of cloves from the barns.

'I've really enjoyed myself these past few days,' she said – feeling, all the same, oddly hollow.

No reply came, only Nick let his hand drop down between them both to find hers. They heard the thump of the generator.

The house lights went up, and then a line of bulbs, fixed to posts along the jetty. Further up, nearer to the house, they saw the black outline of a table, with a single chair next to it.

'That's a lonely sight,' said Nick, and they began walking towards it. He squeezed her hand.

His observation, and the action that went with it, seemed designed to ask for more of a response than Miranda felt appropriate. She remembered when he first started emailing her the tone of his messages had also been somewhat like that – lacking a little in social graces. But then, she thought, emails did change the rules. There was something about them which provoked a condition of intimacy before it was valid. They beckoned one on, inviting risk, drawing back the veil of personality further with every exchange . . .

Her thoughts were interrupted by the noisy arrival of Leggatt, carrying a bottle and shot glasses on a tin tray. He was shouting for Sayeed to fetch two more chairs from the veranda.

'Thought we'd have a little drink out here. I usually do of an evening. Next time you come over,' he said to Miranda, confidingly, 'you might do me the favour of bringing a bit of this. Johnnie Walker, if you can.'

Unusually cheerful – Miranda suspected his grouchiness was partly an act – Leggatt filled and then handed her one of the little glasses.

'Because it's my firm belief that when a body wants to lay down of a night, a drop of Johnnie keeps the demons away. I can only get it on the mainland though. Talking of demons, did I tell you about the *papabawa*, Nick? That's what they call the Zanzibar vampire. It's pretty much like your common or garden Dracula-type vampire, except that it's got white skin and lives in the clove orchards. Where is he with those chairs?'

He was silent for a second, pipe clenched between his teeth as he concentrated on filling his and Nick's glasses.

'You will have heard some of the locals call us *muzungu*. Well, they also call us *papabawa*. There must be a lesson there, though what it is I couldn't say. Here you go.'

Nick took the whisky from him, and immediately put it down on the table so he could unwrap a packet of Marlboros.

'I'll leave you guys to have your smoke,' Miranda said.

'It's my first all day!' Nick exclaimed.

'It's not a problem. Just . . .'

Sipping her drink delicately, she moved away a little from the two men. Leaning her thighs on the jetty railing, she looked out over the dark expanse of the ocean. She could hear its melancholy roar and also, ear-close, the faint squeal of mosquitoes.

'What do you think they were up to, those guys in the boat?' she heard Nick say. 'It didn't look like the kind of craft your average poacher could afford.'

Sayeed was making his way over from the house with the other chairs.

'No . . .' Leggatt sucked loudly on his pipe. 'It certainly didn't. We should go out tomorrow and see what they were about. Don't drag them, Sayeed.'

'Can't do it tomorrow. I've got to take Miranda to the airport . . . Hey, you OK?'

'I'm fine,' she replied, over her shoulder. 'Just thinking. Last day of my vacation is all.'

'Time's wingèd chariot,' Leggatt intoned. 'Are you going on the Cessna or the Beechcraft?'

'I'm not sure,' she said. 'The Air Rafiki one.'

'I see.' Leggatt didn't elaborate further, but it was clear he disapproved.

Not that Miranda was really paying attention anyway. Pensively apart, she was listening to the waves lapping against the stanchions of the jetty and, further away, the wider sound of breakers on open sand or reef. Leggatt said something in Swahili to Sayeed. She felt the jetty bounce, heard the wooden boards creak as the boy ran behind her.

'Rafiki is a strange outfit,' she heard Leggatt say. 'It hooked up with a Russian firm called Air Yazikov, which a pilot friend from my mining days told me is rather questionable. Apparently been making ghost flights out of Entebbe into the Congo.'

She could smell their tobacco. It was something she'd always hated.

'Ghost flights?' she heard Nick ask.

'These aircraft are painted all-over white and do not have registrations. They operate at the same time and under the same call-sign as planes with legitimate flight plans – hence ghost.'

Miranda looked out into the darkness as she listened to them.

'What are they doing?'

Then, louder: 'You OK?'

'Just fine,' she said.

'Leave her be for heaven's sake,' said Leggatt. Then, whispered: 'If you know what's good for you.'

She heard Nick laugh quietly and conspiratorially, and that irritated her. Again the jetty bounced and swayed; once more Sayeed's feet clattered past on the wooden boards. Only this time she was conscious of a strange light threshing the night sky.

'Smuggling diamonds out of the Congo, guns in, that sort of thing. Enabling the killers.'

Sayeed was bringing the storm lamp, she realised. Waves pulled gently at the jetty. The tide was going out, and the air growing colder.

'The Russian who runs Yazikov is an ex-MiG fighter pilot. Veteran of the Afghan war who came back, saw the Berlin Wall fall and didn't like the way things were going. Hop, skip and jump and suddenly he's in Africa with a load of cargo planes stolen from the Russian Air Force.'

She wasn't really listening any more. Looking into the night, she was thinking about the day. About Nick. And about Lyly. Out in the ocean, somewhere there – she couldn't place it now – lay the island.

She heard the clink of a bottle, glasses being filled. 'So you see, the Cold War's still putting a spanner in the works, even though it ended over a decade ago. And your lot aren't angels, from what I hear.'

Miranda shivered. Her mind was feeding on Lyly and what had happened there: in particular on the idea of a snake slithering about amid all that loveliness, and on the story of the slave caves. Nick and Leggatt were still gassing the way men do. Yet for a moment it was as if her companions didn't exist at all – as if they had been carried away along with the receding sea. She looked up at the pale moon, and could almost imagine Leggatt's vampire flying across it. What was its name? Papa-something. The half-legendary aspect of this place was seductive. But the unreality of the islands and the weekend she had spent on them was also coming home to her. A cold consciousness, a tough knowledge that undid any idea of her and Nick as a potential couple. There were reasons. She had a job to do; she'd be moving out in eight months' time. She wasn't even sure if she was really attracted to him now anyway. He could be kind of charmless sometimes. Of course, he called her over exactly then.

'Come and see Ralph's watch, Miranda. It's one of those fake Rolexes!'

Sayeed was sitting cross-legged and silent in the shadows. The storm lamp was in the middle of the table. She moved across and looked at the watch in the flickering light: at the second hand going round, at the old man's hand, its bleached hairs and liver spots. She sat down, and then Nick found *her* hand under the table. That assumption of ownership clinched it. She didn't remove her hand, but she could hardly bear to be near him.

Leggatt poured more drinks; she felt like her soul was pouring away. Tomorrow, anyhow, she'd be gone. Back to herself and her responsibilities. For it was, she knew now, just a holiday romance. Not even that: just a shadow of one. *I don't believe you!* she imagined Ray saying. Then Nick let go of her hand.

19

The first sign, in the sky, of the coming change was a ragged tuft of greasy warm cloud. Brown, streaked with red and yellow tints, it had hovered above the ocean for two days, rising in temperature and gathering an ever more powerful charge of negative ions. It must have been about three o'clock in the afternoon of the third day that this stained, suspended rag – like the cloth of a cook or a mechanic – began to roll about itself. Cold air rushed into its warmth from all sides, creating a partial vacuum and a magnetic commotion of oppositely charged particles.

Birds were already flying inland – not to Zanzibar, for this presage of bad weather was as yet far away, but to Mombasa and Malindi. Long ago, they had felt a disturbance in the atmospheric equilibrium, sensing the change of monsoon that would occasion cyclones and hurricanes.

Winds began to eddy round the lone cloud, drawing others to it, swirling pouches of aqueous vapour. Elastic and compressible, each one brought a new colour to the original oily roll. Its reds and yellows multiplied in shade, black and purple were added, layer upon layer, streak upon streak – till the whole, driving across towards the mainland, presented that ugly and threatening appearance which enabled the rainmaker to bring the monsoon he in fact foresaw.

The elders of the Kenyan coast were wrong, this time, to say 'the rains are coming'. The accumulating storm, diverted by the island of Lamu, was sucked back out to sea. Gyrating, gathering in size all the while, it moved horizontally across the waves, travelling northwards, now dark red, the burnt umber of the painter's palette, now grey, with the appearance of a ball of smoke.

As it travelled northwards, along the Tanzanian coast, the cyclone increased its velocity and collected ever more violent winds about its centre. Smaller whirlings knitted to the initial motion; became larger themselves; gathered further gyrations in their turn.

So in a continuous, circling, progressive action, this remarkable mass of cloud and vapour, about forty-five miles in diameter, made its way towards Zanzibar. Of the power and nature which, according to the law of storms in western lands, is called a hurricane squall, this weather pattern is known, by the fishermen of the Swahili coast, as the *chamchela*. They would also know that the cyclone's northward movement was unusual – tropical storms tend to move southerly – and therefore all the more worrying.

At the cyclone's heart, even now as it impinged on an exposed bluff off Macpherson Cove and, forced to one side, was bounced once more out to sea, raindrops began to gather. They mixed with a fine mist of saltwater, spoondrift as mariners once called it, which was caught up from the crests of waves as the cyclone progressed. Its direction was a small atoll beyond Macpherson, an islet where turtles have been known to lay their eggs.

Below the *chamchela*, as it drove along, low over the water, the sea began to swell, rising heavily, sending eddies of increasing violence towards Lyly's shore – where, as if to taste the salt that was filling the air, a bulky figure emerged from the ruined cottage.

Some way off, Nick Karolides floated in the tugging water, tensing himself for every wave. He had been there for about three quarters of an hour, spying on the men. For his island was now peopled. There were seven: the three men from the motor cruiser – those whose faces he recognised, those who were armed – and four others who had come in two small dhows.

The wooden fishing boats were pulling hard at their anchors in the Lyly lagoon. As with the poachers' boat, they had been narrow enough to get through the gap in the reef. These were less rough in construction than the other dhow, but their unplaned, grey timbers and tattered sails still made them look like the marine equivalent of shanty-town dwellings. The cruiser itself was beached, its dark green pennant fluttering in the rising wind. He watched the figure go back inside the cottage.

From his vantage point, down in some reeds near the rocky outcrop that led out to the entrance of the underwater cave, Nick could see most of the beach. It was uncomfortable, lying in that muddy spot with his mask just above the surface. His legs were numb and he was worried that the silty water would clog his breathing apparatus – but otherwise it was a good place from which to watch.

There were a large number of crates on the beach in front of the cottage. The men were packing canisters, about the size of catering tins, tins of beans or juice, into the crates.

Not all the Arabs were doing this. The figure emerged again from the house. Nick could see the outline of a sub-machine gun hanging from a strap round his neck. The man was staring out to sea. To Nick it seemed as if he were staring directly at him. This man, bulky and unshaven, appeared utterly alert. It was almost as if he knew he was being watched.

Nick suddenly realised that the temperature had dropped, and the sky had darkened considerably. The lagoon, too, had changed colour, its blue trailing into black. A sudden, heavy wave lifted up the dhows.

The clouds were a sombre tangle, spinning rapidly through the lowering sky. He knew the signs now, he had been in the tropical belt long enough. A storm was coming in. He'd better get back to the yacht. Slowly, silently, he eased himself out of the reeds. There were crests of foam on the waves. A strong wind was

211

blowing, and the current was running hard. It began to rain just as he dived, the big grey drops plummeting into the water like lead shot.

Leggatt had anchored some way off on the other side of the island, so they couldn't be spotted, but Nick had plenty of air in his tanks. He swam deep to avoid the swell and detection – swam over sea fans, groupers and blennies, a carousel of trevally and a lone turtle flipping its way to calmer reaches – swam over these, but was thinking all the while about the metal canisters and the men with guns. He was panicking a little, if truth be told.

He was also thinking about Miranda. She had been back on the mainland for two days before he and Leggatt had managed to return to Lyly. There had been one email in the interim, thanking him for 'a lovely weekend', but it was rather formal and cold, he thought, as if signalling that nothing would come of what had happened. He felt disappointed, let down, having been under the impression that something deep and passionate might have been in the works.

The keel of the *Winston Churchill* was dark in the water. He swam round to the other side, to the rope ladder. Breaking the surface, he realised that the wind was much stronger now. He banged on the hull three times with the heel of his knife, to alert Leggatt. Climbing out of the water, he became conscious of the weight of his tank. Sounding on the metal, rain was falling heavily now. The boat was rocking from side to side in the current.

His blond mane flying in the rising wind, the old man was at the top, gripping the gunwale with one brown hand and holding out another to Nick.

'You better come below!' Leggatt shouted, as Nick released his harness and lowered his tank to the deck.

The rain was lancing into Leggatt's face. 'I don't much like the look of this. Barometer's dropped like a stone. I've had to reduce canvas twice already.'

Inside the cabin, rubbing himself with a coarse towel, Nick began telling the Englishman what he'd seen.

'They had guns. They were packing crates –'

But the old man, he realised, wasn't really listening.

'Tell me later. I'm going up. I think it's a cyclone.'

Once he was dressed, Nick joined Leggatt in the wheelhouse. The storm was gathering rapidly, wind battering against the wheelhouse door. Large grey waves cruised the surface as if they were something other than water – something of another order entirely. Rain hurled down.

Leggatt gripped the wheel. 'We're going to have to sit it out. We can't heave anchor now, not in this.'

There was a clap of thunder, like God stamping his foot. Another wave unfurled itself against the deck. Its crest swept over the timbers. Straining on its chain, the *Winston Churchill* creaked fearfully as it absorbed the blow. The two men tried to keep their balance in the shifting wheelhouse. There was a brief moment of stillness – except for the lamp, which swung from side to side. Nick looked at Leggatt. Grim-faced, he was struggling with the wheel, the lamp casting its shaken light on his worn face. Another wave came, and the boat shuddered. It was terrifying how quickly the storm had risen.

'Is there anything I can do?' asked Nick, looking out at the thick clouds of broken water that rushed towards them.

Leggatt grunted, chewing anxiously on the end of his pipe. There was another peal of thunder, long and syncopated this time, petering out like a drum roll. The two of them stared out of the wheelhouse window. A jagged dart of lightning spurted across the sky. Lyly's palm trees and lighthouse were invisible now. Fog had descended on the island, and a torrent of slanting rain. A blow hit the yacht. The noise of the storm itself was suddenly interrupted by a tearing sound, quite different from the groans of the timbers.

'Oh Christ!' shouted Leggatt, reaching for his cap where it hung on a hook and clapping it on his head. 'That's something down. You take the wheel. I'll tie it when I get back. I'm going to have to take in more sail. We're still quite close-rigged, and if I don't take it all in we'll drag.'

Nick gripped the varnished wood of the wheel. In spite of the anchor, it was still fighting the current. The *Churchill* was tilting. He didn't know how it should feel, but this felt wrong, like a dancer out of kilter. He heard Leggatt sliding about on the deck behind him. He stared out of the rain-lashed glass. Through the window of the tiny cubicle, over a teak board spread with stained charts, binoculars, a sextant and other instruments, he could see waves bounding towards him. He found himself thinking suddenly about the Arabs on the island – how were they coping with this? – when another crashing sound came. Then a faint cry.

Hurriedly tying the wheel with a length of rope, Nick ran outside into driven water, to find Leggatt lying on his side next to a bollard. A fallen spar lay nearby, together with a tangle of sail and rope. There was blood in his blond hair. Either he had hit the bollard or the spar had hit him. Nick rushed over and knelt beside him, but the old man was already sitting up.

'Get back down. I'm all right. Get back down. Carried away the jib.'

Nick ignored him. Quickly taking off his shirt, he pressed it to the wound on Leggatt's head. The yacht began to heel to starboard.

'The wheel.'

The old man was silent then, his head lolling forward onto his chest. For a few seconds, the storm seemed to lull again. There was a breath of cold air, and then Leggatt's numbed eyes were opening, widening, looking over Nick's shoulder.

The old man lifted his hand. Nick looked himself. An enormous sea was racing towards them. It was as if a mountain were bearing down on them, only it was *alive* – animal, foam-flecked, intense. There was something mesmerising about it . . . but Nick knew he had to get Leggatt inside. Gathering his arms and legs, he dragged him over the slippery deck towards the wheelhouse.

As he did so, however, the Englishman seemed to come to his senses.

The approaching wave towered above them, a rising world of water.

'Rope,' gasped Leggatt. 'Get us in the guide rope.'

The two of them slid over to the safety rope that ran along the gunwale. Leggatt, whose face was streaming with blood, pulled the rope over his chest, and Nick followed his example. Above them, the wave curled, then tore down from its crest. They were flung against the rope as the water struck. Nick felt the *send* of the wave bodily, as its momentum moved everything on board. They scudded on, following the big wave like a toy boat. And then, as they swept along, there was a screech of timber, followed by the sound of inrushing water.

Something had stove in. Slowly but certainly, the *Winston Churchill* started to tip over.

'Wait!' shouted Leggatt, as Nick tried to scramble clear. 'Wait till she's gone.'

If it hadn't been so dangerous, and Leggatt not injured, it might have been comic – something out of Chaplin or Harold Lloyd, the way the two of them, becoming ever more pendulous, hung from the guide rope at the top of the capsizing sloop.

As the mast hit the water, Leggatt shouted in Nick's ear. 'We have to get to the dinghy . . . if it isn't torn off!'

Nick looked towards the bow. The little boat was still there – tugging at its leash, storm-tossed and filled with rainwater – but still there. Like a pair of monkeys, dangling crazily in mid-air, feet scrabbling against the streaming deck, they inched along the rope. The *Winston Churchill* was done for. Nick knew this; he felt shocked by the turn of events: the awareness that, less than an hour ago, the yacht had been floating peacefully. In a few minutes, it would sink like a block of concrete. And – if they didn't reach it in time – take the dinghy down with it.

They made it with seconds to spare. Nick hauled the smaller boat alongside and dropped down into it, twisting his ankle painfully. Leggatt followed, falling in a heap on top of him.

'Cut the rope!' Leggatt shouted hoarsely, fumbling in his pocket and handing over his penknife.

Nick – God knows what had happened to his own knife – did as he said. Suddenly they were free. But not out of danger. Such a small boat was hardly up to the exigencies of a tropical storm. Yet there was no time to waste in consideration of their chances. Leggatt had already begun undoing the buckles that held the oars. Once they were unshipped and installed in the rowlocks, Nick began to heave the dinghy away from the crippled sloop. It was exhausting work in such heavy water, and they had not gone twenty feet before the last of the *Churchill* settled lower into the sea. There was a brief pause. Then, with a drawn-out creak, it disappeared beneath the waves.

Nick expected Leggatt to say something, but he was silent. Perhaps he was faint from the blood he had lost. He must, anyway, the younger man reflected, be devastated to see his pride and joy go down like that. Like losing a child. But he seemed oddly unmoved.

The storm, at least, was showing signs of abating. Although the waves were still very large, and there remained a danger of them being swamped in the dinghy, the rain had ceased. The sky had begun to clear. If he twisted round, Nick could just make out the pinnacle of Lyly's lighthouse. At least they had a landmark. That was something. In the circumstances, that really was something.

Still shaken by how quickly it had all happened, Nick rowed on a little further. The dinghy slid up the waves – and then pitched down again. It seemed pointless, they were making so little progress. The boat might as well have been a beetle in a bathtub. Leggatt still hadn't said anything.

Nick himself spoke. 'I'm sorry, Ralph.'

Wild and bloody, Leggatt looked up and laughed out loud.

'I'm less worried about the boat than those fellows with guns.' Then he laughed again, manically.

Had the knock on the head made him delirious? Unnerved by the mirthless laughter, Nick replied slowly. 'Do you think we should head for the mainland instead?'

The Englishman grunted, and looked down into the bottom of the rowing boat, where dirty water was slopping to and fro. Then, as if the sight of it had brought home to him their true plight, he suddenly returned to his customary solidity.

'In an eight-foot dinghy? We'd never make it. I think we should carry on for Lyly, lie off it out of sight till nightfall, then steal one of their dhows under cover of darkness. Or the cruiser?'

It sounded a far-fetched plan, but without saying anything, Nick began rowing again, arching his back against the pressure exerted on the wooden blades. The sea had fallen silent now. The only sound was the rattle of the oars and the quiet lap of water against the bow. The sky was like the inside of a red shell. Behind him, he knew, loomed the shape of the island. But in his imagination its familiar features were obscured by the silhouettes of men. Their figures moved across the blooded air. Their postures were determined. Also, as Leggatt said, they were armed.

20

Khaled stood barefoot on the white, wrack-strewn shore, stood on the gleaming, purring sand looking out to sea. Even though the waves came with some regularity, the foam broke into patterns that were slightly different each time. This seemed a very holy thing to him, as if each wave were craving admission to that perfection comprehended by Allah alone.

Legs apart, feet deeply planted, it was strange to think that just two hours ago the sea had been black and raging. They were lucky that the dhows, protected by the lagoon, had not been overly damaged. The crew were fixing the sails now. The only remaining signs of the storm were the seaweed on the shore and the white tufts of foam that still rode the tops of the waves.

He was wearing his favourite T-shirt, which had a picture of a monkey in a frame and the English words 'Talking Heads'. He had picked it up on a second-hand market stall in Dar, years ago. He didn't know what the words referred to, but he liked the picture.

He remembered coming here as a boy, with his father or his friends, Ali and Juba. It was near to here that he had seen the great turtle that night. But that was long before, like a great many things. That was other water, and he knew if he thought of it he would surely drown. The Koran spoke of Allah letting free two bodies of flowing water, one sweet and palatable, the other salty and bitter. *And He has made between them a barrier and a forbidding partition.*

His father had told him that various people had lived on this little island in times gone by. In history. In succession. Together.

Apart. Swahili and Arab and Portuguese and British. All *pekete-vu*, he had said. All mixed up. Sometimes all *shambuliana*, he had said. All bombarding each other.

After the revolution his father had taken possession of Lyly on behalf of the state. Except the state didn't know and it effectively became his own place. In time, during the early nineties, he quietly sold it to the agent of a rich Arab who had started bringing alms to Jambangona, their village on Pemba. His father had put the money, which was surprisingly little – although sufficient considering he was poor and the island had not belonged to him in the first place – into a motorised fishing boat. Khaled remembered the day it had emerged from Turtle Mo's dockyard, gleaming and new, and he and his father had journeyed in it to Jambangona.

The agent who had come initially was, he would later realise, none other than Zayn. Over the next few years messages would arrive for Khaled's father from the rich Arab via the same route, and extra money. Eventually another fishing boat was bought. Then disaster struck.

It chilled him to remember the terrible mat, the scene coming back like a hollow shriek: the faces smeared crimson, the strange shape of the cuts, the dismal feeling – when he came round, surrounded by the horror – that all the love he had ever known had drained away with their blood.

He spent a hellish year trying to persuade the police to investigate, to no avail. He sold the two boats and used the money to live, spending freely, taking trips to Dar and Nairobi with Ali. They visited prostitutes in the Kenyan capital. They drank alcohol. They piled up sins to the horizon of heaven.

Then Zayn came, and all was changed. He began another life, one that took him from Zanzibar to Sudan all the way to Afghanistan – and, now, back here again. All in the name of jihad, a holy programme, a sacred work. Zayn, when he had shown him all those videotapes of what the US was doing to their Muslim brothers in Iraq – bombing children, he said, poisoning the water supply, he said – told him one day that he, Khaled, would get his revenge. *You will join us on a jihad job.*

Now he was here, on that jihad job; although in fact, he had done very little. Apart from organising the rental of a Nissan truck in Dar – for which he had used the satellite phone – he had, if truth be told, done almost nothing. The grinding of the TNT, with a portable generator and a household food mixer set up on the cottage table – all that had been done by Yousef and Zayn. Looking out to sea and listening to the surf, he remembered the whining noise of the machine over the past day and a half, and the smell of chemicals in the air. Khaled was glad Zayn had put him on guard duty. It seemed like a dirty business. Once they had finished, Zayn, his shirt covered in granules of explosive, had come over and given him a great bear hug, lifting him off the ground, saying, 'How lazy you have been while we are working, timid finch – when your wings are larger we will expect more of you!' Then he had dropped him to the ground.

Khaled wondered what his father would think of the work. How hard it was, these days, even to picture his face! While the thought of his death pained him, it was comforting to recall the happy times. His mother also. But they were gone now, it was all past joy. He needed a future, a life to come, but all he could see was more death. That was the programme. That was the work. And the only balm it offered was the balm of glorious doom. *Mbuga za peponi.* The gardens of paradise.

Since his return, the words were coming back. The words and the phrases and the names. His beloved Swahili. But it wasn't enough. He was confused. The world was confused also. Only the pain was the same. That was the fate of all human beings. Only those who were believers could escape it. And among believers, only those who undertook jihad were guaranteed a place in paradise. The thought of it frightened him.

Sometimes, when he was scared like this, a voice came to him, quiet at first then louder between his temples. A rough kind of chattering, growing in volume and not always intelligible. He had heard it first years ago as a child, six or seven, by the sea, when he had fled down the strand after being scolded by his father. Then its grating roar had told him, *go into the water, go into the water*. And he had gone in, covering his shins – and then his father, who had followed, was behind in the water, lifting him up and carrying him back to their house, talking sweetly to him, telling him he was a good boy, a good boy, over and over again.

He looked up at the declining sun, then was startled by a noise, like rustling paper. He glanced nervously behind him, into the mysterious perspectives of the forest. He almost laughed at himself when he realised it was only a large red coconut crab, moving across the beach. Its carapace was almost exactly the same colour as the sunset. The sound came from the frond of palm leaf that the crab had gripped in one claw and was dragging behind it. Calm again, Khaled observed its strange movement for a while.

Then he raised his eyes to the curtain of trees, scanning it till he found the gap he had noticed the previous day. Someone had hacked through, quite recently, and while he was on guard duty he'd wandered down the path they had made. It led to something he knew about but, in all the intervening years, had quite forgotten: the opening to a series of caves that ran beneath the island. He used to play in them with Ali and Juba. His father had once said they were cursed, and it was true there were bones there, but he and his friends had never been frightened.

Hearing voices, he turned back to look at the cottage. Zayn was standing by the door, his great bulk obscuring the entrance. At his feet knelt Yousef, fiddling with the catches of a briefcase made of hard black plastic. It was the satphone by means of which they communicated with the Sheikh, the one he had bought units for in Peshawar, the one he had used to rent the truck in Dar. That had been exciting, using the device. It still amazed Khaled that it was possible to communicate without wires, even though he had seen many astonishing things on his travels and during his military training. He watched as Yousef lifted the lid of the briefcase and put his hand inside. A few seconds later, a silver rod rose from a corner of the open case. The top of the rod began to open and a web of shiny metallic fabric extended – like a small umbrella, upside down.

Yousef drew out a telephone handset on a curly cord of black plastic. He handed the telephone to Zayn, who presently began to speak. It struck Khaled that Zayn was quite prepared to use Western technology when it suited him. He'd often had the same thought during his training, when they were handling weaponry: rifles from America, explosives from Italy, grenades from Britain. Yet the Palestinian also had a kind of rage against it. Earlier that day, Zayn had first played one of the records on the wind-up record player they had found in the cottage. Then he had smashed the machine against the wall, saying, 'Come and see how it sounds now, Shaitan's noise!'

Khaled wondered what their orders would be. They still didn't know the exact timings of their mission. Soon enough, he suspected, they would know. The work was nearly done. The loads had been carefully packed into the cans, then into crates. Tomorrow they would float them over to the dhows on pontoons and pull them aboard.

The four crewmen of the dhows, plain Swahili sailors who knew nothing of the great task they were undertaking, were now dozing on the beach, wrapped in their kikois. They were wise to get up their strength for the journey ahead. For those bound for Mombasa port, from where the crates would be offloaded to continue by road to Nairobi after being met by other members of al-Qaida, it was a long and arduous journey. Khaled wondered whether he would be assigned to Nairobi or Dar. There were a lot more crates for Nairobi, which Zayn had described as 'the big number'. Ahmed the German was the leader of those taking care of things in the Kenyan capital.

He looked out to sea again. As his eye drifted to the edge of the island, he saw something unusual. A black patch. Was it? Yes, a small boat, rounding the headland of green forest where it stuck out into the ocean. He turned and ran back towards the cottage.

'A boat! There is a boat!'

Zayn, who was speaking into the phone, looked up and waved him away angrily. He clearly did not wish the Sheikh to hear of any trouble.

'Come!' Khaled said, urgently, tugging at Yousef's sleeve.

The two of them ran down to the beach where Khaled had been standing. They looked out over the low, humming waves, Khaled pointing in the direction of the headland. That was there, a long green arm – pointing out, just as Khaled's own arm was. But there was nothing else. Even the flecks of foam had gone now. All that could be seen was the forbidding totality of the ocean.

'There *was* a boat!' Khaled said, panting. 'I saw it!'

Yousef looked at him and smiled, the charcoal moustache creasing on his upper lip.

'You are dreaming. We would have heard the engine.'

'It was a rowing boat, I think.'

Yousef looked at him again, and then shook his head. At that moment, hearing Zayn's heavy tread behind them, the two younger men turned round.

'Well?' asked the cell leader, folding his thick arms and thrusting his head forward impatiently.

'He says he saw a boat.'

'I did see a boat!' said Khaled. 'There.'

He pointed again, and Zayn's iron gaze followed.

'I see nothing.'

'But I am certain,' urged Khaled. 'I think –'

Zayn contracted his heavy black eyebrows.

'I think you are a fool. But fools can be wise, even ones like you, from this godforsaken place. You think you saw something? Fine, you search the island.'

He unslung the machine pistol from his shoulder.

'Take this. If you see anyone, anyone at all, kill them at once. Now get out of my sight.'

With that, laughing, the two others turned and left Khaled standing on the beach, the heavy gun in his hands. He looked at the great red dome of sky above the two figures, its immensity pierced only by the shadowy spear of the lighthouse. *Mnara. Al Manar*. The lighthouse – in Swahili, in Arabic. Sometimes he didn't know which language to use. In all the tongues of man, oblivious to their divisions, night began to fall.

21

'Put up the sunshine, Nick.'

The oars' narrow blades spread wide either side of the boat.

'What's that?'

Leggatt shook his bleeding head. 'It's no use disguising the fact. If we don't get through the door before nightfall, we're crucified. We might as well drown ourselves right now.'

Nick, whose habit it was to dwell in possibility, was more optimistic. Even in adversity he remained full of hope. He continued rowing as hard as he could. The skin began peeling off his palms.

This time, at least, his efforts were vindicated. At dusk itself, immeasurable moment, the low outline of the island neared from darkening haze to actuality, resuming the image they knew. Speaking in a hoarse whisper, Leggatt guided Nick between two heraldic rocks in the crook of the headland, where the reef joined Lyly proper.

The rocks marked deep water and a break in the reef. Without Leggatt it would have been impossible to proceed. But they did find the place, and it was through this *mlango*, or 'door', as the gap in the reef was called in Swahili, that the dinghy of the stricken *Churchill* finally landed.

They stood listening to the waves sucking softly at the sand. It was good to be on solid ground. Nick's body was still full of the pulsing of the oars.

He looked at the old man. 'So now we try for one of the dhows?'

'I suppose so. The cruiser's engine would make too much noise.'

'It would probably have a key, anyhow, rather than an ignition button.'

'Some do, some don't. Anyway, that's all a bit previous. Whatever we take, it will be no picnic getting through that lot.'

Leggatt gestured up at the dark blur of the forest. There was no other way through to the lagoon. Looking at the trees, Nick's resolution weakened a little too.

He steeled himself. 'We'd have no chance with the dhow in daylight. It's got to be now. Delaying would be dangerous.'

'Right. Let's do it then.'

They set off. Nick went in front and Leggatt followed close behind, limping from his injuries. The moon was rising high, stars beginning to shine brightly in the cloudless sky. As soon as they entered the forest, however, this clarity was obscured. They could see hardly more than two or three paces in front of them. After only ten minutes or so of pushing their way through ferns and branches, a bough struck Nick a stunning blow on the forehead.

He sat down heavily, blood streaming from a deep cut. It was then he realised the true craziness of their mission.

'Up you get, soldier,' said Leggatt, grabbing his arm and hauling him to his feet. And so he moved on, and Nick moved on behind.

They pressed forward, guided only by a faint, tree-filtered glow of moon and stars and the occasional application of Leggatt's lighter. It was astonishing that it worked after the soaking they had taken. But it did, and its brief glare lit their way through whenever they reached an impasse.

All the while, Nick wondered whether it was worth continuing. They were making a hell of a noise, crashing into branches and stumbling over logs. The dense forest gave good cover, but it was difficult to move through it with anything like speed or safety. It was sinister at night, the coral rag; there was something unearthly about it, especially when the leaves rustled or a fern touched your face. Nick, whose forehead was still bleeding, found himself remembering Leggatt's stories about the slave caves, and the Zanzibar vampire.

Eventually, after an hour's hard bushwhacking, they broke through to a ridge of dunes above the cottage. It looked peaceful in the moonlight.

'Good God,' whispered Leggatt. 'We could be in Cornwall if it wasn't for those monkeys down there.'

A firelight glowed orange from the interior of the cottage. They must have cleared out the old fireplace. In the lagoon, perhaps forty feet out, Nick could see the shapes of the dhows. He felt Leggatt grip his arm again.

'We *can* do this you know. We just have to get past the outlook of the cottage. If we get down –'

He walked towards the edge of the dune and lay on his belly. Nick followed suit. The two men proceeded to crawl on their stomachs, worming their way out of the shelving dunes down across the beach. It was tense work. Every now and then a figure moved across the orange light in the cottage, and they froze, the taste of fear rising in their throats.

It was their concentration on the cottage that was their undoing. Once they were out of direct sight of it they stood up and started walking across the beach, looking over their shoulders every now and then to check they had not been spotted. Leggatt – Nick could see his faint outline – was doing this when suddenly he tripped, over a rock as Nick thought, and fell heavily.

Then the rock moved and, with a howl of surprise and fear, got to its feet. Suddenly Nick realised there was a man there in the moonlight with them, a kikoi flapping around him.

As Leggatt was standing up, the man – he smelt strongly of fish oil – demanded something loudly in Swahili. Three other forms rose from their beds in the sand and began shouting.

'Run for it,' Leggatt urged. 'I'll meet you at the dhow.'

Before the drowsy men could lay hands on them, the two of them started sprinting down the beach. But it was too late. The door to the cottage had opened and a powerful flashlight was flicking across the sand. Nick saw its beam fan their running feet. He could hear Leggatt's breath rasping behind him.

Another sound came, so ear-splitting and intense it could hardly be characterised as a sound at all, more like a feeling deep in the gut. Someone was shooting at them from the cottage. Nick felt the bullets whistle past, spitting at the sand round his feet. The light flashed again.

'Get down!' he cried to Leggatt over his shoulder, as another volley of bullets swept over them.

Nick flung himself gasping on the beach and looked back anxiously, worried that the old man had been hit or had not been able to keep up with him. He saw a wild-haired figure in the gleaming spotlight. Then the bullets sprayed again, tugging up the sand so it filled Nick's eyes. He wiped it away, in time to see Leggatt lurch to one side, trying to move out of the light. He seemed to have managed it. He was astonishingly agile for an old man. Then there was a thud and, with a deep groan, Leggatt pitched over and fell face first in the sand.

Nick stood up and ran towards him. There was another series of bangs, very close this time, and immediate sudden pain – a bullet creased his temple and tumbled him over.

* * *

The next thing he remembered was being dragged up a staircase. His head bumping against every step, blood streaming from his face. Then ropes binding him. Two lights: the bright one of the flashlight, electric white; the flickering, piss-coloured one of a hurricane lamp. Face down, dusty planking in his mouth, as they tied and tied. Voices speaking in Arabic.

Then somebody lifted him up like a doll and flung him against rough masonry. Finally, a heavy door dropped shut, and the darkness was complete.

* * *

He woke with dried blood stuck to his face and throat. It covered most of one side, like a mask. He tried to move, then remembered his hands were tied. There was something else, too. A noose around his neck. Passing through his bound hands and behind his back, it was linked to another rope, one that held his ankles together. He panicked, throwing himself from side to side on the wooden floor and hyperventilating.

Calm yourself, his own voice said to him. *Breathe*. Slowly, he curbed his anxiety a little. He rolled back to his original position, slouched against the wall – limbs and rope in a single insoluble knot. He could feel the stippled surface of the rough-plastered wall in his back. Air touched his face. Air and sun, streaming in through a square, glassless window. He was in the lighthouse. Yes. It was the same window out of which he and Miranda had gazed, only a few days previously. He could see the burner in the middle of the room, beside it the trapdoor that opened from the stairs. Then the memory of what had happened the previous night rushed in upon him: Leggatt's face falling in the flashlit sand, the sudden pain of his own wound. Blood in his eyes.

He knew that Leggatt must be dead. Not just because the Englishman wasn't trussed beside him in the lighthouse. It was the way, like lumber just struck, the old man had fallen. Nick realised that tears were streaming down his cheek, softening the bloody mask.

Maybe he was wrong? Maybe Leggatt was OK, and they were keeping him elsewhere. But already he knew this hope was false. The old guy – his habit of mind as outmoded as some dog-eared sticker on a leather suitcase – he wasn't coming back. Or if he was, it was as a voodoo revenant, lifting the grave's lid in the dead of night. Or flapping hideously out of the mangroves like the *papabawa*.

Nick knew it was more likely that there was no grave, that these people, whatever they were doing, had left the body there on the sand. He shuddered at the thought of crabs and seabirds tearing at the old man's flesh. It was then he heard the footsteps on the tower stairway. His stomach churned as he counted them.

The trapdoor lifted. A fat, shaven head emerged, followed by a pair of meaty shoulders.

The man who stood in front of him was enormous. Nick recognised him from his surveillance. But at a distance he hadn't quite taken in his size, his bull-like aspect. The man was dressed in jeans and a denim shirt. On his feet were a torn pair of sneakers. But it was his face – and something in his hand – that drew Nick's attention. The high-domed forehead, stubbly at the hairline, the flat, wide nose and tiny, set-back ears. Most of all the eyes: the hazel disguise of two black points of hate.

The thing in his hand was a panga. It swung back, then down, towards Nick's leg.

At the last second, it seemed, the man changed his grip. It was the flat of the blade that hit Nick's knee. He cried out as metal struck bone, and rolled over on his side. The man crouched down beside him, yanked him up by the neck-noose.

'Who are you? Why you watch us? You American, yes?'

Nick thought quickly. 'I'm Greek!'

The man stood up. A little smile curled his lips. Again the blade came down. The other knee this time, only the grip was slightly wrong. Or right. It made a gash. Almost losing consciousness with the pain of it, Nick gave a series of jolting whelps. Then tried to worm his way down into the wooden floor of the lighthouse.

'Oh no, mister. I think you are in a mistake. I think indeed you are American. I think maybe your government has sent you here to spy on us. American!'

He knelt down close, so close his breath was on Nick's face.

'Mister, do you know what that means?'

His tongue lolling out like a dog's, Nick shook his head in desperation.

'It means you are the devil's shit.'

Laughing, his belly shaking, the man stood up once more. He pulled Nick's rope, dragging him across the floorboards.

'OK,' the man said. 'I have work. We talk tomorrow. Why I don't kill you? So we can see what you know in your agent's head. Today, tonight, you rest.'

He took another length of rope and attached one end to Nick's ankles and the other to the lighthouse cast-iron burner.

'Yes, devilshit. You rest nice. Then tomorrow you can tell me all about it.'

With that the giant Arab suddenly crouched down again and, scooping Nick up bodily, bundled him out of the lighthouse window.

The rope snaked out behind him.

Nick was so surprised he didn't realise what was happening – blue sea and sky and green forest tumbling round him in angled planes. The rope attaching him to the burner jerked tight. His head banged hard on the white-painted stonework of the lighthouse.

Concussed, dangling upside down, Nick Karolides began to take leave of himself. As his battered body swung to and fro, all manner of confusion filled his mind. A woman's body (Miranda: he tried to catch her to him, a preservative from evil), his work (two lobsters in companionable conversation), something of Leggatt (an old British navy sextant he kept on the chart table of the *Winston Churchill*), something of his mother (her passion for decorative flowers). He could see sky and forest and the rough

231

stone face of the lighthouse, but it was all chopped up, chaotic, following the wild hurry of his mind.

Flashes of lucidity came and went. His limbs trembled. The last thing he saw, high up there beyond the flaking paintwork, was a swirling mass of birds, making a pattern in the blue sky. Tiny, riding the amazing dark cloud of themselves. Leggatt had spoken of this. Of a species acting out – something called a dread – in the sky. What were they? He couldn't get the name now, not now, not now. *Quaglia? Gwalia?* Something like that. It didn't matter any more, anyway. The cloud of birds was breaking up, retinal signals disintegrating into black spots of thought, the animation of consciousness itself, intense and almost indescribable. Then – dancing, fading, finally absent – the pattern itself was gone, to be replaced by something utterly unnameable. His bound throat gave a little gurgle.

* * *

During the night, it all came down on the lighthouse. Rain and lightning and hail. Another storm. On guard, Khaled sat in front of the fire they had made in the cottage. He huddled closer, trying to keep warm in the chill the storm brought with it. He had always hated thunder.

Every now and then, he went to the door and looked outside. Once, when the sky lit up, he saw the shape hanging from the lighthouse. He supposed the American was dead by now, like his friend. It made him feel bad. There had been too much death on this mission already. Not the death which was their aim, but accidents, arrivals that had to be dealt with.

The day before the whites came, two Zanzibari fishermen had landed on the island: looking for turtle eggs, Khaled suspected. Yousef, who had been wiring up – detonation cord and blasting caps strewn over the table in the cottage – quickly covered everything with a blanket. Zayn had been friendly at first, telling

Khaled to give the visitors cups of tea. Then, as they were drinking these – sitting on their haunches outside the door, chatting to Khaled in Swahili – Zayn had approached them with stealth from inside and slit their throats. The blood went all over the step, and they had to throw down sand after dragging away the bodies. Now there were three corpses hidden under brush at the edge of the beach.

The fire crackled. Rain swept down on the roof. The manner of the fishermen's death – the crooked cuts in their throats like that – had disturbed Khaled greatly. It made him wonder. It gave rise to doubts.

Next door, Zayn stirred dimly – then returned to a regular snore.

'You can bury them tomorrow,' he had said. 'Or weigh them with rocks and take them out to sea. With the other.'

'You didn't have to do this,' Khaled had said. 'You could have just let the fishermen go on their way. They were plain men, simple men, they would not have understood what we are doing here.'

'They could have talked, brought policemen from Stone Town.'

Zayn had clapped him on the shoulder, jovially at first and then again, harder and harder, his voice rising as he spoke.

'Are you soft, my friend? Perhaps you are not strong enough for this work? Not committed enough. Is your faith weak? Perhaps I need to talk to the Sheikh about you. He will be very disappointed if you are shown not to be worthy of this mission.'

The big man had finally pushed him to the ground, and walked back up to the cottage, where Yousef was boiling rice over the fire. Khaled had lain there for a while in the sand, his shoulder aching and tears welling up in his eyes. Then he had joined them for supper, at which both he and Zayn acted as though nothing had happened.

Now, as the other two slept on the floor in the bedroom next door – the Nairobi dhow had left, with the other men – Khaled kept watch, sharpening a piece of stick with his knife and poking the fire with it. He felt angry and afraid. Tomorrow they would begin their own journey, perform their holy task, once the crates had been lodged in the second dhow. He and Yousef would sail it to Dar-es-Salaam port – mainly him, since he knew how to sail the things – that had been agreed. Zayn would follow at a discreet distance in the cruiser, until they neared the port, at which point he would veer off up the coast and moor in a cove and wait.

They would make their escape in the cruiser, eventually meeting with a cargo ship in which two berths had been arranged through a marine broker. Or two of them would. There was still another matter to be resolved, the most holy and terrible part of all the work. Either he or Yousef had to drive the truck in which the crates would be loaded. It was a mission that truly served the cause of jihad, for it meant certain death. There were buttons in the cab. Only one person would be joining Zayn in the cove.

Khaled looked into the fire. It had not escaped his attention that Zayn had somehow been counted out of the reckoning for this aspect of the mission. Something else was still disturbing him too. The expressions on the faces of the dead fishermen, the shape of the gashes in their throats, the blood on the floor . . . The horrific scene of his discovery of his parents came back to him powerfully, bringing to the surface of his mind things that had been bubbling under during all his training, things that he had tried hard not to think. Why had Zayn been so vague about the killings? What was it his father had done that had angered the Americans so much? A terrible possibility flitted through Khaled's mind. He dismissed it quickly and thought about his own standing in the organisation. Zayn's questioning of his abilities and commitment had raised strong feelings in the young man.

It was these feelings – though he could hardly disentangle the anger and the wounded pride and the fear and the pity, for himself and for others – it was these that made him, on catching another lightning flash of the hanging man, suddenly stand up. He took down the hurricane lamp from the doorpost and, putting his knife in his waistband, began walking along the path that led to the lighthouse. The rain hissed on the hot lamp, threatening to snuff it out. But he walked slowly, letting the rain stream over him, as if its cooling waters might wash away all confusion and aid understanding. Either side of him, the spectral forest twisted in the wind.

On reaching the foot of the lighthouse he looked up at the black shape of the man. For an instant he thought he could hear him moaning. Maybe he was still alive?

It was probably the wind. Khaled opened the lighthouse door and stepped inside. He began climbing the stairs, his uncertainty mounting with every step. On entering the upper chamber, he held up the lamp. Flickering on the mirror of the burner and bouncing off the walls, it made the place seem beautiful, a world of light. Then he saw the rope – a taut black line leading from the burner to the window.

He put down the lamp and started pulling on the rope. The body was terribly heavy. He had great difficulty lifting it over the sill into the room, whereupon it dropped like a bale of meat.

The man's head hit the floor with a loud thump. Khaled began to worry that Zayn might discover him. Doing – what? He still didn't know exactly. It was inexplicable to him. Maybe the reason was that hideous possibility concerning his parents, that possibility which he could not consciously acknowledge, did not dare to fully recognise – since it would make him tragic, or someone who had been manipulated by evil, or someone who was just a dupe. He could accept none of those things. They made the voice in his mind speak too loud. Or maybe it simply struck him that the death of this man could no more be part of jihad than the death of the fishermen, and would therefore be a sin. On the other hand, if Zayn spoke the truth, the man was American, and in Khaled's mind all members of that nation stood charged with the murder of his mother and father . . . At least, they had until recently. He was confused. The sea wind was roaring in the trees outside. He reached out and touched the man's cheek. It felt cold, but that might have been just from the rain. Then he gave a start and trembled. He brought the lamp closer. He was being foolish. He knew now what he must do.

* * *

Khaled was woken by a kick in the ribs. Zayn's face was in his. Stubble. Night breath.

'So. You slept. And now the man is gone. Our prisoner. I believe he may have been an agent of the United States government. I had wished to interrogate him further before his death. And now –'

Another kick. Zayn was bare-chested. Black hair covered his heavy torso like the pelt of an animal. It was darker than his shaven head, and softer looking.

'And now he has escaped.'

He took Khaled by the collar and forced his face down into the smouldering coals of the fire.

'Maybe that is what you are also. A spy for the Amerikani.'

'No! You know that is not true. I can explain, the man . . .'

'I must punish you.'

Khaled felt the flesh on his face begin to blister.

'Wait!' he spluttered, into the hot ashes. 'I have something to show you.'

Zayn paused, and lifted him up.

'What can you show me? You are a coward, and lazy. You do not believe, in spite of the injustice done to your family. You dishonour their memory with your laxness and bad actions.'

236

'Let me show you.'

The bare-chested Palestinian loosed his grip. 'Very well. What?'

Khaled got to his feet, his scorched face grey with ash. He reached into his pocket, drew out something and proffered it: a severed human ear, roughly hacked.

'The man made noises in the night. He was trying to undo his bonds. So I killed him with my knife.'

A slow smile spread across Zayn's face as he studied the ear lying in Khaled's palm. But then he frowned.

'So where is the body?' he asked abruptly.

'You said we were to deal with them. So this morning, at first light, I picked rocks from the beach, to weigh them like you said, and took him and the old one out in the small boat and sunk them, together with those of the fishermen.'

He waved the ear in front of Zayn, a red-fringed petal between finger and thumb.

'I kept this to show you, uncle,' he said imploringly. 'So you know I acted well.'

Zayn looked at him distrustfully. 'I wanted to question the Amerikani.'

'I thought you would be pleased,' Khaled said anxiously.

As Zayn's hard eyes fixed on him again, Yousef emerged from next door in a pair of white underpants.

'What is happening please?' he asked bemusedly, looking from one of them to the other.

'Nothing,' shouted Zayn. 'Go, make your ablutions. Then we must pray, eat our food and set off. The day is here. There is no time for all this talking.'

He turned back to Khaled. 'You I will deal with later.'

'You leave one task unmentioned,' said Yousef, quietly.

Zayn looked at him, nodded gravely, then went into the bedroom to put on his shirt. Yousef, draping a towel over his shoulder, went down to the beach to wash.

Relieved, Khaled looked at the ear in his hand. It was changing colour, browning as cells popped, as blood oxidised in vessels. He was no scientist, but he knew what the matter was. Decaying flesh. Soon it would shrivel, turn leathery and hard. He had seen, every day, something similar in the upright racks of drying fish in his father's village. But the picture that the severed ear raised in his mind right now came from another world entirely. The look of it made him think of a tiny hamburger. He had seen one of those once, normal-sized he supposed, in a place in Mombasa that tried to be American. It had had ice creams and – what do they call those machines? A jukebox.

He stared at the ear for a few seconds, ragged-edged in his palm. Then he went outside, walked a little way – up to the top of the beach, where he flung it into some bushes. There was no need to be pious. It was just a piece of flesh. The job was done.

Shortly afterwards the three of them squeezed into the little mosque and prayed. Then they came back to the fire for breakfast. Yousef – who from the start had taken the domestic role in the team – proceeded to cook some maize meal, together with a pot of coffee.

They ate in silence, all three conscious of what was to come. Everything was done now, more or less. They were ready to set off, more or less. All that remained – the task Zayn had not mentioned – was for Khaled and Yousef to draw lots. Concerning the driving of the truck that awaited them at the docks. Concerning death.

After the meal, they all went outside and walked up to the dunes on Zayn's instructions. Telling them to wait there, he went over to some bushes, whereupon he bent over and broke off two small pieces of twig. Standing with his back to the others, he fiddled about with them.

Khaled looked out to sea. Further down, on the beach proper, he could see a strange structure of upright sticks.

There was a shout. Khaled turned and saw Zayn give a little jump. It was an almost comical movement for such a big person. He came hurrying back over, nodding his head and grinning oddly.

'A snake. I saw a snake! Now . . .'

His voice trailed off suggestively. Khaled looked at Yousef. The diminutive Syrian smoothed his moustache with the back of his hand, and gave Khaled a shy smile. Trying to take his mind off what was about to happen, Khaled turned and looked again at the strange structure, trying to work out what it was. The morning sun, already a little too much to bear, screwed down on the three men, making short, squat shadows of their bodies in the sand.

Zayn spoke, finally. 'Who is to pick first?'

Sweating, Khaled looked at his feet.

He heard his own voice. 'I will.'

It was all over with very quickly. Zayn's big fist was in front of his face, with the two brown ends of twig, evenly matched, sticking out. Without thinking, Khaled reached out and picked one.

He held it up. It looked very short indeed.

Zayn walked over to Yousef. The Syrian paused for a second, smoothing his moustache again. Then he pulled the remaining twig from Zayn's bunched hand.

'Now you measure,' commanded the cell leader.

The two came close together, as if they were about to embrace. Already one was condemned, by devices arbitrary or natural. Already one was murmuring dry-mouthed devotions, trembling and shredding his twig in his hand. Already one was being both comforted and congratulated by the other. For was it not an honour to die like this? Was it not a prize beyond price to go into paradise?

22

P-p-peep.

Somewhere in the office, Miranda could hear an alarm going off. She wondered whose it could be. It was eight o'clock in the morning, and most people had not yet arrived for work at the embassy.

P-p-peepit!

She imagined the person, whoever it was, rummaging through their briefcase or daysack looking for the rogue machine.

With the slow dawn of recognition, she became aware that it was *her* alarm, *her* bag. She had thrown her coat – mornings in Dar-es-Salaam could be kind of chilly – over her bag, muffling the sound and making it seem further away. And now it was she who was rummaging around.

She pressed the button on the top of the little black square, remembering only then how she had set it for that time. She hated wearing a watch, and always tossed the clock into her bag before leaving for work. She was sure that she had cancelled it. It must have been jogged in the jeep, making the button come up again. She turned back to her computer and began typing, resisting the temptation to check her email program to see if Nick had replied. That kind of thinking wasn't helpful. She hoped he understood from her tone that it would go no further. She could have written that it might have done, under different circumstances, but that was a hard thing to communicate without committing yourself. Still, he was the first thing she had thought of when she'd woken up that morning, very early.

It was builders that had broken her sleep, not the alarm clock. In fact, she hadn't really needed the alarm any day that week and now wondered why she'd set it at all. A group of labourers had lately begun work on a new house opposite her own in Oyster Bay. They started at five-thirty after sleeping amid the steel sticking out of the bare concrete. The foreman roused them by banging a stone on the metal ring of a tyre, and this was what had been waking her. Hung from a tree by a bit of old rope, it made a noise like a bell.

In truth, she didn't mind. She liked getting up early in Africa, throwing back the patterned sheets she'd bought from an Indian draper in Dar. Then she would put on a towelling robe and step out onto the veranda while the air was still relatively cool. In those moments she could feel, just for half an hour or so, before the sun got truly up, that she was back home.

It wasn't exactly homesickness. It was just that she liked to be able to measure things against an idea of home. Which mainly meant her father. And he was gone. Her mother, on the other hand, had never really been there at all. She wasn't even with her as a ghost as he was – inmate, inhabitant, a guest in her mind – but lay somewhere beyond the reach of conception. It didn't help that there were hardly any photographs. Miranda wondered if she had not been scarred by the absence of that deep, strong, inexhaustible force that she'd heard said was a mother's love.

There were some things, however, that could be defined by their absence. Or suggested by it at least. She'd realised a strong idea of America since coming to Africa. It was not a positive idea – since the country was too vast and complicated to be thought of in that way – but a negative one. Those shacks roofed with plastic bags, those pastel-paint signs in Swahili and broken English, that smell of wood smoke from the breakfast fires of crouched old women – those things all told her: this *isn't* home. This is far away. This is different.

The perimeter wall, the tubular-steel gates of the embassy's inner sanctum, and the main guard booth with its buzz-cut marine inside – Corporal Rossetti that morning, sleeves rolled up high over his rifle-toting biceps – they weren't home either. Although strictly speaking, they all stood, gates, booth and Corporal Rossetti alike, on what counted as US soil. The same went for the phalanx of heavy plate-glass windows in the three-storey concrete building and the titanium satellite dishes up above. 'Cupcakes of the gods', Ray called them, and like many things at the embassy they felt alien to her.

It was Ray whom she'd imagined looking for the alarm, his heavy moustache thrusting over his lip. He was usually in by now, his holdall slung over his shoulder and his considerable belly swinging along in front of him.

The office was weird without anyone in it, acquiring a sort of mystery – ordinary objects and fixtures demanding a different kind of attention when not surrounded by humanity. Some of the lights in the room had their own circuit. They hadn't come on when she'd pressed the communal switch. In those parts, the blue circle behind the American eagle shone eerily in the gloom: the State Department screen saver. The machines were humming quietly. There had been a security directive about logging off before you went home, but few people took any notice of it. Dar was the furthest thing from a high-risk posting that could be imagined. Most people just used ordinary, unencrypted PCs. There were only a couple of the shielded 'Tempest' machines in the whole place, and these were rarely used. It hardly seemed likely there was a terrorist or foreign agent outside among the street traders, reading embassy computer screens by means of an electromagnetic emanation monitor, which was what the Tempest system prevented. You only had to look outside, at the chaos of Africa, to know how unlikely that was.

She went over to the coffee machine. After fetching out the jug from underneath, she crossed to the sink to pour away yesterday's leftovers and fill it with water. Returning to the coffee machine, she tipped away the old grounds with their sodden skirt of paper and fixed a new filter. Then she opened a new foil packet of coffee with her teeth, shook its contents into the filter cone, poured the new water into the machine's steel trap, and put the jug back underneath. The machine whirred. A green display said BREW.

She stood for a moment, watching the first brown drops come through. It was PX coffee of course, not local. All the good stuff was exported, apparently. The packets laid out for sale on the pavements of the bustling streets outside the compound were just factory-floor sweepings. Ray had told her this.

It was a strange city, Dar-es-Salaam. African, yes, but shot through with its Arabic past. *Haven of peace.* That's what the words meant in Arabic and Swahili. It sounded nice, and sure, some bits of the town were OK. But the history was not so great. It was called that because in those old days it was a good port for slave ships. She remembered the caves on Lyly.

Her long hair over one shoulder, Miranda leaned against the smooth concrete pillar next to the coffee machine's stained table. She thought of Nick. In some ways she was glad there had been no reply when, feeling lonely, she had rung him yesterday. It was just a momentary blip. She didn't want to get into a big relationship. She hoped he didn't feel led on, or that she'd consolidated anything by letting him kiss her in the garden like that: it was just one moment, in which she didn't want to dwell, wanting instead to make her way.

It would take work, she knew it would. Her father had taught her that. She often remembered something he had said, when, as a girl, she'd complained about the difficulty of some her book reports. *Of course it's difficult. That's the point. What do you think they should do with you? Put you in a glass case and throw sugar at you?*

There was movement on the other side of the office. It was Clive Bayard coming in. He waved at her before heading for his desk. Clive was the embassy's only black face – African-American that is, as opposed to the Foreign Service nationals. That was the term for the local personnel whom it was her job to manage. Clive was the embassy archivist. Officially his title was Research and Documentation Provider. His role was to make sure that all paperwork in the embassy was properly sourced, stored and secured. Ray called him the paper boy, even though he was over fifty. Clive had a paper shredder by his desk. A good deal of his work consisted of destroying papers with high-classification dockets pinned to them. The shreds had to be burned in a furnace afterwards, just for good measure.

It used to be Nisha Ghai's job to do the burning, but a directive had recently come over the wires that only American nationals could handle high-classification remnants. It now fell to Miranda herself to do it. Nisha had been pretty upset about this reduction in her responsibilities, thinking that it was somehow her fault. It had taken all of Miranda's charm to persuade her that it wasn't.

'It's just one of those DS directives,' she had said.

She remembered how Mrs Ghai had anxiously twisted the large ruby ring she wore and looked at her, fierce and frowning.

'It is nothing to do with your work,' Miranda added. 'We're entirely happy with that. It's just that the documents have to be kept secret.'

'It is hardly as if you yourself are proper secret service,' the proud Asian lady had replied, before walking out.

Only one member of chancery was. The big embassies, like London, where Miranda hoped to work one day, were said to be thick with intelligence staff. But here there was just one guy. His main tasking, currently, was dealing with issues arising from the presence of Congolese rebels on Tanzania's north-west border.

There was a messy war in this region, in which the US had potentially lucrative mineral interests. The guy's objective was to secure future mining concessions with possible successors to Laurent Kabila, who the previous year had ousted the awful Mobutu Sese Seko – another client of the US in his time. Since there were some twenty rebel groups there, all with shifting alliances between themselves and neighbouring countries, he had quite a job on his hands. Hardly ever in chancery, Lee Denham kept a low profile. Ray, who had once dined at his house, said he kept a large collection of bowie knives in a glass cabinet. Miranda smiled to herself as she remembered the horrified, theatrical whisper her friend had adopted to convey this information. Yet Ray also said he found Denham kind of desirable, despite this disturbing sign of a violent personality. Or perhaps because of it. His greatest passion was for the crewcut Corporal Rossetti, whom he said had more virility than any man he knew – and, possibly, the best physique. But then, Ray often said such things.

The coffee pot was almost half full. Taking a polystyrene cup from the box next to the machine, she held it under the drips with one hand while pouring from the jug with the other. On the way back to her desk, she switched on the photocopier. It began to chug. She could never understand why it took so long to warm up.

The papers on her desk were mostly contracts for local staff. It was part of her job to recruit them and check them out for security. Every dimension of embassy support, from laundry to gardening to the outer, first-ring guards in the perimeter booths – who were supplied by a local security firm – came under her aegis. In practical terms, all this made her quite an important person in the embassy, even though officially the position she held was relatively junior. Too junior, she felt.

As well as its own generator, motor fuel and food supplies (in case of siege, as had happened in Khomeini's Iran), the embassy had its own emergency water supply. The tanks had recently been tested. Their contents had turned out to be brackish – the supplier had clearly used sea water for at least one top up – and a new firm was now being tried out. Its tanker was due in at ten-thirty, and she hadn't even prepared the contract yet. She moved her mouse, dislodging the screen saver, and started to type . . .

It was probably the noise of her fingers scampering over the keyboard that stopped her from hearing anyone come up behind her. A pair of hands grabbed her shoulders suddenly, and she almost jumped right off the chair.

She whirled round – only to find not an intruder but the moustache and twinkling eyes of Ray Delahoya.

'Got you,' he sniggered.

'Don't *do* that!' she said, clasping a hand to her chest. 'You know I hate it.'

'Couldn't resist. What are you doing in so early anyway?'

She swung back round on her swivel chair and started typing again, refusing to answer.

'Oh, be like that,' Ray said in mock disdain, and walked off.

The open-plan room where the lower grades of chancery worked began to fill up as staff filtered in. She carried on typing. It was clearly going to be a bad day. She could already feel the dull ache in her back which she tended to get while working on the computer.

A little later, Ray brought over a doughnut and another cup of coffee.

'Peace offering.' He put them down on her desk.

Smiling, she swivelled round. 'It's OK, I'm just a bit edgy. I haven't been sleeping too well.'

'Know why that is . . .?' He winked at her, then wandered back to his desk.

Shaking her head in half-amused desperation, Miranda returned to her work. She had, eventually, confided in Ray about

Nick, and now she was wondering whether it had been a good idea. Like the kiss itself. It wasn't that their embrace hadn't been pleasurable. It had, very much so, and that was the problem: she was afraid it would distract her.

At ten-twenty, with the newly completed contract in her hand, she made her way down to the motor pool, nodding at colleagues as she passed them on her floor. Denying herself the lift as usual, she took the three staircases briskly. A mop and bucket stood on the last step. George the cleaner's. Another one of her charges, he was missing as usual. She went out into the sunlit car park. It was full now, mainly of four-by-fours: approved-for-access stickers on their windscreens, dust on the covers of their back-door tyre mounts. Beneath the dust she could make out the logos of the US shippers: Brunner GM, Chicago; Hober Mallow, Philadelphia's Premier Ford Dealership. All parked in the alien corn here, she thought, all a long way from God's own country.

As she crossed the motor pool, she thought again about Nick, alone himself, out there on Zanzibar. The past few days she'd been feeling regretful she hadn't made love to him while on the island. But – he wasn't right for her, and that was that. He was, she reasoned, the sort of person who would keep building sandcastles even though he knew the tide was coming in. A dreamer.

Corporal Rossetti gave her something between a wave and a salute from the guardhouse. She took a path across the lawn, over the woodchips, which – it occurred to her – looked like some kind of breakfast cereal. The sprinkler was whirling round again. She felt the drops on her open-sandalled feet. Where she was headed was a booth. A booth and a vehicle boom. A point of entry and exit.

The gate was one of two in the second, lower perimeter wall. Alternating concrete pilasters with metal pickets, this outer wall separated the embassy grounds from the street. Manned by local staff, the booths at the two gates in this wall were really just mild deterrents to keep away curious townsfolk. The real protection, which came under the direction of the Marine Security Guard and was nothing to do with her, happened further in. Having a setback/standoff zone between two lines of defence like this was an important part of security strategy at all US embassies. Going by the book, at less than a hundred feet this one wasn't quite wide enough – but in most ways the security systems and procedures at Dar exceeded the standard requirements.

She smiled at Juma, the local security guard on duty. His job was to receive visitors and to register cars as they came in and out. As usual, he was looking at the CCTV camera that was permanently trained on his booth and the vehicle boom next to it. Juma was known for gazing at the gizmo's little black eye with alarming frequency: as if he were the audience rather than the subject. The Gunnery Sergeant's men – Corporal Rossetti and the other members of the MSG – monitored these outer booths through such cameras. From time to time they had had to gently remind poor Juma that he was there to screen visitors to the complex, not to imagine himself on screen in some sort of action adventure. It struck her Nick was a bit like that – all that nonsense about living dangerously.

Miranda suspected that Juma's habit came from a fascination with the videos that were sometimes shown by the embassy's film society. Though it sounded grand and art-housey, in reality stuff like *Die Hard* and *Lethal Weapon* was the staple fare. But occasionally more old-fashioned thrillers made it onto the schedule – *Chinatown*, *The Thirty-Nine Steps*, that kind of thing. Every Christmas, too, there was apparently a tradition that the whole chancery staff, both US and Foreign Service nationals, gathered together for a showing of a *It's a Wonderful Life* or *The Wizard of Oz*. These film nights were meant to break down barriers, but she wasn't sure they were such a good idea. They just encouraged the impression – common among uneducated Tanzanians – that every American had, somehow or other, something to do with Hollywood. It was as if the US existed only iconically, on a screen, and that Miranda, Ray, Corporal Rossetti, all Americans in fact, were nothing but cinematic characters made flesh. This was partly, Miranda reckoned, because the wealth gap was so big. For the average African, to own what an American owned did, after all, amount to dreaming an impossible fantasy. She was terribly conscious of how even little things, such as the texture of their clothes, gave Westerners an extraordinary aura. At Mto Wa Mbu, children had run and felt her skirt between finger and thumb.

Juma would have to be careful, in any case. The Regional Security Officer had been over from Nairobi lately. He had made a point of insisting that the local guards be more vigilant. And, furthermore, that their vigilance was itself better scrutinised. '*Quis custodiet*?', as Ray said cheerfully on hearing this, and Miranda had to ask him what he meant. 'Who will guard the guards?' he'd replied, adding that he himself was prepared to take personal charge of Corporal Rossetti.

The new instructions were part of a general review of security. Every week now, the embassy held alarm drills to identify contingent dangers. But since Dar was rated a low-threat embassy, really this was just a case of occasionally letting out a short burst on the Selectone blooper.

As it happened, the blooper had gone off just before Miranda came down. Corporal Rossetti had announced over the loudspeaker system through the embassy that they would be hearing alarms for a fire, for a bomb or a terrorist attack, and then the conclusion was the all-clear signal. Everyone had patiently waited to listen to these four different sirens going on as part of a normal drill, then had got on with their work.

She walked a little way alongside the outside of the wall, until she came to the big faucet that connected to the water tank. The tanker truck hadn't arrived. She wondered whether to go back upstairs and call the firm. But in the event she decided instead to take a few minutes in the sun. She went across the road to a little news stall and bought a copy of the Tanzanian *Daily News* from the boy behind the counter.

'CLINTON'S GIRL TAKES THE STAND,' read the front-page splash. It detailed the latest advance in Kenneth Starr's sex-and-perjury investigation of the President, in which Monica Lewinsky had begun testifying before a grand jury. Miranda turned the page. The Tanzanian media weren't going to tell her anything she didn't already know about that from other sources.

Overleaf another headline declared: 'GOAT LURES MEN TO DOOM, CHICKEN FOLLOWS.' In the mountains near Iringa, three men had died trying to retrieve a goat that had fallen down a mineshaft. Each one had been lowered into the shaft on a rope. When the first didn't come back up, another followed to rescue him, and then the next. Only when the villagers tied the rope round the neck of a chicken and lowered that down – and brought it back up, dead – did they realise 'this hole must be evil', as the newspaper queerly styled it. They wrote like that. Police later established there was poisonous gas in the shaft.

She had hardly finished the article when the tanker truck drew up. It began reversing into the gateway. Folding the newspaper under her arm, she strode over to it.

'You're late,' she said, trying to sound stern.

'I'm sorry, madam,' replied the driver, looking down from his cab. 'I could not get diesel.'

'Right. Well, come on then. I've been waiting.'

He got down from the truck. She could see his skin through torn blue overalls.

'How long will it take?'

'Quick, madam, quick.'

He slapped the side of the tank, making it resound deeply.

'This very fast pump. And I have rushed fast here also.'

He shook his head sadly. 'Diesel is a big problem in Africa.'

She suspected that the driver had, in truth, come directly from his village. One side of the cab was piled high with bright green maize cobs. He was clearly bound for the market after he had emptied the tank.

She watched the driver begin uncoiling the hose. The steel nozzle was in his hand. There were oil stains on his ragged overalls. She walked over to the pipe, which was in the wall, and he followed – walking backwards, pulling the heavy hose behind him, like a player in a tug of war. With slow, heavy steps, he fought the resistance of the drum on which the hose was wound.

She watched him unscrew the cap from the projection from the wall, attach the nozzle to it, then walk back to the truck to turn on the flow. The hose grew fat as the water began to run.

'Well,' she said. 'I'll leave you to it. Don't forget to put the cap back on.'

She began to walk away, and then remembered the contract. 'Oh, and you can give this to your boss.'

He folded it and stuffed it into the long trouser pocket of his overalls.

It'll get oily, she thought, wondering whether she should say anything. She paused for a second, then abandoned the idea. As she turned away, another truck pulled up behind the water tanker, which was now blocking the gateway. The driver had a slight moustache and pale-brown skin. He looked at her through the window. The truck had a canvas cover over its trailer. The driver seemed familiar. He also seemed a little agitated, mumbling to himself. One of his hands was on the wheel, the other out of the window, hanging down, tapping the outside of the door. He would just have to wait, she thought.

She walked back up the wood-chip path towards the chancery.

She could hear a jackhammer from over the other side of the building. Construction workers in the compound. There was to be a swimming pool. That was why the driver of the other truck seemed familiar. He'd been bringing the tiles for the swimming pool.

She passed a gardener digging a flower bed. Working his trowel quickly, he was throwing up earth in a way that reminded her of the snake on Lyly. Thinking about Nick tossing the reptile into the bushes so fearlessly, she went back into the chancery building and began climbing the stairs. Maybe she had, after all, been a bit too undemonstrative in the email she'd sent thanking him for the holiday. Perhaps she should have given herself more of a chance to let things happen if she changed her mind in the future.

Feeling a little downhearted, she let her eyes drop to the dull grey concrete of the steps. George the cleaner's mop and bucket were still there. She frowned. Old George liked *chibuku*, the local beer, more than was good for him. It wasn't worth making a fuss about. He was only a cleaner, after all.

The entrance to each section of the chancery had little plastic signs – *Shipping, Community Liaison, Visas*. Her own department was Administration, which sounded boring, but was in fact the heartland of the chancery. Not that it seemed it as she walked in. A man from the Political and Economic section was holding a discussion about Clinton with two or three other staff at the entrance. Hung on the wall nearby, a portrait of the President looked down at them, smiling broadly. At the other end of the room, Ray had his golf club out. He was putting down the carpet between the rows of desks. As she got closer, he managed to get the ball into the polystyrene cup into which he was aiming. He gave a loud cheer.

Miranda bent down to pick up Ray's cup and ball. The room went white. A flash, like a sheet of lightning, came in through the windows above her. She heard a deep rumble. Next, a thud. The windows exploded inwards. The wall to the side of her bulged horribly, bellying, breaking up into chunks of masonry. Glass blew over her head. She saw it pass in slow motion, even though it took only a split second – passing over everyone and landing on them, not small shards but lumps linked to mylar ripped in thread-lines through the air – like strips of sticky tape, only long and ragged and in ribbons.

She was swung off her feet. Desks and chairs were knocked over, a computer sailed through the air. Thousands of sheets of paper swirled. The place was full of dense dust and smoke. Pieces of concrete and glass, streamers of mylar – the protective anti-shatter film that covered the windows – were all around her. There was an intense heat.

Dazed, curled up on the carpet, she felt as if someone had hit her in the chest with a shovel. Tinier fragments of glass, ones that had come free of the mylar and were being carried up in the clouds of dust, began to rain down. She put her hands over her head, shaking uncontrollably. There was glass in her hair. Her mouth was full of dust.

Outside more explosions began going off, every few seconds. She wondered if they were under fire, if it was gunfire she was hearing. Everything seemed disconnected – her torn dress, her hurting ears, a teacup that kept rattling, rattling, rattling.

A sudden quietness came, for a few seconds, then terrible screams. She felt the carpet on her cheek. She opened her eyes. The smoke stung them. She closed them again. There were small cuts all over her hands and arms. She could hear groans and, further away, more hysterical screaming. 'God give me strength,' she said, aloud, spitting out dust.

After a few minutes, she opened her eyes again, squinting through the dust cloud. There was a strange, industrial, oily smell, and a gritty texture in the air. Paper floated down. Rubble was everywhere, and shards of glass with strips of mylar attached. She tried to make things out in the stinging smoke.

What she saw was Ray. He was flat on his face, legs buried under two large blocks of concrete.

She stood up slowly and hobbled towards him, through the tumbled furniture. Something had hit her leg, she realised. Ignoring the pain, she leant over Ray. His hair and shirt were soaked with blood. It was he, she realised, who had been groaning. Someone else was still screaming, awful and rhythmic. She tried to lift off one of the blocks. It was too heavy. She panicked, not knowing what to do. *Breathe*, he must be able to breathe. She started clearing away bits of stone and plaster from near his mouth. She tried to move his head a little so that he wasn't face down. But didn't they say you shouldn't do that? She began carefully taking the smaller chunks of concrete off his chest.

'Please,' came a familiar, if muffled voice. 'That hurts.'

'Oh God, thank God,' Miranda said. She kissed his blood-wet hair. 'You're alive.'

'There's something on my legs,' he said, into the carpet. 'I can't move.'

'You're trapped. You need help.'

She looked behind her. Figures were moving in the smoke pall. Behind them, as she looked, a portion of wall fell away, revealing blue sky. Between her and the sky was a litter of desks, computers and filing cabinets. One of the computers burst into flames. A woman in the distance was still screaming – screaming and screaming.

None of the people around her were as badly injured as Ray: the mylar had saved them, although some had quite bad gashes. The man from the political econ section shouted down the room. 'What's the State Ops Center number? We've got to let Washington know.'

Ray gasped. 'My fucking legs are busted,' he said, as if he had just realised.

'What's the number? Anyone know?'

Blood from Ray's legs and head was mixing horribly with rubble and masonry dust on the carpet next to her. She held his hand helplessly.

Someone shouted the number up the room.

The man from pol econ spoke down the phone. He said there's been a huge explosion here, he didn't know the nature of the explosion but there's been a huge explosion here.

Corporal Rossetti burst into the room. Miranda could hear the screaming again, from elsewhere in the building. The marine had a large gash down his face. His rifle was in his hand.

'All those who're able, proceed to the evacuation point immediately!'

'Ray's hurt!' shouted Miranda. 'He can't move.'

The room was filling with fumes from the burning computer. There was another explosion outside, then two more.

Miranda jumped each time. Threads of smoke were coming up through the floor.

'Gas tanks,' said Ray, feeling her tense. 'I know it from Liberia.'

He chuckled crazily, then groaned again, flinching as something fell on his face. It was water, dripping down on them from smashed pipes in the ceiling.

'We need help here!' called Miranda, her forearms streaming with blood from her little cuts now. 'Urgently.' The flow of water was getting heavier; she couldn't tell what was wetness from the roof, what from the cuts.

Rossetti ran down the room, his big soldier's boots nimble in the glass and concrete. He knelt down beside them, his hands moving over Ray's torso. He lifted off the blocks. The bones of Ray's knees were sticking out, clearly visible amid a mess of blood and cloth and concrete dust. Miranda stared at them, stupefied with horror.

Rossetti spoke into his radio. 'One down on the third floor. Pretty bad. Send medic.'

'You go,' he said to her, producing a dressing from his kit. 'I'll stay with him.'

'I can't,' said Miranda, still transfixed by the bones.

'Out,' Rossetti barked. 'Now!'

Cowed by the abrupt military tone, she stood up and made her way unsteadily through the wreckage. There was still a large cloud of dust, mingling with fumes from the computer's melting plastic. At the end, where the missing wall was, she could see black smoke rising from burning cars below. She edged a little closer, uncertain of her bearings and trembling with shock.

'Away from the wall!' called the man from pol econ. He had a wound on his forehead.

'Come on, quick! The floor could go.'

His voice sounded numbly in her ears; the noise of the explosion had deafened her a bit, she realised, as the pol econ man took her hand. *I'm going to fall*, she thought, *I'm going to tumble down all these storeys*. They ran out into the corridor, joining a crowd of fleeing staff. Everybody squeezed through the narrow hallway towards the stairs, which were obstructed with fallen blocks and hanging pieces of wood. There was debris on almost every step, making it difficult not to trip.

It was a hushed procession; everyone was dumb with shock. On the way, Miranda noticed first George's upturned mop and bucket, then, a few steps further down, the cleaner himself. Half of his skull had been dashed away. A fallen beam lay nearby. Blood and brain matter were pooling into the stairwell.

She felt herself about to throw up, but the pol econ man grasped her hand more tightly and dragged her on, over the pieces of cement that covered the stairs. Eventually they made the exit, spilling out with others equally panicked. Some had facial injuries or deep cuts on their arms. One woman was holding a hand to her eye. John Herlihy, the maintenance manager, was sitting on the ground, his plump cheeks striped with soot.

He looked totally bewildered.

The motor pool and chancery gardens were scenes of devastation, filled with confused people. Some were screaming, others weeping, others shocked and silent. Miranda felt choked up. She was still bleeding from the little cuts. Many people were bleeding. Nearly everyone was dishevelled, their clothes ripped and covered with dust. Cars and jeeps – all sorts of vehicles – lay thrown on their sides or roofs, blazing fiercely. Those further away, that hadn't been blown over, still had seared paintwork and stoved-in windows.

Everywhere there were piles of broken wall, splintered pieces of wood, twisted auto parts, glass and concrete – an accumulation of loose materials sometimes four feet deep – and scattered bodies. One, lying in the courtyard where Ray's bench used to be, was headless. Another was totally blackened, charred like meat. Another was missing a hand. She saw it was Mrs Ghai, and then she did vomit, going down on her knees.

Another corpse, Miranda realised with mounting horror, once she had recovered, was that of the gardener she had passed on her way back from supervising the water tanker. His chest had been crushed under a scorched block of concrete. It had spread-eagled him in the middle of his bed of soil and broken blooms. Several trees nearby had been knocked over; bushes and flowers had been ripped to shreds. The whole lawn was strewn with woodchips from the path, blown up into the air by the explosion. Debris was still fluttering down – pieces of paper and fabric swirling in the vapour of corrosive fires.

She jumped as a tyre exploded with a pneumatic pop.

'Come on,' said the pol econ man. 'We better get out of here. There could be another blast.' His forehead was oozing thick gouts of blood.

'You're right,' she said. 'The underground fuel-storage depot could go up . . .' She tried to focus. 'We better warn somebody.'

She ran over to tell a marine, hurting her feet on the carpet of fragments that covered the ground.

'OK,' he said, his face clown-like with dust. 'You get out now.'

But how? The main gate was impassable. Its steel bars had twisted, some of them fused together by the heat. A truck lay near to the guardhouse, the walls and windows of which were totally smashed. It had been stripped of everything but its chassis. The iron skeleton of the thing was glowing hotly. Next to it was a large crater. Miranda was slowly becoming aware how very great the force of the shock wave must have been. At first, she thought the glowing truck was the remains of the water tanker. But it was the other one that was glowing, she realised, the one with the canvas cover that had pulled up behind. The water tanker itself was now over by the chancery building, up against the front wall. Having been carried over the lawn and the motor pool, it had evidently taken much of the blast. The tank had been squashed inwards like cardboard tube. The driver must certainly be dead, she thought. Chilled, she realised she had escaped by a matter of minutes. Had she waited to see the water tanks filled, she would have been at the heart of the explosion, and reduced to particles. As it was, the blast had taken out the walls on each of the chancery's three levels on the facing side. The building was now charred a deep black, full of gaping holes. Smoke was still billowing out of the holes and the remaining window frames.

The motor pool was especially chaotic. Fire engines were arriving, ambulances were arriving. There was more smoke, from burning cars. Some members of the marine detachment were trying to secure the area, kneeling down and training their guns on the Africans who were gathering at the edge of the compound. Others were trying to herd embassy staff away. One marine, having grabbed a ladder and put it up on the perimeter wall, was ushering folk over. The wall itself was cracked and, in some places, covered in blood from where wounded people had touched it. They were a sorry-looking bunch, those waiting anxiously in line for the ladder. One muscular young man – it was the secret-service guy, Denham, Miranda realised – had only one shoe and was limping badly. Others in the line, which she herself joined, were calling emergency services, colleagues and relatives on their cellphones. As she waited, she heard the sirens of more ambulances and fire engines.

On the other side of the wall, the Peace Corps people, who had rushed over from their nearby complex as soon as they heard the bomb, were waiting in vehicles to ferry people away to hospitals. Two Peace Corps nurses climbed over the wall to help the injured who were still in the compound. On the pavement outside, the embassy's physician, Dr Macintyre, was treating those who needed immediate attention. Two people, both Tanzanians, were lying on makeshift stretchers – doors blown off their hinges at houses and offices nearby. Many of these buildings had caved-in walls and roofs, and all had lost the glass in their windows.

A helicopter droned overhead. Beneath it, a vast crowd began to converge on the scene, running up to look inside the compound, horrified at the damage. Firemen were beginning to hose the building, sending up plumes of steam to mix with the smoke and dust. Here and there, shafts of sunlight were coming down through the palls.

After making sure that Macintyre knew about Ray, she went in one of the Peace Corps vehicles to the house of the chargé d'affaires. It had been agreed that this was to be set up as a temporary headquarters. On the way, suddenly aware that she was still trembling with shock, Miranda heard the news that there had also been a near-simultaneous bomb at the embassy in Nairobi. It was by all accounts a much worse and deadlier explosion. As they sped through the city, she shivered at the thought that anything could be worse than what she had just experienced.

Looking back, she saw a cloud of black smoke rising into the air, carrying up shreds of paper and cloth. The vast crowd was now running away from the scene.

She told the lady in the front, leaning forward urgently, as if it were something with which either of them could help.

'They must be frightened too,' the woman replied. 'There's rumours of secondary bombs going round. Kampala and Khartoum as well, they're saying.'

'Who do you think it is?' Miranda asked, wincing. Her eardrums were hurting badly.

'Must be the Islamics. Got to be. The Tanzanians have no axe to grind with us.'

At the chargé's house, more Peace Corps people were on hand with coffee and sodas. She drank a Coke, feeling light-headed – and guilty at having left Ray behind. Someone brought her a facecloth soaked in disinfectant with which to dab her cuts. She was still trembling, she realised.

After gathering her wits, she set about trying to help as further staff appeared. There was so much to do. First of all they had to account for everyone, locate them, and try to work out how many had been injured. Miranda assisted with the list-making, finding out contact details of relatives in the United States. This was then read down the continual open line to the Operations Center of the State Department: the name of the employee and family, the name of the person to call, the phone number, which was then rung by State so that people wouldn't wake up in the morning and hear it on the news. A similar list was made on behalf of Tanzanian employees, but many did not have phones.

By six o'clock they had ascertained that at least ten, maybe eleven people had died at Dar. Over eighty others had been injured. One of these was Juma the guard, whom the blast had plucked from his booth and thrown bodily into the air. Just after he had landed, a car had fallen next to him, less than a metre away. The glass in the car's windows had shattered and entered his body like buckshot. The doctors said it would take months to remove all the tiny fragments. Several of the other local guards were dead.

It was no consolation that US nationals were not among the fatalities at Dar. As two-way radios crackled and mobile phones warbled their incongruously cheerful signatures, it became increasingly clear that the situation in Kenya was far bleaker. The Nairobi death toll rose throughout the day. The figures were still hazy, but it seemed that over two hundred people had been killed, twelve of them Americans. Up to five thousand Kenyans had been wounded in the streets and offices around the Nairobi chancery.

As the afternoon wore on, more and more people crowded into the chargé's house, sitting on cushions on the floor or huddled together in small, blood-soaked groups. An improvised first-aid station was set up on the first floor of the chargé's house, where Dr Macintyre, with the Peace Corps nurses, could attend to those who didn't require immediate hospitalisation. Many people needed stitches or were hysterical and had to be calmed down. In between comforting people and making cups of tea and coffee, Miranda helped a medical orderly dispense tranquillisers. She heard that Ray had been taken to hospital and that his condition was stable. She tried to keep busy, not to think about the bodies of Mrs Ghai, or George, or the gardener.

Each new arrival brought some fresh horror story. At about five-thirty, Corporal Rossetti arrived, pale and dishevelled, still carrying his M16. He was utterly exhausted – reduced to near incapacity by the effort of rescuing people, assisting the badly wounded, and protecting what remained of the chancery. This included the task of destroying classified documents and equipment. After seven hours, Rossetti had – wisely – agreed to hand over guard duties at the embassy to a mixed force of military staff from a number of third-party diplomatic facilities based nearby (including the British and the Israelis), in conjunction with the Tanzanian police.

He related in more detail the scene that Miranda had briefly witnessed from the back of the Peace Corps vehicle: how the crowd of onlookers on Laibon Road, nearly a thousand strong, had been successively driven away by scares and, in turn, attracted by the terrible fascination of catastrophe.

'I nearly had to fire over their heads,' said the Corporal, whose own head was in his hands. 'We had to get control. It was like a huge wave. They kept to-ing and fro-ing. Rushing at me, and then falling back in a mass movement.'

There were other movements, other spheres. High in the sky, above the carnage at both sites – above the dead in their ungainly postures, above the maimed and the punctured, above the broken buildings and the still-billowing palls of smoke, above the looping sirens and the nervy crowds – the most sophisticated communications network known to man was responding to contingency. Naturally, the President had been informed at once. At the White House, at the Pentagon, at CIA and FBI headquarters, emergency meetings had been hastily convened and action plans laid down. Secretary Albright and the Department of State's Operations Center were charged with coordinating the response.

Later that afternoon, President Clinton himself, along with Secretary Albright and other notables, telephoned the chargé's house to express their sympathy. Later still, Miranda and the others were told that planes were on their way from home. The secret-service man, who still had only one shoe and a sock full of blood, stood on the chargé's dining-room table to give a briefing.

'We now have a twenty-four-hour open line to the State Department,' Denham said. 'You may have heard there were bombs in cities other than here and Nairobi. I am pleased to say that that is not the case. There were threats, but these have been neutralised. People have been picked up. But Nairobi is very bad. Much worse than here. The good news is that hundreds of government employees – FBI, Army, doctors, post-disaster experts and secret-service personnel – are on the way. All need to be found accommodation, vehicles and phone lines. What I suggest is that everyone who is able and not deemed essential personnel goes home and gets some sleep. But don't leave this house unless you have some means of keeping in contact. Keep a low profile anyhow. In the morning, get back here and help man the phones and fix stuff up. Bring your mobiles. We're going to need people to liaise with the hospitals, with Washington, with expediting stuff through the airport.'

Miranda didn't go home in the end. Oyster Bay was too far, and she was still too shaken up anyway. She slept on the floor under a blanket, waking to television pictures from Nairobi of the rescue effort. It had continued through the night. There was rubble everywhere, interspersed with chunks of metal, pieces of cars, bodywork, engines, all twisted out of shape and black with soot. Under rows of bright arc lamps, a crane was pulling away blocks of masonry too heavy for pickaxes and crowbars. Acetylene torches and angle-grinders were being used to cut through steel rods. The TV microphones picked up clearly the voices of those who were trapped, crying out for help.

She stayed until lunchtime helping with the phones and organising the installation of further lines. In the afternoon, famished and weary, she went to the hospital in a taxi to visit Ray, buying a take-out (something she never normally did) from Jambo Snacks under the clock tower and eating it on the way.

Ray was to be evacuated to London that night, Britain being nearer than the US. She wept when she saw him there in the hospital bed with both legs in casts, even though he maintained his customary spirit.

'Don't cry, sweetie. I've been lucky really. My internal organs are OK. And my dick, thank the Lord.'

'What about walking?'

'Ah yes. Mobility. Well, they go all quiet when I ask them about that. Apparently my kneecaps are crushed.'

An image of broken eggshells went through Miranda's mind as she remembered the bones she saw. Tears started to run down her face again.

'Come on now,' he said. 'Give me a kiss and go do something useful. I'm sure those Brits will sort me out.'

She kissed him, but was still crying when she got back in the taxi. Instead of returning to the chargé's, she asked the taxi driver to drop her at a local rental place, where she hired a new car. Her own, like those of most of her colleagues, had been wrecked by the blast. Then she drove quickly back to the house, where she was due to staff the open line again. On arriving about three o'clock, she ran into Clive Bayard. She realised she hadn't spoken to the archivist properly since 'the event', as the Op Center was now calling it. It was he who had taken yesterday's call from Clinton.

'It was weird,' he confided to her a little later, over coffee and doughnuts in a brief moment of downtime. 'I've never been much of a fan of the President, especially not since this stuff with the women. All that business offended my sensibilities. But when I heard his voice on the phone asking me my name and giving his support and saying what a terrible thing it was that had happened to us, I knew that he meant it right from his heart. He was genuine. You know, I don't care what that guy does now, he can seduce every American woman possessed of dark hair and breasts between Montana and New Mexico, and damn me if that doesn't include you, Miranda.'

She stared at him, amazed. Clive was a strict Baptist and she had never heard him blaspheme or mention sex before. He had taken off his spectacles and was continuing in the same vein, holding the glasses in one hand and gesticulating with a half-eaten doughnut in the other.

The image stuck in her head as she drove back to Oyster Bay. Clive wasn't alone in seeming out of character, volatile. The bomb was having strange effects on many people – jolting their self-images, altering personalities and relationships. More strangely, it seemed to be jolting time and place, too, which had the appearance of chopping back and forth as the event jumped and quickened in the memory. It was disconcerting, she thought as she collapsed on her bed the second night after the bombings – like a movie that messed with appearance and reality.

Only this was real . . . Back in her familiar patterned sheets, back in her own bed at last, Miranda Powers was about to slip into the toils of sleep. She reached over to the bedside table. The last thing she saw, as she turned off the light, was the baby turtle shell Nick Karolides had given her on their way back from Lyly.

PART THREE

23

The least consequence of what transpired at 10.39 a.m. on Friday August 7, 1998 – date never to be forgotten, time branded on her memory– was the loss of her alarm clock. Miranda threw the sheets aside quickly, realising that she had overslept – on such a day. She had woken up easefully, thinking of Nick and the twanging guitars at the night club on Zanzibar, and the sweet air of the garden afterwards, where he had kissed her. Then her thoughts turned, in a single, self-punitive flash, towards poor Mrs Ghai, George the cleaner, the gardener, Ray, the body without a head. Towards the hundreds of others in Kenya, some still trapped beneath the rubble, alive or dead.

After dressing quickly, and grabbing a few mouthfuls of yogurt and muesli for breakfast, she rushed back to the chargé's house. She had to fight her way through. Once the bomb had gone off, the world's media – CNN, BBC and many more – had quickly started to gather round the ruined chancery. Now they had begun to concentrate on the emergency op centre at the house.

During the night, a public-affairs strategy had been devised by the Department of State. Orders were given that the media were to be kept away from evidence-sensitive bomb sites and prohibited from conducting on-camera interviews with victims. But it was too late: a number of images were already out and flashing round the world. Some of them were deemed too grisly for the international networks, and were shown only on African TV. These included one of a hand with a ruby ring still on one of its fingers.

Mrs Ghai's. Miranda fled to the bathroom, holding her own hand over her mouth.

Later she saw another image, from Nairobi, of bloody handprints on a wall, which she guessed were those of an injured person dragging themself to safety. Again she had to turn away. The chancery public-affairs officer tried to clamp down on such broadcasts. Instead, proper briefings, stand-up press conferences, were to be given to the hundreds of journalists who now congregated in Dar.

Miranda watched President Clinton and other members of the government make statements on CNN. 'These acts of terrorist violence are abhorrent,' said the President, standing in the White House rose garden. 'They are inhuman. We will use all the means at our disposal to bring those responsible to justice, no matter what or how long it takes.'

'Terrorists rejoice in the agony of their victims,' said Defense Secretary William S. Cohen. 'What we want to do is take the joy out of their celebration, and we will do everything in our power to track them down.'

Secretary Albright announced a $2 million reward for information leading to the conviction of those responsible for the bombings. 'Our nation's memory is long and our reach is far,' she said.

Miranda could not bear to think what it was like for those families who had lost sons or daughters, mothers, fathers. In Nairobi, it had taken over twenty-four hours of constant digging by Marines and special-forces personnel to remove the bodies from the rubble. The TV showed Marines and Kenyan soldiers standing by the ruined building, which was now ringed with coils of barbed wire and piles of sandbags, in anticipation of further attack. Behind the barrier a bulldozer pushed a jumble of debris. Miranda saw bodies being wrapped in plastic or having numbered aluminium tags attached to their ankles for identification. She saw coffins, made of red wood, being loaded onto the backs of pickups and, as was the custom for the Africans, being taken for burial to their home villages.

* * *

The Administration acted promptly to deal with the crisis, initiating a rescue plan and taking steps to apprehend those responsible. Not surprisingly, however, things were a bit chaotic. It was not until forty hours after the bombings that the C-17 Globemaster III carrying the Tanzanian FEST (Foreign Emergency Search Team) arrived in Dar. The regular FEST plane had been despatched to Nairobi and it was only later, as the scale of the tragedy became apparent, that it was decided to send a separate one to Tanzania. The delay was partly to do with accessing an appropriate aircraft and partly to do with the availability of a second stream of equipment: radios and telephones, search dogs, tools for the excavation and extraction of buried personnel, medical supplies, next-of-kin records and other emergency documentation. It took a lot of work to get all this together.

In addition to the FESTs, a variety of service members were despatched by the Department of Defense, which called on its resources from all over the world. A fifty-man Marine Fleet Anti-Terrorism Security Platoon was sent by Central Command to each city; a thirty-man Navy Seabee unit was deployed from Guam to help with recovery operations in Nairobi; European Command sent a twenty-man surgical team, a seven-member Army-combat stress-control team, a critical-care transport team and a seven-member Air Force aeromedical evacuation crew. From south-west Asia, more medical personnel and a mortuary affairs team were deployed, split between Dar and Nairobi.

But it was mainly FBI staff – medical and explosives and engineering experts as well as investigating agents – who were first to arrive at the two sites. Under federal law, the FBI is mandated with investigation of crimes committed on United States property

271

abroad, and this was why Mort Altenburg touched down in East Africa. Jack Queller, rushed from Cape Cod to Washington by light aircraft, was another who came, having been called in personally by Secretary Albright as a Center for Terrorism Control adviser to the FEST.

Queller and Altenburg went to Nairobi first. Both men were shocked by the quantity of debris at the site when they first visited it. There was glass, a lot of glass, mounds of brick, twisted pieces of charred metal, huge slabs of concrete. The walls of several buildings had been completely ripped away, like a cross-sectional diagram. Webs of vapour still hung over the site. Kenyan construction crews, their picks and shovels ringing on stone and steel, continued to dig for human remains.

Altenburg threw himself into investigative searches and interviews. Queller stood back a little, trying to get a picture of how it had happened. He noticed that some of his colleagues were riding roughshod over the personnel from the Kenyan Criminal Investigative Division. He himself took special care to listen to what the African policemen had to say as they went about their own examinations of the crime scene, in the wake of the FBI's technical experts.

The forensic procedure itself involved mapping out a boundary, a demarcation about six hundred yards from the putative centre of the blast, and working one's way in. What the technical agents were looking for first of all were pieces of metal that showed a close proximity to the explosion – such as might have come from the vehicle in which the bomb was carried, if that was the case. There was a characteristic pitting and cratering of surfaces, and thinning and rolling of the metal itself from the amount of energy and pressure exerted on the object at the time of detonation.

Later they would swab for trace elements, explosive residue: minute particles of chemical produced when the explosive reacted and changed from a solid to a gaseous state. Having been isolated and dissolved in acetone, the particle would then be separated, using gas chromatography, and its chemical constituents identified with an electron microscope. Only then would they know exactly which ingredients had been used to make the bomb.

There was so much to get through that the FBI set up tents in a parking lot next to the embassy, laying out trestle tables inside, on which they could study fragmentary evidence. It was here the torn pieces of metal were examined, having been carefully picked up from where they had come to rest.

Queller stared at them. It was hard to get a sense of how these blackened pieces, carried by the shock waves at thousands of feet per second, had moved through the air as the explosive expanded; how energy moving at such a high rate of speed could take metal, heavy metal like an axle or a piston rod, twist it, churn it, puddle it, flatten it, or form a knife-like edge even as it travelled.

The following day, on a visit to the hospital, he saw some of the damage that had been done to human flesh by these projectiles, and by the billions of particles of glass, concrete and other material that the explosion had flung around in concentric circles.

He walked the beds with an Asian woman doctor. Torn limbs. Corneal laceration. Shrapnel littering flesh. Teeth sheared off. Holes in the skull. People who had lost parts of their jaws or shoulders. There was one man, a driver at the embassy, who had lost an eye, an ear, and half of his forehead. The ambassador herself had a badly torn lip and other injuries. Many others, from what the doctors told him, had glass buried so deep in their bodies it would take eight or nine operations to remove it.

Queller was most moved by those who had lost limbs. One man had lost a hand. The doctor told Queller how he had come in with the hand dangling from the threads of its neurovascular

273

bundle – a lone figure in the sudden surge of humanity that had descended from buses and cars in the immediate aftermath of the explosion, overrunning the triage area and covering its walls and floor with blood as they slumped and lay and sat down all along the hallways, waiting for attention.

He left the place trembling and had to stand in the car park under a red-flowered tree before he could gather the strength to drive back to the bomb site.

* * *

Over in Dar, Miranda was at the scene as the first wave of FEST personnel arrived, to begin collecting evidence there and initiating a programme of interviews. She watched the agents as they checked in at the chargé's house, where she was still working the phones. There were as many women as men among them, and African–Americans, Asians, WASPs – a broad spectrum – but all seemed somehow the same: the same youth and iron-hard fitness, the same sober business suits half concealing shoulder holsters and handguns, the same logic-chopping, Quantico brains. The response teams went into the blast sites first with picks and shovels, then wearing surgical gloves, carrying Q-tips and tiny plastic bags. They all wore protective Tyvek suits – all-over plastic suits to prevent contamination of evidence. They must be boiling in those, she thought, under the African sun.

The mandatory security inspections conducted by the FEST included rigorous questioning of the chancery staff. Held at the Kilimanjaro, these were something of an ordeal, but everyone agreed they were necessary. One by one, those who weren't too badly injured were called to the hotel.

By the time it was Miranda's turn, Queller and Altenburg had arrived from Nairobi. It was they who conducted the interview. She was surprised to see the two men together. She didn't know what to say as she was escorted into the room by another agent.

Queller was friendly from the start, rising to shake her hand, offering her his good left one, which threw her a little even though she remembered about the prosthesis.

'We met before, didn't we?' he said, with a smile. 'I'm sorry that we have to meet again under such tragic circumstances.'

Altenburg was colder in his manner, studying her impassively from behind his spectacles. It was he who asked most of the questions, sitting directly opposite her at the formica desk. There was a pile of files, and a tape recorder. Queller sat a little apart with his legs crossed, the empty sleeve of his missing arm hanging by his side. The agent who had escorted her in stood at the door. She felt like a criminal under guard.

At first the interrogation was technical. 'What colour was the smoke from the bomb? Are you able to describe its smell?'

She tried as best she could to remember. 'Well, it was just black really, black with streaks of grey. I don't know how to describe the smell. The only time I ever smelt anything like it was when some kids burnt a car in my cousin's neighbourhood back home. Only it was more, kind of chemical. And you could smell the masonry dust too.'

There were a few more questions like that, and then Altenburg began quizzing her on matters of security.

'Had anyone, before the Friday, asked you questions about your working day, or about protection protocols at the chancery?'

'Stuff like – what are the MSG's schedules and so on?' Queller put in helpfully.

'No,' she replied. 'Anyway, I know very well not to answer questions like that.'

'What did you see on the day of the bomb? Did you see anything suspicious? Any people or vehicles at the perimeter?'

She began telling them about the water tanker. 'I had to go out and deal with the water-supply man, he was late you see, and I had to hang around . . .'

'Forensics have been right over the wreck of it,' Altenburg said. 'We think the other truck was the core of the blast. Can you tell me anything about that?'

'It was coming up as I left. I wondered what was in it. I thought it was stuff for the swimming pool.'

'What?' Altenburg said.

'We're having a swimming pool built and construction vehicles have been coming in. I thought it was one of those.'

Altenburg wrote something down.

'OK,' said Queller.

'It was waiting to pass the water truck. I remember being surprised because usually the Tanzanian drivers honk their horns like crazy and this guy didn't. He just waited there. Well, you know, he was a little agitated. I think . . . I mean, he was patting the side of the door with his hand.'

Both Queller and Altenburg sat up.

'Can you remember his face?' asked Altenburg.

Miranda shrugged. 'Not really. He had pale-brown skin. He did seem familiar, I remember thinking that. I thought he was part of the construction team.'

'Try harder,' Queller urged.

She closed her eyes. She tried to visualise. 'He had a moustache, I think. I didn't really look.'

'That was unfortunate,' said Altenburg. 'Considering how things turned out . . .'

He opened one of the files in front of him, lifting it up so she could see her name on the cardboard cover.

'It's your job to vet local ancillary staff here, isn't it?'

'That's right,' she replied.

'Any reason to suspect any of them?'

'Not at all,' she said. 'They're all highly committed.'

Altenburg leafed through the file. 'You think you vetted them properly?'

'I followed the standard requirements for medium- and low-threat sites.'

'It's clear to me that those requirements did not anticipate a vehicular bomb attack.'

'If I'd anticipated it I might have been able to do something about it!'

She paused, trying not to bristle at his insinuation.

'I implemented the security requirements to the maximum extent feasible. I applied risk management as I was taught – looking into the backgrounds of everyone, from gardeners to mechanics to . . . just about everyone.'

She realised she was floundering. She felt guilty. She didn't understand why she felt like this. She glanced at Queller, who gave her a slightly grim smile of encouragement. He lifted his stump off the table and rubbed it with his good hand.

'Let's play a little game,' Queller said. 'Let's try to put together an identikit of the guy you saw in the truck. Break up his face and tell us about each element in turn.'

She closed her eyes and tried to do as he said. 'He had a small, thin nose. His eyes . . . they were kind of brown, I think. The mouth – well, the moustache as I said. Like, a pencil moustache.'

'What do you mean?'

'Like, er, straight and black. Not much of it.'

Altenburg turned impatiently to Queller. 'This isn't getting us anywhere.'

Queller rubbed his stump again.

Altenburg addressed himself to Miranda. 'I still don't understand why you didn't check the truck.'

'I wouldn't normally have done so,' she said, with some agitation. 'I wouldn't have been out there if it had arrived at another time.'

'You don't think it was strange that he was sitting right behind the other truck. It seems to me things could have been much worse, that they planned to drive in behind a truck that was coming in much deeper – into the compound proper.'

'I didn't think it was odd, no. Lots of trucks come in. As I said, the reason I thought the truck was bringing in supplies for the construction workers was that the man's face seemed familiar.'

'Really?' Altenburg said. 'And yet you can't remember it?'

'I only saw it for a few seconds.'

Altenburg leant back in his chair and put his arms behind his head.

'What would you say if I said you failed in your duty by not checking that truck? You don't feel any responsibility in that direction?'

'None whatsoever,' Miranda replied, aggressively. 'It isn't my job to check vehicles. That's a crazy idea!'

Inside, even as she spoke, she was not so sure. Should she have checked? Was she to blame? Would Mrs Ghai, George the cleaner, the gardener – would they all still be here if she had?

'I think we are putting the wrong complexion on things here,' Queller said, addressing Altenburg. 'We're not here to apportion blame. We're here to find the perpetrators.'

She spat the words. 'Is that what people are saying? That this is my fault?'

Altenburg closed her file. 'That will be all for now. Don't leave town though.'

'That's enough,' Queller said. 'Jesus Christ, Mort . . .'

And then, more gently: 'Miranda, these are just general questions of the kind we are putting to everyone. You are not under suspicion of anything.'

'Well –' said Altenburg, coolly, '– no more than anyone else.'

Miranda stood up, looking at Queller as she did so. Angry with Altenburg first and foremost, she was also angry with him, for not supporting her more. She summoned up as much dignity as she could muster.

'One friend of mine was killed in that blast,' she said, thinking of Mrs Ghai. 'Another was badly injured. I will not be held responsible for these things. I take great exception to the way in which I have been questioned.'

With that she left the room, ignoring the agent at the door and the next person waiting for questioning on the other side, who was Clive Bayard. He gave her a surprised look.

She ran in tears out of the building to the hire car. She didn't stop crying all the way to Oyster Bay, her sobbing drowning out the noise of the tyres as they hummed along on the hot tarmac, her body hunched over the wheel as she drove.

Back in the interview room, once they had concluded the rest of the day's investigations, Queller turned on Altenburg.

'What the hell did you think you were playing at with the Powers girl? You surely don't think she can be blamed for this?'

'I have my reasons.'

'Her role's only administrative security. The truck would've been checked by the Marines at the second wall.'

'As I say, I have my reasons.'

'Which are?'

Altenburg sniffed, then gave him a hard look. 'I wanted to press her a little. I'm going to have a full audit done on her.'

'I think you'll be wasting your time.'

Altenburg ignored him. 'I've got work to do, if you don't mind, Jack. I want to run through what's left of the chancery CCTV footage.'

They did a little shuffle at the door as both tried to leave at the same time.

Late the following afternoon, Miranda was called back for further questioning by the two men. During the day she had worked herself up into a rage, furious that her competence had been called into question. She was determined to meet their questions head-on.

Queller looked up and smiled encouragingly as she entered. Altenburg had a video-media program running on the computer in his room – software that allowed him to modulate digitally converted images from the ordinary video player that was wired up next to it. He was in shirtsleeves, his jacket on the back of the chair. On the desk, next to his bare, brown-haired arms, Miranda recognised a pile of tapes of the type used in the embassy's CCTV cameras. It looked as if he had been going through them and downloading whatever he needed onto the computer.

'Miss Powers,' he said, 'we have been going through footage of all contacts made by embassy staff in the months preceding the blast. Much of it has been destroyed, but I would like you to comment on two small portions of the visual record.'

He clicked an icon on the screen and a moving image came up in a box. It showed Miranda in the car pool, talking to a man in a T-shirt. Queller bent forward to look at it, leaning on the desk with his stump again.

'Who's this guy then?' asked Altenburg, silkily, clicking on pause to freeze the screen.

To the surprise of both men, Miranda burst out laughing, throwing back her head.

'You don't think . . .? That's great, that's priceless. He's a US citizen.'

'Your boyfriend?' asked Queller, in a hopeful tone.

'Well – I guess you'd call it a fling.'

'What's his name?' asked Altenburg.

'Nick Karolides. He works on a USAID project on Zanzibar. We just kind of met.'

Altenburg signalled to the agent at the door, who went out to check Nick's name on one of the bigger computers that had been set up in some rooms nearby. Having been brought in on the FEST flight, they were now connected directly to a range of US government databanks. There was a brief silence in the room while the three of them waited for the agent's return. Eventually, Altenburg spoke up again.

'When did you first meet him?'

She pointed to the screen. 'Right then. Well, a few hours before. On the beach. He was over here to collect some stuff from back home. We just got talking. Then I went over to Zanzibar to see him.'

'Tell us what happened.'

She hesitated. 'On Zanzibar?'

'On Zanzibar.'

Miranda sighed and gave Queller an imploring look.

'Well?' Altenburg said.

'We toured. We took a boat trip.'

She waited for him to reply, but Altenburg just slid his mouse round on the desk, pointing the cursor at Nick's face.

'Are you asking if we slept together? Are you going to haul me up for that too?'

Queller smiled thinly, as if he enjoyed seeing Altenburg get a run for his money.

'I took a long weekend –' Miranda explained, in a more reasonable tone, '– went over to the island for a few days and met up with him there. When I came back, I decided it wasn't going anywhere. So what? I got clearance. The trip's logged in the day files. Did they survive?'

'Rather to my surprise,' said Altenburg, 'they did.'

'The MSG put them in a fireproof safe, right?'

Altenburg nodded. The agent came back in and passed him a printout. He took off his glasses and read it.

'Well?' enquired Queller.

'I guess he's legit,' replied Altenburg. He sounded vaguely

281

disappointed. 'Now, there's another tape I would like you to look at.'

Miranda tossed her hair.

'I'm just doing my job,' Altenburg responded primly, as he cued up the new tape.

He pressed the 'PLAY' icon, and they waited for another image to appear as the computer counted up the bytes. When it did, what the screen showed was a man with light-brown hair standing opposite one of the gateways to the embassy: the one where the water tanker and the bomb truck had come in. Juma's post. The man was wearing a baseball cap with the words 'SPORT TEAM OSNABRÜCK' on it. Most of his face, which was brown-skinned, was obscured by the video camera he was holding up. The image only lasted a few seconds, before a bus passed and he was gone.

'Do you know anything about this guy?' asked Altenburg, rewinding and playing the stream again.

'I remember the incident. One of the security guards alerted me to it and I came down. But the man had gone. I made an incident report in the day book.'

Altenburg removed a piece of paper from her file. 'Yes, I've dug that out, as I said. Your report in the day book. In which you recommend no action be taken. Why was that?'

'There was not much we could do. He was gone. He told the guard he was a tourist.'

'Indeed. That is what it says. Now, of course, it looks different. It looks like he was conducting surveillance of a target.'

'You don't know that for sure.'

'But am I not right in thinking that DS regulations state that in all cases of surveillance of a diplomatic institution, Washington should immediately be notified?'

Miranda hesitated. 'I . . . believe that is correct – but I didn't think it was surveillance!'

She looked at Queller. His face betrayed not the slightest emotion.

'I'm telling the truth,' she said.

Altenburg put his hands together and stared at her across the desk. She could see, in his hard blue eyes, the scepticism invited by her assertion.

Eventually he spoke. 'I'll be frank with you. This does not leave you in a good place. I will be putting in my report that you were possibly negligent in your duties in not checking the truck. I have already recommended to DS your suspension from post until the matter has been gone into further.'

'You're shitting me,' said Miranda, feeling something waste inside her.

'I most certainly am not,' said Altenburg.

It was then he dropped his bombshell. 'In fact, my recommendation has been accepted. The suspension comes into effect immediately.'

Miranda could hardly draw breath. It was all so sudden. She felt a hot rush of blood to her face, and tears come to her eyes.

'This is very precipitate,' said Queller, shaking his head. 'Surely any disciplinary matter should wait till after the investigation?'

'Let me remind you who is chief investigating officer here,' Altenburg said, standing up. 'Your role is only advisory.'

He picked up his jacket off the back of the chair and folded it fastidiously over his arm.

'I suggest you return home, Miss Powers, and wait to hear from us. And now, if you will excuse me, I have to go.'

As Altenburg closed the door, Queller went over to comfort her, lightly placing his hand on her heaving shoulder.

'Look, I swear I had no idea he was going to spring that on you.'

She shook her head several times from side to side.

'Come on,' said Queller. 'It'll sort itself out.'

'Can't you do anything?' she said, chokily.

'Do you want me to drive you home?'

'I can drive myself.'

'I'll drive,' Queller insisted. 'You're too upset. Leave your vehicle here.'

Acquiescing, she went out down to the lobby with him, passing other embassy staff waiting for interview. Some of them, recently released from hospital, were bandaged. Miranda avoided their eyes, feeling the stain of guilt that Altenburg had laid upon her.

It was dusk. They found the jeep Queller had been supplied with on arrival. He drove out of the city and, following Miranda's muttered instructions, east along the coast road to Oyster Bay. The vehicle was an automatic, and he had already attached the stainless-steel bulb to the steering wheel, which allowed him to drive more easily with one hand.

The flame trees that grew around Miranda's bungalow were glowing a deep orange in the dying sun.

'Beep the horn,' she muttered, when they pulled up outside the gates.

He did so, and the old nightwatchman, dressed in ragged khaki and carrying a staff, emerged from his booth and let them in. Hands shaking, Miranda found her keys and opened the door. She went straight over to the sofa and lay down on it, clutching a cushion to her chest like a child.

'Got anything to drink?' asked Queller.

She nodded at a corner cupboard. He took out a bottle of bourbon and two shot glasses.

'Don't worry about this,' he said, handing her a glass. 'I'll fix it. Where's your phone?'

'Bedroom. Bedside table.'

He went through and sat on the unmade bed. There were bits and pieces of feminine underwear and other clothing strewn about. He felt like a voyeur. The room smelt sweet, and as he dialled – holding the handset under his stump – his eyes scanned the dressing table under the window. The usual crowd of perfume phials and make-up stuff. Also – by the bed – a little shell of some kind, rather beautiful. He could hear the muzz and gap of the long-distance line, then a beep: 'Department of State. How can I help you?'

In the lounge, staring numbly at the wall, Miranda listened to Queller's half of the conversation.

'Put me through to the Secretary. Clearance 78034 JQ.'

'Maddy? Jack Queller here.'

'Dar. Pretty grim, but not so rough as the other place. It's a big job, as you know. We'll get them though, eventually . . . I'm just hearing statements. Listen, you know that FBI guy I mentioned to you when I agreed to come out on this? Well, I've run into a problem with him already . . .'

Miranda listened as he explained what had happened. Her ears were still hurting from the blast.

'He's gone way overboard on this, and had the poor girl suspended. I'm convinced she's clean.'

'You can take my word for it.'

She felt a rush of gratitude, but wondered how, as an intelligence pro, he could be so adamant. Why should they believe him, anyway?

'I know you won't want to intervene in an ongoing operation, but can you do me a favour? Her name's Miranda Powers, she's a junior in Diplomatic Security.'

'That's right. P-O-W-E-R-S.'

'No, you don't have to overrule Altenburg directly. The disciplinary aspect will run its own course. There is no case for her to answer. In the meantime, I want her reassigned to me as a local adviser. I know it's non-procedural but –'

There was a long pause during which Miranda imagined the distinguished other party speaking from her Washington office, raising objections and qualifications.

Finally Queller spoke again.

'Thanks, Maddy. I won't let you down on this.'

'Yeah, me too.'

After telling Miranda his plans for her, Queller insisted she ate some sandwiches, going to the refrigerator and making them himself. They drank more bourbon, it got late, and then she didn't want him to leave, so he agreed to sleep on the couch, making her laugh through her tears when he said it wouldn't be so cramped for him as he only had one arm. She went through to her bedroom, got undressed, and into the sheets. As she sank into sleep, she wondered what it would mean, exactly, to be his local adviser. She would ask him in the morning.

When she woke up, hung-over, he was gone. Wandering into the kitchen in her white towelling robe, a thousand thoughts rushed through her head, varying and shifting like a mist. Unsteady, she made herself some coffee and went through to run a bath.

Usually she took brisk showers, but that was in the time before: the time when her integrity and professionalism were intact and she believed herself worthy. The bath was a refuge, and right now that was what she needed.

Her face in the mirror had a sickly, greenish hue, and was still covered in numerous small scabs from the glass. The marks were like tiny zippers, the crust breaking at regular intervals as the skin underneath healed. She shuddered. Some people had suffered terrible scorching burns that would mark them for life. How could it be her fault?

Lying in the tub, head pounding, her thoughts continued to turn. The interview session replayed itself, flashes of memory veering, backing, cannoning into each other. Then Queller's fixing that she work for him directly. At least this was some kind of solution; at least it meant she wouldn't be mooching around until the hearing.

Steam rose about her, clouding the window. Beyond the glass, in the thick bush they loved and sometimes descended upon in their hundreds, the quelea birds were singing. The flowers on the bush made her think of Zanzibar and the Macpherson gardens . . . Nick Karolides.

She slipped under the water, closing her eyes against the enamelled brightness, her scratched skin stinging. Should she call him? He must have heard about the bombs. Was it fair to expect him to have tried to call her, considering how she'd effectively brushed him off on her return to Dar?

She came up for air, then stood up and soaped her legs. She liked the idea, heard somewhere or other, of distributed memory: the body remembering, every piece of it thrilling with information deeper and more primitive than conscious thought. And what it said was this: Nick's strong hands moving over her. She imagined him swimming through the water, or simply floating, the wave motion lapping him.

And now she was down in the water again herself, filled with melancholy and longing. Her feet were up on the taps, her little toes curling. The sponge danced gently, an island on her stomach.

24

Over the course of the next two days, in a stuffy room at the Kilimanjaro Hotel, Miranda worked with Jack Queller. Computers and secure phone lines had been installed. Everything was on a direct satellite uplink to Washington. The job was to process. To sift and analyse. Data was beginning to come in from the bomb sites, as the FBI gathered fragments of physical evidence, analysed photographs, and interviewed witnesses. Traces of ammonium nitrate and TNT were found at Nairobi on analysis of cotton swabs taken at the blast site.

'That is the primary blasting agent in many home-made bombs,' Queller told her on their first morning together. 'The next thing will be to find evidence of the detonators, which can range from anything like Casio watches with nine-volt batteries to mercury tilts and complex electronic timing devices. Usually blasting caps and detonation cord are used. It's like a rope, det cord, made of another explosive that ignites easy. About ten centimetres of det cord is good to ignite five kilos of TNT. Or one blasting cap for the same amount.'

In Dar, the men in the Tyvek suits had also found remnants of TNT. There had been some arrests. Fourteen foreigners had been picked up by the Tanzanian police and turned over to the FBI for interrogation: six Iraqis and the same number of Sudanese, plus one Turk and one Somali. Queller said he thought these men would turn out to be innocent.

'There's always a kind of panic after something like this. A need to pin down likely culprits.'

'I had noticed that,' she said, and Queller laughed.

Miranda started going through massive caches of data under his instruction, applying various filters and keyword searches. It was all SIGINT, or signals intelligence, that had been sent over that morning. The National Security Agency had scoured its digital and other records of recent global communication, using satellites, ocean cable taps, electromagnetic listening devices and direct feeds from Internet servers. Expert cryptological linguists had been going over hundreds of hours of phone calls, radio transmissions and emails, in particular from the main terrorist 'host nations', including Libya, Lebanon, Sudan and Afghanistan.

The room smelt of old fabrics, the traffickings of life. She imagined businessmen coming and going. Deals done, exchanges made. She stared at the screen. She felt disconnected. Not the same person as she had been before. There had been a loss of continuity. Everything seemed fragmented, speculative, unstable. There was a weird sort of incongruence about her: today's and yesterday's self asking each other, *Who are you?* Raw emotion was the only corrective to this feeling that nothing seemed to have any foundation any more. Now and then, waves of cold anger swept over her as she thought about her suspension. Then she would put herself straight and try to think rationally about what had happened. About victims. About perpetrators.

At least two terrorists had been killed in the Nairobi blast, it was thought. Their bodies had been partially recovered. The rescue operation was still continuing, but hopes of finding anyone left alive under the rubble were fading fast. Rescuers had been pumping oxygen into collapsed areas. They had been working like maniacs, but were becoming despondent about the chances of anyone having survived. Sniffer dogs, heavy-duty balloons, pneumatic jacks, and cutters capable of slicing through cement and iron had all been employed. But again, it didn't seem likely now that they could do any good.

Queller was certain it was the group led by Osama bin Laden that was behind the bombs. But he still hadn't been able to persuade Altenburg of this. Miranda remembered Queller talking about bin Laden back in Washington all those months ago.

'Why wasn't something done, if you knew he was such a threat even back then?'

'I knew. As I said, others were not convinced. They still aren't.'

He told her that SIGINT had picked up several potential threats to US diplomatic installations in the meantime, but that the intelligence machine had not acted on them.

'Why on earth not?' she asked, experiencing again that strange sense of disjunction. She had a feeling that whatever came out of the rubble of the bombs, it would not be clarity.

Queller's answer confirmed her suspicions.

'Traffic work is like netting chaos. There are hundreds of thousands of interceptions every day. You've got to think of the size of the NSA's collection system versus the amount of information in the world. Even at high speed – chomping through billions of bits a second – it is never going to cope. You can't have total awareness, so you have to put in filters. Then you miss stuff because the filters might be too specific. Very few inputs of information meet the criteria for forwarding to analysis.'

Miranda looked at the one-armed man, and felt a sense of awe about the hidden world he was describing. A world that was a sort of deepening gulf, a place where information was endlessly proliferating, resistant to explication or validation.

'And then, when we do get a hit, we can't be sure it's not degraded intelligence. High-level targets very often know we're on to them. I've been monitoring bin Laden data for years and I've learned that he just likes to taunt and provoke. He even gave an interview on CNN – less than a year ago. There was even one in *Reader's Digest*.'

'Does he think he won't be caught, going on TV or speaking to people like that?'

'He thinks Allah is protecting him.'

'So he's kind of open about his plans?'

'He uses a portable satellite phone, like those used by ships or explorers. Yes, he chats away. But he is open about particular operations only in the most rhetorical way.'

'I don't understand.'

'This might give you an idea,' Queller said. He dug around for a piece of paper. 'British MI6 sent this through yesterday. "To kill Americans and their allies, both civil and military, is an individual duty of every Muslim who is able, in any country where this is possible, until the *kufr* armies, shattered and broken winged, depart from all the lands of Islam." That was sent to a London Arab paper in February. *Kufr* means unbeliever. It is a reference to our forces in Saudi Arabia.'

'So where is bin Laden now?' she asked, lifting her hand to touch one of the healing scratches on her face.

'Still in Afghanistan, I guess. We have a satellite that passes over one of his camps there. But it's hard to tell where exactly. Probably some other hideout in the mountains. Or in Yemen, where his family are originally from. Or somewhere in Kashmir, hoping things will flare up between India and Pakistan. He can't go back to Saudi – he grew up there – they've expelled him and withdrawn his passport. He had operations in Sudan at one point. And sleeper cells all over the world, from which he can draw support if need be.'

They took a break for coffee. She went out into the car park to ring Nick on her mobile, but she could get no sense from the manager at the hotel on Zanzibar, who just kept saying he was not there and that he didn't know where he was. He said he thought he had perhaps gone back to Lyly. Or was on a visit to the USAID headquarters in Nairobi.

Worried, Miranda walked back to the lobby of the Kili. She had been missing Nick more since the bomb, and was surprised he hadn't called; he *must* have heard about it. Again she wondered if it was too much to expect him to have tried to get in contact with her. Her heart grasped at the possibility that it was simply that the phones were inoperative. The idea that he might have got caught in the blast in Nairobi was too horrible to contemplate; his name wasn't on the list of American dead, anyway.

She was surprised how powerful the need for him was, considering how lukewarm she'd become at the end of their time together on the island. She found herself wondering whether it was anything special about him that was drawing her to him now, or simply the bomb's levelling circumstances – its effect of making one want to preserve every emotional connection, however slight.

Some news came through just after she got back to Queller's office. A group calling itself the 'Liberation Army of the Islamic Sanctuaries' had claimed responsibility for the killings, in statements faxed to Radio France International and the Cairo bureau of Agence France Press.

'*Jaysh Tahrir al-Muqaddasat al-Islamiyyah,*' said Queller, enunciating the group's name in Arabic. 'That isn't one of the usual al-Qaida pseudonyms, but the pattern is the same. Bin Laden has always been calling for US forces to leave Saudi Arabia because he believes they tarnish the holy places. Mecca and Medina. In previous despatches he's said he would pursue US forces and strike at US interests everywhere until that demand was satisfied.'

'How would that help him, if he's in Afghanistan and been expelled by the Saudis, like you say?'

'I think the strategy would be that if he could throw the US military out of Saudi and the whole Gulf, he'd be able to establish an extremist Islamic government there, and hold the West to ransom by restricting the supply of oil.'

Miranda went and checked again that Nick's name wasn't on any of the casualty lists, either at Nairobi or Dar: what if he had been coming to see her? He wasn't – all US citizens at the two sites had been accounted for. But where was he then?

During the afternoon, the Nairobi investigators had two lucky breaks. The first came just as Queller and Miranda were coming back from lunch. One of the men picked up by the Kenyans had been identified in a police line-up as the terrorist who had jumped out of a pickup and thrown a grenade at guards minutes before the Nairobi truck drove towards the embassy gates. Later, information came through from Karachi that Pakistani immigration officials had picked up another man coming off a flight from Nairobi. He had been travelling on a false Yemeni passport, and had tried to bribe the officials when they spotted it.

The breakthrough in the Dar investigation didn't come till the following morning. Another security camera on the roof of the building had been found intact. Altenburg, who had already been through the images, sent them across to Queller with a scribbled note:

> I suppose you had better let that girl watch this, since she is on it. It covers the fifteen minutes before the explosion. See if it prompts anything. Jack, I hear that you have had her attached to you as an assistant. That is against protocol, and a matter I will take up once this investigation is concluded.

It took a while for the right software to be loaded. A technician had to be called. As with the two previous tapes, the recording had been downloaded onto a computer file that enabled its image to be modulated more easily, and Queller's computer didn't have the right application. Once it was installed, they were able to watch the whole thing: Miranda walking across to the water tanker, the second truck approaching, the detonation

293

itself. After that, the screen went blank. It sent a chill through her to see it all recorded in this way, but what worried her most was something else, something niggling at her mind that she couldn't identify.

'We're lucky to get this,' Queller said. 'All the Nairobi tapes were destroyed and most of the ones at Dar were only on real time – just whirring away for the guards to look at – rather than recording.'

'Can you show it again?' Miranda asked, frowning.

Queller streamed the video a second time.

'Can we zero in on the face of the driver?'

He pressed the pause button, then fiddled with the controls. The frozen spectacle enlarged, losing definition as he altered the settings.

'Damn thing,' Queller said.

Moving his hand swiftly between keyboard and mouse, he zoomed out, moved the cursor up, then zoomed in again. Finally the image she wanted came up full-screen. There, indistinct through the windscreen of the truck that had pulled up behind the tanker, was the face she had glimpsed a few minutes before the explosion – and, through a telephoto lens, a fortnight previously. She was realising why the face seemed familiar. It was one of the men she'd seen on the white cabin cruiser on the way back from Lyly. The man whose picture she had so nearly taken. The man with the pencil moustache.

25

'What is the purpose of your visit?'

The official in the ill-fitting blue uniform examined her passport photograph extremely carefully, as if he expected to find another underneath. Security had been stepped up everywhere in the wake of the bombings.

'Vacation.'

A lie, but under the circumstances, easier than having to explain. To explain how she and Jack Queller had matched the image of the truck driver with a file photograph of a known bin Laden associate: Yousef Mourad, a Syrian bombmaker. Or how Queller had sent her to Zanzibar to check out the Arabs who had been on the boat. Or how she had rung Nick numerous times to tell him she was coming, but had got no reply.

The man looked at her from behind black-rimmed glasses. 'Which hotel are you staying at?'

'Oh. I'm staying with a friend. Nick Karolides. He works here – on the coral-reef project.'

The official nodded, as if it were perfectly obvious, and reached for his stamp.

Walking out into the car park, Miranda looked around for Nick's motorbike, even though she knew it was foolish to hope. A row of minibus taxis tooted their horns. She accepted the blandishments of the first driver who caught her eye.

'My name is Rashidi,' he told her, with a wide grin. 'Your destination please?'

'Can you take me to the Macpherson Ruins Hotel?'

'Twende!' he shouted, and started the engine.

'What's that?'

'Let's go! Is Swahili, mama.'

She fidgeted during the journey, as the driver avoided potholes and cyclists. All the things she had seen before – the cloistered streets of Stone Town, the women in veils with copper pots or bundles of faggots on their heads, the endless rows of palms and flashes of blue ocean – they just got in the way now, pressing on her attention. She wanted answers, fast. Where was Nick? The anxiety was now cutting into her deeply.

Miranda soon got some answers, but not the ones she wanted – standing in the dark foyer of the hotel talking to the Indian manager, with his white suit and sleek black hair.

Yes, he remembered her. And yes, he too had been wondering what had happened to Nick.

'Because you see, madam, he is owing me for his room, and his belongings are still there. It is you who has been telephoning?'

'Yes. When did you last see him?'

'Over a week ago, madam. The English gentleman, Mr Leggatt – I think you met him, yes?'

Miranda nodded impatiently.

'Well, he came here in his boat, and they went off. And that was the last I saw of them. I thought they had gone to Lyly, and then taken a longer cruise. But now I am beginning to be anxious. I am beginning to think that it is happening again.'

'What?'

'We had an accident here before, madam. With Mr Nick's predecessor. Didn't you know?'

'No. What happened?'

The Indian's face took on a pained expression. 'He drowned, madam.'

Miranda shook her head, as if to rid herself of the thought. 'Have you spoken to anyone? People at the docks? Leggatt's house?'

'No, madam. You see, Mr Nick was often away for periods. With his work. He recently went to Lyly, as I said, our small island over there.'

He pointed in the direction of the sea.

'Yes, I know. I went there. You didn't think to send a boat to Lyly?'

He hesitated, then raised his hands. 'As I say, madam, Mr Nick is often away.'

She wondered what to do. It occurred to her she might visit the policeman Nick had once mentioned. She couldn't remember his name. But the best thing would be to go find Leggatt. If anyone knew where Nick was, it would be him.

'Would you like some refreshment? A cup of tea? A glass of soda?'

The manager looked at her hopefully, as if the forms of service might resolve their problem.

'I want you to check me in,' she said. 'I'm going to go to Mr Leggatt's now to make inquiries.'

She showed him her passport and filled in the check-in form. Then they went outside, the sun straining her eyes as they emerged from under the thatched eaves into the sandy car park. The manager gave the taxi driver directions to Leggatt's farm.

The journey took about three quarters of an hour. It had seemed less on Nick's motorbike. As they arrived, a dog ran out. It started barking at the matatu – snapping at the tyres as they drew up in front of the house with its tin roof, and its lawn running down to the sea. She saw the wooden jetty where she had stood in the dark after the trip to Lyly. Behind the house, through the taxi's window, she could see rows of sheds and, stretching up as far as the eye could see on hills above, the green terraces of clove plantations. It seemed a far more welcoming place than when she had last come, in the rainstorm.

She wound down her window. The dog was standing nearby, growling. Rashidi switched off the engine and turned back to her.

'Danger from this beast,' he said, with great seriousness, though he was still grinning.

She ignored him and got out of the vehicle. Continuing to growl, the dog lowered its head and looked up at her – but there was something more tentative about the noise it was making now. She felt confident it wouldn't bite. She swung her bag at it, and it slunk off away. It was the rolling tyres that did it, she thought, that had excited the animal's curiosity. Poor Ray had said the same of the little white bobbysox on the antelopes they had seen at the game park: the flicking, the instinctual binary code of these white anklets, is what triggers the lion or cheetah to pursue, he had told her. She thought of him lying in hospital, with his bandaged, shattered knees. Then of Mrs Ghai and the others who had died. She wanted to find the people who had done this.

She noted that the *Winston Churchill* wasn't in the bay, nor was there any activity in the clove-drying barns. She approached the bungalow and banged on the porch door. There was no piano music this time. The door was locked and the whole place seemed deserted. She was just about to leave when a small black figure appeared from the direction of the dilapidated drying sheds.

'Could you tell me where . . .?' she began loudly, then realising he couldn't hear her, walked quickly towards him.

She recognised the boy. It was the one who had been on the sloop with them the day they went to Lyly. Sayeed.

Already he was shaking his head rapidly. He seemed a bit startled and frightened to see her. The only information she could get from him corresponded with that supplied by the manager at the Macpherson.

'Bwana and the young bwana went away in the big boat. I have been waiting!'

'It's all right,' she said. 'You're not in trouble.' She reached out and touched his shoulder.

The boy smiled at her shyly and poked a finger through one of the holes in his ragged T-shirt. 'They shifted to the place we were before. Lyly.'

She considered him for a moment, assessing his usefulness. 'Would you be able to get another boat and take me there?'

The boy made a helpless gesture with his hands. There was a silence, during which he looked to one side, showing the whites of his eyes. Finally comprehending, Miranda reached into her bag and took out a billfold. She peeled off a hundred dollars in low denominations and handed them over. They instantly disappeared into his grubby shorts.

'You come to the hotel at Macpherson Ruins tomorrow morning, early, and we go to the island. Yes? You understand?'

The boy nodded.

'I give you some more money when we return. OK?'

He nodded again. 'Yes. I take you.'

She returned to the Macpherson. After paying the taxi driver, she went to the lobby to ask the manager for her room key. He wasn't there. She rang the bell. As she was waiting, it struck her that she might as well ask to stay in Nick's room. It wasn't a question of not paying for two – more that she might gain some clue as to what had happened. Maybe he had left a note or something.

Hesitating at first, the manager finally assented to her request.

'As you are . . . his friend,' he said, haltingly.

The admission of her intimacy with Nick clearly didn't fall into his usual professional patter, and he seemed almost relieved to turn and fetch the key off the rack behind him. Nick must have left it before he went, she thought. At least that meant he was planning to return.

They walked across the lawn to the chalet. Once the manager

had opened the door, Miranda stepped inside. It was gloomy, and the Indian walked over to draw the curtains.

Evening sunlight, corn gold, streamed into the room. Miranda saw that there were some lumps of driftwood on the windowsill, and a pile of shells, including a large conch. The walls were hung with sponges. There must have been at least twenty of them.

'Mr Nick, he collected those things,' the manager explained, seeing her look. 'So . . . I will leave you. Please lock the room if you go outside. We have been suffering the problem of burglary.'

She looked round the room. The bed was made, but otherwise the place looked as if Nick had just popped out for a minute: clothes thrown on the back of the chair, some of his scuba equipment piled up in a corner. She went over to a calendar on the wall, to see if anything was written on it. She lifted the pages. Nothing. Just pictures of Gettysburg, Graceland, New Orleans's Jackson Square – a picture of Andrew Jackson's statue and street revellers. Beside the photograph was a caption: 'From Civil War to Mardi Gras – on both sides of the platform of this statue of Andrew Jackson are written the words "THE UNION, IT MUST BE PRESERVED."'

On the desk, Nick's laptop was open, in front of a line of marine biology textbooks propped against the wall. She turned it on, looking through a few documents. But they all related to his work. Her eye fell on a postcard of Drew Barrymore. She turned it over. It was from someone called Dino in Florida, whom she vaguely recalled Nick mentioning. The postcard mentioned scuba equipment. It also said, 'Your ma is improving – I might even take her out! Anything to keep that Torrance guy away from her.' It gave no clue as to where Nick might have gone.

She went into the bathroom, took in what was there. A tube of toothpaste, the cap off, a little pink worm of the stuff on the porcelain. A pair of nail clippers, slightly rusted. His shaving kit was also on the sink. She reached out and touched the soap-stiff brush, imagining his warm cheek against hers.

She studied herself in the mirror. She looked exhausted. Her hair flopped lifelessly about her ears and neck. There were dark circles under her eyes, and deep crease-lines either side of her nose. The last week had taken more out of her than anything in her life since the loss of her father. Nothing, she reflected – certainly not her training, which seemed like a joke now – could have prepared her for it.

She went back into the bedroom. After hefting her suitcase onto the bed, she stripped off to her bra and underpants, thinking she might take a shower before unpacking.

But first she went over and looked out of the window. It was covered in mosquito grille, yet she could still see the white expanse of the beach and the ocean's shimmering stripe of green, swelling and flashing in the low sun. Also, but indistinctly, she could make out the black bodies of a group of boys, glistening as they splashed about in the surf. Through the mesh, and the sea's background noise, she listened to their cries and laughing voices.

Her hand found the conch on the wooden sill. She picked it up and examined it. The opening was as pink as the toothpaste. She lifted it to her lips and blew – the sound that came out was so low and mournful that it made her feel uneasy.

She put it down and went over to the desk. Leaning on it, face to face with Drew Barrymore. *Ever After*. There must be some clue in the room. She looked at the line of books. The spine of one was different, older. She reached and picked it out – a heavy green ledger, stained and swollen from contact with water. It was his journal.

She traced her finger under his handwriting, neat and blue except where water had made it run. The last entry was some time ago, and it mentioned her.

July 20. Lyly with L. and M. Usual (fishwise anyhow!) except for snake of course. Mamba, L. said. Think M. was quite impressed . . . She's marvellous.

She smiled at this, but already the tears were starting to prick, and the questions. Where was he? Was this how he felt? She wondered if she herself could ever have anything like the same depth of feeling. Her stomach twisted. Now she was here, seeing his words, she felt close to him again. It was strange, because she'd thought he was almost as hesitant as her before, and now she felt her heart losing its own hesitancy as she became aware of his true feelings.

She has a great laugh. Laughing and her hair blowing in the wind as we walk along the beach. In love? Think, hope, God knows.

Moved, intrigued, leaning over the table in her underwear, Miranda flicked back through the pages – back through the days and the weeks, back to their first meeting at the embassy, and the account of his earlier trip to Lyly. These were the images she took to bed with her, once she'd taken a shower: Nick stomping about the island looking for the cave mouth, or lying in the cottage watching the lighthouse beam fan across the sea.

So it wasn't surprising, when she and Sayeed arrived at Lyly the following morning – when they searched the cottage and the beach, and the boy came running, saying there was a body, there was a body washed up on the shore, and it was *muzungu*, white – that she was convinced it was Nick.

She turned the body over and cried out in horror. The face was half eaten away by maggots, and the upturned eyes gleamed with a dull, grey sheen. One ear was missing.

26

'His name is Leggatt. He was washed up on the beach.'

'So what are you telling me?' Mort Altenburg replied, leaning across the desk in his office at the Kili. 'That she's found the body of some old English guy with his ear cut off and this has something to do with the case? I can't see what. It's probably just a routine murder, a robbery gone wrong. What about the boyfriend?'

'Nothing yet,' Queller said, relating what Miranda had told him in an anguished phone call from Zanzibar. 'She's still looking. But this is all part of it, I'm sure. I know we've had our differences, Mort, but I'm certain she's on to something. They saw some Arabs heading out there a few weeks ago. I think one of them's this guy.'

He passed Altenburg a photograph across the desk.

'Yousef Mourad. It's from our files. He's the same one who was on the security video. In the truck. She thinks she saw him on a motor boat heading for the island earlier.'

'I grant you he looks a bit like the one on the tape,' Altenburg conceded. 'And yes, given what we've got from the guy picked up in Karachi, I'm beginning to come round to the idea this might be a bin Laden operation.'

He took off his spectacles and rubbed his eyes. 'But the Zanzibar side of it's just speculation. It's not certain he was the man on the boat.'

Queller set his face. 'Well, I'm going to check it out.'

'Wonderful. You do that. I can't wait to put in my report how Jack Queller, the great terrorist hunter, wasted his time after the bombings kicking around the beaches of Zanzibar. Meanwhile American citizens are arriving back home in body bags. To be met with honours by the First Lady and the President and their grieving relatives. It's on CNN, Jack.'

Queller didn't need telling. The rolling-news station had been showing the same pictures all day: the Presidential couple and the families of the bomb victims waiting expectantly on the tarmac at Andrews Air Force base, outside Washington. Queller had watched it twice already in his room. The camera zooming in. The President silent, tears running down his cheek as the honour guards unload the flag-draped caskets. As a military band plays 'Nearer My God to Thee', the names of the dead are announced in sombre tones. To Queller's mind, the repetition diminished the pathos. Broadcast so many times, the event became almost unreal.

'– not to mention,' Altenburg was saying, 'the 220-plus non-Americans who've died. What are you going to say to them, Jack, when you get back from the beach? That you're the guy who trained bin Laden? I'm sure they'd really like to hear that.'

'If you hadn't pulled my operation we might have stopped this. I gave you fair warning.'

'The threat scenarios you prepared were flawed. As for the other thing, you're lucky you weren't put on a charge.'

Queller gathered up the photograph from the polished wood, scrabbling at it with his hand. Without saying anything further, he turned and left the room. Breathing heavily, he walked down the stairs to the Kili bar. He needed a drink. His stump hurt.

As he crossed the lobby, which was busy with guests arriving and departing, something odd happened. A young, pale-faced woman in orange robes approached him, carrying a bunch of carnations. Without saying anything, she held one out to him. Frowning, he shook his head. She smiled beatifically and approached another man, the father of a family of tourists – just arrived from England, by the sound of the children's babbling voices. This man, too, waved her away, whereupon the hotel's manager emerged from behind the desk and escorted her outside. Shaking his head, Queller went through to order his drink.

He sat in the bar with a whisky, looking out of the window and trying not to think about what Altenburg had said. The sight of the relatives on TV – one young girl sobbing loudly as the pall-bearers passed by – had sent a thick black jet of guilt coursing through his veins.

He stared out over the Kili car park. It was dusk. There was a strange vehicle there, kind of a long jeep, painted coffee-brown, with a raised dais. Two men dressed in khaki fatigues were clambering into the back. Whites. One was carrying a rifle case. It was a modern version of a shooting trap, Queller realised, a converted long-wheelbase Land Rover with the top cut off. The men looked sleek. Perfect male specimens. He himself had been like that once. He watched as a Tanzanian driver ran across the car park and, after an obsequious performance in front of the two white men, who were cussing him for being late, jumped into the cab.

They must be white hunters, Queller reflected, as the trap drove off. He'd read in a magazine someplace that there were still hunting concessions in northern Tanzania. Arusha way. Places where rich men – it was nearly always men, and nearly always his own countrymen, too – came to shoot lion, elephant and zebra. There was, if he recalled the article correctly, a sliding scale of costs for the trophies.

He thought about the cost of his own involvement with bin Laden, realising as he did so that the same CNN footage was playing on the TV in the bar.

'They are a portrait of America today and of America tomorrow,' President Clinton was saying, of those who had died.

Queller remembered America's yesterdays, a time when he

himself had nearly died in the service of his country. It felt such a long time ago, a whole world away. But it was only the eighties. Escorted by Green Berets and sometimes members of the British SAS, he had made a number of trips across the Pakistan border to link up with units of the Afghan mujahidin.

'Each of them had an adventurous spirit, a generous soul. Each relished the chance to see the world and make it better.'

Since the invasion at the beginning of the decade, the Afghans, together with groups of Arab *wahhabi*, of which bin Laden's was the best known, had been holding out against the might of the Soviet army. As an intelligence officer, it had been Queller's role to assess the training and supply needs that the West could offer them.

'No matter what it takes, we must find those responsible for these evil acts and see that justice is done,' Clinton continued. 'There may be more hard road ahead, for terrorists target America because we act and stand for peace and democracy.'

Queller had met with bin Laden a number of times. The Saudi had become a kind of all-round logistical resource for the Afghan fighters, providing food and weapons. These were paid for mainly by an inheritance of around $300 million (his father's civil-engineering firm had made a fortune building accommodation for pilgrims to the Holy Places in Saudi Arabia), but also by a system of donations from Muslim governments, communities and individuals around the world. Bin Laden had brought in bull-dozers and explosives from the family firm to blast new roads and build redoubts, landing strips and weapons depots for the Afghans. His operations included a vast network of tunnels in the Zazi mountains, in Bakhtiar Province, that became a large hospital for guerrillas injured in the fighting.

Later, he had begun fighting with the mujahidin himself, becoming something of a legend for his bravery at the head of a contingent of Arab and Afghan troops. He fought and ate alongside the ordinary soldiers in the mountain trenches in those days, distinguishing himself in hand-to-hand combat. On one occasion, the story was told, he had driven a bulldozer at a Soviet position while being strafed by helicopter gunships. Queller himself remembered the horror of those things – the way the cartridge cases fell out of the chutes at thousands of rounds per minute, the orange flame that spurted, hellishly, from the muzzles.

He swished the whisky round his mouth and looked down the bar. The man behind it was filling a bowl of peanuts, holding an expression of fierce concentration as he poured them from their plastic bag into a steel container. Above him, the television boomed and flickered.

'Terror is the tool of cowards,' intoned his old friend Secretary Albright on the television, adding her message to Clinton's at the ceremony. 'It is not a form of political expression. It is certainly not a manifestation of religious faith. It is murder, plain and simple.'

Bin Laden's support – arms and money – didn't just come from Arab organisations, like the Saudi Red Cross and the Istakhbarat (Saudi Intelligence). Through Queller himself, the CIA had supplied him with Stinger anti-aircraft missiles to bring down Russian gunships. Queller had also been instrumental in providing US funding for a cave complex bin Laden had built – to a CIA design – at Tora Bora, deep in the Afghan mountains. British MI6 had supplied advisers for other schemes.

There had been another side to it. Not only had American tax dollars (to the tune of $500 million a year) and British pounds paid for military equipment and training, they had also facilitated the rise of a drugs empire that went hand in hand with the military operation. Queller had been only tangentially involved in this, but he had seen with his own eyes the shipments of raw opium go out in C-130 cargo planes under the auspices of ex-SAS and South African mercenaries. Ostensibly there to train mujahidin, the mercenaries had been in the opium trade up to their necks. They were loosely linked to an organisation called Keenie-Meenie Services, so named from the Swahili for the movement a snake makes through grass. KMS had friends deep in the heart of the British military establishment, but government complicity was totally deniable. In this way it was useful for both the UK and the US: members of the same outfit had been hired to mine Managua harbour during the Contra business. In Afghanistan – sometimes with Green Berets, sometimes without – Keenie-Meenie taught mujahidin the use of explosives and timers, and how to deploy anti-aircraft weapons. And in the background always were two men: Osama bin Laden, 'Mr Sam' as a South African employee of KMS christened him, and Jack Queller.

Over the years, Queller himself had watched bin Laden's astonishing metamorphosis. When he'd first known him, he was a soft youth laughed at by other mujahids. He and other Arab scions of wealthy Gulf families were known as 'Gucci muj' by the Afghans because of their fine clothes and shoes. But by the time of the siege of Jalalabad, the key battle of the war, the young civil engineer had become a very different figure, a tough commander in traditional *shalwar kameez* and carrying a Kalashnikov, like the other Afghan leaders. As many as ten thousand fighters from all over the Muslim world – Algerians, Saudis, Egyptians, Filipinos, even Chinese Uighurs – passed through his camps.

It was these, or loosely affiliated cells of the same, that now formed the basis of al-Qaida. Moving his base of operations to Sudan, bin Laden (now known as 'the Sheikh' or 'the Director') bought land for training camps, set up factories and farms to produce income streams and – as was now all too clear – set up bases and safe houses in Kenya, Tanzania and elsewhere. On Queller's advice, the CIA knew that there was more to bin Laden's operations than met the eye. The Ladin [*sic*] International Company wasn't just an import–export concern. Taba Investment didn't just trade in currency. The Themar al-Mubaraka Farm didn't just grow sesame, peanuts and corn. Hijra Construction didn't just build bridges and roads.

When bin Laden resurfaced in Afghanistan in 1996, after being forced to leave Sudan by the Khartoum government, many of these businesses reverted to their ostensible functions. Queller sipped his drink. That was one of the frightening and unusual things about al-Qaida – the way it could slip to and fro, over relatively long periods of time, between the routines of everyday life and business and the extraordinary world of a terror organisation, whose very purpose was to subvert the everyday.

But was the everyday quite so explicable and dependable, anyway? The grievances of the sort of people who joined al-Qaida were as twisted into what we think of as ordinariness as the weave in a carpet: the ordinary, sometimes murderous activities of his state and their own – it was from these things that the terrorists drew their strength and self-justification.

Yet it wasn't just politics, there was a perversion of religion there too, that lure of the sinister, that combination of otherworldliness, brutality and fantasy which bin Laden himself embodied. The fantasy part was important, and in a surprising manner: Queller had established that bin Laden named al-Qaida after Isaac Asimov's *Foundation* books, which had been translated into Arabic under that title. Set over a vast timescale, the saga comprised a series of tales in which a group of savants took it upon themselves to save the galaxy from chaos and corruption. Their leader, a so-called 'psycho-historian', could see patterns in time and so predict the future.

Now the fantasy was factual, all too factual. In the years after his association with the renegade Saudi, it infuriated Queller that the intelligence community had ignored him when he'd warned them about the global scale and ambitions of bin Laden's enterprise – how his front companies were procuring weapons and stockpiling chemicals for explosives. Training impressionable youngsters in hijacking, kidnapping, assassination . . . But in the eyes of Mort Altenburg and others, he was already a dinosaur, a one-armed creature from the Cold War lagoon.

A mass delusion or dissimulation had taken place, Queller believed. Once the Soviet threat had diminished, it seemed a period of unparalleled prosperity had begun. The West feasted like Belshazzar on what was called the 'peace dividend' – but the writing was on the wall the whole time. Now all of them, himself included, were paying the price.

So were others. More stories were beginning to emerge from Nairobi. The pedestrian whose head was blown open. The woman who was standing in his shadow when it happened and escaped unharmed. The buried man who could feel the bodies of dead people all around him in the darkness, who tied his broken leg to his good leg and dragged himself, inch by suffocating inch, to where the rescuers could hear his cries.

Queller watched an advertisement for a chain of prestige hotels roll down the TV screen. In diverse locations worldwide, all the group's establishments were vaunted aloud as being of 'unparalleled excellence and luxury'. He shuddered. Normal living, never mind luxury, seemed an alien concept in the present situation. Bin Laden, he thought, must have had some expectation of how many Africans, as opposed to Americans, would be killed, yet they could in no way be seen as a worthwhile target. He shook his head and sipped more whisky. There was no point in looking for logic in that quarter. Yet it was natural to do so. Even when one was aware that poison filled his bloodstream, it was hard to accept that one's adversary acted not just on moral convictions at variance with one's own, but a different kind of intelligence too.

And a different theology. Queller had long maintained that Islam lent itself to distortion by terrorists because of the low value it placed on the material world. If you believed something, the human frame included, was merely an illusion, it was easier to destroy it. Although, by the same argument, what would be the point?

The two great religions tensed, like wrestlers entwined in a pose, over the question of what constituted man's fall. It was a topic that fascinated Queller, and he planned to make it the centrepiece of a lecture he had been invited to give to the Islamic Studies department at Rutgers University. Though what audiences really wanted, he'd gathered from previous lectures, were stories of guns and bombs, and glimpses of grand conspiracies.

In Christianity, the expulsion from paradise involved humanity's disobedient desire for knowledge. In Islam the loss of Eden also came from eating the forbidden fruit, but the fault was Satan's. Adam and Hawwa's fall was caused by their seeing the world as real in its own terms rather than acknowledging there was no reality but Allah. Acceptance of this (literally *islam*: surrender) was the fundamental pillar of the faith and the route to redemption, allowing humankind to pass across that bridge which separates the two worlds.

La ilaha Allah. There is no God if it is not Allah. The phrase itself was a kind of bridge.

To Queller's mind, Islam had more mystic force than Christianity, because it struck at the core of one's everyday perceptions. In a distorted form, this force could become a tool for psychic attack. So it was with al-Qaida, whose members were encouraged or coerced into believing they were renunciating a polluted world. Like the leader of a cult, bin Laden used Islam's innate mysticism to bewitch his followers in this way – despite his professed brand of Islam, Wahhabism, strictly forbidding esoteric practices. Even music was banned.

Queller believed that as well as fostering them in others, bin Laden suffered from such psychic attacks himself. The twin Islamic doctrines of the illusory nature of creation, and the need for self-abnegation, had some resonance with the psychological conditions of delusion and repression. Disregarding all authority but one's own definition of Allah could, in a diseased mind, lead to a massive expansion of belief in the power of the will, and the assumption of mythological proportions.

Then again, the ingredients for a hell-broth of hatred and trouble could be found in many religions. Feeling irresolute, Queller watched two waiters move a bamboo screen away from a raised platform at the edge of the room. There were large loud-speakers on the platform, and a drum kit and a microphone attached to a pole. There was, it was clear, going to be music in the Kili bar that night.

He had seen the germ of the hatred long ago. As it became clear the Soviets would withdraw, Queller had begun to notice a change in bin Laden's attitude to him. In the early years, he had been warm and welcoming. Later, his manner cooled. He started to conflate the Soviets and the Americans even in Queller's hear-ing, seeing them all as infidel superpowers – unbelievers who threatened the Muslim world. What irked bin Laden most was how the external policy of the Saudi regime had so swiftly attached itself to America as the US grew in power after the Second World War. Throwing off the yoke of the British, they should, in bin Laden's view, have tried to develop an indigenous Islamist policy rather than associating themselves with the *kufr*.

The word meant, literally, 'cover' – hiding from truth – and sometimes Queller thought it appropriate that his nation had come to be its prime example in the Muslim mind: since the tri-umph of the Second World War at least, there had been some-thing like a mass self-willed illusion that American destiny proceeded by way of a special providence. Shifting 'reasons of state', underwritten by an assumption of being God's own coun-try, had been used as an excuse for all sorts of evil abroad, often with a total disregard for local considerations.

The mistake the Reagan administration made, back in the eighties, was to see the anti-Soviet jihad as an expedient geopolitical strategy, an expression of the Cold War, oblivious that to others involved it was the direct expression of the will of Allah. The crisis point came on Queller's final visit to Afghanistan in 1989, between the Soviet retreat and the fall of the Berlin Wall at the end of the year. The mission had been implemented by the CIA's commercial directorate after consultation with a number of leading American oil companies.

The aim was to persuade bin Laden to use his influence on America's behalf with whoever emerged to fill the power vacuum in Afghanistan following the Russian withdrawal. At the time everything was up in the air as factions fought to take control. Back then it seemed viable, even logical, that an American client state could be established in the Hindu Kush. The irony was, communism was beginning to collapse even as the mission got under way, and soon America would have client states right across the east. It still amazed Queller that the intelligence agencies had not predicted this. Then again, he'd been no wiser. If he had, he might not have gone to Afghanistan hunting oil contracts that October.

Queller remembered the visit like no other. Shrugging off time, all the life that had flown in between, it would creep smokily into his head. Even to think of the episode made his stump ache, as if the nerves beneath its web of scar were alive to the memory of their own severance.

In a cold mountain dawn, a convoy of about ten Landcruisers had wound its way through the rocky slopes above Khost, to where Queller was waiting with four Green Berets as a token escort. The convoy stopped a little way off. Bin Laden came forward at the head of a group of heavily armed Arabs wearing a mixture of discarded Russian camouflage and traditional dress.

'What are you doing here?' he had asked, narrowing his fierce brown eyes. He was holding a nine-millimetre-calibre automatic pistol and had a Kalashnikov strapped across his back.

'I've come to talk,' Queller had said, eyeing the pistol and aware that the other Arabs had their rifles out. 'We need to establish what our relations will be now the Russians have gone.'

Bin Laden laughed, his long beard shaking. 'There will be no relations now. We do not want you here. We do not want you in any Muslim country. Your presence in any such place is a disgrace.'

'Look,' Queller had said. 'I've come here to confirm our friendship, to ensure we remain on the same side.'

'Listen to me. You are not welcome here. In alliance with Israel the Jews in your government have come to take command of our holy places. Because of this emotions are raised in me, and in many Muslim people. We know now that when we buy American arms or allow Americans to dig for oil in our territories, we are accomplices of evil. That is why, with Allah's help, I have decided to establish a front to carry out jihad against Jews and American Crusaders. You are a Crusader, Mr Queller. That is why you must leave, now. If I see you again, I will kill you.'

'You're kidding me,' Queller had said, smiling, desperate to defuse the situation.

The morning sun, rising above the hooded, grim mountains, glinted on bin Laden's face.

'I will show you how serious I am.'

He shot Queller in the elbow. The Green Berets raised their weapons but, seeing they were hopelessly outnumbered, had lowered them again immediately.

'Now understand that I aim to turn your country's presence in the holy lands into a myth, just as I did with the Russians here in Afghanistan. In the religion of the Prophet – Allah's blessing and salutations upon him – as I think you know well, Queller, there is something called jihad. A special place reserved in the

Hereafter for those who participate in it. And the enemy of jihad?'

He spat at the rocky ground, where the Green Berets were squatting in a circle round Queller and his shattered arm, forty AKs trained upon them. Even through the disruptive patterns of the camouflage cream on their faces, and the net of his own pain, the dismay and fear of the American soldiers had been clear to behold, Queller remembered.

More of bin Laden's words came back to him. 'The enemy is the Zionist–Crusader alliance under the banner of the USA. The enemy is the iniquitous United Nations. The enemy is *you*.'

Swallowing the last of his whisky, Queller stood up. He glanced at the television. Now William Cohen, the Defense Secretary, was saying his piece.

'We can never allow terrorists to diminish our determination to press on with the inspiring work of those who have been taken from us. Their sudden loss must only strengthen our sense of purpose.'

Then the anchorwoman switched to coverage of independent counsel Kenneth Starr's investigation into the question of whether President Clinton had committed perjury or obstructed justice in trying to hide his relationship with Monica Lewinsky, and the possibility of impeachment proceedings in Congress. All that stuff, it seemed to Queller, was hotting up at a hell of a lick.

He went back up to his room on the top floor of the Kili. Whatever he thought of the government's past role in the sponsorship of bin Laden, including his own part, his conscience prompted him – like divine authority speaking in his head – that he had to pursue this matter to the best of his ability.

The antagonisms had to be faced as they stood. History was history. It had to be amputated: what was past was prologue, nothing more. The important thing now was that those who'd been bereaved, Americans and Kenyans and Tanzanians alike, had a chance of justice.

As soon as he could, Queller resolved, he would fly over to Zanzibar and join Miranda. It would be strange to go back, after so many years. He looked over at the minibar, wondering if it was wise to have another drink. *I mustn't*, he said to himself, and lay on the bed, realising he was exhausted. But temptation had already begun, by insensible gradations, to make its way into his soul.

Later, around three-thirty, he was still sitting on the bed drinking from the bottle, wondering if he would have peace before the rising dawn. Or ever, until he saw – his thoughts were blurry now – the Lote Tree of the Uttermost Limit, at the zenith of the seventh heaven: the edge of Being where the Prophet on his Night Journey received God's instructions before returning to earth.

The edge of Being, beyond which his Lucy was. He swigged the care-drowning, grief-dispelling Scotch till he gasped.

27

Nick Karolides awoke, cried out and lurched forward in surprise. Seized with panic, he clutched at the sides of the boat, making the little craft tilt precariously. He was parched. There were no oars. Nothing but himself and the ocean.

He tried to work out what had happened. Half-conscious then as now, he had barely understood that someone was pulling him into the lighthouse. He remembered being dragged down to the beach in the dark, strange hands pushing off the dinghy in which he and Leggatt had made their landing. There was something else – a thin man in the boat moving quietly, corpses crushed next to him, the man hauling the bodies over the side, along with the oars . . .

Around him the sea lay still and mysterious. Patches of brown sargasso weed and bright red jellyfish floated past, like little islands. But he could see no land. He listened to the water as it lapped at the side. Lap, lap. No land. Just the ocean rolling on and on. He moaned and lay back down in the bottom of the dinghy, curled like a foetus under the glaring sun. It must be some kind of nightmare. He remembered that the man had climbed over the edge of the boat, swimming. Why had he left him?

Hours went by. When he awoke, it was cooler. A light rain was falling, pattering on the fibreglass of the dinghy. He opened his mouth. The thirst was awful. There was a thick line of blood on his temple where the bullet had grazed him. His limbs ached, too, and were covered with rope burns. His knees, where the big Arab had hit them, were especially painful. There was a cut in one – the salt made it sting viciously – and heavy bruising on both. He wasn't quite sure which was worse, to be stuck on Lyly with those men or out here on the sea. He remembered more now, remembered being flung out of the lighthouse, dangling . . .

He felt helpless, but knew he had to make an effort to save himself. His tongue was swollen. He made a cup with his hands to try to catch the rainwater. But it was fruitless, and he ended up licking his palms. Then, just as he was wondering if he would die of thirst, the rain intensified and he was able to take a few worthwhile mouthfuls.

But the Lord giveth and the Lord taketh away. As the clouds opened, and the sky darkened, the waves increased in size. The dinghy slithered up and down, slapping loudly as it dropped into the troughs. As the rising wind gusted in his face, Nick began to worry about water coming in. For with each wave that swept towards him, a mass of spray was cast into the boat. He tried to bale it out with his hands, but it was no use.

No use! The sea began to surge around him. The waves grew ever larger in size, each one bearing down menacingly on the little boat. There was always another, and another, and another. He was powerless to prevent them. As the waves sent the dinghy bounding down, he gathered himself each time. It was always the same. There was nothing to be done. The dinghy lifted – was briefly in space. Then the hull banged. The fibreglass shuddered.

A wave swept right across, nearly knocking him over. He gripped the gunwale, and a fearful thought came to him. At Nantucket, he'd read, the cliffs were receding six feet a year as the waves battered them. What hope had the dinghy, such a puny thing by comparison to those great walls of rock? An oyster in its shell had more chance than him.

But after some time the immediate peril ceased. The wind declined, the fighting sea called a truce with itself, and the sun went down. Glowing crimson on the dark blue ocean, it took his heart with it as it declined. As the darkness gathered, Nick – a hunched, lonely figure – began to accept that this might be the end. Drifting for forty hours in an open boat had finally cured Nick Karolides of pursuing the phantoms of hope.

During the night he became very cold. He couldn't sleep. His teeth chattered. The boat rolled along in the darkness. He thought of Miranda. But all that did was increase his sense of being abandoned, totally alone.

The dawn broke red. That must be east, he realised, squinting through salt-inflamed eyes. He looked around. The sea was calm again. But no land. His bones hurt. He seemed to be cold in his very heart.

He thought: if that was east, then he was drifting in the wrong direction. For the island must be west. Frantic, he stumbled aft and began paddling with his hands to try to turn the dinghy around.

Exhausted, he gave up this effort to control his own destiny and allowed himself to be taken wherever the current went. He sat motionless for an hour – was it? – watching the sea slide by. He tried not to think of Leggatt. He tried not to think of death. He remembered the old man prodding him with his pipe stem, to emphasise a point.

The sun grew hot again, tightening his skin painfully. Blisters had begun to rise on his back and arms. Once, the water roiled nearby and he thought of sharks. The tigers and hammerheads that he knew cruised here. That gave him an idea. He rallied a little, summoning the energy of despair. He was more thirsty than hungry, but if he could catch something there would be fluid in it. He took off his shirt and tore off lengths of cotton, tying them together. Then he removed his belt and, nearly breaking a tooth in the process, prised off the spike of the buckle and bent it. Tied to the end of the cotton it would, he reasoned, serve as a lure. He dropped it in the water.

Waiting, Nick found himself imagining fish down below, intrigued by the fragment of metal as it glittered behind the boat. Surely one would bite soon? It occurred to him that the things most easy to imagine are more often than not those impossible to achieve. He pulled up the links of cotton. Nothing. But he mustn't give up hope. He mustn't.

He watched cormorants diving, flying up high then dashing their bodies down on the sea, like something trying to find a way to die. But they came up with fish; he was the one more likely to die.

Maybe he would have more luck trying to distill seawater. He devised a contraption, made from a funnel of the same shirt fabric – tied between the rowlocks – that he hoped would drip fresh condensation into one of his shoes. But the material sagged, and the water ran straight through. The sum consequence of his efforts at survival was, through the removal and employment of his shirt in such a way, to reduce what little protection he had from the sun and spray. His skin blistered even more. The accumulation of his hours at sea etched itself on his body.

And on his mind. He had given up hope of being sighted. Now there was a wicked stillness on the water, which moved past the hull in large sheets of oily liquid. He began to think about his death. The biggest adventure of all, he reflected miserably. Yet maybe – he was delirious now – maybe it was not so bad to be summoned away like this? How different, after all, was being cast adrift in an open boat from man's average experience of life on earth? His head lolled forward. The dinghy wallowed, and was still again. Or did it edge forward? He no longer knew.

He woke again, raising his eyes in expectation of further futile progress, another little indefinable scratch on the sea's forbidding totality, its grey, luminous slate of horror. What he saw was something else. Something that disturbed the tilting horizon of sky and ocean.

A ship! He stood up unsteadily, his arms stretched upwards. He tried to shout, but at first all that came from his throat was a dry croak. He tried again, and this time some noise came, but hardly enough to carry across. He shouted more, and started leaping up and down. He nearly fell into the water. Eventually his voice gave out and he stopped shouting.

They had spotted him long ago, in any case. He saw ropes flutter. A boat was coming off the davits, cranking down on heavy pulleys. Exhausted, swaying, he watched men climb into the boat. They began to row towards him. He felt faint, light-headed. They were coming towards him, weren't they? He toppled over and fell into the bottom of the dinghy. There was a thud as the other boat came alongside. They pulled him over the gunwale into it, then tied a lanyard to his dinghy to tow it behind them.

Of the journey back to the big ship he knew nothing, returning to consciousness only as he collapsed on its iron deck.

They took him below. There was a smell of unwashed men, rough tobacco, bad cooking. A stove spluttered in a corner. He could see eyes peering at him in the yellow light. His ears were filled with voices speaking a language he understood but rarely spoke himself these days. *Get some water here. What happened to him?*

Someone pulled off his ragged clothes. Somebody else held a tin cup to his mouth. Water. Sip sip. He clutched for the cup, but they held it back. Sip sip. Then a bucket was brought and a sponge and they were washing the salt from his face and neck. After that he fell asleep.

On waking, Nick was given more water, hot this time and mixed with rum. The man in front of him was a big guy with jet-black hair and a steady gaze. Taking the cup in his hand, Nick slowly came to his senses. The sailor studied him curiously for a second, then climbed back up, his boots clanging on the spiral stairway.

Nick took in his surroundings. He was in a kind of hole,

wrapped in blankets smelling of catsup. He could feel bolt-tops through the blankets. Opposite him were other holes, compartments of sorts, cubbyholes of iron sheeting sticking out from the sides of the boat. Seamen's berths, he realised, seeing yellow oilskins and other items of clothing hung on lines above the divisions. In the berth directly in front of his own a poster of a half-naked young woman had been pasted above the bedhead. He stared at her dyed blonde hair, her insecure smile and pneumatic breasts. He could hear the rumble of a diesel engine. The motor's tremble, and the sea's swell, they came home to him bodily – from iron through blanket to flesh and bone.

A tall, moustachioed man in a captain's hat and a tight-fitting jacket came down. He put a can of Heinz spaghetti hoops on the stove and started questioning Nick in faltering English as he warmed it.

'What happened to you? Why were you adrift?'

To the man's great surprise, Nick answered him in Greek.

'By God!' the man said, stirring the spaghetti hoops with a tea spoon. 'I didn't expect to find one of my own countrymen floating in the middle of the Indian Ocean. What a story!'

'Where are we, exactly?'

'Off northern Tanzania. Tanga way.'

He brought over the tin, guarding his hand against the heat by wrapping an old sock around the bottom.

'Pepper?'

Over the next half-hour Nick learned that the vessel which had rescued him was a small cargo ship called the *Pearl of the Ocean*. It was on its way from Suez to Beira, where it was due to exchange its cargo of Egyptian potatoes for one of Mozambican sugar. The man talking to him was Captain Phillipos and nothing gave him greater pleasure than Nick's Greek ancestry.

But when Nick mentioned taking him back to Zanzibar, the captain grimaced, his moustache folding.

'We'll be going by the island, very soon,' he said. 'But if we put in, they'll have us for port fees, which is fair enough, plus a host of bribes for false customs discoveries, which isn't. I'm sorry – you'll have to come to Beira unless you are able to put up two thousand US.'

'I don't have anything,' said Nick. 'You saw how I was.'

'Well, that is the way of it,' said the captain. 'At least you didn't drown!'

He went back up on deck. Nick spooned the last of the spaghetti hoops into his mouth and looked wretchedly at the picture of the naked woman. Beira? What use was Beira to him? He listened to the churn of the propellers and – pulling the yeasty blankets about him – wondered where he had gone wrong in his life.

A little later, the captain came down again with a bundle of clothes.

'You better put these on. I've had an idea, but it will take a little effort on your part.'

'What?' Nick asked, clutching at the clothes the captain was flinging at him. A pair of canvas trousers. An old blue sweater. A pair of rubber boots.

'Well, we can't put into Stone Town harbour, it's hard enough for us to make a profit as it is. But we could stop just outside of it. And well, we have your little boat and I don't see why we couldn't find you a new pair of oars.'

'You mean, row in?'

'I do indeed,' said Captain Phillipos. 'We'll be going by Stone Town in about two hours' time. One of my men will clean up your dinghy.'

'To be honest,' said Nick, putting a leg into the canvas trousers, 'it would be more useful if you could drop me at Ras Macpherson. That's Macpherson's Point, north of Stone Town.'

The captain shook his head. 'Never heard of it. But I'll look on my chart.'

With that Captain Phillipos climbed the stairs. Pulling on the high rubber boots, Nick followed him up, emerging onto the sun-lit deck. At first the crew, dark men with hard-lined faces, eyed him warily in his ill-fitting seaman's kit. The ocean swelled gently around the rusty old ship. Up on the foredeck, a scowling man was emptying Nick's dinghy of water.

Then one of them said, in Greek, 'He looks like a circus performer.'

'Well, they're your clothes,' replied Nick, in the same language. 'And they don't smell too good.'

They all laughed, pointing at the man cleaning Nick's dinghy. It was his kit. His sombre face brightened as he joined in the laughter.

The crewmen spoiled Nick after that, giving him chocolate and cigarettes and asking him about his family. He played up the story of his father's and grandfather's lives a bit, but they didn't question the truth of what he told them. An assumption of common experience – of the Greek merchant marine and its tough, ancient history– ran through the conversation. Nick felt proud to be accepted by these men. There was a touch of fable about them.

Later, Captain Phillipos emerged from his wheelhouse to confirm that he would drop Nick off at Ras Macpherson.

'You'll have to make your own way through the reef, though. I can't risk going into the lagoon. Fetch some oars, Eleutherios. Our visitor will be leaving us soon.'

Nick went up to the stern. The day was almost over and the sun was setting. He leaned on the taffrail and looked out hopefully for Zanzibar. In a cloud of diesel fumes, the *Pearl of the Ocean* continued. The waves darkened, chopping black under the golden light.

28

It was evening, and Miranda was drinking rum and coke alone at the Macpherson. She shook the ice in the glass and remembered, regretfully, the time at Leggatt's farm when Nick had been drinking with the old man and she had allowed herself to drift away from him.

On the television, President Clinton was dealing with some personal issues of his own. Earlier in the day, he had testified to a federal grand jury for over four hours as part of the investigation into whether he had perjured himself or tried to persuade others to perjure themselves.

'I did have a relationship with Miss Lewinsky that was not appropriate,' he said, from the White House Map Room. 'In fact, it was wrong. It constituted a critical lapse of judgment and a personal failure on my part for which I am solely and completely responsible. I know that my public comments and my silence about this matter gave a false impression . . .'

Miranda's eye wandered past the President's grim face to the historic room behind him. It was in the Map Room, the CNN reporter had said earlier, that Franklin Roosevelt had directed Allied forces in wartime – 'liaising with British leader Winston Churchill in his own Cabinet War Rooms in London'.

It made her think of the dead Englishman's boat. And of Leggatt himself: his upturned face, the missing ear, the striations beneath the skin where the maggots had begun burrowing across his cheek and neck.

'Now is the time – in fact, it is past time – to move on. And so tonight I ask you to turn away from the spectacle of the past seven months, to repair . . .'

* * *

In Florida, Mrs Karolides, Nick's mother, was one of millions watching the speech across America. The TV flickered with the President's contrite countenance. Above her a standard lamp produced more honest light. She wasn't paying much attention to the broadcast anyway. Her hands were busy, and she was thinking about her son. It worried her terribly that she hadn't heard from him since the bombings. Even though she knew that they had happened on the African mainland and not on Zanzibar, it seemed very near when she looked in the atlas. The news of the outrages had, in fact, shocked her from her customary religious stupor. These days she was having nothing to do with her crazy church. She had even put away her shrine.

She was thinking about Dino, too. He had been so kind to her in the past few months. And she was thinking about her work. The floor of the lounge was littered with tissue paper, starched cotton, waxed crepe paper and coloured cellophane. Beside her on the sofa were a pair of scissors, some wire cutters, a roll of sticky tape, and some coils of garden wire. On her knees was a book, *A Step-by-Step Guide to Making Artificial Flowers*.

'The flowers in this book were all inspired by real flowers, but are not meant to be an imitation of them,' she read. 'People will not walk into your house, touch the flowers you have made and ask, "Are they real?" But they will certainly be impressed . . .

'You can't improve on Nature, everyone knows that. But, by developing an awareness of the possibilities, you can make flowers that look nearly natural from materials that might otherwise be wasted.'

On screen, a cluster of experts were picking over the President's address. 'It's a question of trust,' declared one of the talking heads. 'He's broken his contract with the public. And once that connection is severed . . .'

326

* * *

Miranda turned off the television and began walking towards her (or, as it was, Nick's) room. She made her way across the Macpherson's tree-lined courtyard, past the beds of hibiscus and jasmine, thinking how she hated the kind of two-bit wiseacres the networks wheeled on. She hated TV in general, anyway. Its breathless coverage of the bombings had been a disgrace. Far more powerful, in its odd way, was a headline in one of the Tanzanian papers, recounting the last words of a woman who had died after being pulled from the ruins. *'Kuta zimebomoka.'* The walls have fallen down.

* * *

Mrs Karolides listened as one of the experts catalogued the gifts the President had given Ms Lewinsky last Christmas. A stuffed animal, a New York skyline pin, a Rockettes blanket, a pair of novelty sunglasses, a marble sculpture of a bear's head . . . What on earth could she want with any of these trashy items? Why would anyone want them? She shut off the foolish babble with the remote and looked to her book again.

'Determined not to ignore today's feeling for mass production, we designed a whole chapter of flowers that can be cut out six or eight at a time. Once round with a pair of scissors, one fold, one twist and you have a rapidly growing pile of flowers to decorate a cone, a hanging ball or a ring.'

* * *

Miranda took off her clothes and lay on the bed like a corpse. She felt like weeping, she was so lost. She let the air of the fan wash over her, thinking about Nick and the false accusations that had been made against her.

* * *

'We can recreate the idea of a holly wreath to hang on the front door,' read Mrs Karolides, under her standard lamp, 'without having to make a wire and moss frame for it –'

* * *

Miranda sat bolt upright. Somebody was trying the handle. Remembering da Souza's warning about burglars, she slid off the bed, wrapping the sheet around her, and looked about the room for a weapon. All she could see, in the moonlight, were the sponges on the walls. The door rattled again. Her stomach churned.

Finally her eye fell on an empty beer bottle next to Nick's computer. She grabbed it by the neck and went over to the door.

'Who is it?' she asked, fiercely.

'Who's that?' said a familiar voice on the other side.

'Nick?'

She opened the door, and took in, framed by the dim light of the corridor, a figure in a blue sweater and sea boots. She felt her heart leap, as if something very precious and wonderful, which she'd thought lost, had been restored to her.

'Miranda!'

She threw her arms round him.

'Thank God. Where the hell have you been?'

'Hell's exactly where I've been.'

He thudded wearily into the room in the heavy boots. He looked terrible.

'I've been looking for you all over for days!' she said, still clutching the sheet and bottle.

He sat down on the bed, drawing violent breaths. There was a large cut on the side of his head.

'Uh, it's a bit complicated . . . You can put that bottle down now. How come you're here anyhow?'

'Because of the bombs.'

'What bombs?'

She gave a little laugh. 'You really have been away, haven't you?'

She sat down beside him, pulling the sheet more tightly around her. 'I was beginning to think I'd never see you again.'

'You nearly didn't.'

'What happened?'

He leant forward and put his head in his hands, pressing his fingers into his skull as if all the punishment in the world had devolved upon it. She realised she had to be practical, that now was not the time to tell him how much his return meant to her. He was too distraught.

'You know, you smell pretty bad. Why don't you go have a shower, then you can tell me what's been going on. And me you. And I better have a look at that cut, too.'

'OK,' he whispered. He went through to the bathroom and started taking off his clothes.

Replacing the sheet, Miranda made the bed. She could hear the sound of the shower coming through. She put on a T-shirt and shorts and went to ask da Souza for a first-aid kit. Back by the time Nick came through, with a towel round his waist, she told him to lie down on the bed.

'I need some clothes.'

'Just lie down.'

She dressed the cut on his temple, which had softened in the shower and was bleeding slightly, and bandaged up the deeper wound on his swollen knee. Apart from the occasional wince he lay there in silence. She could hear the waves washing quietly outside as her hands moved over his body.

Later, as the fan whirred above them, they talked, lying face to face on the bed as they recounted to each other the story of their recent days, each equally full of astonishing facts. Later still, by which time the generator had gone off, the fan ceased its gyrations, and the moon waxed stronger, diffusing its light over the immensity of the gently whispering ocean – later still, touching, murmuring, surging, they made love.

* * *

'Or we can imitate,' read Mrs Karolides, 'those blossoms of Arabia that blush unseen in the desert air, without having to cover them under hothouse panes. In the diagram below, you see how a heart of rose petals can be arranged within a triangle of leaves, conveying an impression of the paradise garden, walled off from the ordinary world.'

Thinking of her pyx, her little wooden box in which a priest had once carried the sacrament, she stood up and went to fetch it.

* * *

Nick turned to look into Miranda's green eyes; they were wet with tears. He felt a wave of panic.

'Are you all right?'

'Just happy.'

'Oh.'

'You growled like a beast,' she said, reassuringly, squeezing his hand.

He laughed. His pains forgotten for a while – loving her for that mercy, and for the adventure of her body – he gathered her into his arms once more.

They lay like that for some time, until he rolled on top of her and brought his face down to her breasts. After another little while he took one of her nipples into his mouth, and raising a hand to the other, let his palm brush over it. She uttered a cry . . . He moved down her body, covering her stomach and pelvis with subtle kisses till, like a hummingbird over a flower, he began flicking his tongue over her.

She put her hands in his hair, whispering his name.

29

Morning dawned, and with it knowledge – for Miranda at least. It was imperative Queller be told about Nick's arrival and what had happened to him on Lyly, but both her mobile and the land-lines were inoperative. Short of flying immediately back to Dar, there didn't seem much she could do. She decided to give it a couple of hours. They had a swim before breakfast, during which Miranda wondered whether she was just delaying her return in order to spend more time with Nick.

After they had eaten, she tried the hotel phone again, to no avail. Nick was in the TV lounge, sitting on the sofa in shorts and T-shirt. She went to join him, dialling on her mobile with her thumb as she walked across the room.

'It's a newsflash,' said Nick, excitedly. 'Clinton.'

Her eyes flicked from the little screen in her hand to the big one mounted on the wall. This time, however, even though his *mea culpa* was still as fresh in the wind as the Macpherson's jasmine, the President wasn't talking about Monica Lewinsky.

'We have convincing evidence these groups played the key role in the embassy bombings in Kenya and Tanzania,' he was saying, in a statement from Massachusetts. 'Terrorists must have no doubt that in the face of their threat, America will protect its citizens. Today, we have struck back.'

'Christ,' said Nick.

'Shush,' said Miranda.

'That was the President speaking from his holiday retreat at Martha's Vineyard,' intoned the announcer. 'In the wake of his grand-jury ordeal, he was on vacation with Hillary and Chelsea.

Now he has cut short his visit there and is returning to Washington. We hope to bring you coverage from the White House shortly of a briefing he will give on the strike.'

They listened to the backgrounder, and watched the graphic displays. At Zhawar Kili al-badr, a complex of three camps associated with Osama bin Laden near Khost, in Afghanistan, twenty-one people had been killed and thirty wounded. At the al-Shifa pharmaceutical factory at Khartoum in Sudan, said to be owned by the terrorist leader and staffed by Iraqi technicians supplied by Saddam Hussein, twelve people had been killed and dozens injured. Some, the screen showed, were still being dug out from beneath the rubble. But the facility thought to be there, for the manufacture of VX nerve gas, had been 'functionally destroyed', said National Security Director Sandy Berger.

Sudanese officials protested that the factory hadn't been making Empta, the chemical precursor to VX. It had, they said, been making cough medicine, antibiotics and simple analgesics (aspirin and paracetamol), as well as veterinary drugs for animals. The factory also produced medicines for diabetes, ulcers, tuberculosis, rheumatism and hypertension, supplying 70 per cent of the drug needs of a country beset with war and disease.

US officials countered that they 'could find no evidence' of all this. What they did have was a CIA soil sample from the factory, a sample containing Empta, they said.

Sudan was also quick to point out that it had expelled bin Laden in 1996 after pressure from the US, sending a hundred of his followers with him to Afghanistan. 'We gave US officials a piece of advice that they never followed,' said the Sudanese foreign minister Salah-el-Din. 'We told them: "Don't send him out of Sudan because you will lose control over him." Now, the United States has ended up at war with an invisible enemy.'

The picture, which had been glowing red with rubble fires at the factory, changed suddenly. The anchorman cut in: 'We can now bring you the President in the Oval Office.'

'Good afternoon. Today, I ordered our armed forces to strike at terrorist-related facilities in Afghanistan and Sudan because of the immediate threat they presented to our national security.

'I want to speak with you about the objective of this action and why it was necessary. Our target was terror. Our mission was clear . . .'

Miranda watched Clinton's jaw move.

'Their mission is murder. And their history is bloody . . .'

'Oh my God, they have bombed?' asked da Souza, coming into the room. He stood next to the sofa, the white arms of his suit stretched out in front of him like those of a supplicant.

'Shush!'

'Our forces targeted one of the most active terrorist bases in the world. It contained key elements of the bin Laden network's infrastructure and has served as a training camp for literally thousands of terrorists from around the globe. We have reason to believe that a gathering of key terrorist leaders was to take place today, thus underscoring the urgency of our actions.

'Our forces also attacked a factory in Sudan associated with the bin Laden network. The factory was involved in the production of materials for chemical weapons.

'The United States does not take this action lightly . . . We will persist and we will prevail. Thank you, God bless you and may God bless our country.'

'That was the President, who will now be resuming his vacation at Martha's Vineyard, after making phone calls to other world leaders to garner their support for the strikes.'

Later in the day – during which Miranda and Nick had the manager bring them pizza and beer – it became clear that bin Laden had been nowhere near the camps when the missiles struck. He was, said his Taliban protectors, 'alive and well'.

According to one report, he had left the camp an hour before the strike. Some said that he hadn't been there for months and that other terrorist groups rented the military-style complex off him. Whatever the case, bin Laden had been on the *qui vive* ever since the embassy bombings, according to an unnamed security source in Pakistan, and had started moving from base to base.

'The word,' vouchsafed the CNN reporter, 'is that he is now at an opium farm south of Jalalabad. It is not at all certain that any of the members of his organisation have been killed. Back to you, Peter.'

'Thanks, Wendy. Now over to William Cohen at the Pentagon,' cued the anchorman.

'We have taken these actions to reduce the ability of these terrorist organisations to train and equip their misguided followers,' the US Defense Secretary said in his briefing. 'Those who attack our people will find no safe place, no refuge from the long arm of justice.'

As he spoke, Miranda realised that Queller's views had rapidly become official US policy. They must have picked up further al-Qaida people while she had been away. Pointing the finger at bin Laden himself, Cohen added, in regard to the al-Shifa plant, that the terrorist leader had 'contributed to this particular facility'.

She went outside into the garden to call Queller on her mobile again, itched once more by the feeling that the need to be close to Nick, and to experience the reprisals as they unfolded on the screen, was a dereliction of duty. The wire-mesh door swung behind her. She walked about in the hot sun, hoping that a signal might come if she changed her position.

It was no good. She looked upwards, as if the weather had something to do with it, and gazed at the immense blue-and-white spread of the sky; the cloud mass was breaking up into tiny points as if – it was her father's phrase, *throw sugar at you*, that drifted into her mind.

She noticed a bushbaby in a mango tree. Putting the phone in her pocket, she walked over and stood under the tree, watching the squirrel-like animal take a piece of fruit between its tiny claws and nibble at it exquisitely.

Its face and the movement of its paws were terrifyingly human. The evolutionary message was clear; there seemed only the filmiest of screens between her and the creature in the tree. Miranda felt, in that deeply interfused moment – interfused with the yellow fruit and sugared skies as well as the animal itself – a kind of astonishment at being alive at all.

Yet as she probed the strange experience, the link between it and the bushbaby broke like a twig; the feeling was gone. She took one last look at the little creature – with its face of an immature human embryo, rounded by an eskimo's furry hood – and walked back across the courtyard.

Inside, the whole madhouse, shrieking thing was still playing out. CNN had switched to a feed from ABC, which had a scoop. 'I have never met him,' the captioned owner of the al-Shifa factory, Salal Idris, was saying of bin Laden. A reporter from the network tracked the businessman down in Saudi Arabia. 'I have never dealt with him. I have never knowingly dealt with any one of his agents.'

'Still can't get through,' she said, hooking her shoulders under Nick's outstretched arm on the sofa. 'Have I missed anything?'

'I don't think so. I can't get a handle on it. What's the point of bombing if it doesn't kill the guy? It doesn't make sense.'

He was right. Getting at the truth behind the spectacle, as the TV ineluctably shaped it, was like looking through a steamed-up window only to find another behind it, and another, more and more to infinity. They could have polished the window till it was thin as tissue paper and they still wouldn't have seen through. Perhaps there was little understanding in it anyway, this endless etcetera of events which led from dead Russians in Afghanistan, via this, that and the other, through dead Africans and Americans in Nairobi and Dar, to the bombardment of a country with some of the highest levels of malnutrition ever recorded.

The deaths to come, in the parched fields of Sudan, would never appear on CNN, or in the *New York Times* – but a lot of work went into them. Over the previous week, progress reports from the investigation into the embassy bombings had flooded into the White House situation room from all over the national security apparatus. Everything, from interviews with suspects to trawls through telephone intercepts and satellite-surveillance tapes, seemed to point to bin Laden. Queller had been vindicated. Even Mort Altenburg agreed with him now – to the extent of saying, to others at least, that he had thought so all along. President Clinton met in secret with six advisers to discuss a counter-attack. The group included, in all probability, Security Director Berger and Secretary of State Madeleine Albright, as well as General Tom Kirby from the Pentagon. They decided that al-Shifa and Khost were the targets to go for.

The planners worked round the clock. Once the targets had been pinpointed by several of the US government's twenty-four global positioning satellites (GPS), the weapons units of six US navy warships and a submarine locked on to the coordinates. Two of the ships were in the Red Sea, the others, including the submarine, were in the Arabian Gulf. They were, assortedly, part of the USS Abraham Lincoln Battle Group, the USS Dwight Eisenhower Battle Group, and the USS Essex Amphibious Readiness Group. The sub was the USS Columbia.

The next stage involved logging the coordinates of the targets into the 'mission-tailored' tracking systems of eighty Tomahawk cruise missiles. These systems comprised, in addition to GPS, Terrain Contour Matching (TERCOM) and Digital Scene Matching Area Correlation (DSMAC). Like Tomahawk® itself, all these had been registered as trademarks by the US Navy, which had lately made its first sale of the package to a foreign country – the United Kingdom had bought sixty of the missiles.

With the systems primed, it was just a matter of waiting for General Kirby to relay President Clinton's final executive implementation order, which was delivered over an encrypted line from Martha's Vineyard. Once the holiday order had been given, initiating the vertical launch systems of the various vessels was a matter of diverse hands turning diverse keys and punching diverse buttons. It was all as safe as could be, and as controlled: the organisation of violence. Every step in the process was as cross-checked and balanced as the government under whose auspices the operation was taking place. And the hands were strong hands, at the ends of strong arms, rolled with khaki, and attached to well-muscled bodies topped with shaven, right-thinking, patriotic heads. Some wore caps, some were white, some were black. One nation under God, indivisible, liberty and justice for all.

In this way, in defence of such precepts, navy weapons officers detonated the solid-booster explosive charges that lifted the Tomahawks from their silos. The missiles rose straight up at first. Then, the optimum altitude having been reached, their casings fell away. Tail fins and wings were deployed, pushed out of slots in the sides of the missiles by automated servo motors. Tiny rockets on the missiles changed the angle of thrust. Then the turbofan propulsion kicked in. After that, the missiles ceased to be projectiles and became something more like small robotic planes, just over six metres in length and half a metre in diameter.

Four score strong, they descended to a lower altitude, to avoid radar detection. Silver specks, cigarette-sized in the sky, they left vapour trails like children's crayons on nursery walls. But the vapour did not last, it disappeared as swiftly as childhood too.

As a Navy press release put it: 'Because of its long range, lethality, and extreme accuracy Tomahawk® has become the weapon of choice for the US Department of Defense.'

Security Director Berger observed that the point of using Tomahawks was to avoid 'giving the show away'. On TV screens worldwide – in a hotel lounge in Zanzibar, in a suburban house in Florida, at a secret location in Afghanistan – he explained after the fact that 'the primary motivator here was maintaining operational secrecy'.

The missiles continually realigned themselves by comparing time and location signals transmitted by atomic clocks in the satellites to their own on-board clocks and computers. From these calculations they extrapolated the ever-decreasing distance to the targets and made adjustments accordingly, also taking into account the shape of the underlying terrain and the prevailing weather patterns.

Detonation was simultaneous with impact, either from side on, or (in which case the missiles were programmed to make a parabola in the last minutes of their journey) directly above. At the factory, observers reported three large explosions. Walls were blown out, and steel and concrete thrown over the compound. At the camps, command and communication facilities, weapon and ammunition dumps and training areas, such as shooting ranges, were destroyed. Twenty-seven people were killed.

It was a terrorist university, and what it taught was death.
From the outside it looked like an ordinary factory, but deep in its
underground bunkers they were making deadly nerve gas.
Keep tuned to CNN for updates on the US missile strikes on
Afghanistan and Sudan!

Miranda and Nick sat together in silence as the reporting gathered pace. As the day progressed, coverage switched from the delivery of the Tomahawks to their effects. In the countries where the missiles had fallen, important officials gave their views. The strikes were 'a gross violation of human rights', declared the Taliban Foreign Ministry in Kabul.

The screen showed thousands of Afghan protesters stoning the deserted US embassy in the city. Then switched to Khartoum, where a similar scene took place, crowds climbing the fence of the embassy building (which had also been evacuated several years ago) and setting light to American flags.

'Down, down USA!' howled the protesters.

'This is a terrorist action,' said the President of Sudan, Omar el-Bashir, more soberly. 'This aggression targets Muslim and Arab people. They have no right to strike Sudan without any vindication or evidence. Clinton and America will have to pay.'

As to the question of whether or not the al-Shifa plant was being used to make nerve gas or other chemical weapons, he remarked: 'Putting out lies is not new for the United States and its President. A person of such immorality will not hesitate to tell any lie.' He went on to call the beleaguered President 'a war criminal of the first degree'.

Elsewhere in the Arab world, the reaction to the missile strikes was no less outraged. 'Lewinsky's dress is no longer the preoccupation of the world after Clinton has discovered Osama bin Laden's *shalwar kameez*,' declared an editorial in Beirut's *Al-Kifah Al-Arabi* newspaper.

'It is a conspiracy against the Muslim world,' said Qazi Hussain, leader of Pakistan's Jamaat e-Islami party. 'We will join the jihad!' shouted demonstrators on the streets of Karachi. They, too, were burning American flags, along with effigies of President Clinton. For good measure – and the cameras zoomed in on this – they stamped the burning embers into the pavement.

The US government responded bullishly to the criticisms. 'In life, there is no perfect security,' explained Undersecretary of

State Thomas Pickering. 'There may be more such strikes. We will act unilaterally when we must, in order to protect our citizens – but we invite other nations of the world to stand with us in this battle.' Some Western states did back the strikes. 'I strongly support this American action against terrorism,' said British Prime Minister Tony Blair.

Officials from the Organisation for the Prohibition of Chemical Weapons came forward to say that, as well as nerve gas, Empta could be used to make fungicides and anti-microbial agents. It was also linked to a process for softening plastics. Other Western scientists pointed out that VX gas shared some of the chemical constituents of cherry flavouring, as used in boiled sweets or cough syrup.

* * *

'I can't talk now,' said Queller when Miranda finally got through, the following morning.

She kept him on the line to tell him about Nick.

'What? You've found him? When?'

She told him.

'What the hell have you been doing since then?'

Forbearing to answer that question exactly, she said she hadn't been able to get through.

'Stay there. I'll be over as soon as I can. Where exactly are you again?'

'The Macpherson Ruins. Outside of Stone Town.'

During the next day, in that very place, the TV remained on whenever the generator permitted. There was to be no more love-making for a while, though there was more pizza and beer. And chicken curry and coconut rice. Over the tin roof above the sofa, bushbabies would thud across, making the aerial dish wobble and the TV picture too. Da Souza would come in from time to time, put down their food and drink on an old tin tray marked

'Property of Union Castle Shipping Company: Southampton, Cape Town, Zanzibar.'

Assuming a posture of horrified amazement at the events on the screen, he would stay and watch for a while.

'Very bad,' he'd say. 'Very bad. They will do, and the others will do, and they will do, and the others will do again. Is there no way we can control this damned crew?'

When he had left, the wooden-framed mesh door would creak on its hinges, and the warm jasmine-scented air stream more briskly through the mesh of the screen. Time passed no less briskly, and still the garrulous reporters and the anchormen, and the witnesses and the commentators and the experts chattered on.

'Let's go for a swim,' said Nick, eventually. 'Before it gets dark.'

Beneath a reddening sun, they went to the room and put on their costumes, then walked slowly down to the beach, towels slung over their shoulders.

Unwatched, the TV babbled in the lounge, then faded to black as the generator went out with a groan. At that moment, more or less, CNN happened to be reporting big news. Osama bin Laden himself had apparently sent a message from Afghanistan to London's *Al-Quds Al-Arabi* newspaper, saying that he had vowed to make further attacks on 'Crusaders and Jews'.

'The battle has not begun yet,' the message continued. 'The response will be with actions and not words.'

* * *

The man who sent that message, prepared long before, in expectation of duress, was far away from where the Tomahawks fell. He was riding a horse through a remote pass in eastern Afghanistan, along smugglers' tracks. Below him – he spurred his mount on, impatiently – rode two of his lieutenants: Ayman Zawahiri, the Egyptian doctor, and Muhammad Atef, al-Qaida's military commander. Behind them, also on horseback, were seven hand-picked members of his personal bodyguard.

The guards were close by the Sheikh at all times, but he took care to keep some part of himself back. Mystery magnified majesty, power was strongest when half hidden. He also kept himself back from revelation to the enemy, sending messages only, or allowing them to see glimpses of himself in the videos made by Ahmed the German, some of which they inevitably laid hands on. It was better to keep in the shadows like this, before emerging with one's full strength. The displayed hand of the thief, as he saw lately in Herat, derives its horrifying influence not from itself but from the want of a body.

Or perhaps a better analogy was the voice that echoed through the pillared city of Iram, warning its disobedient people. Ignoring it they were turned into stone and drowned in sand, surrounded by all their useless wealth. *Hast thou not seen how thy Lord dealt with Ad, at Iram adorned with pillars, whose like have not been reared in these lands!*

It was cold – there were drifts of snow caught in pockets of rock on either side of the pass – and he was glad of his woollen coat. Tonight they would sleep in a shepherd's barn, perhaps killing a goat to eat with the rice they had brought with them. He was hungry already though. He reached into a pocket with his long, slim fingers and, taking out a date, put it into his mouth.

Chewing the sweet flesh, he halted his horse – its hooves clattering on the rock – to look again at his companions below. He had a sudden vision, then, of putting on swift wings and flying down to them, scouring the side of the mountain. He closed his eyes against the glitter of the rocks, spat out the stone of the date, and encouraged the visualisation further, pulling on the silken threads of his consciousness like a spider in its web. As if by mental effort alone he might fly as high as the gates of the paradise or, swooping down, spy on inhabitants of the fire. Even, shaving the oceans with level wings, betake himself to the land of the Adversary – that would itself, in time, being of time, be in the fire.

He put another date in his mouth.

* * *

'I take refuge in God from Satan, the stoned one.' So whispered Khaled al-Khidr, kneeling in a mosque in Jambangona. On the island of Pemba, it was the town of his parents, who were no more. Outside the mosque, he could hear a goat bleating, waiting to be milked.

His disavowals were over. The convalescence of memory had concluded. Truth, that highest thing a man may keep, had come clearly, like the ringing of a bell that penetrated his very heart. His own history, that night of destiny – marked like writing in the particular cuts on their throats – had all descended, unclouded, manifest, into the translucent casket of his soul.

Why had he left it locked so long, escaping into other thoughts, when the key had lain so plainly in front of him all the time? Was it because he had *wanted* to collude in Zayn's story? That he had *desired* not to know the truth?

He pressed his forehead to the floor.

For whatever reason – the adventure of jihad, freedom from his family and the narrow circumstances of Zanzibar – he had gone along with something that at the time appeared to ease the affliction of their death. Yet the salve was also the cause, and in allowing it to be applied he had brought greater affliction to himself and others.

He clutched his head, doubting now whether he could have any destination but Gehenna, that fire whose fuel is men and stones. All the Sheikh's talk of a pleasing Paradise, *a walled and lofty garden*, he'd said, *its clusters nigh to gather* – this was nothing but words, false resemblances designed to wind into one's mind, covering havoc and ruin with cloying murmurings. And all this he had known before, even as he had entered on that savage path.

About him, the other worshippers were following the proper devotions, according to the Koran. He tried to gather himself. Calling on Allah and hoping on Allah, he prayed that being condemned to sin might, in fact, have been a way of arriving at Him. Yet he knew, that no more than the sun could rise in the west, he had no warrant to make this claim on the Lord.

Read out! In the Name of thy Lord who creates, who creates man from a blood-clot.

Read out! For thy Lord is the Most Munificent who teaches by the pen, teaches man that which he knew not.

The mullah was expressing the uncreated, self-sufficient power of the Koran. The essence of the Book was Allah's name – written *alif, lam, lam, ha.* Yet it surpassed the words by which man calls on Him, being a door to the essence of He who created the heavens and the earth with the truth, who splits the grain and date-stone, and holds the keys of the Unseen.

The times and speakings of the devotions jumbled in Khaled's head. He felt afraid. There is no terror like that of God, who brooks no presumption, no division, is all and everything, ever has been and will be, absolute entire.

We have distinguished the signs for a people who know . . .

We have distinguished the signs for a people who understand.

Khaled felt a wave of resignation wash over him. One day, he knew, He that looses the winds and stirs up cloud, raising even the bones and broken bits of the dead to live again, would in his mercy reveal the explanation for all that had happened. Like – yet not like, exceeding similitude and the idea of similitude – a man of light coming into a dark room, He would show He contained the darkness of the room before He entered, comprehending all things.

Khaled heard the mullah's voice from the steps of the *minbar*, echoing through the building, bouncing off the walls and smooth, pink-marble pillars.

The time would come, he knew: that dreadful hour when the earth was rolled like a scroll and the sun and moon brought together. The mountains would be plucked as wool-tufts and the limbs of the dead testify as to their deeds, good or evil.

Those who had turned away would be snatched by the scalp into the furnace, while those who were on the right hand, who were not in illusion or slumber, who performed their witnessings and preserved their trusts – they would enter the gardens, high honoured, one nation, indivisible, returned to God together.

And He would tell them, then, all the People of the Book – Muslim and Christian and Jew – of that whereon they were at variance. And so all would drink from that lake at the entrance to Paradise, the Single, the One, which is another name of God.

With prayers over, the crowd funnelled Khaled to the door, slowly at first then surging once people gained the main street, dispersing their individual ways. He blinked in the light. Fields of cocoa and nutmeg, limes and ginger, lay before him in the shimmering haze. Above the fields, carpets of jungle-bush covered rounded mountains.

He walked through the centre of Jambangona – past stone houses, mud huts, a small coconut-oil factory. Across the square, he could see his parents' house, but he didn't go to it. He could not face meeting their ghosts just yet. He saw, moreover, that there was an old man sitting outside. He recognised him as a local – a half-witted vagrant who lived by mending other people's nets; he must have taken up residence there.

Unsure what he was going to do, Khaled made his way across a field to the river, which was shaded by mangroves entwined with creepers, and overhung by bundles of knotted liana. The holes of coconut crabs dotted the banks. The water was stagnant, the green of unripe bananas.

There were flowers everywhere, of every colour. He could smell their sweetness; bound up with it was a ghastly scent of putrefaction, where the roots of the mangroves rotted down into the wet, black soil.

It was, he remembered from childhood, a place where snakes were found. Once, he and his friend Ali had thrown rocks at a mamba till, pinned down, it was eaten by the coconut crabs emerging at dusk from their holes.

He looked into the water; its green surface was perfectly still. Suddenly overcome with panic, he fell to his knees and began to weep uncontrollably. He began touching the palms of his hands on the damp earth and passing them manically over his face and arms. He was hearing the voice at this time: *go into the water, go into the water . . .*

He tried to hang onto himself, to calm down and not catch the earth on his palms, not let his distress turn a ritual of purification into a deliberate soiling. He'd wanted to cleanse himself before returning to his parents' house, to make his peace with their ghosts and deal with the vagrant. He wanted to find Ali, too.

The rite was the *tayammum*, purification by sand or stone – or, failing those, earth – when water was not available or unhealthy. In his distress, he was doing it wrongly, mixing earth with tears and sweat. The point was just to touch, not rub with earth. He should, in any case, have performed the ablution before prayer and not afterwards. It was, he reflected miserably, yet another sign of his sinful condition.

30

Zayn Mujuj manoeuvred the cabin cruiser past a rock in a creek, on the eastern side of Pemba. A cigarette hung between his lips. Sweat ran down his shaven head. Unfamiliar birds and animals were calling out to him. Yet he remembered this journey. He had been here before. He remembered how there were too many birds and animals and plants in this place. It was deep green, and he didn't like it. He was more comfortable in treeless acres of barren ground. Palestine, Sudan, Afghanistan. Places of ochre. Places of rock. Places of the skull.

He was looking for Khaled. Once the bombs went off, the two of them were supposed to take the cabin cruiser from the quiet cove near Dar where it had been moored during the operation to rendezvous with a cargo ship in the ocean in the afternoon. This would take them to Muscat in Oman. Then Dubai again, Karachi, overland to Peshawar and across the border into Afghanistan, back to the Eagle's Nest.

But it didn't happen that way. The cargo ship hadn't shown. They waited till dusk, then motored to Pemba, it being the nearest land to the rendezvous point. They would stay there for a week. Another deserted cove. Each night, Zayn called the Sheikh on the satphone. Where is the ship? *It is coming.* Where is the ship? *There is a delay.* Zayn was surprised at his own anxiety. In the mornings, he would send Khaled to buy fish from a village. They ate. They waited.

One bright day, everything changed. Zayn woke up in the cruiser, in the quiet cove. He could hear the sea's quiet conversation, see the splashing, sparkling water, but it had little effect on him.

Nor did the brilliant red-and-yellow woodpeckers in the palm trees, or the pelicans that swooped down over the sand. It was not in his nature to find such experiences pleasant. He resisted ascribing symbolic value to them, and was a wonderful killer exactly because of this, because he took the same approach with human beings. Yet sometimes, sometimes beauty played on him, disarming him momentarily, like bare-legged Sheba. Afterwards he hated again: all the more fiercely, for having chanced the loss of hate. He would die if love assailed him, if – like someone slipping into a tempting lake on a hot day – he allowed himself to forget what had happened to his family in Beirut.

One drop had poisoned him, turning everything to pain and woe. The slaughter had been carried out by the Israeli air force and the Christian Phalange, but the deeper blame lay with the United States, which had supplied much of the Israeli armoury and consistently maintained the line that the Israelis were 'partners for peace'.

Zayn spat through the window into the water, remembering his brother's body, beaten with iron bars by the Phalange till it was an unrecognisable mess of blood, remembering his holy dread of the Israeli jets tearing over the rooftops. The bombs they dropped on Abu Chaker street felled one apartment block after another, till they came to his home, burying his father, mother and baby sister under tons of concrete.

It was for this he hated the US and its mart of destruction, it was for this, for the better cause, that he had murdered Khaled's parents, punishing the father for embezzling al-Qaida money. Seeing a potential recruit, he'd then ensnared the young Zanzibari. He wasted no time feeling guilty about it: like shame and regret and hesitation, guilt was for fools.

He turned over and looked at the other bunk. The boy was not there. He must have gone early to buy fish. Zayn stood up, buttoned his jeans, and went up on deck. He looked sullenly across the waves at palm trees dappled by sun, rustled by wind. A dark switch chastised his conscience: these seaside sights and sounds were unreal. Only the task existed, which was in Allah.

He waited two hours. Then he knew Khaled had fled. That was a risk. He took out the briefcase to dial bin Laden on the satphone again.

Macerations of silk, the tone interrupting the thin hiss of the static; and then his master's voice, no less soft, like the brush of a raven's feather. *Who?* To other ears a blast of evil, to Zayn it was honeydew.

He told him that Khaled had become a security threat, had disappeared. He said he did not know why, but always thought the boy was weak.

They spoke in a crude, thinly veiled code. Osama was 'the manager'. He was 'comfortable'. He was 'at his ease'. Yes, the Talibs, 'the owners of the company', were still happy with him. Khaled was 'the timid finch'.

The manager said the timid finch must be killed if he will not return to Afghanistan with Zayn. *He knows too much.* And the ship? *It will not come now.* Why? *There are delays. There are some problems in the organisation. A man has let us down.* Zayn paused. *Shush shush*, went the satellite. *Come soon*, he heard the voice say. *I have work for you here.*

Suspecting Khaled had returned to his family's place, a village – almost a town – up the creek, Zayn set off there in the boat. He took the cruiser up this narrow inlet choked with reeds and mangroves. Wild pigeons were calling at him from the banks, but he ignored them. Tree-coneys and monkeys were jumping about in the green tresses hanging over the water, a pygmy antelope came down to drink – but all these, too, he ignored.

Reaching Jambangona, he moored at a dilapidated quay, then began to search the market. Here were sesame seeds, tomatoes, cashew nuts, here were guavas, durians, yams, here were oranges, pulses, pods of kapok and vanilla, here were limes, cassava root, grapefruit all piled high in profusion. But he disregarded them. He ignored the donkeys also, wandering between the stalls, and the women with copper pots on their heads. This was why the Sheikh, the Director, Mr Sam prized him. Because he was implacable. Because he saw only the task at hand, which was Allah's hand.

* * *

Jack Queller had arrived on Zanzibar the previous night. He joined Nick and Miranda for breakfast at the Macpherson. Da Souza began serving them coffee, sliced pawpaw, toast. Do they want eggs? The atmosphere was a little tense. Queller was having difficulty spreading butter on his toast. Nick was grilling him.

'Couldn't you have done something sooner? If you knew the dangers?'

'Well I –'

Queller's mobile rang, saving him. It was Altenburg, brusque. He had news from the listening posts at Langley.

'SIGINT has picked up a series of calls off the island of Pemba. To bin Laden we think. You are the nearest agent. Can you check it out?'

'Do you have a grid?'

Altenburg gave him the map reference.

'We are sending a helicopter. Some men. But you might get there quicker.'

Why is he doing this? Queller wondered. What is he up to? If there is a prize to be found on Pemba, why doesn't he just take the credit himself? Queller had lived among secrets so long he could see only what was clandestine, hush-hush: hidden plans, ulterior motives, strategies that sucked righteousness to themselves like a sponge sucked water. He could not see, for instance, that Altenburg might not be a ruthless empire builder. That he might be just an ordinary man doing his job.

'How can we get to Pemba?' he asked his breakfast companions.

Da Souza brought the egg, a pitiful thing, the white unravelling from the yolk. Queller felt a strange sympathy with it. Now Miranda was quizzing him about the call.

'There's a lead there,' he said. 'Calls have been traced. We need to go right away. We need a fast boat.'

* * *

Zayn moved round the ancient masonry, his shaven head ducking under lintels, fringes of straw. He was searching the stone houses, huts, the mosque at Jambangona. Curious faces watched him from windows. At a small coconut-oil factory the dust from milled husk made him sneeze and sneeze. A killer in blue jeans sneezing, an adept of the difficult trade of death sneezing: it was like the laugh of a demon. He had a knife in his tall boot, rage – bright as the white phosphorus of Israeli shells – burning in his brain. He made his way down to the river.

* * *

It took a little time. Nick borrowed his Belgian friend's big motor boat, the *Cythère*. They travelled to Pemba. It was a very different island to Zanzibar, much hillier and heavily wooded in some parts.

Nick was at the wheel, Miranda was beside him. Queller sat a little way back, looking out to sea. The prow of the boat slapped down on each wave as it came. The green mass of the island loomed. From the midst of it, perched on the edge of hills, smoke rose from beehive-like stone buildings.

'Copra kilns,' Nick explained. 'A friend of mine,' he shouted back to Queller, 'said the English pirate Captain Kidd hid his treasure here in the seventeenth century.'

351

'Which friend?' asked Miranda.

'Leggatt,' said Nick, from the side of his mouth.

They fell silent, remembering the dead Englishman.

* * *

There was no one at the river. Zayn returned to the house of Khaled's parents. He'd pulled his knife out of his boot here, once before, slashing two throats in the darkness with savage efficiency. But this time there was no one there except an imbecilic old man mending a net. Zayn picked him up and shook him – but it soon became clear that the man, who nearly passed out with fright, knew nothing of Khaled's whereabouts. *That family died! That family were murdered!* This was not the information that Zayn required. The old man was dropped and left trembling on the floor. Zayn took the boat up another shallow-water creek, further inland – past fishing villages, past ruined palaces hung with vegetation. The creek widened to a river, the river to an estuary, the estuary to a bay.

He was by the sea again, a town called Chake Chake. It was a port, there were fishermen, cranes, warehousing; it was also a holiday resort, there were tourists, knick-knacks, antiquities. He could see white faces among the black. Women in bikinis lying on the beach. Men in Bermuda shorts, haggling with boys selling pineapple chunks. They wore trays with straps made of plant fibre, had long wooden skewers loaded with pineapple. There were kayaks for hire. It all infuriated the Arab beyond measure. Sweat was pouring down his shaven head again. The sun was up. There were two cannons. There were decorated pillars. He was sweating for the Director. He was sweating for jihad.

He left the boat in the harbour, not deigning to check in at the port office. His eye fell on a beggar here, on a boy there. He pushed his way up the busy main street, Zayn Mujuj, killer in blue jeans. A briefcase in one hand. A knife in his boot. There was a sign, *Main Street*. Carved items were arranged on the pavements for sale. There were stalls with fabrics, shells, bangles. Zayn didn't stop to look or buy. But he remained watchful, ever vigilant, scanning the streets for Khaled. If necessary, he would wait. He would complete the task.

He searched for another hour, then booked himself into the Hoteli ya Chake. After saying his prayers, kneeling on the floor of the room, he took a shower. Then he came downstairs and ordered grilled octopus. He wondered, looking out of the window, why such a crowd had gathered in the square.

* * *

There was nothing at the map reference. Just a deserted cove. A fishing village where they were directed further inland. Another small town. Yes, a stranger has been here. *He injured an old man. He went up the Chake River. He went to Chake Chake.* Queller shook his head and followed Nick and Miranda back to the boat.

They took to the water again. The green river debouched, into a blue bay. There was a town over there, some kind of port, some kind of resort – a lazy, tropical, sprawling place, with houses made from shattered coral, thatched with papyrus.

The empty sleeve of Queller's missing arm flapped in the wind, pulling at his light cotton jacket where it was attached with a large safety pin. On the same side – though hidden under the jacket – an automatic pistol sat snugly in a brown leather shoulder-holster. He joined the other two by the wheel. The sun was up.

'This,' he said, as they crossed the dazzling bay, 'is a beautiful spot. It's not the kind of place in which you'd expect to be hunting terrorists.'

A pair of tourists whizzed across the bay on jet skis. Not long afterwards Nick drew in the throttle, and they chugged towards the entrance of Chake harbour. There were many dug-out canoes with outriggers, four or five big wooden dhows and a few modern boats with motors and fibreglass hulls. There was also, at a separate wharf, a steel ship of larger tonnage, berthed under a crane that was lifting crates of cloves off pallets lined up on a cement platform, outside a commodious warehouse.

Standing on white stone plinths raised above the quays, a pair of ancient Portuguese cannon guarded the entrance to the harbour. On both sides fishermen were releasing their catch – tuna, kingfish, mullet, shrimp and lobster, all glistening in the bright sunlight as they slithered from the nets into low wooden pens set out on the flagstones.

'Would you look at that?' murmured Queller.

Elsewhere in the bay there was a beach, upon which some jet skis and a few kayaks were pulled up. Nearby, stuck on iron poles in the sand, a sign, misspelt and faded, declared *Kizunguzungu Motor Sports, Pleasure Croft for Hire.*

As the *Cythère* passed between the cannons, Nick pointed, lifting a hand from the wheel. 'Look! That's the boat, the one that was at Lyly.'

They moored a few boats away from the cabin cruiser and disembarked. By the port office, a beggar with a bad case of jiggers thrust out a swollen foot as they walked by. Next to him a young Swahili boy was trimming the sails of a toy boat made from the hollow shell of a baobab fruit. Queller was right. It didn't look the kind of place where murderers might hole up. But the cruiser was there.

In the distance, they heard the sound of ululation.

They passed a malodorous shark, strung up on a bamboo frame waiting to be skinned, and wandered through a confusing knot of dank alleyways. To the casual observer – say a red-eyed fisherman coiling a rope in the porch of his house – they must have looked no different to the other *muzungu* tourists roaming about.

The ululation grew louder.

They finally found Main Street. Here, too, various items – copper trays and coffee pots, baskets and mats woven from reeds, carved wooden spoons and Arab chests made from ebony or mangrove and studded with brass – were all laid out for the tourists to inspect and, with luck, purchase. There were also colourful collections of cowries, piles of other, tinier shells, plus a few Arab swords and daggers. Miranda noticed a stall hung with silks and Persian rugs, and another with malachite bracelets and anklets, and beads made from ivory and amber.

They walked on, past a man doggedly pushing a barrow of pineapples towards the beach, into the centre of the town. There was a crowd in the square, also a couple of large black bulls, held in a stockade. Gated, the stockade funnelled into a kind of grandstand.

'What is happening here?' Miranda asked a little brown man selling polystyrene cups of coffee from a wooden tray hung round his shoulders.

His eyes filled with amusement. 'You do not know? It is *mchezo wa ngombe*.'

'What's that?'

'The game of the bull. Will you buy some coffee? It's ginger-flavoured.'

Miranda obliged, and the others followed suit. Having no option, hemmed in on every side now by the buzzing crowd, the Americans stood on a crumbling white wall under a casuarina tree to watch the bullfight. The custom was, said Queller, a strange remnant from the days of Portuguese influence on the islands. Miranda remembered him telling her about this back in Washington.

Another place, another time . . . was where the bulls seemed to rush from too, charging into the grandstand raising billowing clouds of dust. The pen was like those into which the fish had been tipped at the harbour, only much taller and sturdier, made from palm-trunk uprights lined with strips of bamboo. Cheered on by the crowd, some of whom were beating drums and blowing horns, African youths leaped in and out of the pen, weaving between the bulls, flicking them with pieces of white cloth. Others, hanging over the edges of the pen, baited the animals with pointed sticks, or tried to catch them with neck-ropes and jump onto their backs.

* * *

The game continued. The crowd was all eyes, and the eyes of the crowd were red from the dust. The bulls had small horns but – snorting, pawing the ground with their hooves – they presented formidable opponents for the bare-chested youths. Each took his turn, the showier ones cartwheeling and pirouetting. Once a young man had been in, he went through the crowd, grinning and covered in sweat and, if he had been wounded, streaming with blood. In front of him, he carried a brass pot into which by way of payment for the entertainment, onlookers dropped coins.

Or, as in the case of Queller and Nick and Miranda, five-dollar bills.

Or, as in the case of Zayn Mujuj, who had been drawn from his hotel into the whooping crowd, nothing at all.

One youth, especially pleased with himself, told the Americans that the bulls were called Bom-Bom and Wembe. The youth himself was called Ali, he informed them.

'What do the bulls' names mean?' Miranda asked.

'In Inglezi,' Ali replied, beaming wildly, 'Bom-Bom and Wembe is Machine-Gun and Razor!'

Before they jumped into the pen, the youths made a barking noise – to get up their courage – the drums beat all the louder, and the women sang and trilled.

'*Kige-lege-le! Kige-lege-le! Kige-kige-lege-lege-kigelegele!*'

Or chanted in unison, clapping their hands: '*Aliye mbuya yangu naanchezele ngombe!*' He who is my lover, he must play the bull.

So Ali explained. The men, meanwhile, were clapping their hands and whistling. Their job – their job was to put *Shetani*, or Satan, into the bulls.

* * *

Another youth jumped into the pen. He was wearing a T-shirt with a picture of a monkey on it. He was thrilled to be back among his people and their customs – to be back with his friend Ali, to be away from all the rigidity of al-Qaida, with its heavy sense of mission, its burden of holy murder. But he wasn't, he wasn't away from it, because Zayn, who had barged his way through the crowd to the front of the pen, had fixed his eyes upon him.

* * *

Through the criss-cross of bodies, through the pall of dust, Nick Karolides saw them both, the terrorists, a vision of half-remembered faces – one shaven-headed, bulky and fiery-eyed, the other delicate and nervous but wanting to prove himself at last in the game of the bull. Faces from a mist of pain, from the memory of Lyly and his ordeal there.

Khaled, in the centre of the arena now, caught hold of a bull's rump and leant on it to goad it back into play. The other bull had been caught in a neck-rope by a youth hanging over the side. It was thumping itself into the side of the pen, making it shake and the crowd call out indignantly.

'That's one of them in the middle now!' Nick shouted, jumping off the wall and forcing his way into the mêlée, in the direction of the pen. 'The other is the big guy across the other side.'

Miranda and Queller followed him, the crowd parting as the *muzungu* pushed through. They reached the edge of the stockade. The bull Khaled was pushing, Bom-Bom or Wembe as the case may be, was still refusing to move. Suddenly the other bull, having disentangled itself from the neck-rope, wheeled round and charged him. He rolled over in the matting and the bull cannoned into the other side – knocking Zayn, who'd climbed up the fence, into the arena, much to the amusement of the crowd.

* * *

Still hanging on to the tail of the other bull, squinting through the dust-cloud, Khaled saw the face of the Palestinian: he was wearing an expression of awful amiability. Horror-struck, Khaled let go of the bull's tail and dashed to the edge of the pen. Zayn, pursued by the other bull, ran after him and started dragging him back down from the side. The crowd cheered loudly, assuming this was all part of the entertainment. The pursuing bull gored Zayn in the leg and he fell to the ground, whereupon the bull started to trample him, snorting of triumph.

The young man climbed over the fence and fled through the crowd. The three Americans ran after him, down Main Street. Khaled knocked over, in the course of his flight, the pineapple man and his barrow, then disappeared into a maze of narrow alleyways. They lost him for a while before Queller – who had dropped behind, stumbling on pineapples – spotted him reappear from a side entrance. Reappear and straight away dodge, on seeing the sprawling white man, thinking himself unseen, into the doorway of a shop. A sign above the door said 'SHELLS AND OTHER CURIOS OF NOTE'.

Drawing his automatic, Queller went inside. Seeing the gun, the Indian shopkeeper gave a shriek of horror and gestured to a back room. There was another room, and a third, till Queller gained the inmost chamber. This was ill lit, a paraffin lamp casting jumpy light on cardboard boxes full of shells. He looked round. There was no one to be seen.

Then he heard a noise and approached a corner, holding the gun out in front of him. Suddenly, a shape moved in the darkness and a hand came out, flinging a fistful of tiny, sharp shells into his face. Momentarily blinded, Queller lowered his weapon. Khaled took this opportunity to burst from his hiding place and bowl him over.

He ran through the shop, past the astonished Indian, and out into the street again: smack into Nick and Miranda, who had backtracked. He sprang up like a cat and, pushing them aside, ran off again. Nick sprained his wrist, falling off-balance into the concrete gutter when Khaled pushed. It was full of stagnant water and floating, all-too-familiar solids. Queller re-emerged from the shop and in no time at all – not even enough time for him to wrinkle his nose at the smell – the three of them set off in pursuit.

It was Nick who caught him, in a diving tackle next to one of the stalls. Queller, reaching them breathless, trained his gun on the youth.

'You're not going to shoot him!' Miranda yelled, stepping forward.

The youth took advantage of Queller's distraction to jump up and grasp one of the Arab daggers on display at the tourist stall. He dragged Miranda to him and put the knife to her neck. Holding her in front of him as a shield, he began to walk backwards away from Queller and Nick. With the point of the knife at her throat, Miranda was frozen in a posture of wide-eyed stupefaction.

Queller lowered his gun again. His empty sleeve flapped in the breeze.

'You can't get far,' he said, his stump crawling with pain.

He only half believed the words himself, deriding himself as he said them, deriding himself also for that same derision, drawing him away as it did from alertness, from senses fully engaged to present danger. He stood helplessly, looking at Miranda with the knife at her throat. He felt old and powerless, a shadow of his former self, the active agent that age and a missing arm and the death of a wife had taken away from him. The gun was in his hand and it was bright and breezy on Pemba, but he was going, Jack Queller, into an area of psychic darkness. He was by his wife's bedside in the hospital again, he was up on the mountain with bin Laden again.

The youth was already running to the dock, dragging Miranda with him, pulling her, clutching her to his monkey T-shirt. There were too many people for Queller to shoot. People were running to and fro in between. Nick was already following, shouting.

* * *

Holding the woman's head beneath his arm, Khaled unwound the rope that moored the cabin cruiser to the quayside. Then he climbed in, pulling the woman behind him. He looked frantically for where Zayn had put the keys. He opened a cubbyhole. There was a gun there, one of Zayn's, a little silver pistol, and there was a flashlight. But no key. He pulled down the sun visor. There they were, where keys are always kept.

He started the engine. All the while the young white woman was held in the crook of his arm. She was very quiet. He had no idea what he was going to do with her. He had no idea what he was going to do with himself. This was not a good situation. How had he imagined he would be able to slip back, undisturbed, into his old life? All he knew, right now, was that he had to get away from Zayn, get away from al-Qaida, get away from the Amerikani.

Queller and Nick ran down to the docks and powered up the *Cythère*. They were gabbling, blaming each other. Queller, his empty sleeve trailing behind him, had lost his safety-pin and his self-possession; Nick was losing his dreaminess, finding himself out at last. Reflected in the windshield of the *Cythère* as it surged forward, he confronted his own image: flecked with spray, the self-portrait was mesmerising, wavy as the sea behind it, wavy and dangerous, too, since he had to drive the *Cythère*, Olivier's difficult boat.

And so two pairs of props threshed the shallows of Chake harbour. Two craft sped out into the bay, hulls smacking the waves, white tails of foam issuing from bows as steel blades cut into the water, each according to its pattern, turbulence marshalled to a single line. The stories could be told second by second, relating the thought of those in the boats, the feelings they had, the words they breathed, accompanied by proper gesticulations of the body – just as the old men of the Swahili, those people of the sea, related their own voyagers' tales from times before, in port shebeens and firelit villages down the coast, now as long ago . . .

Some short time later, a wounded figure, streaming blood, stumbled out of the glowering firmament down to the harbour. He gave a roar of anger on seeing the boats bounding away in the distance. Clambering across, Zayn tried a few of the outboards on the fishing boats, ignoring the shouts of their owners. Out the cords came, in they snickered. None would start. Seeing a tourist pull up on the little beach next to the harbour, a young white man with a Scandinavian look, Zayn splashed out into the surf and relieved him of his jet ski. When the puzzled Swede protested, Zayn cuffed him like a bear, knocking him into the breakers.

31

The boat ahead swept up to the foaming ruff of the reef, drove alongside for a short while, then – angling in at a place where the foam subsided – passed into the lagoon.

'That's the *mlango*,' Nick said. 'Gap in the coral.'

The young African had tried to evade them in his boat – steering from side to side and hiding behind other islands – but it had not been difficult to follow him to Lyly. The *Cythère* was more powerful, but the cabin cruiser had too much of a head start for them to overhaul it.

'This is where they put the bomb together?' asked Queller.

'Yes. Christ, I hope she's all right. Can you see inside the cabin?'

Queller lowered the expensive binoculars kept on the *Cythère*. They were heavy to hold with one hand. He had to shout to be heard above the sound of the engine.

'No, I can't. I'm not surprised he's come back here though.'

'Personally,' said Nick, keeping the boat steady as it bounced across the waves, 'I've had it with this fucking place. If he does anything to her . . .'

Queller said nothing. The white tower of the lighthouse came into view. Its outlines hardened as they approached. Queller noticed there was a house, too, and another building. Almost everywhere else, the forest covered the island like a thick green carpet.

'Why do you think he has–' he heard Nick say, as the other boat beached, 'come back here?'

'They always go back. Like a dog to its vomit. It's a criminal pathology.'

'Maybe he's run out of fuel,' Nick shouted.

The *Cythère* sped up to the door in the reef, then suddenly swerved to one side.

'Shit!' Nick said. 'She's too broad in the beam. She won't get through.'

He eased off the throttle.

'Give me those.'

Queller handed him the binoculars – but it was easy enough to see what was happening with the naked eye. The man was dragging Miranda up the beach, towards an opening in the forest.

'He must know them,' Nick said, desperately.

'Know what?'

The engine throbbed in the water.

'There are caves on this island. I couldn't find a way in, not above water. Leggatt cut a hole through. That opening. That's where he's taking her. We'll have to swim.'

Queller looked down at the outline of the coral beneath the water. The clearance they needed was only a matter of a foot either side. Struck by an idea, he opened his jacket and produced his pistol.

'We could shoot it away.'

Nick looked aghast. He seemed to hesitate, for some reason Queller couldn't understand, then nodded. 'All right.'

Queller slipped off the safety catch and aimed at the edge of the coral. There was a boom as he pulled the trigger and a tall splash as the bullet hit the water. A large piece of reef dropped away to the ocean floor. Then he did the same on the other side. Another white shadow spun down. Now there was plenty of room. Queller put his gun back in its shoulder holster.

Nick let out the throttle, executed a circle in the water, and they passed through easily. He drove the boat directly onto the beach.

'Easy,' Queller said.

Nick cut the engine.

'I'll go in.'

They hit the sand with a heavy thump. Queller was knocked off balance and, with only one arm to steady himself, half fell onto the deck.

'I'll go in,' Nick repeated. 'Into the cave. You stay.'

'Wouldn't it be better if we both went in?'

Nick shook his head.

'You wait here. Keep watch. Leggatt said there were various openings, he could come up any one of them.'

'Where are they?'

'I – wasn't able to find any.'

Queller frowned. 'I better come.'

'Stay here. He could just reappear and take our boat.'

Nick picked up the heavy rubberised flashlight Olivier Pastoreau kept in the cabin of the *Cythère*. Queller took the binoculars and hung them round his neck. They climbed out of the boat and began jogging up the sand.

'If that's how you want it,' Queller said, short of breath. 'You better take this.' He reached into his jacket and produced the gun.

Nick looked at it askance. 'I've never really shot guns much. I could hit her.'

They reached the opening that Leggatt had hacked out in the forest curtain.

'Just take it. This is the safety catch.'

Nick took it and weighed it in his hand for a second.

'Be careful,' Queller said.

But the younger man had already set off down the passage through the trees, at the end of which an oval opening could be seen through mossy green rocks. Queller walked back down to the beach, anxious, feeling that he should have pressed harder about going into the cave.

He waited by the shoreline at first, looking out at a sandbar appearing to the west. Noticing a strange, circular structure at the place where the arm of the sandbar joined the beach proper, he walked over to it. The thing was like a little fortification. Sticks in the sand, shored up with heavy rocks right round. He peeked over and looked inside it, but there didn't seem to be anything but sand.

* * *

The flashlight was still in the crook of wet rock where he'd placed it. It sent light skittering over the green walls of the cavern. Miranda was afraid. The young African man pushed her against the algae. He held the point of the knife at her throat with one hand, the other gripping a fistful of hair. Gasping for breath, she told herself again and again to keep calm.

All the way, as they had wound and slid along corridors of rock he seemed to know well, he had been talking – to himself or her she could hardly tell – in a garbled mixture of English and Swahili. One thing she had been able to pick out constantly was the phrase 'jihad job'. He kept asking, in a sing-song voice, *This jihad job? Or no jihad job? What this thing? This jihad job?*

But now, holding the point of the knife to her throat, he was definitely speaking to her.

'You must help me escape from here,' he said. 'You must come with me as hostage and tell your friends to go away.'

The knife was shaking in his hand. He seemed to be trying to master himself. Calming the pure fear inside her, Miranda locked her eyes on his in the shivering light.

'They're outside.' She struggled to keep her voice calm. 'My friends. You saw them coming. You must give yourself up. It will be better for you.'

He stared back, tilting his head to one side. He looked crazy.

'If you don't help me, I will kill you. That is what voice says. Away from all. Kill all if necessary. Away from hunt. Execute all action. In the name of Allah, forgive!'

* * *

Queller walked over the island sand, checking whether they had surfaced anywhere. He went into the forest at another place, taking a different path. There seemed to be a hell of a lot of blind alleys that someone had cut through. Birds were whistling in the trees above him and light shone down on the forest floor. But the way the green pressed in gave an eerie atmosphere, a deadly stillness that seemed to suggest that the glades in which he paused and the defiles through which he passed had a presence beyond the merely human.

He was relieved to come back out and walk down to the sea. Then he saw something strange. Out on the edge of the sandbar, the surf was tugging at some kind of object. He lifted the binoculars. Through the lens he saw a jet ski lying on its side, the light waves washing over it.

* * *

The man pressed the point of the knife a little harder against Miranda's throat. Her mind jumped desperately from word to word, option to option, the damp cave wall against her spine. Then it came to her.

She spoke softly and slowly. 'Giving yourself up is what Allah would want. You have done enough harm. It must stop now. Let it stop now.'

He moved away from her, and began shaking his head from side to side. She slid down the wall, raw-nerved, terrified.

He lowered the knife, as if exhausted, and when he spoke it was if he just wanted to unburden himself.

'They killed my parents. I realise it now. Al-Qaida killed my parents. Zayn killed my father and my mother. I wanted kill him, when I realise it. But when I saw him – I was too afraid.'

He repeated himself, shouting. 'Too afraid!'

The phrase echoed round the cavern.

'You did the bombing, right?'

He nodded, his head bobbing in the green light.

'But I was not the main. It was others – there is a man, Zayn . . . that man I said. And I shall be killing him.'

'It is time to stop killing,' Miranda said. 'The time for killing is over.'

He raised the knife again.

Miranda tried to keep her voice as even as possible, to put into practice all she had learned, in books, in classrooms, about dealing with a hostage situation – bonding with the hostage-taker, trying to make him feel you were on his side, that you understood his concerns.

'You haven't told me your name. What is your name?'

* * *

Queller swung the binoculars round, scanning the horseshoe of the beach – until he saw the little stockade he had peered at earlier. Looming over it now was a large man, his torn shirt covered in blood. Queller recognised him as the Arab in the bullring. He thought about the gun he had given to Nick. But the man – who had just pulled one of the pieces of wood out of the palisade – was too far away to get a decent shot anyhow.

He watched the Arab drag himself monstrously up the beach, leaning on the stick for support; then something strange happened. The huge man paused, lifted up the stick and began thrashing the sand. This went on for about a minute, before he continued on his way. He seemed to be heading for the lighthouse. Queller looked around the boat for some kind of weapon. His eye settled on a long steel spike, a fishing gaff, marlinspike. He picked it up and began walking in the direction the man had gone.

* * *

Nick hurried through the caves, sliding on the algae, switching the gun from side to side. He was glad he had brought it now, and had taken off the safety catch. He kept finding alcoves and openings, but they were empty. He carried on, breathing hard, cave moisture dripping down his face. He stopped, listened. Voices in the distance. A drop of algae fell from the ceiling onto his nose. He listened again for the voices. Sometimes they seemed far away, sometimes near. He called out her name.

The shout echoed, reverberating amongst the hollows and angles of the cave, impossible to decipher or locate as it overlaid and repeated itself. *Miranda! Miranda!* Deeper in the cave, the echoes themselves seemed to twist over again, knitting and meshing knotting tighter and tighter together. *Miraaanda . . .*

* * *

Khaled stood up suddenly, dropping the knife. She saw it turn, tip-topping in the beam of the flashlight before disappearing into the dark. Khaled was spinning now, swivelling round in the cave, something silver glinting in his hand that he'd whipped from his waistband at the back – it was the tiny pistol he had taken from the compartment in the boat, she realised. He was all jangly again now, a bag of nerves. All her good work had been undone.

She stretched a foot across the slimy floor trying to hook the knife and bring it closer. The man stopped spinning round. He gave a peculiar sigh and walked over to the flashlight. For a moment she saw his face in the phosphorescence, his eyes full of a wild light of their own, a strange, serene smile playing about his lips.

She felt the knife under her foot.

He picked up the flashlight and swung round, shining the beam full in her face. He took two quick steps then, and all was dark.

* * *

Next to the palisade Queller found the body of a large green snake. That was what the guy had been hitting on the ground, he realised. It must have tried to bite him. He followed the footsteps in the sand. There were drops of blood. The bull must have gored him pretty badly.

He wished he still had his pistol. It was an Arcadia Machine & Tool .45 – no elephant stopper, since he preferred a light weapon these days, but a whole lot more use than a marlinspike. The tracks led to the lighthouse, then seemed to disappear.

Holding the gaff in front of him, Queller was about to go inside when he heard a noise to his left. He turned to see the Arab lifting the thick length of wood he had taken from the beach. Queller jabbed the steel spike forward, but it was too late. The rough wood smacked him in the face, knocking him to the ground. The Arab bent to grab the spike, then lifted it over his head. Blinking away the pain, Queller saw two huge hands where they gripped the shaft, and he could see the steel point, too, as it plunged down.

* * *

Deep in the labyrinth, Nick entered a large cavern. The gun in one hand, he swept the beam of the flashlight around with the other. The light, bouncing off the green walls like a laser show, suddenly fell upon a figure crouched in a corner. As it did so the figure moved.

'Please,' said a voice. It was Miranda.

'It's me,' he said, squelching across the floor. 'It's Nick, baby.'

He knelt and shone the flashlight at her face. Her mouth was slightly open and her face was smeared with algae. But she looked OK otherwise. He put the flashlight down, reaching for her, drawing her head to his chest.

She started to sob. He put his hands round her and lifted her. Her arms went round his neck. A shot rang out above them.

* * *

Queller stared at the sky. There was a terrible weight on his chest. He looked up at a few clouds crossing the blue in the place where, some seconds ago, he had seen a shaven brown head, a face with a wolfish expression, and two hands pulled back above, holding the gaff. It had glinted in the hot sun as it came down.

Then all that had gone. There was gunfire. A small report, not his AMT but something lighter still, maybe a Derringer.

A red hole had opened in the Arab's forehead, liquid spurting onto Queller's face and, before he understood what had happened, the man's heavy body had pitched forward onto him. The gaff was planted in the sand behind his head – so close it had grazed his skull and pressed in strands of his hair. The Arab's head was across Queller's shoulder.

A shadow came over him and he felt the gaff being pulled out of the ground. He saw a young African face looking down: the face of the youth who had taken Miranda.

'I guess I owe you a debt of thanks,' Queller said.

The youth was still holding the gaff in one hand. In the other was a small pistol of exactly the type Queller had envisaged.

'Do not thank me. Thank Allah. His voice spoke me. It spoke me and told me to give up this trick. To do some things I should have done long time before. Now I go to do more work. Not against America. True work for Muslim people.'

Queller tried to wipe away the Arab's blood from his eyes, but he couldn't get his hand up.

'Wouldn't it be better,' he said, trapped under the dead man, 'if you came with me back to Dar and we talked all this through?'

The youth touched Queller's forehead with the point of the lance.

'Because I no longer trust al-Qaida – you think that means I must trust America?'

With that he lifted the gaff, turned and was gone.

Queller tried to lift the dead Arab off him. But it was impossible with only one arm. He was too exhausted, too old. A few minutes later he heard gunshots. Then the noise of a boat starting up. Not long after that, Nick and Miranda were lifting off the dead man.

He leaned on them as they walked down to the shore. Khaled, as Miranda told them he was called, had taken the *Cythère*. He'd also removed the spare fuel jerry from the cabin cruiser and taken it with him. It wouldn't have been any use to them anyway. The shooting Queller had heard was explained by a ragged line of holes beneath the waterline of the cruiser. Far across the water, the *Cythère* was nearly out of sight, its motor only faintly audible.

'Olivier won't be very happy,' said Nick, as they watched. 'That boat's worth about a million. It had sonar and everything.'

'Oh, the agency will see to that,' Queller said, sitting down on a rock, rubbing and holding his chest.

'Where do you think he's gone?'

Queller looked out to sea. There was no sign of the boat now.

'Who knows?' he said. 'How the hell are we going to get off this island? Any ideas?'

He looked round at Nick and Miranda standing hand in hand on the beach, the forest at their back and the lighthouse stretching up behind them.

'Do you know you're both covered in some kind of green stuff?'

Nick grinned, and gave Miranda a sidelong look. 'Maybe we should go into the sea and wash it off?'

Queller smiled. 'I shall avert my eyes and go up to that little house over there.'

An hour later, clean and glowing, Nick and Miranda joined him in the cottage. They slept there that night. The following morning they were woken early by the sound of helicopters.

32

The story was out. CNN and several other networks had got wind of it, well before the rescue helicopters reached the mainland. Accordingly, when Queller, Nick and Miranda arrived in the drab, echoing halls of Dar airport, a phalanx of flashbulbs and bulbous TV microphones was there to greet them. They disembarked like a trio of pop stars. The impression of celebrity was strengthened by the presence of Altenburg's men who, together with the brown-uniformed Tanzanian police, made a kind of gangway for them between the bawling reporters.

There was also someone else there to greet them, a miraculous oddity, someone out of place who perhaps because of that, because of the flowing surprise of her bright orange, Hare Krishna robes, was able to burst through the cordon and press something into Queller's only hand.

A red carnation. He looked at her pale, blank face – white as peeled almonds, framed by long brown hair – and found himself saying, 'Why thank you very much!' It struck him, making an odd connection with the big Arab, that they were usually shaven-headed.

As quickly as she had appeared, the Krishna was swept away by security. Queller, Miranda and Nick were rushed out into the car park, bundled into a Landcruiser, and driven to the FEST control at the Kili. Altenburg sat in the front passenger's seat. Several vehicles followed behind, carrying FBI agents and Tanzanian government employees. In one of these lay Zayn's massive corpse. It had been brought in a helicopter from Lyly. Lacking a coffin, they had had to use a fish crate. The Tanzanians who had organised this mainly comprised members of the General Service Unit, as their intelligence service was called. There were also a couple of policeman, including Ernest Chikambwa, who had gone in one of the helicopters to guide the Americans over the islands as they searched for Queller and company. The convoy got under way, travelling along the road from the airport towards the city, past maize plantations and shouting children.

'So what the hell has been going on?' Altenburg demanded, turning round and gripping the faux-leather headrest. 'I want a full debrief you know, Jack.'

'There'll be plenty of time to give you all the information later. We've been through quite a lot.'

'You are one stubborn guy!' Altenburg exclaimed. 'I want to know exactly what happened out there.'

'We had a chase, one guy dead, the other got away. Isn't that clear enough for now? You can debrief me back at the hotel. First I want a bath and a drink.'

Interrupted by a radio call reporting the progess, or rather lack of progress, in the search for Khaled, Altenburg let it drop. Fingering the stem of the carnation, Queller looked at Nick and Miranda. Not exactly lovers in pretty springtime, he thought. They both looked wrecked. Miranda was staring dumbly at the shanties and shop signs running by the window; Nick had fallen asleep, his head on her shoulder.

Queller needed to think straight. In half an hour they would be in the centre of Dar, approaching the keyboards and microphones of the FEST comms centre where the whole thing would have to be chopped up and reported in such a way that Washington could understand it. A smooth narrative, appropriately processed, free of the amorphous raggedness that was reality itself. After that would come the real report, the analysis that could take months, that put back in all the disruptions in the pattern of recollected events and tried to understand them.

He held the carnation up to his nose and smelt it. Only the faintest scent. The bud was still half closed. On an impulse he reached across his thighs and placed it on the empty seat beside him – under the dangling sleeve that hid his stump. It was hurting from his fall on the boat, and so was his face where the Arab had slashed him with the stick. It gave Queller some satisfaction to think that his would-be murderer was lying in a fish crate in one of the vehicles behind. At least something good had come out of this mess, even though it was scant compensation for those who had been injured in the bombings, or the relatives of those who had died.

But then, what would be? Assassinating bin Laden? Hunting down every member of al-Qaida and executing them? It wasn't possible to work out a calculus of loss in this way. Revenge might be a kind of equation – an eye for an eye, a tooth for a tooth, even an arm for an arm – but not justice. Especially when there was always the danger of creating martyrs and inflaming the situation further. Organisations like al-Qaida had the monstrous typology of the hydra, growing eleven heads for every two you cut off. In any case, their effective strength was not measured merely by counting heads.

Outside, thickening from fields and villages to shanty town and warehousing, the rural landscape shaded into urban. Altenburg was issuing orders over the radio. Queller listened: Queller the all-hearing, Queller the veteran Arabist who had coined the phrase 'The Age of Acronyms' to describe the post-Cold War security situation, who had devised in his seminars what he believed to be the first application of organisation theory to the new world order.

The truth of it was that those 'thousands of hell hounds called terrorists' (Edmund Burke), those 'cocksucker terrorists' (Oliver North), had over time a tendency to move towards a mirror image of the intelligence communities to which they were opposed, imitating their methods and behaviour. The acronyms of one side – ARM, PLO, PFLP, IRA – found their opposite numbers on the other – FBI, CIA, DST, SIS. This underpinned a wider thesis: that a terror organisation's increasingly rigid structure would, eventually, over time, lead it to the negotiating table.

Now, however, sitting in the rear of the FEST Landcruiser – exhausted, a throbbing scarlet stripe across his cheek and a carnation by his side – he was not so sure about this line he used to spin. The argument just seemed like a set of vague axioms now. It didn't really apply to al-Qaida anyway. The structure of bin Laden's organisation was based on the idea that structure itself should be resisted – that one cell of the organism should not know what the other is doing. He could never see Uncle Sam sitting down to peace talks with Mr Sam. Or the Taliban allowing bin Laden to be extradited and tried – not unless the sanctions the US had already imposed on Afghanistan really began to bite.

Queller stared at the back of Altenburg's head. Brown hair cut square at the nape. A little spot. He was telling the driver something up front. How the government had printed tens of thousands of images of bin Laden's face on leaflets, together with notice of a reward (it had been upped to $5 million). The Air Force was going to parachute them over Afghanistan in the next few weeks.

Would they ever catch up with him? Bin Laden would be moving his camp every few days, Queller reckoned. Right now he could be setting off once more: in a convoy of shiny four-by-fours not unlike this one, disappearing into Afghanistan's epic landscape, winding like a metallic snake into the mountain labyrinth, long before more Tomahawks, relentless but never infallible, could pinpoint him again.

He looked across at Nick and Miranda. She had fallen asleep as well now, her face grey under the heavy dark fringe. Whenever

376

they hit a bump or pothole or swerved to avoid a cyclist, the eyes of one or the other would flicker open, register Queller for a second and then close again. Between them on the seat, their hands lay limp like two dead fish. Queller wondered whether they would last as a couple. All that stuff about adversity bringing people together – he wasn't sure he believed all that.

The convoy had passed into Dar's commercial district. The traffic was pandemonium. Queller stared out of the window, watching signs and billboards flash past like a rapid series of hallucinations: *Envi Skin Cream* – 'YOU TOO CAN LOOK LIKE THIS' – *Nido Milk, Kargill Seeds, Standard Bank, Shell, Kahawa by Nestlé*: 'THE STRONGEST BREW', *Carlsberg Green and Carlsberg Brown*: 'BEST FOR THE TOWN AND THE COUNTRY'. The signs didn't tell the whole tale, to Queller's mind. There was something missing, some knife or razor, some way to cut through the endless web of the companies that produced these goods.

Of one thing he was certain. The worldwide spread of trade was in the main a force for good, but it often came with a price. Sometimes it seemed to force nations into a kind of splendid vassalage, where the restraining element outweighed the beneficial one. The erosion of local enterprise, unfair pricing systems, the replacement of democracy by corporate power, a general loss of identity and will . . . While the multinationals were often either stepping into the shoes of corrupt and brutal regimes, or simply going hand-in-glove with them, all these factors contributed to the growth of fundamentalisms, even if they were not directly responsible. It was an expensive way to grow your business, if one took a long view.

Taking the war to the terrorists when they struck wasn't cheap either, and as likely to make things worse as better. Organisations like al-Qaida might grow stronger if they were attacked – like weeds which, sprayed with tonnes of pesticide, grew resistant to it – as their political consciousness, and capacity for pain, was raised to ever higher levels of intensity. The Israeli situation was a prime example, though since the Oslo Agreement things seemed to be looking up a little.

Maybe there could, in the future, be something like an ecology of terrorism? It would be a planting, a forestalling, a readjustment in the way things were ordered, causing a readjustment in how they were ordained. Was it possible, by replacing economic exploitation and political vandalism with actions that planted seeds of hope, to avoid this kind of thing happening again? A world determined by hope would be forever green; a world ruled by force, continually bursting into flames.

Effects emerged from causes – the fire hidden in the wood, as the Koran had it – and theoretically at least it should be possible to create conditions of improvement. Queller had a vision of a grand redemption, one great system – costly to all, but bringing forth much more good than its price.

Happiness, knowledge, virtue, the real wealth of the human race . . . these were inestimable gifts, but why should they not be successfully propagated?

It was, he knew, a pipe dream, something that would work only through the sympathy of many governments and corporations. The future was as imponderable as ever. Even with the sophisticated quantative modelling now available, the far-off event one was planning to avoid would dissolve and fade away, lost in the digital chatter of permutation.

Maybe, in any case, it was irresponsible to think of an imaginary period for the removal of evils, and better to think of improving the present. But interventions of any type – military, economic, political – often just seemed to compound the problems. However judicious the planned course of action seemed at the outset, it frequently ended up entwined with the cause, and the good intended held as a prejudice against those who attempted it. Somalia was a prime example: that poor pilot torn to pieces by the mob.

So far as the cause of terror itself went, Queller thought, putting it down to globalisation alone was usually way too simple. It certainly was in this case. Driven by many forces, the reasons for the bombings swarmed as thickly through time as bats from a cave. It was impossible to track the process, to fix where each contributing factor, itself the result of infinite combinations, would brush the future air. And that was not even to begin to consider the psyche and motivations of al-Qaida's members, or those of its leader, that inward world where – fanned by the rustling wings of repression and desire – the flame of fanaticism grew to a conflagrant mass.

He looked out of the window, where a small boy was pushing along a toy car made of twisted wire. There was innocence in every place, but here among the African poor, whose vicissitudes were so much greater, it glowed star-bright. The continent had its own intense griefs and did not deserve the used griefs of others. How much better, he thought, to be innocent than penitent. Feeling a kind of gluey despair, as if he'd fallen into a pit of tar, he wondered how any good could come of the imminent briefing with Altenburg.

The agent driving the Landcruiser gave a blast on the horn. They were dead in the centre of the city now, next to the clock tower, and here there were more signs still for his eye to absorb: *Jambo Snacks, Zanzibar Drop* – 'COLD AND DELICIOUS'. The largest poster, gaudier, flame-licked, advertised something called the *Holy Spirit Fire Church*. 'ON SUNDAY JOHN NATHAN TORRANCE TALKS HERE ON THE END-TIME AND THE LIFE TO COME.'

The Landcruiser moved forward, weaving in and out.

33

People were walking around, congregating by the Reflecting Pool or stretching out under the cherry trees. Miranda went over and dipped a hand in the water. Then she climbed the steps and stood between the columns of the edifice, posing for the photograph that no one would take. It was like a promissory note in her head, the thought of that photograph, like a cheque that would never be cashed.

After coming down, she walked along the Mall past the Vietnam Vets Memorial. A wall of polished black granite covered with names. An order of death. There were a number of Powers there, she noted. She carried on further, into the centre of the city, pausing awhile under the impressive obelisk that was the Washington Monument. There was a slightly eerie quality to the structure, as if it were a place of consecration or sacrifice.

She thought about the people who had died in bombings; then, seeing something in the stone, she thought about herself. Some 150 feet up the obelisk was a clear delineation in the shading of the marble: she wondered if her life was going to be like that now. Before the bomb/after the bomb. It was a very different Miranda Powers who had gone to Africa. Yet in another way she felt a kind of resentment against the world for not having allowed her to move on.

She continued on up towards Federal Square, till she stood in front of the brown, fortress-like FBI headquarters – the J. Edgar Hoover building where, the previous day, she'd had an appointment with Mort Altenburg. Further debriefing. What had caught her attention most were the posters of the Bureau's Ten Most

Wanted Fugitives, chief among them Osama bin Laden. There was something disturbingly saintly and seductive about the man's eyes. He looked more like a Greek icon – John the Baptist or someone – than a James Bond-type evil genius. It was hard to envisage that he had been the cause of all the havoc and the slaughter, just as it was hard to imagine that he might never be brought to justice.

Altenburg had told her the investigation was ongoing, and that they had a lead on Khaled. Bin Laden himself had issued further threats. Altenburg had added that Jack Queller was under investigation 'for various reasons', but wouldn't go into details. All inquiries into her own competence had been halted. There was to be no disciplinary hearing. Currently on discretionary leave, she would take up a new post in a month – in Washington itself, Kirsteen's department, the one that looked after visiting diplomats and heads of state.

Hungry, she went to a Starbucks a little way down from the Hoover building. She didn't usually go into them, they were too regimented for her, but there was nowhere else nearby. Ray, who was out of hospital now, hated the chain with a passion. He'd left the service, and gone to live in San Francisco on a State Department pension. The city was, he said in a letter, 'like a second Eden' – but she suspected he was just putting a brave face on things. He would have to use walking sticks for the rest of his life.

She ordered a skinny latte and a granola bar and sat thinking about Nick. She'd tried to persuade him to stay in Washington, but he wouldn't. It was inevitable, she guessed. They had been thrown together by events, and now events had drawn them apart. But it hurt her still, she was surprised how much.

She opened her purse and took out the little turtleshell he'd given her. She let it rest on the palm of her hand. The interleaved shell was full of soft orange fires, each layer ministering light from the down-lamps of the table. It made her sad to look at it, so she put it back. But the sad, solitary thoughts came all the same . . . She couldn't, after all, allow herself to believe that it was merely circumstances that had brought them together. Her feelings had grown too strong and, according to his diary, so had his. Had they both, in their separate moments, been deluding themselves about what they'd had? If not, what had it all been *for*?

This was where her resentment came in. Progression ought to be the order of the world, she believed, but she felt that with Nick at least she hadn't been allowed to progress. It was as if she were a pendulum continually striking the sides of the clock that contained it, but never breaking through.

She hadn't been able to get much out of him; he seemed more self-absorbed than ever. He'd said he still had work to do, that maybe when he had finished his contract they might get something together. She told him if he loved her he'd stay here, and instantly regretted saying it. He said she could equally come out to Zanzibar if she liked, and that it was selfish of her to think her job more important than his. That annoyed her, and then she told him there was no way she'd join him.

Was that true? She wondered now. Success in the department had been her goal for so long that she took it for granted as her horizon. But maybe the bombings ought to have changed that; maybe she ought to concentrate on things more valuable than work. Yet it was also true that her work had become – one only had to think for a second of the stricken victims of the attacks – more important than ever now.

And so, hiding her frustration, she had resigned herself to the situation, and turned away after his final kiss, making a safe, straight line back across the asphalt frontage of the DS building. She had watched him, then, from an upper window, crossing by the tennis court and getting into his rental car. All at once she'd felt angry and sad, in love and out of love, tossed like a cork on the ocean.

She glanced at the long noticeboard that ran down one side of the Starbucks. Alongside little cards advertising t'ai chi classes and apartments to rent were pinned pages of that day's *Washington Post*. She had read it earlier in the day. The President had vowed not to resign, saying that 'every American has been broken by something in life'. They were powerful, piercing words, appealing to a general mercy that would free all of fault; yet still she had her doubts about what would happen.

Leaving the Starbucks, Miranda walked up the broad sidewalk a little further, until part of it dipped down, near the Navy Memorial. There was a sunken area there, with a map of the oceans set into the ground like a mosaic. She went and stood over where Zanzibar should have been, and was surprised to find it marked. But then, it was an oceanographic map, and only things like islands and ports and currents were shown.

On either side of her, as she stood on Zanzibar, was a display of bronze statuary, attached to the walls around. One image in particular caught her eye – a petty officer in his bell-bottoms, reefer coat and cap. She walked over to it. The seaman's hands were in his pockets, his duffel bag by his side. He was gazing into the distance, as if waiting for a ship to arrive at the dockside. The sculptor had ingeniously made the hems of his trousers and the collars of his coat curl in the sea breeze.

She stood there for what must have been half an hour looking at this man. He was slightly hunched, forever waiting on that liberty boat to release him from his prison of bronze. There was something truly heroic in his eyes, something excellent, something of an America where gods still dwelt. Like a child, Miranda reached out and touched his face. Behind her, the wind thrummed the wires on a line of flagstaffs.

She thought of the war the statue commemorated, how those who die in a great cause never really fall. And then, again, she thought of Nick, wanting her to throw it all in. Feeling a stab of sadness, she began walking quickly up the incline, to where the sidewalk retained its normal level. Below her, in the sunken place, the flags continued to wave.

* * *

FBI SEEKS BOMB SUSPECT
by Seymour Ong
Washington Post Staff Writer
Sunday, October 18, 1998

LAST week the FBI narrowly missed capturing a man suspected of involvement in the attack on the US embassy in Dar-es-Salaam on August 7. Sources named the suspect, a citizen of the East African island of Zanzibar, as Khaled al-Khidr, 23. A complaint seeking his arrest has been filed in the Southern District Court of New York.

On Wednesday, FBI agents and Comoros Island police swooped on a house he had rented in the Comoran capital of Moroni, 200 miles off the east coast of Africa. He had fled there by boat from Zanzibar, the sources said. Al-Khidr, for whom a $2m reward has been posted, had vanished by the time the agents arrived in Moroni.

Since the swoop, al-Khidr has eluded capture, but the wide-reaching FBI investigation into the August 7 bombings is gaining ground. Mort Altenburg, the top FBI official in the investigation, told reporters that 'amazing advances' had been made. Altenburg said, 'We're starting to unpick a far-flung conspiracy orchestrated by Saudi militant Osama bin Laden and his al-Qaida organisation,' adding that it was the largest overseas investigation in the history of the FBI.

Intelligence analysts and law enforcement agents are still trying to determine the global scope and structure of bin Laden's organisation and the character of its leader.

'Some folk think al-Qaida is like the FBI. Others think it's completely disorganised. I'd say we're somewhere in between,' said Altenburg.

'It's not the powerhouse it's made out to be. But they do have some capabilities.' Altenburg added that the agency was using pattern analysis to compare the August 7 bombings with previous terrorist events. 'It may be that al-Qaida is responsible for more outrages than we'd thought.'

* * *

Bare-chested, Queller sat on the sofa in his cabin on Aquinnah. The date was October 18. He had collected two items from the post office in Vineyard Haven that morning, and mailed one himself. One of the things he collected was a new arm, the latest model to which he was entitled under the terms of his insurance plan. The other was a letter from the FBI, ordering him to attend an in camera hearing concerning US government links to bin Laden under the Reagan administration.

For some weeks he'd wondered how he might extricate himself, knowing full well he was being set up as the fall guy. But he was weary of evasion. He had told too many lies in his life, lived too long in betrayals, become accustomed to a world where what was under cover found justification in nothing but its own secrecy. Now it was time to stop: to open a door of light. He would be like al-Khidr, the Green Ancient who explains mysteries to ordinary men, making everything public which had been veiled by night.

His familiar bird was singing on the locust tree outside. It made a wavering note, as if falling through gravity. He had spent the previous night writing his version of events – a version which, while it might not have lifted him out of ignominy, at least put another side to the story than the one which, he knew,

Altenburg would be telling. It was this text that he had mailed in the Haven – to Miranda Powers. He had sent it to her because he trusted her. Probably that was foolish, but the image of his wife he saw in her face gave him reason enough.

He'd not said what he intended – that he was ready, now, to take his wages: in the present life, in the life to come, in plain view of He from whom not one secret is concealed, who assays all bias, on the right hand and the left, and hears every soul's whisper. He'd only asked that she do her best to make public the extent to which the US government had, through Pakistan and directly, relations with bin Laden during the eighties and early nineties.

The bird outside flew up, singing so sweetly as it ascended that it might have been entering not the sky but that beloved republic where all are equal, free and undivided. Queller began unrolling the new arm from its bubble wrap. *The purpose of this appendage is prosthetic. It must not be used for any other purpose.*

It had a specially padded socket, supposed to be the most comfortable on the market, and an advanced gripping mechanism. He strapped it on, then went through to the bedroom of the cabin to look at himself in the mirror. A slight pot belly, freckled, rounded shoulders – over all of this ran the cream-brown straps. Well, it was a little more comfortable than anything he'd had before. He went over to the chest of drawers and, picking out a hand at random, clipped its ratcheted steel prong into the arm. It made a satisfying noise, the noise of something meant to do business. He returned to the lounge.

On the coffee table in the middle of the room stood a glass of whisky. Next to it lay his AMT automatic pistol. He went over to the table and, using the prosthesis, picked up the glass and drank from it. Good. Having put the glass down, flexing his shoulder muscles to control the angle of elevation and strength of grip, he reached out once more.

He picked up the gun. Then, thinking of his wife in the way a homing bird yearns for its destination, he lifted it to his temple and pulled the trigger.

* * *

Nick found a little split cocoon on the wooden boards of the veranda. That was putting it rather grandly. He had made a kind of deck for the cottage on Lyly, which was all cleaned up and very accommodating now. He flicked the cocoon with his toe and watched it bounce down the steps. He didn't consider it symbolic that it was split – he had long ago left that side of himself behind. What he had now was occupation, responsibilities, the satisfaction of getting up and doing his work each morning, a chronicle of day by day. Those days to come: he vowed he would eat them like fruit now, tasting them slowly, drawing from them what meaning he could, undeceived, without expectation.

It would have been so easy to stay in America: to shut the door on Africa and forget all about it. And he had very nearly done so. Then he had made a trip down to Florida to see his mother and Dino. They were together now. He had talked everything over with Dino, and this time the old guy had tried to persuade him to stay. But it was the voice of another old man, Leggatt, that spoke loudest. Nick felt indebted to the Englishman, and the only way he could repay him was coming back here and looking after the turtles. Sometimes, when he went to check the nests, he imagined Leggatt by his side: upright, leonine, puffing on his pipe.

Nick looked out to sea. The light of the evening sun glowed above Zanzibar's main island, bruising the clouds as they passed. It would be dark again soon, but the night held no terrors for him now. He lit the lantern and began walking down to the beach, to the palisade he had made with Leggatt and Miranda.

He thought of her often, and sometimes wondered if he had made the right decision. It would have made a nice end to a love story. But then, what they had was never a love story, even though they might have been in love. He'd accepted that now. Just as he'd accepted Zanzibar was not paradise, and never had been. It wasn't really a resignation. He felt happier these days, in the main. He'd a sense of inner calm, a feeling things were going his way – one he immediately corrected, knowing it was the old thing creeping up on him. It wasn't enough to dispel one's delusions one time only; they constantly threatened, always ready to take over, building anew on the memorial of their former condition.

With lingering steps, he walked down the beach. He could see the lighthouse and, perched on its summit, a fish eagle. He stopped and stared at the white-capped, imperious bird for a while, wishing he had a fish for it. Then it struck him it might be waiting for the turtles. He was about to clap his hands and make it fly away, when it took wing of its own accord – lifting towards a window in the high cumulus. He watched till it disappeared in red-orange streams of light, issuing from sun to sky like molten iron from fire.

He sat down by the palisade round the nests. Looking towards the darkening gulf of the horizon, his resolution faltered a little. It was so hard to live in the present, as it slipped glassily by, so hard not to fall into presumptious hopes of how the future would be sent to you, so hard not to be tricked by an ideal conception of one's own personality. Having another human being by your side didn't necessarily make it any easier either.

He felt a pang of loneliness all the same. The truth was, he missed Miranda. However much they had been swept up by everything that had happened, they had, even though it was just for a short time, climbed a branch of the tree of life together. Why had he lopped it off?

He hardly knew now. The tale he'd been telling himself, the arguments he'd been rehearsing – about turtles, about Africa – didn't run so smoothly through his mind as before.

The beat of the waves filled his ears. It was not regular, not quite clear – he lit a cigarette and saw her face – but there was a pattern all the same. The fourth or fifth wave was higher in pitch, the process itself – he felt an urge to speak her name – rising in little ridges of elevation and then, though it was hard to tell when, falling again.

Was there, looking at things dispassionately, a chance for them? There was certainly time in the world. But nothing would come of nothing. Without the hand of providence, or some other fate, if neither was moved to make a change, what they had would go out like a fire from want of fuel.

Nick made a gap in the palisade, as he had done the past three nights. Spray settling on his brows and hair, a dying sun fusing a new moon's spectral light, he sat waiting there. Cool beneath the sand, oblivious to his paternal care, smooth eggs waited too. When their time came, a kind of tremor would pass through the tiny bodies in their caskets, and they would start to hatch: to immediate threat – the gulls that were whirling above even now, the predatory crabs that ceaselessly patrolled the sand. So against all odds, having broken the shell, burrowed up four feet, and completed a fraught passage across the moonlit beach, the turtles would enter the ocean. But not yet, not yet.

Acknowledgements

I would like to thank the following for their advice, help and support at various stages in the period of this novel's gestation: Claire Armitstead; Will Atkinson; Phil Baker; Anna Borzello; Zev Braun; Lorraine Breen; Steve Caplin; Angus Cargill; Alex Clark; Victoria Coleman-Smith; Peter Couzens; Jim Crace; Michael Downes; John Dugdale; Bridget Frost; Nick Harris; Rachel Hore; Veronica Horwell; Julian Hunt; Derek Johns; Martin Kettle; Julian Loose; Joanna Mackle; Chris McLaren; Ian Pindar; Steven Poole; Eva Sallis; Ian Sansom; Linda Shaughnessy; Elaine Showalter; Paul Theroux; Kate Ward; Sarah Wherry; James Wood. Thanks are also due to Officer Jeremy Young for filling me in on details of the Boston Police cap badge, and to Sarah Spankie for commissioning the article that took me, at the time of the bombings, to Dar-es-Salaam and Zanzibar in the first place.